W9-CBR-275

STAR TREK®

FEDERATION

STAR TREK®

FEDERATION

Judith & Garfield Reeves-Stevens

POCKET BOOKS

New York   London   Toronto   Sydney   Tokyo   Singapore

POCKET BOOKS, a division of Simon & Schuster Inc. 1230 Avenue of the Americas, New York, NY 10020

This book is published by Pocket Books, a division of Simon & Schuster Inc., under exclusive license from Paramount Pictures.

ISBN: 0-671-89422-6

First Pocket Books hardcover printing November 1994

10 9 8 7 6 5 4 3 2 1

POCKET and colophon are registered trademarks of Simon & Schuster Inc.

Printed in the U.S.A.

FOR OUR BROTHERS—

Bill, who never missed an episode of *The Original Series,*
and Sid, who *still* hasn't seen one.

HISTORIAN'S TIMELINE

2061   Zefram Cochrane returns to Earth's solar system after the first successful faster-than-light voyage to Alpha Centauri.

2079   Earth endures the Post-Atomic Horror as it recovers from World War III.

2117   At the age of 87, Zefram Cochrane leaves his home in the Alpha Centauri system and disappears in space.

2161   In the aftermath of the Romulan Wars, the Federation is incorporated and Starfleet is chartered.

2267   In the second year of Captain James T. Kirk's first five-year mission aboard the *U.S.S. Enterprise* NCC-1701, Kirk and his crew discover the Guardian of Forever. In the third year, Kirk, Spock, Dr. McCoy, and Federation Commissioner Nancy Hedford encounter Zefram Cochrane and the Companion. Later that year, Ambassador Sarek comes aboard for passage to the Babel Conference.

2269–70   Following the completion of the first five-year mission, Kirk is promoted to admiral; Dr. McCoy and Spock retire from Starfleet.

2295   The Excelsior-class *U.S.S. Enterprise* NCC-1701-B is launched from spacedock on its maiden voyage.

HISTORIAN'S TIMELINE

2366   In the third year of Captain Jean-Luc Picard's ongoing mission aboard the *U.S.S. Enterprise* NCC-1701-D, Ambassador Sarek comes aboard for passage to Legara IV. Several weeks later, the Borg attack Federation territory for the first time.

2371   Captain Picard returns to Earth's solar system following the incident at Veridian III.

Rest enough for the individual man, too much and too soon, and we call it death. But for man, no rest and no ending. He must go on, conquest beyond conquest. First this little planet and all its winds and ways, and then all the laws of mind and matter that restrain him. Then the planets about him, and, at last, out across immensities to the stars. And when he has conquered all the deep space, and all the mysteries of time, still he will be beginning.

—H. G. Wells
Things to Come
1936

PROLOGUE

☆

ON THE EDGE OF FOREVER

ELLISON RESEARCH OUTPOST
Stardate 9910.1
Earth Standard: ≈ Late September 2295

Kirk knew his journey would be ending soon.

That feeling overwhelmed him even as he resolved from the transporter beam and felt the gravity of this world reassert its hold on him—a hold it had never once relinquished over all the years, all the parsecs, which had passed from that first time to now. All that had happened since that first time was but a heartbeat to him, as if his life were dust streaming from the tail of a comet, without mass, without consequence, measured only by the moment he had first arrived at this place, and by the moment of his return.

It had been twenty-eight years since he had first set foot here, and Kirk had no doubt that he would never do so again. He could hear Spock's patient voice in his mind, blandly noting the illogic of that conclusion, given that the unexpected was all too common in their lives. But in some matters emotions took precedence. Which is why he had returned. Everything *was* coming to an end. No matter what Spock concluded, no matter how McCoy argued, Kirk's heart knew the truth of that feeling.

This is the last time for so many things, Kirk thought, falling into the litany that had grown in him since his retirement. Soon would come his last passage by transporter. His last look at

3

starlight smeared by warp speed. His last glimpse of fleecy skies and Earth's cool, green hills. He thought of the old song for space travelers, written before spaceflight had even begun on Earth. He was saddened that he could not recall all of it.

"Captain Kirk, we are honored by your visit."

The words caught Kirk by surprise, though he knew they shouldn't have. The speaker was a young Vulcan woman, Academy fresh, standing at attention before the slightly raised transporter platform in the outpost's central plaza. Kirk guessed her age as no more than twenty-five years Earth standard. He hesitated on the platform, thinking back. When she had been born, he'd been returning *home*. The first five-year mission almost at an end. An admiralty waiting for him. Kirk cast back to the memory. He had not gone gentle into that good night. His time as a deskbound admiral had lasted less than two years. Two years of going to bed each night on Earth knowing that *she* was orbiting above him, being readied for another mission. And each night he had known that *she* would not leave spacedock without him, Starfleet and all its admirals be damned.

Kirk had been right.

V'Ger had come to claim the world and Kirk had beaten the odds again. As he always would.

No, Kirk thought. *Had. Past tense.* He was sixty-two years old. McCoy told him he could look forward to one hundred and twenty, even more. But the trouble with odds was that you could never really beat them, just avoid them for a while. Spock would be the first to admit that, in time, everything evened out. That was one way of looking at death, Kirk knew, the inescapable evening out of the odds. The thought brought him no comfort.

"Captain Kirk?" the Vulcan began, a polite query in her tone. "Is everything all right, sir?"

"Fine, Lieutenant," Kirk said. Even though he was finally, unthinkably, retired from Starfleet, a civilian again, however unlikely, the Fleet always remembered her own and this, his last rank, would be his forever.

He stepped down from the platform, hearing the whisper-soft grinding of fine red dust beneath his boot. He smiled at the Vulcan, and because Spock had been his friend for thirty years, he could see an almost undetectable shadow of emotion cross her face. Kirk blinked and looked again at the rank insignia on the white band of her tunic. He corrected himself: "Lieutenant *Commander.*" He supposed he should wear his glasses more often. But a lieutenant commander at twenty-five? Could the Academy really be making them that young now? *Could I really be that old?*

"May I show you to your quarters, sir?" The Vulcan nodded to indicate a collection of prefab habitat structures a few hundred meters away, assembled within a clearing in the ruins of the city . . . or whatever it was. A quarter-century of study by the Federation's best xenoarchaeologists had been unable to reveal the purpose of this place, only that its primary structures were at least one million years old, and the age of its oldest structure was exactly what Spock had later surmised: six *billion* years.

There was a time when the significance of such antiquity had been overwhelming to Kirk. The central stones of this place had been carved and assembled before life had ever arisen on Earth, before Earth herself had coalesced from the dust and debris surrounding her sun. But now six billion years was merely an abstraction—a mystery he would never comprehend in his lifetime, just another fact to be placed aside, abandoned, with so many other unattainable dreams of youth.

"No, thank you," Kirk said. "I'm afraid I won't be staying long enough to make use of any quarters. The *Excelsior* will be arriving shortly to pick me up."

"The staff will be disappointed to hear that, sir." Kirk noted that the Vulcan hid her own disappointment well, as she did her disapproval that Starfleet's flagship had been relegated to providing a civilian with taxi service. That's not how Captain Sulu had viewed Kirk's request for a favor, but Kirk understood how others might see it.

"As you are one of the few people to have interacted with the device," the Vulcan added, almost boldly, "we had looked forward to hearing of your encounter in your own words."

Kirk looked around the plaza, anxious to continue without further conversation. "It's all in my original logs. I'm sure they offer more detail than I could recall today."

5

JUDITH AND GARFIELD REEVES-STEVENS

In what was, for a Vulcan, surely a near act of desperation, the lieutenant commander impassively asked, "Is there nothing we can do to have you extend your stay with us?"

"No," Kirk said. It was that final. In less than two months the Excelsior-class *Enterprise* B would be launched from spacedock. Kirk wasn't certain what was drawing him back to Earth for that occasion. He had no intention of ever again setting foot on a starship as anything other than a passenger. He still recalled too well the haunted look on Chris Pike's face when they had spoken the day Kirk had taken command of the first *Enterprise*. From that first day, that first hour, somehow Kirk, too, had known that that was how his own journey would end. With the *Enterprise,* or her namesake, going on without him. Even here, it made him uncomfortable to contemplate that moment to come in his future. There had been so much he had wanted to accomplish, so much he *had* accomplished, and yet the two never seemed to overlap. Forty-six years in Starfleet, and his losses still seemed to outweigh his gains.

Kirk caught sight of a distinctive pillar at the far edge of the plaza. Floodlights had been set up on slender tripods around it, changing the dark color of the stone he remembered to something lighter. There was writing on it as well, intricate lines of alien script like the overlapping edges of waves on a beach. He didn't remember having seen writing there before, but no doubt the archaeologists had cleaned away the encrustations of millennia.

"That way, isn't it?" Kirk asked, already walking toward the pillar, knowing what he would find beyond.

"Yes, sir," the Vulcan said. She fell into step beside him, her tricorder bouncing against her hip as she hurried to match his stride. "If I may, sir, as you know, it gave no indication that the conversation of stardate 7328 would be its last communication with us."

"And that surprises you?" Kirk interrupted. He picked up the pace before she could answer. He felt he was swimming in sensations—the taste of the bone-dry air that drew the moisture from his lungs, the lightness of the gravity, the slight reediness of sound distorted by the thin atmosphere. He was thirty-four again,

6

filled with purpose, pushing eagerly at the edge of all the boundaries that encompassed him.

"Surprise connotates an emotional response," the Vulcan said primly, "which has no place in a scientific investigation."

Her response, all too predictable, wearied him. Such earnestness was best served by youth. Let her devote the next four decades of her life to this mystery if she would. Kirk no longer had that luxury.

"Instead," she continued, "it could be said we were perplexed by its silence, especially in light of the conversations you reported with it, and its apparent willingness to answer any—"

"Yes, fine, very good, Lieutenant Commander." Kirk let the sharp words spill out of him, anything to have her stop talking. "If I could just have a few moments . . ."

He sensed her falter beside him and he walked on, alone, past the pillar and the floodlights, around a fallen wall, a tumble of columns, and—yes!—there—right where he remembered it. Right where it had remained through all these years, haunting him, forever haunting him, just as its name had foretold.

The Guardian of Forever.

A large, rough-hewn torus, three meters in diameter. A repository of knowledge. A passageway into time. Its own beginning and its own ending. A mystery. Perhaps, *the* mystery.

Kirk paused and gazed upon the Guardian. Like the pillar, its color was different, changed by the floodlights that ringed it. There were sensor arrays nearby as well, sheets of gleaming white duraplast on the ground around it to keep the soil from being disturbed by the many scientists who toiled to learn its secrets.

Kirk gazed upon the Guardian, and remembered.

A question. Since before your sun burned hot in space and before your race was born, I have awaited a question. . . .

Those had been the first words the Guardian had spoken to him. An investigation of temporal distortions had brought the *Enterprise* to this world. McCoy had accidentally injected himself with an overdose of cordrazine and in fleeing his rescuers had passed through the Guardian into Earth's past. There he had changed history so that the Federation never arose, so that the

Enterprise no longer flew through space, so that Kirk and Uhura and Spock and Scott were trapped in this city, on the edge of forever, with their only chance of restoring the universe they knew waiting in the past.

Kirk closed his eyes, the cruel memories still alive within him.

The universe had been restored. The *Enterprise* returned to him. And the price had only been the death of one woman. The one woman he had truly loved.

Her name formed on his lips.

"Edith," he whispered.

Kirk knew the Vulcan would hear him, but he no longer cared. Caring was for youth, and at this moment, Kirk felt as old as the stones of this place.

He walked across the ruddy soil until he came to the duraplast sheets. A permanent static charge repelled the dust and kept the sheets clean. His boot heels clicked across their hard, slick surface. He heard the Vulcan follow.

Now, no more than a meter from it, Kirk stopped to study the mottled surface of the Guardian. It had glowed when it spoke so many years ago, pulsing with an inner energy no one had ever been able to trace to a source, just as they had been unable to replicate whatever mechanism had initially allowed the Guardian to act as a gateway through time. The most detailed sensor scans possible consistently reported that the Guardian was no more than a piece of granitic rock, hand-carved, and that was all.

"Perhaps you could ask it something, sir," the Vulcan suggested, after a moment of respectful silence.

There were a thousand questions Kirk could think to ask. Perhaps that was why he had returned. But for now, none seemed worth asking.

"Do you really think it would do any good?" he asked. He glanced behind him and saw the Vulcan staring intently at the Guardian, as if that simple question asked in a familiar voice might stir the intelligence locked within the stone.

"The Vulcan Science Academy spent years in conversation with the Guardian, sir. It offered virtually infinite knowledge, ours for the mere asking. But—"

Kirk held up his hand to stop her. He knew the story. The

Guardian did claim to be the repository of infinite knowledge, present, past, and future. But it seemed that there were inherent limitations to the languages of the Federation and the minds of the scientists who had engaged the Guardian in conversation. Too many times the Guardian had said it was unable to respond until a more precise question had been asked, yet it provided no clues as to how particular questions might be framed more precisely.

A human scientist had summed up eight years of frustrated research by equating the total of recorded conversations between the Guardian and humans to an exchange that might be expected between a human and dogs. The smartest, non–genetically engineered dogs might have a vocabulary of five hundred words, and comprehend a handful of actions and even abstract concepts such as direction and the duration of short periods of time. But what about the other hundred thousand words a dog's master could use? What hope did a dog have of understanding its master's philosophy and biochemistry and multiphysics? How could a dog even attempt to respond to its master in the human's own spoken words? It was frustrating and humbling for humans to be relegated to the status of mute animals, knowing no way to reach up to the Guardian.

The scientist had bitterly concluded that the researchers at Ellison Outpost had spent eight years conversing with a stone, and had gotten exactly the same results as they might get from asking questions of any rock. A few months later, the Guardian had ceased to respond to questions at all, as if confirming the scientist's assessment.

The Vulcan kept her face blank, but her next words, to Kirk's attuned ears, were a plea by any other name. "I would find it most interesting if you would ask it a question, sir."

Kirk nodded. It was a small enough request. In a few minutes, a few hours at most, he would be gone, but the Vulcan would still work here. Why leave her with regrets?

He turned to the Guardian, focusing on its wide opening through which the other side of the plaza was clear and unobstructed. The ruins beyond stretched to the horizon.

"Guardian," Kirk said in a firm, commanding tone, "do you remember me?"

The Vulcan betrayed her extreme youth by holding her breath in audible anticipation. An instant later, she remembered the tricorder at her side and brought it up to check its readings of the mute stone.

"Guardian," Kirk repeated, "show me the history of my world."

The space bound by the circle of stone was unchanged.

Kirk turned to the Vulcan. "I'm sorry," he said. And in an abstract way, he was, even though the mysteries of the Guardian had moved beyond his concern.

"Thank you for trying, sir," the Vulcan said. Then she switched off her tricorder and stood with her hands behind her back, as if she were stone herself and had no intention of leaving his side.

In the past, Kirk might have paused to consider a polite way to ask what he asked next, but time had become more important than hurt feelings these days.

"Lieutenant Commander," he said, "I would appreciate it if you would leave me alone here."

The startled Vulcan hid her surprise again, though not as well as the first time.

"Is anything wrong, sir?"

"I wish to meditate." It was a lie, of course, but one with which no Vulcan would argue.

"Of course, sir," the Vulcan said. She began to walk away. Kirk turned back to the stone. Then he heard her footsteps stop. He looked back at her. A wind had sprung up. Her severely cut hair fluttered against her pointed ears.

"Sir," she called out over the growing wind, "this outpost has standing orders that personnel are never to step through the opening in the Guardian. We do not know if or when it might become operational again."

"Understood," Kirk called back, and the Vulcan left him. He was alone with the Guardian. He stared through the opening. *Is this what I've come back for?* Kirk thought. *With no more future before me, did I hope in some way to return to the past?*

The wind gusted and Kirk felt himself pushed toward the stone, caught in a swirl of obscuring dust that made his eyes water and his throat raw. He reached out a hand to steady himself. The Guardian was cold to his touch.

He felt tired.

He thought of the stateroom Sulu would have for him on the *Excelsior*. A soft bed. He could even turn down the gravity to ease the ache in his back. The old knife wound he had gotten just before the Coridan Babel Conference so many years ago had been coming back to taunt him of late. Assisted by too many other past injuries, too many sudden transports into different gravity fields.

"Has it come to this?" Kirk asked the wind and the dust. "Will there be no more worlds to explore? No more battles to fight?"

The Guardian was silent.

Just as Kirk had known it would be.

There would be no more miracles for him in this universe. He had captured a part of it in his life, imprinted a thousand worlds in his mind, had experiences and adventures that humans of centuries past could not conceive, and which humans of centuries to come could never repeat.

He should be content with that, he knew.

But he wasn't.

For all his confidence, his bravado, his skills and talent and drive to be the best, in his heart, at his core, there were doubts.

Too many words left unsaid. Too many actions left undone. Too many questions gone unanswered.

And now, with the journey's end in sight, with the knowledge that it was time to put aside those things left unfinished, Kirk was not ready.

His doubts tortured him.

Edith, his love, in a roadway of old Earth, the truck rushing for her . . .

David, his son, on the Genesis planet, with a Klingon knife above his heart . . .

Garrovick, his commander, and 200 crew facing death on Tycho IV . . .

For all that Kirk had done, had he done *enough?*

Could anyone have done enough?

Or was it all without meaning? Was life a simple tragedy of

distraction from birth to death, with no more purpose than this stone before him?

Kirk knew his journey would be ending soon, and this far into it, he still did not understand what had driven him to take it, nor long to continue it.

Alone, he whispered a single word to the wind and the dust. "Why?"

And for the first time in two decades, the Guardian of Forever answered. . . .

Part One

BABEL

THORSEN

The Eugenics Wars of the late twentieth century were more than fifty years in the past, but the evil that had spawned them lived on. Hatred, intolerance, unrestrained greed, all those qualities which defined humanity so well, proved fertile ground as always.

A generation unborn at the turn of the millennium grew up with a fascination for those who had promised order and salvation in the midst of chaos. In the world of the mid-twenty-first century, crumbling beneath the environmental outrages of the twentieth, that promise was a heady dream. A perfect world was possible if only the mistakes made by Khan Noonien Singh and his followers could be avoided.

Adrik Thorsen was one of that generation determined not to repeat the mistakes of the past.

He heard the call of the supermen whispered through the ages, predating even Khan. He rallied beneath the red banners and dark eagle of the Optimum Movement. He wore the red uniform of Colonel Green. He awoke each day with the knowledge that the destiny of the world, of all humanity, lay in the hands of those who had the will to take drastic, necessary action.

Adrik Thorsen had that will, and in the mid-twenty-first century, in pockets of despair, regions overcome by anarchy and hopeless- ness, Thorsen was allowed to enact his policies.

His quest for perfection began with the weeding out of the unfit. Those who were less than optimal, by infirmity, by genetics, then by religious beliefs and political persuasion, were the first to be coded for deletion. In those early days, killing children for the sins of their parents had been distressing to Thorsen. But in time he came to see the anguish he experienced, and then transcended, as a sign of his own growing perfection.

True to his own theories, Adrik Thorsen was becoming optimal. If the world would only follow in his footsteps, he could lead all humanity to an era of peace and prosperity that would surpass all understanding.

But his progress tormented him because he knew that whenever great men such as he dared dream great dreams, inevitably there were those who would attempt to drag them down. By their very opposition, he considered his opponents to have proven themselves less than optimal. Thus, they, too, could be coded for deletion with all the others unfit to share the world.

As he journeyed on his own inner search for the Optimum, Adrik Thorsen's dream consumed him. Then it consumed his own pocket of the world. In time he was certain it would consume the world itself, and Paradise would follow from that moment as surely as night followed day, as constant as a law of nature.

But first Thorsen understood he must vanquish the laws of history. The biggest mistake that had been made by Khan's supermen was that they had lost. Adrik Thorsen would not permit that mistake to be made a second time.

Thus on the morning of March 19, 2061, Thorsen himself led the mission against the WED Research Platform, geostationary orbit, Earth. Six carbon-shelled, single-passenger orbital transfer units carried Thorsen and five trusted troopers to within two kilometers of the corporate space station, undetected by proximity radar. The transfer units were jettisoned and the final approach was made in membrane suits, using nonignition maneuvering units.

They made magnetic contact with the station's hull at 01:20 GMT, precisely as scheduled. Their induction scans showed that no alarms had been triggered.

FEDERATION

At 01:27 GMT, they detonated the first spinner charge on the uplink dish, shutting off all communications with the platform's corporate headquarters. Eight seconds later, a series of secondary detonations flashed along the staff module, splitting it in two.

Thorsen watched with satisfaction as he counted seven platform crew members expelled from the resulting hull breach, arms and legs kicking frantically, mouths horrifically gaping with silent cries in the vacuum. As he had suspected, two of the crew members wore the blue and white uniforms of the New United Nations peacemaking forces. It was clear that Thorsen and the Optimum Movement were not the only ones who knew what breakthrough had been engineered at this facility.

According to the operations manifest Thorsen had obtained, ten researchers and an unknown number of peacemakers remained on the platform. By now, the platform's automated emergency decompression procedures would have sealed internal airlocks. It would be at least five minutes before any remaining peacemakers could don their own membrane suits and launch a counterattack. Thorsen and his troopers were unopposed as they jetted directly to the outermost arm of the platform, where the revolutionary new test vehicle was stored in its own docking module.

Thorsen knew he could not explosively decompress that module without risk of damaging the vehicle itself. And it would be suicide for any of his troopers to attempt entry through the personnel airlock, where they would become a captive target. Accordingly, Thorsen ordered one of his troopers to the airlock to deploy an inflatable decoy. The decoy was the size and shape of a trooper in a membrane suit, and would draw the attention and laser fire of any crew members inside. At the same time, Thorsen commanded two other troopers to assemble an emergency evacuation blister on the outside of the docking module, sealing it to the hull and pressurizing it. Now his forces could breach the module's hull without loss of internal atmosphere. The vehicle inside would be safe.

At Thorsen's signal, the first trooper cycled the inflatable decoy through the personnel airlock as the troopers in the evac blister used cutting lasers to breach the hull.

The two troopers floating near Thorsen, ten meters away from the module, watched for the approach of peacemakers from the other airlocks.

But whoever remained inside the vehicle storage module did not share Thorsen's respect for rational military action. Before Thorsen's troopers in the evac blister could finish cutting their entry point, a gout of crystallizing moisture exploded from the vehicle airlock doors at the end of the module. Debris blew out with it, meaning both the interior and exterior doors had been opened at once.

Thorsen guessed what desperate strategy was being attempted and instantly moved to counteract it. He and the two troopers with him jetted to the open vehicle airlock door. The first trooper to arrive was cut in half by a particle beam, his suit and flesh rupturing in an explosion of instantly frozen blood.

Thorsen directed a fly-by-wire flare pack to the lip of the vehicle airlock door and ignited it. Anyone inside who had seen the flash would be blind for at least thirty seconds. Then he and the remaining troopers flew into the docking module, lasers on continuous fire, tuned for membrane fabric, not for metal or carbon.

There were no peacemakers inside, only unarmed researchers, all but one cowering in their pressure suits. Soon, only that one remained alive. She was in the vehicle itself, a reconfigured Orbital Fighter Escort with a single particle cannon on its nose. The modifications that Thorsen knew had been made to the fighter's vectored impulse drive unit appeared to be all interior. From the outside, it was no different from any other fighter he had piloted.

Thorsen's troopers on watch outside the airlock door reported that no peacemakers had yet emerged from the other modules. Thorsen conferred quickly with the troopers in the module with him. They could see the researcher in the fighter through the vehicle's flight-deck windows. It was difficult to assess what she was doing on the control consoles, but it was apparent that the fighter was still locked into position on its launch rails and would not be able to leave without a manual release.

Then Thorsen's induction scans alerted him to impulse circuits cycling through their ignition sequence. The researcher was attempting to power up the fighter's main drive. Thorsen knew that when the researcher activated it, the plasma venting would kill everyone in the docking module, including her, and the mechanical strain against the launch rails would tear what was left of the entire platform apart.

Thorsen admired her for her willingness to die for her ideals.

He nodded at her with respect as he tuned his laser to optical frequencies that would pass through the fighter's flight-deck windows. Though he forgave her the terror she showed as she saw the muzzle of the weapon point at her; she died badly, without acceptance of her fate at the hands of her superior. She was obviously not optimal. Thorsen thus had no regret as he watched her lifeless body slowly spin in the fighter's cabin.

Within ten minutes, the troopers had removed the researcher's body and Thorsen was strapped into the pilot's chair. Despite the modifications to the vehicle, there were no major changes to the flight controls. He approved. The best innovations were always the simplest. Efficiency was always optimal.

Thorsen's troopers released the fighter from its launch rails and Thorsen used the maneuvering thrusters to gently guide the vehicle from the storage module. He told his troopers he would use the particle cannon to decompress the platform's remaining intact modules; then, when the danger of a peacemaker counterattack had been neutralized, they could board for the next phase of the mission.

It took Thorsen three minutes to destroy the platform. Bodies floating everywhere, a cloud of death surrounding the distant Earth, as it always had. In two more minutes, he had used the particle cannon to neutralize his own troopers as well. History had too often shown that great men were brought down by those who dared to share the glory for others' actions. Thorsen felt no remorse because none was warranted.

At 02:11 GMT, Thorsen sent a coded signal to an Optimum listening post on the moon. The listening post responded with a flight plan that would guide the fighter to Thorsen's meeting with destiny. And Thorsen's meeting with destiny would be humanity's turning point as well.

Because, as of March 19, 2061, the key to total victory over the Optimum's opposition, and to the resulting emergence of a new order and salvation for the world, lay in the hands of a young

JUDITH AND GARFIELD REEVES-STEVENS

scientist named Zefram Cochrane, who was poised on a threshold from which he would forever change humanity's place in the universe.

Driven by the wings of history and dreams of salvation for all who were worthy, and determined not to repeat the mistakes of the past, Adrik Thorsen flew for Titan.

His plan was simple, efficient, optimal—whoever controlled the genius of Zefram Cochrane would control the future of humanity.

And as of March 19, 2061, the future of humanity belonged to Adrik Thorsen.

ONE

☆

CHRISTOPHER'S LANDING, TITAN
Earth Standard: March 19, 2061

For just one moment, a fleeting instant of the time his life would span, Zefram Cochrane thought he heard the stars sing to him.

He could see them overhead, through the transparent slabs of aluminum that formed the dome over this part of the colony of Christopher's Landing, Earth's largest permanent outpost in near-Saturn space. Beyond the dome, the frozen nitrogen winds of Titan swept away thick orange streamers of crystallizing methane and hydrogen cyanide, as they chased the terminator to clear the dense atmosphere for only a few minutes between the clouds of day and the mists of night, allowing, briefly, dark bands to appear in the sky above. In that darkness, the stars flickered for Cochrane, creating a shimmering jeweled band around the dull yellow arc of Saturn that filled a quarter of the sky, so far from the sun that the light reflecting from it made the enormous planet almost imperceptible in Titan's twilight. Its rings, head-on in the same orbital plane as the moon, were invisible.

In that narrow window of time, between the beginning and end of a day unlike any other in human history, Cochrane stared at stars he had known all his life, and they were unfamiliar to him.

21

Alone among all humans now alive, as far as he and most others knew, he had seen them as no one ever had.

Blazing in deep space.

Orbiting a world belonging to another star.

Four and a third light-years from Earth.

Four months ago.

Cochrane closed his eyes to see the stars as he had seen them then, the constellations familiar to billions of his fellow beings shifted to new perspectives never seen before.

Four and a third light-years. A world so far away the fastest impulse-powered probes took more than two decades to reach it, and then took more than four years longer to transmit back the data they recorded.

And Zefram Cochrane had gone there and returned in two hundred and forty-three days.

Faster than any human had ever traveled before.

Faster than *light.*

Cochrane blinked open his eyes at the sudden feeling that the stars here were staring down at him with shock and approbation for daring to invade the sanctity of their domain. In response, he felt laughter rise up in him. He couldn't help it. He stamped his foot into the engineered soil beneath his boots and unexpectedly bounced a few centimeters in the moon's half-gravity.

The awkward moment as he waved his arms for balance broke the previous moment's spell, and he finally realized that the pleasing harmonies he heard were not from the offended stars above, but from the string quartet that played in the assembly hall of the governor's home adjoining the domed field. The faint melody, festive even over the perpetual background hum of the immense air circulators and muffled howl of the outside winds, sounded like something by Brahms, but he couldn't place it.

Cochrane looked down at the bare soil beneath him, the crushed and sterilized decomposed rocks of an alien world in which Earth bacteria worked to change its composition, cleansing it of Titan's octane rain and hydrocarbon sludge. Someday grass and trees would grow here, so that children would run in play and lovers would stroll and old people would sit in contentment on benches by a splashing fountain as they grew old together, gazing up at the stars and knowing that others like them looked back from different distant worlds.

Now the laughter that had been growing in him faded and he felt tears form in his eyes for no reason he understood. What books would he never read that were still to be written on those different distant worlds? What poetry would he never understand? What music? What paintings, what sculpture, what histories unimagined would play out without him now that the human stage had been expanded to . . .

"Infinity."

Cochrane jumped at the word so aptly spoken, startled by the unexpected company. He recognized the voice, of course. His ship, the *Bonaventure,* had cost more than 300 million Eurodollars, and the precarious state of the world was such that government agencies were not inclined to turn over that level of funding to thirty-one-year-old physicists who had the audacity to question the most basic tenets of nature. But the voice belonged to the man who had paid for his ship—Micah Brack.

Brack owed allegiance to no government funding committee or board of directors. The debit slips the tycoon had authorized over the eight years of Cochrane's single-minded pursuit to overturn the Einsteinian mind-set of the Brahmins of modern science had come from Brack's own pocket. Considering that most data agencies placed him among the ten wealthiest individuals in the system, with holdings on every planet and moon humans had colonized, that pocket was virtually without limit. Most of Christopher's Landing existed because of Brack's foresight, *and* his impatience with those who merely looked up at the stars, unable to grasp the promise they held. In Micah Brack, Cochrane had found a champion, a backer, and most importantly, a friend.

"Sorry to startle you." Brack put his hand on Cochrane's shoulder, glancing up to see what Cochrane had seen, so far away. He nodded to the sounds of the reception coming from the lit doorways and windows of the governor's metal-walled home. "But they're about to notice the star of their party is missing."

Cochrane knew that as well. Since his return to the system, less than fifty hours ago, he had had no time to himself. He wasn't used to that kind of intrusion. He didn't like it. Never had. And

23

he had no intention of ever getting used to it, even though Brack had warned him about the public's probable reaction to news of his accomplishment almost three years ago. At the time of that conversation, they had been out past Neptune, with Sternbach and Okuda, literally bouncing off the walls of the *John Cabal,* an old lunar ice freighter Brack had refitted as Cochrane's microgravity lab. The freighter had allowed Cochrane and his team to conduct their research light-hours from Earth's military surveillance nets and the gravimetric disruptions of the sun's gravity well.

Brack had been with them that day, on one of his infrequent trips from Earth—the day the team's first, hundred-kilogram, fluctuation superimpellor test sled had literally warped itself into a smear of rainbow-colored light and streaked off into something other than normal space-time. Eight minutes later, Cochrane's scanners had picked up the distinctive radiation signature of the miniature particle curtain he had rigged to self-destruct the sled one minute after launch. It had been a drastic measure, but at the time he had known of no other way to cause a continuum-distortion generator to reenter normal space at a precise moment, had no precise idea of how far the sled would travel, and had no way to predict in which directions it might drift while not in normal space.

When the signature had been confirmed, the vast, hollow drum of the *John Cabal*'s science bay had echoed with cheers. The sled had traveled eight light-minutes—more than 143 million kilometers—in sixty seconds.

The prototype superimpellor was massive in proportion compared to the initial test devices Cochrane had used in his twenties at MIT to accelerate electrons to twice the velocity of light. But its size had not lessened the effect of the distortion and it had transported the sled at a pseudovelocity eight times faster than light, corresponding to a relativistic time-warp multiplier factor of 2^2!

That day they had toasted farewell to the Einsteinian universe, drinking hundred-year-old cognac from squeeze tubes—microgravity was no place for effervescent champagne. It wasn't

24

that Einstein and Hawking and Cross and all the other giants of physics had been proven wrong—the universe had simply opened another window onto its infinite, unpredictable nature for humans to peer through, and a whole new science had to be created to describe phenomena that earlier scientists had never seen, and that some, like Einstein, had refused to imagine.

In that refusal, at least, Einstein *had* been wrong. Because, as Cochrane had predicted, and as he had finally given up trying to explain to nonscientists, whose eyes inexplicably yet inevitably glazed over whenever multidimensional equations entered the conversation, the effects of relativity were limited to normal space-time alone. Cochrane's subsequent bench tests on rapidly decaying particles had shown that once the superimpellor had entered a fluctuating continuum distortion, the well-known time-dilation effects of very fast-speed travel no longer occurred.

Because there was no way for information to be exchanged between the normal universe and the volume contained within the distortion—for *now,* his team continued to remind him—time could progress within the continuum distortion at the same rate it had progressed when it was last in contact with normal space-time, without contradicting anything that had been established about light-speed being the fastest anything could travel.

Of course, Cochrane knew that eventually, given enough fluctuation-superimpellor-driven ships visiting enough distant stellar systems with their own rates of relativistic time, variations in timekeeping would mount up. He could see that eventually, given enough superimpellor-driven spacecraft visiting enough distant planets, a whole new technique of timekeeping and date-recording would have to be developed to account for those local rate-of-time variations and relate them to each other in a meaningful, if complex, way. But by slipping the bounds of Einsteinian space-time, time dilation was no longer a limiting factor to the human exploration of space. More importantly, Brack had observed that day, neither was distance.

However, Brack had gone on to warn, there was a price that would have to be paid. When Cochrane returned from the stars as the first human to have traveled faster than light, his name would be uttered in the same breath as Armstrong, Yoshikawa, and

Daar. He would no longer be able to lead a normal, low-profile existence—he and his life would belong to the world. To the universe.

Judging from Cochrane's reception in Christopher's Landing, everything Brack had said had come true. Cochrane sometimes wondered about the insight or science behind his friend's ability to predict the future. He did it so often and so well. But Brack himself denied having any special gifts. "The events of the future are reflected in the events of the past," he often said. He claimed only to be an attentive student of history.

Cochrane looked back up at the dome, but the brief twilight clearing had passed. The mists of Titan's night billowed beyond the transparent slabs, roiling in the external floodlights, as if the colony were a lone oceangoing vessel, plying Earth's North Atlantic in the winter. Cochrane tried not to think about icebergs.

"What was that you said about infinity?" he asked his friend.

Brack grinned and the years dropped from his face. Cochrane guessed the billionaire was in his fifties, middle-aged for the citizens of Earth's industrialized nations. His short hair was white—Brack paid no attention to fashion or fads—and worn in a style reminiscent of the Caesars. But his eyes sparkled like those of a much younger man, and the smile in his rugged face was always full of the promise of youth. Cochrane guessed having enough wealth to affect the course of human history might give a person reason enough to feel young and energetic, but he often thought there was more complexity within Brack than the man would ever reveal.

"I saw you looking at the stars," Brack answered. "So wasn't that what you were thinking? About the new limits to human growth? Or, should I say, that now there are *no* limits."

"But how did you know that *was* what I was thinking?"

Brack glanced away, a smaller smile flickering at the corners of his mouth. Cochrane recognized the expression. Brack wasn't going to answer the question. Instead he asked one of his own. "What are the prospects for a colony?"

"At Centauri B II?" Cochrane was surprised by Brack's sudden change of subject. He was operating in his business mode now.

26

FEDERATION

"Those surveys were complete before I left," Cochrane answered. "They were complete practically before I was born, weren't they?"

The whole world knew the prospects for a colony at Alpha Centauri were good, and had for decades. Of the hundred or so known solar systems detected beyond Earth, the Centauri system was the most thoroughly mapped, primarily because it was also the closest solar system to Earth's.

Seen with the unaided eye, Alpha Centauri was the third brightest star in the sky, though only visible south of latitude +30°. Its brilliance was due to its closeness and to it being, in fact, a ternary system composed of three separate stars. Alpha Centauri A was a spectral-type G2 star, a close twin to Earth's own sun, gravitationally locked to Alpha Centauri B, a slightly larger and brighter K0 star. Alpha Centauri A and Alpha Centauri B orbited each other about the same distance apart as the diameter of Earth's solar system. The third stellar component of the system, Proxima Centauri, was a much smaller red dwarf star, in excess of 400 times more distant from A and B than they were from each other.

Just after the turn of the century, astronomers on Earth, using ground-based, adaptive optic telescopes, had resolved at least two additional bodies in the Alpha Centauri system: two large planets caught up in a complex, oscillating orbital pattern around the A and B stars. The scientific world was shocked by their discovery because common wisdom presumed that no planet could maintain a stable orbit between two such closely situated stars.

In the decades that followed, a new generation of astronomers employed liquid vacuum telescopes on the moon's farside to resolve three more planets in the Alpha Centauri system. One, about the size of Mercury, was locked in an eccentric orbit around Alpha Centauri A. The other two Earth-size planets occupied interweaving orbital paths around Alpha Centauri B, in a region roughly corresponding to that defined by the orbits of Mars and Venus in Earth's solar system. Such an orbital pattern was, of course, also considered impossible. The charting of the Alpha Centauri system made it a fascinating time to be an astronomer.

27

Lunar-based spectroscopic interferometry analysis of the five Centauri planets eventually confirmed that one of the two Earth-size planets orbiting B exhibited a strong oxygen-absorption line. Since the planet's size and mass and, therefore, gravity were only a fraction higher than Earth's, and since oxygen is a light enough gas that it would dissipate within a few thousand years under Earth-type gravity, the strong concentration of oxygen in that planet's atmosphere could mean only one of two things—either a completely novel chemical reaction was occurring on the planet's surface, constantly replenishing the supply of oxygen—

—or there was life.

The news electrified the world. In the solar system, only on Earth had life taken hold with such success. Mars had merely shown promise. The microfossils excavated from its ancient seabeds had shown the existence of early forms of plankton and archaeobacteria—suspiciously similar enough to forms that had evolved on Earth to lead several scholars to suggest that some agency other than catastrophic meteoric impact had been responsible for the same seeds of life being sown on Earth and Mars together.

As the new century progressed, uncrewed probes were launched toward the Alpha Centauri system. Most met the same fate as the disappointing Nomad series at the turn of the century, rapidly and inexplicably failing after passing the heliopause surrounding Earth's solar system. The development of efficient, vectored impulse drives led inevitably to a second and third generation of probes launched toward Centauri and other likely extrasolar systems at substantial fractions of light-speed. Though some of these new series also met with unexplained failures and disappearances, dozens of probes did succeed, blazing past alien worlds as they transmitted relativistically attenuated data back to Earth.

By the time of Cochrane's own birth in 2030, scientists were as certain as scientists could be that a fully evolved, self-regulating, Gaia-type ecosystem was flourishing on Centauri B II, just as on Earth. So certain were they that crewed expeditions were launched. But a further series of mysterious failures, culminating in the tragic loss of telemetry from the NASA vessel *Charybdis*, brought an end to the first attempted wave of the human exploration of extrasolar space. Some commentators fond of conspiracy theories even put forward the idea that Khan Noonien Singh and his followers were not frozen in some long-lost sleeper ship, but were prowling the outer solar system, blowing up space probes, keeping their genetically inferior conquerors planet-bound.

Whatever the reason for Earth's initial difficulties in pursuing advanced exploration, as the political tensions of the mid-twenty-first century worsened, funding for purely scientific endeavors became less popular and harder to obtain. As had happened so often in human history, Brack assured Cochrane, even with the potential rewards of cooperation and exploration so obvious, humankind once again turned in on itself, becoming insular and distrustful and forgetful of the need to look beyond the immediate.

There was always a weariness in Brack when he spoke about the incessant repetition of failure in human affairs. Cochrane detected that same weariness now.

"I know what the scanners say," Brack continued impatiently. "I've seen the simulations, read the reports, the speculations." He gestured dismissively. He was a man who only wanted results. "But what I came out here to ask you, Zefram, is what did Centauri B II *look* like to you? What did it *feel* like?" He held out both hands as if beseeching Cochrane. "I know what the oxygen percentage of the atmosphere is. But what did it *taste* like to breathe alien air? Do you think a man could live there and call it *home?*"

Cochrane recalled the tang of that air: sere, dusty, but filled with the scent of life. After the fact, he knew he had been a fool to slip off his breathing mask even for the few minutes he had allowed himself. Computer analysis had shown the ecosystem of Centauri B II to be DNA-based with the same range of amino acids—more fuel for the fire of those who thought Earth and Mars had been deliberately seeded. There was no way of knowing what kind of bacteria and viruses he had exposed himself to with those lungfuls of air never before tasted by humans. But other than two days of sinus discomfort, and some stinging grit in the corners of his eyes, Cochrane had suffered no ill effects. Maybe he had been lucky. Or maybe humanity was meant to go to other worlds unencumbered.

"Yes," he told Brack, numbers and scanners aside. "No night for half the year, but it's a place where people could live with no more hardship than desert equatorial regions on Earth."

"Good," Brack said. He winked at Cochrane. "You remember the law of mediocrity?"

Cochrane understood the law was a much misunderstood scientific principle, which translated to the lay public as "things are pretty much the same all over." If chemistry behaved a certain way on Earth, then the law of mediocrity suggested that chemistry would behave the same way on a planet a thousand light-years distant, or on Earth a billion years in the past. Cochrane knew what Brack was getting at.

"You're thinking that if the first planet we visit in the first solar system we explore has an Earth-like planet, then the galaxy is filled with them."

Brack nodded. "And humans will be like dandelion seeds blown on the wind, filling them all."

Cochrane smiled at his friend's grandiose dream. "You know how long it would take to establish even a single colony in another solar system—even *with* the superimpellor? You know how much it would cost?"

Brack didn't smile as he answered. "One billion Eurodollars." He held up the fingers of one hand, the thumb folded in. "Four years."

Cochrane stared at Brack as the industrialist spread his arms to indicate everything around them. "Think of it, Zefram. A Christopher's Landing–type colony. Fusion generators to begin. Solar and thermal in the second decade. Hospitals, libraries, self-building factories. Drone mines. Even an orbiting space platform for mapping, communication, and ship maintenance and repair. I'm assembling the modular components on the moon as we speak."

Cochrane was startled by the news, and by Brack's audacity. "You were that certain I'd succeed?"

"If you've been in business as long as I have, you learn how to pick winners."

Cochrane's eyes narrowed. He wanted to ask exactly how long Brack *had* been in business, even though he knew from experience that that was another topic Brack didn't like discussing. But there were other questions. "Why the hurry, Micah?"

Brack thought about his answer, pursed his lips, stared up at the dome, but focused on something only his eyes could see. "In 1838, a British steamer, the *Great Western,* crossed the Atlantic, Bristol to New York, in fifteen days." He looked back at Cochrane. Cochrane shrugged. He didn't see the point. "It was the first fully steam-powered vessel to make the crossing. Another ship arrived the same day, but it had taken nineteen days to cross from London. Now, the sailing clippers could make the crossing faster if the winds were right, but the *Great Western* moved independent of the winds and the weather. It was technology. Dependable. Repeatable. Fifteen days from London to New York. A trip that used to take months."

Cochrane waited. "I sense an analogy building."

Brack rubbed at his temple, as if he were caught up in a memory instead of reciting facts he had studied. "You know what the American newspapers—they were the data agencies of the time —you know what they said?"

"I'm at a loss."

Brack quoted. " 'The commercial, moral, and political effects of this increased intercourse, to Europe and this country, must be immense.' "

"They were right, weren't they?" Cochrane asked.

Brack's eyes burned into him. *"And,* they said, because of the expansion of business, the rapid spreading of information, and the resulting reduction of prejudice, it would make 'war a thing almost impossible.' "

Cochrane shrugged. "Simpler times."

"No," Brack said emphatically. "There's never been a simpler time. Never. In all of human history, everything has always been as complex as it is right now. The people change. The technology changes. But the . . . the forces at work, whatever it is that drives us to *be* human, that's always the same."

Brack looked back at the governor's home. The quartet still played. Cochrane could hear faint laughter mingled with the music—a cocktail party on Titan. He wondered what the newspaper data agencies of 230 years ago would have thought about that.

"Eighteen thirty-eight," Brack continued. "That same year, the Boers slaughter three thousand Zulus in Natal. British forces invade Afghanistan. Eighteen thirty-nine: Ottoman forces invade Syria. Britain and China start the Opium War. Eighteen forty: the Treaty of London unites Britain, Austria, Prussia, *and* Russia against Egypt. Steamships didn't do a thing except get troops into battle more quickly. It's *never* going to end, Zefram."

Cochrane thought he saw where his friend was headed with his argument. "You're worried about what's going on back on Earth, aren't you? Colonel Green. The Optimum Movement."

But Brack went on as if he hadn't heard Cochrane. "A century later, *nineteen* forty-four: World War *Two.*" He rolled his eyes in mock exasperation. "We actually started *numbering* them. And all eyes were on television. You know what the data agencies said about that?"

"You tell me."

"Exactly what they said about steamships!" Brack held his hand to his eyes, recalling something he had read. Or heard. " 'Television offers the soundest basis for world peace that has yet been presented. International television will knit together the peoples of the world in bonds of mutual respect.' " Now Brack rubbed his hand over his eyes, as if overcome by a sudden wave of fatigue, not just weariness. "Television! And after Korea, and Vietnam, and Afghanistan, and Africa, and Khan, and Antarctica, war was *still* with us. And television . . ." Brack snorted disdainfully. "It's been twenty years at least since anything's been done with it on an international level. It's dead. Steamships are curios for collectors. But people are still people."

Across the domed field, the concert ended. Cochrane heard the polite applause. As Brack had said, the guest of honor would be missed soon.

"What's your point, Micah?"

"They're going to say the same thing about what you've done."

"That the fluctuation superimpellor will bring an end to war?"

32

Brack's wry smile didn't do anything to warm his grim tone. "I promise you that that will be the lead editorial on a hundred services by the end of the week."

"Well, why not?" Cochrane asked. "I mean, wars are fought over resources, and the superimpellor opens up the galaxy. There's no end to resources now."

Cochrane followed Brack's gaze to the governor's home. There were silhouettes in the windows. People looking out, trying to find the man of the hour. Of the century.

"Wars are fought because that is what people do," Brack said. "Resources are an excuse, nothing more."

Cochrane felt frustration rising in him. Usually, he was all for these philosophical talks with Brack. The industrialist could go on as if time had no meaning for him. But Cochrane was about to be pulled back into the governor's reception. Who knew when he would have five minutes to himself again?

"Micah, the superimpellor has no military function, if that's what you're worried about. It can't even be used out here by Saturn without getting twisted up with the sun's gravity well. On Earth, it can't function for more than a nanosecond without self-destructing. Remember Kashishowa?"

Brack's expression hardened. "I know it has no military function—the little 'accident' at Kashishowa Station notwithstanding. I would never have funded your work if I had thought otherwise. But no matter what the editorialists say over the months ahead, the superimpellor has no *peaceful* function, either. It's technology, Zefram. Neutral. It's only what humans make of it."

At last Cochrane saw the question to be asked. "And what should we make of it?"

"An insurance policy."

Cochrane didn't understand.

"War won't end, Zefram. The superimpellor won't do it. Matter replication or teleportation won't do it. Nothing on the thousand drawing boards I fund ever will. But what the superimpellor *will* do is make sure the next war won't cause humanity's extinction."

"There won't be a 'next' war. The New United Nations—"

"Are a joke. There will *always* be a next war. And each next war brings crueler weapons. And the more cruel the weapons, then the more cruel the person who uses them." Brack stepped closer to Cochrane. Someone was in the open door of the governor's home, waving her arm as if calling Cochrane in. "We're ten years from World War Three, Zefram. Twenty at most. The New United Nations is destined to collapse like its predecessors. And a third world war fought with twenty-first-century technology is going to be something from which Earth might never recover."

Cochrane frowned as he finally understood what Brack meant. "But Centauri B II will be far enough away not to get involved."

"Centauri B II and a half-dozen others within the decade. Perhaps twenty within the same number of years."

Cochrane gave his friend a skeptical look. "Not even you can afford to spend twenty billion Eurodollars on twenty extrasolar colonies."

"You're right. But I can get four or five started. And when my competitors see me doing it, they're going to think I see profit in it, so they're going to try and beat me at my own game. They'll form consortiums. Sell shares. Attach superimpellors to every probe sled and impulse freighter in the system to flood the nearby systems with a wave of exploration . . . and I intend to give them the patents to do it."

Cochrane nearly choked. *"Give* them the patents? After what you spent to develop them?"

Brack patted Cochrane on the back. "You've made space travel quick, now leave it to me to make it inexpensive. Trust me, my friend, by the time I'm finished with giving your invention away, they'll be naming planets after you. And by the time any of my competitors figure out I'm just throwing my money away on colonies, with no hope for any kind of reasonable return, it will be too late. A whole industry based on interstellar exploration will have emerged." Brack's eyes narrowed as his most serious tone returned. "An industry that will be able to survive the collapse of Earth."

"You're telling me all of human history is a race, aren't you?" Cochrane asked. "That we've always been running away from our own worst instincts, and that we always will be."

Brack gave Cochrane a look the physicist knew too well. A

34

surprise was coming, and it wouldn't be pleasant. "Zefram, Colonel Adrik Thorsen left Earth two hours ago. He's coming here. To see you."

Cochrane felt a chill that had nothing to do with the chill air of Titan. Thorsen was one of Colonel Green's cadre. He was rumored to have quelled a ration demonstration in Stockholm by deploying battlefield pulse emitters designed to be used against armored infantry. The civilians taking part in the demonstration had had no radiation armor. Hundreds had been killed. Thousands left impaired, their synaptic connections sundered at a molecular level.

Then Thorsen had joined with the Optimum Movement in the Pursuit of Perfection. Perfection was whatever Colonel Green and those of his countless analytical committees said it was. And if something, or someone, or some group of people wasn't perfect, then that thing, or that person or group, didn't deserve to exist.

Cochrane understood what Brack had said about history repeating itself. The coldly efficient bureaucracies of Green's Analytical Committees, the stark design of the interlinked OM triangles, all were just new skins for an old and hideous ideology that should have been consigned to its ashes more than a century ago.

"I've had nothing to do with the Optimum," Cochrane said. "Why does he want to see me?"

"Don't flatter yourself. He wants to see your ship."

"Our ship."

"The point is, he wants to make it *his.*"

The answer seemed obvious to Cochrane. "But we won't let him."

Brack sighed. "There have been a great many changes while you've been away, Zefram. The Optimum Movement has been expanding its influence. Rapidly. There are some nations on Earth that don't like the way things are going. They're the ones clinging to the illusion of order the Optimum offer, and ignoring the price they'll have to pay."

"Well," Cochrane said, his mind working quickly, "if Thorsen left two hours ago, then we've still got a few days before he gets here. We can work out something tomorrow."

"Colonel Thorsen will arrive on Titan in nine hours."

Cochrane's eyes widened. Whatever vehicle Thorsen was in, he was traveling at almost five percent the speed of light. Impulse drives could boost a space vehicle to that kind of velocity in less than an hour, but the rapid acceleration would crush any living thing on board into a thin organic paste against the aft bulkhead. True, there were specially constructed impulse ships designed to operate at multi-g accelerations with humans aboard, for military or emergency rescue missions, but those required the pilots to be suspended in liquid-filled command capsules, "breathing" an oxygen-rich saline solution to prevent their lungs from being crushed. Crewed ships could reach light-speed velocities without harming their living cargo only through *gradual* acceleration. But even at a constant, military-standard three-g acceleration, it would take almost five days to achieve the speed with which Thorsen was coming to Titan.

"What's he sending? An artificial-intelligence surrogate?"

"He's coming himself, Zefram."

"Not in nine hours, he's not. This time of year, we're thirty-seven light-minutes from Earth. No human could survive that kind of impulse acceleration."

A handful of people were walking across the bare soil to Cochrane and Brack. They only had a minute left to talk undisturbed.

"As I said," Brack said emphatically, "there have been a great many changes since you left."

Cochrane's eyes widened as he realized what Brack was implying. "Inertial damping?"

Brack frowned. "I've spent a fortune trying to develop *that* over the past thirty years, too. And the breakthrough came out of the R-and-D section of a chain of simulator theaters, of all things." He looked away to gauge the approach of the party guests. "But on the bright side, between your superimpellor and control of inertia, there's not a place in the universe humans can't travel."

Cochrane felt as if he'd been kicked. Control of inertia put the full power of vectored-impulse space travel in the hands of human crews and passengers. The solar system could be crossed in hours. An Earth-moon flight would be little longer than a maglev train trip between San Francisco and New Los Angeles, with more time spent getting out of Earth's atmosphere than traveling the next 380,000 kilometers in vacuum. And Adrik Thorsen, the Optimum, was already using that technology.

A part of Cochrane wished he could see the specs of an inertial damper. The device, if it were real, might help him overcome some of the superimpellor's engineering shortcomings. But it was human shortcomings that concerned him now. "After all you've just told me about human nature, do we really want the Optimum to spread into the universe?"

Brack shook his head. "The Optimum aren't interested in the universe. They're interested in control. And how can they have control if the superimpellor can whisk their potential subjects light-years beyond their influence?" The reception guests were almost upon them. "I'm guessing Thorsen's coming here to see if he can *suppress* your invention."

Cochrane clenched his fists at his sides. Alone in space, it was easy to convince himself that science was as pure as the numbers glowing on a scanner screen. But being back among the madding crowd, he was once again reminded of how impossible that ideal was. As long as people remained blind to the clarity with which the universe was laid out, there would always be those who would seek to obscure and twist its truths for ugly political and philosophical goals. Cochrane could see Brack read that growing sense of resentment and anger within him.

"Don't worry," Brack said. "There's no chance he'll be able to suppress anything. I'm giving away the patents, remember? As soon as you download a systems assessment I can include as an engineering supplement, I'm going systemwide to transmit your design theories, your blueprints, and your manufacturing log. By the time Thorsen arrives, the information will already be on its way back to the inner planets. By the time the editorialists start pontificating on the end of war, millions of people will have access to your work. The genie, so to speak, is out of the bottle and will never go back in."

Cochrane felt overwhelmed. After so much time alone, his emotions were too rarefied. Though he had never admitted it to anyone, indeed, had taken great pains to deny it, he *had* looked

37

forward to a scientific triumph. He especially had wanted to hear the apologies from those who had scoffed at his work years ago. "I had hoped to publish in the normal way," he said hesitantly. "Peer review. A data conference upon publication. That sort of thing. I . . . I don't know what to say, Micah."

"That's why you're with me, my friend. I do. And this is not the time for things to be done normally. I want humanity to explode out of this system as if a dam had burst."

Cochrane wanted that, too. More than ever. More than anything. "So what do we do about Thorsen?"

Brack lowered his voice as the approaching partygoers came within earshot. "Leave Thorsen to me. In two hours, my yacht will be prepped for launch at Shuttlebay Four. She'll take you back to the *Bonaventure*. I've got a tug up there now replenishing her." Brack suddenly turned to the approaching guests and held up his hands. "Ladies, gentlemen: an indulgence, please. I'll return him to you in just a moment." Then he put his arm around Cochrane's shoulder and guided him across the soil, away from the excited and slightly annoyed buzz of conversation that grew behind them.

Cochrane was annoyed, as well, as he pictured strangers' hands on his ship. "Micah, please. The antimatter field containers are still too sensitive. And I've *got* to do something about the lithium converter. It only runs at twenty-two percent of—" But Brack cut him off.

"There's no time for that, Zefram. Put it in your engineering download. The point is, when the *Bonaventure*'s fueled and stocked, I want you to leave."

Cochrane stopped dead. He could tell Brack didn't just mean Titan or near-Saturn space. "As in, leave the system?"

Brack nodded. His expression was grim as he heard the partygoers swarming toward them again. "That's right. Far enough out that you can use the superimpellor again."

Cochrane grimaced. It would take him two weeks to get far enough away from the sun's gravity well. Two more weeks of being alone in space.

"Not for long," Brack added, obviously sensing Cochrane's

unspoken reaction. "Just enough that the military nets will lose track of you. Because when Thorsen arrives and finds you gone, they *will* be tracking you."

"And then what?" Cochrane asked.

Brack quickly laid out his flight plan, telling Cochrane to reenter the solar system opposite Saturn's present position, then come in like an Oort freighter on a long-fall passage, to rendezvous with asteroid RG-1522. "I've got a manufacturing setup there," Brack explained. "You can get started on the second generation of the superimpellor. Get the fields up to the volume of a freighter."

"And be safe from Thorsen?"

"I'll be honest," Brack said. "Thorsen's just a puppet. I want you safe from the Optimum."

"When will that be?"

"When they realize that anyone with a few hundred thousand Eurodollars can retrofit an existing space vehicle to make a faster-than-light vessel. And that anyone with a few hundred Eurodollars can book passage on one. When Colonel Green and his cohorts realize they can't stop the spread of the superimpellor, they'll lose interest before they'll admit defeat."

There were footsteps immediately behind them. Chiding voices told Brack he had monopolized Cochrane long enough.

"Come with me, Micah," Cochrane said impulsively, as if the two of them were still alone. "See what I've seen."

Brack smiled with no hidden meanings. "Soon, but not now." He gestured to the bare soil around them. "I've still a lot of work to finish here before I move on"—he waved his hand at the dome and what lay above it—"out there."

"What kind of work?"

For a moment, the weariness left Brack's eyes. "I want to see the grass grow here, Zefram. A billion kilometers from where it evolved." He patted his friend's arm, almost in a gesture of farewell. "And then, I want to plant a fig tree."

Someone handed Cochrane a drink. He felt hands on his arms and back. Conversation, a dozen questions, flew around him. But he looked over at Brack and asked, "A fig tree?"

Brack looked almost sheepish, being parted from Cochrane by the throng that gathered. "From which the Buddha drew enlightenment. It reminds me of home," he explained. He touched his fist to his heart. "A man's entitled to that."

Brack nodded once, then stepped aside with an expression of finality as the crowd bore Cochrane away in triumph, as if he had safely tossed Cochrane into the currents of history but must himself forever remain on the shore.

Through the long hours that passed that night, until he stood at the airlock doors of Shuttlebay 4, Cochrane thought of all that Brack had told him, and of Colonel Thorsen hurtling toward him with a technology that had not existed a year ago. But most of all, he thought of Brack's final words.

What more could any person want than a home? And what was the purpose of Cochrane's work if not to make the entire universe humanity's home?

The thought of home brought back memories of the small house outside London where he had lived with his parents on their last posting. Sitting in the back garden, a few days after his eleventh birthday, playing with a simple plastic wand and tub of soap solution, he had cast shimmering bubbles into the air. The colors had transfixed him that day, along with the reflections caught within reflections when one bubble formed within another. And for some reason he still did not understand, his mind's eye had suddenly conjured an image of a different sort of bubble twisting around another so that they both popped up in a somewhere-else his young mind could *see* but not describe.

It had taken Cochrane twenty years to work backward from that moment of intuition and create the technology that could do what he had seen so clearly. All because he had sat beneath a tree.

Cochrane thought of fig trees then, as Brack's yacht was buffeted by Titan's winds, lifting through them. As the clouds were left behind, Cochrane stared out a porthole to see a distant star, brighter than any other but a star nonetheless, not easily resolved into a disk. Somewhere near it, too faint to be seen, was the home of all soap bubbles, all fig trees. Cochrane's home.

Planet Earth. It would be seventeen years before he returned to it, and he would never see Micah Brack again.

The ancient race humanity ran to escape its own worst attributes continued, but on this day, unlike any other in human history, for the first time the race's destination was in sight. And though he had not yet fully grasped his position in what would unfold, it was now up to Zefram Cochrane to lead the way.

TWO

U.S.S. ENTERPRISE NCC–1701
IN TRANSIT TO BABEL
Stardate 3849.8
Earth Standard: ≈ November 2267

Kirk knew the inevitable could be avoided no longer. There was no time left to consider the odds, to devise strategies, or even to change the rules. He had to take action and he had to take action *now*.

His opponents stared at him, their thoughts unreadable. All Kirk could hear was the faint hum of the environmental system's fans, the slow sighs of his ship while she slept, late on the midnight shift. Kirk allowed no emotion to show on his face as he reached forward. All eyes were on his hand.

He dropped five tongue depressors onto the pile on the shimmering fabric of the medical diagnostic bed, and in his most authoritative voice, he said, "I'll see your five."

Without expression, Sarek of Vulcan, son of Skon and grandson of Solkar, turned over his cards.

Kirk lost control of his own expression as he stared at the ambassador's poker hand.

A pair of sixes.

Kirk sat back in the chair he had set up beside the ambassador's bed in the *Enterprise*'s sickbay. "You were bluffing," he said.

Sarek blinked. He looked over at Spock, who sat placidly in a second chair, wearing his blue medical jumpsuit and black tunic as if they were a formal uniform. "It is the nature of the game, is it not?" Sarek asked.

Spock nodded sagely. "Indeed."

Kirk didn't like the sound of that. There was something wrong here. "Spock, I thought Vulcans couldn't lie."

"Though we are capable of it," Spock explained, "we choose not to. In most circumstances."

Kirk narrowed his eyes at Sarek. "But isn't bluffing a form of lying?"

Sarek's expression remained bland, though Kirk was certain that something in it had changed. The more time he spent around Spock, the more he had convinced himself that Vulcans betrayed just as much emotional information in their faces as humans did, though in a much subtler fashion.

"In this case, Captain, bluffing is an expected strategy of the game. Indeed, it is encouraged. Therefore, by betting in a manner inconsistent with the actual value of my cards, I am, in fact, following the true intent of the game, which therefore, by definition, cannot be false."

Spock nodded thoughtfully. "Well put, Father."

Sarek lay back against his pillows. "Thank you, my son."

Kirk wrinkled his brow. Not two days ago he had heard Sarek tell his wife Amanda that it was not necessary to thank logic. He didn't know how, but something told Kirk his leg was being pulled. Perhaps being cooped up in sickbay with him for two days was beginning to take its toll on the Vulcans.

"So this *isn't* the first time you've played poker?" Kirk asked accusingly. Chess was more his game, and he enjoyed the never-ending tournament he and Spock had fallen into. But with three players to account for, poker had seemed a better way to socialize with his fellow patients. To Kirk's chagrin, however, the pile of tongue depressors was deepest on the blanket beside Sarek.

Sarek maintained his maddening composure. "My wife taught me many years ago, after Spock joined Starfleet. The insights it afforded me have been beneficial in certain negotiations with . . . certain species."

43

I bet they have, Kirk thought. "Coridan's going to be admitted to the Federation, isn't it." He made it a statement. If Sarek negotiated as well as he played poker, the other delegates to the Babel Conference didn't stand a chance against him.

"I will argue for admission," Sarek acknowledged, "but my wishes are in no way an indication of what the result of the final vote will be."

"With that much dilithium on the planet," Kirk continued, "how could Coridan not be admitted? The Orions were willing to start an interplanetary war over it." The knife wound in Kirk's back was a direct result of Coridan's dilithium. Orion smugglers had conspired to prevent the planet's admission to the Federation in order to maintain their illegal mining and smuggling operations and profit from supplying both sides with dilithium in the war to come.

But Sarek did not agree. "It is true that dilithium is the lifeblood of any interstellar political association. Without it, warp drive can never be exploited to its full potential. But, it has been my experience that wars are seldom fought over resources. At the time, the question of resources may appear to be a valid excuse for hostilities, indeed, a rallying cry. But upon reflection, most conflict is inevitably based in emotion." Sarek fixed Kirk with a steady gaze—an emotional signal of some sort, Kirk was certain. "I mean no disrespect," Sarek concluded.

Kirk mulled over that last statement, which from anyone else would have meant the opposite of what it appeared to mean, and despite the ambassador's recent heart attacks and cryogenic open-heart procedure, Sarek had never once lost his mental edge. Kirk wondered if there was such a thing as Vulcan humor. He looked back at Spock, trying to detect any sign of hidden Vulcan laughter.

But Spock merely raised a quizzical eyebrow. "You have a question, Captain?"

Kirk couldn't bring himself to ask the obvious. He knew he could talk with Spock about Vulcan emotions, but it might be too embarrassing a topic for Spock to discuss in front of his father. If Spock could feel embarrassment, that is. Kirk decided that changing the subject was a better tactic. "Did your mother teach you how to play poker, too?"

Spock shook his head. "Dr. McCoy did, after our encounter with the First Federation ship."

"Actually," Sarek volunteered, "I have often thought poker would be a useful exercise for Vulcan children, to help them learn to control the display of their emotions."

Kirk saw his opening and pounced. "Gentlemen, it sounds as if you're suggesting that the famed Vulcan reticence to display emotion is nothing more than a prolonged bluff itself. In fact, it could be said that for a people who pride themselves on choosing never to lie, their whole demeanor is, in fact, just that." Feeling proud of himself, Kirk folded his arms.

Sarek and Spock exchanged a look. Spock spoke first. "Captain, what you have suggested is not logical."

Kirk didn't understand. "Yes, it is."

Spock was about to reply when Sarek interrupted. "Captain, the 'pot' is still unclaimed. We have yet to see *your* hand."

Damn, Kirk thought. He had hoped they had forgotten. He turned over his cards. A pair of fives.

"It would appear you were bluffing, as well," Sarek said, with just the slightest hint of smugness in his tone.

"He is quite good at it," Spock offered.

"Indeed."

Kirk looked from father to son, realizing that *they* had successfully changed the topic on him. Kirk decided that whatever effect the past two days were having on Sarek and Spock, they were certainly beginning to take their toll on *him.*

Sarek reached out to scoop up the tongue depressors. "I believe the cultural incantation required at this time is 'Come to poppa.'"

"That is correct," Spock said.

At the sound of those words coming from the revered Vulcan diplomat, Kirk clamped his hand to his mouth to try and contain his laughter, but he knew he wasn't going to make it. It erupted from him with a barely contained snort. He tried to cover his unfortunate reaction with a series of coughs, but that just made

45

the knife wound in his back flare with sharp pain, bringing tears to his eyes.

In their most subdued Vulcan manner, Spock and Sarek looked alarmed.

"The incantation is not 'Come to poppa'?" Sarek asked.

Kirk waved his hand. If he even tried to open his mouth, he'd go on a laughing jag that could set Earth-Vulcan relations back by a decade.

"Captain?" Spock said with Vulcan concern. "Are you all right?"

Kirk nodded. He wiped the tears from his cheeks. "Water," he gasped in what he hoped was a convincing simulation of something caught in his throat. He started to get up from his chair.

The door to the examination room puffed open, taking Kirk by surprise. It was too early for Nurse Chapel and far too late for Dr. McCoy.

But it was McCoy who entered, eyes bleary, hair mussed, uniform obviously just thrown on. Kirk instantly knew that whatever had brought McCoy to sickbay at this hour, it had also wakened him unexpectedly.

The ship's surgeon came to a stop in the middle of the ward. He stared at his three patients with an open mouth. "What in God's name are you two doing out of bed?!"

Sarek folded his hands in his lap. It was clear the doctor was referring to Kirk and Spock.

Spock answered the question. "Playing poker."

McCoy's eyes dropped to Sarek's bed, took in the deck of cards, the piles of tongue depressors. "So help me, I'll sedate the lot of you! Put you in . . . *restraints!*"

Kirk finished getting to his feet. "Bones, it's all right. Your treatment made us feel better even faster. . . ." But then he winced. The knife wound in his back seemed to twist in place, as if the knife were still in it. He felt the blood leave his face. From the look on McCoy's face, it was an alarming departure.

Kirk suddenly felt Spock's arm slip under his, steadying him. But McCoy disapproved of that, too. He grabbed Kirk away from the science officer and manhandled the captain across the ward, telling Spock to get back to bed before he was put into isolation.

Kirk flopped back on the medical diagnostic bed and felt his breath escape him. McCoy activated the diagnostic board and Kirk heard his own heartbeat racing. "I told you this could happen," McCoy snapped as he held a whirring medical scanner over Kirk's chest.

Kirk mouthed the words "What could happen?" Now he really couldn't talk. He felt as if the bandages around his chest were solid duranium, slowly constricting, cutting off any chance he had of breathing again.

"The knife was treated with a protein inhibitor." McCoy deftly clicked a drug ampule into a hypospray. Kirk heard his heartbeat accelerating. "It's an old Orion trick. Keeps the wound open and bleeding with no poison to show up in an autopsy. Makes sure there's no blood left on the weapon, either." The cold tip of the hypo pushed against Kirk's shoulder and he felt the sudden pinch of its high-pressure infusion. "Fortunately, you were lucky enough to get in here before you needed an autopsy. *Barely.*" Though Kirk didn't feel as if his condition had changed, the sudden caustic tone in McCoy's delivery told him he was going to be all right. He felt his breathing ease. His heartbeat began to slow. He recognized the effect from his last visit to Vulcan. "Tri-ox?" he whispered.

McCoy glared down at him. "When I hear that you've earned your medical degree, I'd be happy to discuss drug therapies, *Captain.* Now stay put."

"Yes, sir," Kirk whispered. He squinted to the side as McCoy spun around and advanced on Spock. "And as for you," the doctor began.

Kirk closed his eyes and smiled as McCoy's tirade continued. Sometimes he thought the doctor was only happy when he had something to complain about, and Finagle knew Kirk and Spock went out of their way to oblige him.

The pain in his back began to lessen, and Kirk guessed that McCoy had included something else with the tri-ox compound without telling him. Just as he hadn't mentioned anything about the protein inhibitor on the knife.

Probably didn't want to worry me, Kirk thought, feeling himself beginning to drift as McCoy and Spock argued over medical procedures, and Sarek maintained an appropriately diplomatic silence.

Kirk slipped back to three days earlier, walking near his quarters on Deck 5. An Andorian had passed him: Thelev, a minor member of Ambassador Shras's staff. Thelev had nodded in greeting. Kirk had nodded in return, eager to get back to the bridge, eager to continue the investigation into the murder of Ambassador Gav—the murder for which Sarek was prime suspect.

In retrospect, Kirk decided it was his eagerness that led him to ignore Thelev's unexpected change in pace. In retrospect, he knew he had distinctly heard Thelev stop, turn, and start again, walking behind him. At the time, Kirk had worried that the Andorian was going to raise yet another matter of concern to the ambassador, as if having 114 dignitaries on board for the past two weeks hadn't given Kirk his fill of ambassadorial concerns. Part of him was still hoping he could make it to the turbolift before Thelev called his name when he felt the first blow to the back of his neck.

Starfleet training had taken over then, diplomatic immunity be damned. But the first blow Kirk had taken had dulled his reflexes, and just as he thought Thelev was finished, he felt the long narrow blade of the Andorian ceremonial dagger rip into his back, grating against bone, igniting shocking streamers of pain like lava through his chest.

What had happened next, Kirk still wasn't too certain. Whatever had transpired, he had ended up in sickbay and Thelev had been taken to the brig.

But the threat to the *Enterprise* hadn't ended with the Andorian's arrest. An unknown vessel was still pacing them. Thirty-two ambassadors whose loss could mean an interplanetary war were its probable target. And Sarek was only hours from death, unless McCoy could operate. Which he couldn't do without Spock's cooperation in providing a transfusion. Which Spock wouldn't provide while Kirk was in sickbay and the *Enterprise* was being followed by an unidentified vessel.

In the end, Kirk and McCoy had convinced Spock that the captain's wound was minor. Spock had relinquished command, donated blood, and Sarek's operation had been a success.

No, Kirk suddenly thought, jerking awake from his reverie. It was too soon to think of success. Thelev had turned out to be a surgically altered Orion. The pursuing ship, also Orion, had destroyed itself when the *Enterprise* had disabled it. But the Babel Conference had yet to take place. Coridan's fate was still in question. What if the Orions had a contingency plan? For all the effort they had put into placing Thelev on the Andorian ambassador's staff, into reengineering one of their vessels for a suicide mission, into sanctioning Gav's murder—it just wouldn't be like the Orions to give up after a single attempt.

I have to talk to Spock about this, Kirk thought. He opened his eyes. McCoy was standing above him. Kirk had a sudden feeling of panic that he had slept. That he had missed something. But McCoy was in as much disarray as he had been when he had caught his patients at their midnight poker game.

"Can you breathe now?" McCoy asked. It wasn't a friendly question.

"Yes," Kirk said. His throat felt normal. The pain of the knife wound throbbed with each heartbeat, but it was dulled.

"Good," McCoy said. "Then get up."

"Up?" Kirk felt a rush of adrenaline as he connected McCoy's command to his unexpected presence here. Something had woken him up. Something had brought him to sickbay to waken the captain. Knowing that, Kirk was instantly alert, the knife wound a memory. "What is it, Bones?"

"Nothing *I'm* in favor of," McCoy complained. "But then, I'm just a doctor, not a fleet admiral."

"Admiral?" Kirk asked as he slowly sat up and swung his legs over the side of the bed.

"Kabreigny," McCoy answered, keeping one eye on the scanner he held to Kirk's side.

Now Kirk was even more alert. Quarlo Kabreigny was one of the most powerful admirals at Starfleet Command, in charge of the entire Exploration Branch. Starfleet had been from its very beginning, more than a century ago, an organization whose prime mission was scientific, whose very charter clearly stated its mandate "to boldly go where no man has gone before." Yet the nature of the universe was such that Starfleet vessels quickly took on responsibility for upholding the law at the boundaries of the Federation's expansion, for protecting shipping lines and colonies, and for maintaining watch over security threats from other, nonaligned systems. The fact that Starfleet and the Federation itself had risen from the nightmare of the Romulan Wars further added an inescapably defensive flavor to its role.

But whenever the critics grew too loud, whenever the members of the Federation Council grew concerned over the ongoing dichotomy between Starfleet's scientific and military missions, Admiral Kabreigny would step into the fray. By the time she had finished addressing her questioners, detailing the impressive scientific advances engendered by Starfleet, and showing how they stood above and apart from its "secondary mission," as she characterized it, which involved phasers and photon torpedoes more than sensors and diplomacy, the debate would end for another year or two, until the next funding cycle.

Without question, Kabreigny was one of the great shapers of the modern Federation, following unwaveringly in the footsteps of those giants who had drafted the Paris Charter in 2161. Books had been written about her and her influence. Hers was a name that was spoken with a respect reserved for Black, Cochrane, and Coon—all people without whom the Federation would not exist.

And she wanted to speak with James T. Kirk.

It was a bit like waking up to find the finger of a god pointing down at you.

"When did the message come in?" Kirk asked. He knew he'd have to reply right away, which is presumably why McCoy had been wakened in the middle of ship's night, to see if the captain was in a condition to receive a communication from Command. Kirk could get to his quarters, into a uniform, and be onscreen inside of five minutes.

"No message," McCoy said. He closed his hand around the scanner, shutting it off. "When that tri-ox wears off, you are going to have such a headache."

But Kirk ignored the prognosis. "What do you mean, no message?"

"She's here, Jim. On the *Enterprise*."

50

Kirk stared blankly at the doctor. Admiral Kabreigny was seventy-seven years old. She didn't leave Earth lightly. She certainly didn't journey all the way to the Babel Conference for a strictly political debate.

McCoy read the questions in Kirk's eyes. "She arrived about thirty minutes ago. No warning. Communications blackout, she says. Showed up at my door demanding to know why you weren't in your quarters and when you'd be fit for a meeting."

Whatever was going on, it didn't sound good to Kirk. Subspace radio was as secure a method of communication as had ever been invented, and it was so fast, its signals propagating at better than warp factor 9.9, that the delay between Earth and the Babel planetoid was only a matter of minutes. What could she have to say that was so critical? And that justified the risk to her health?

"Did she give any indication of what this was about?" Kirk asked.

McCoy frowned. Clearly, he knew something. He glanced over his shoulder at Spock and Sarek. Kirk saw them watching the proceedings with indifferent expressions, but was certain their Vulcan ears had picked up every word that he and McCoy had said. "Excuse me, Ambassador, Spock."

"Of course, Doctor," Sarek said magnanimously.

Then McCoy pointed at Kirk, followed by a quick gesture at the door to the examination room. "And you, in there."

Kirk gave McCoy a half smile as he started for the door. "I'm not going to be your patient forever, Bones. You keep that attitude up and I'll have you swabbing decks."

As the door opened before him, Kirk heard Sarek speak in a low voice. "Can he do that?" the ambassador asked.

As the door slipped shut behind him, Kirk heard the beginning of Spock's answer. "I believe he would like to, but regulations clearly state—"

Kirk took a deep breath as he faced McCoy in the privacy of the examination room. "All right. What's going on?"

McCoy's eyes darted around the room, looking everywhere but at the captain. "I think it's pretty bad, Jim. You see, this passenger liner has . . . disappeared."

Kirk tried to understand what that would have to do with Kabreigny's unprecedented visit. "Sabotage? Piracy? Important passengers? What, Bones?"

"None of that," McCoy said hesitatingly. "It's *where* the liner disappeared that has the admiral concerned."

Kirk held up his hand. "Just a minute. You're telling me that the admiral has come all this way from Earth under a communications blackout and suddenly she's telling everything to the ship's surgeon?"

The irritation was gone from McCoy. Instead, he just looked nervous. "I think it involves me, too, Jim. And Spock. But he's in even worse shape than you are right now."

Kirk was starting to feel dizzy, but whether it was the medication or straight frustration, he couldn't be sure. "All right. *Where* did the liner disappear?"

"The Gamma Canaris region."

Kirk sat back against the examination room's diagnostic bed. He was afraid he could see where this was going. There was only one way out, a slim one. "Command doesn't think the disappearance has anything to do with hostilities on Epsilon Canaris III, does it?"

"If that's what Command thought, I doubt if the admiral would be here right now." McCoy dropped his voice to a whisper, even though they were alone. "You know what Kabreigny suspects just as well as I do, Jim. *I* was there. Hell, the three of us were there."

"You didn't tell her, did you?" Kirk asked, then immediately regretted having done so. "Of course you didn't. I'm sorry. I'm . . . tired."

"That's nothing compared to the way you're going to be feeling in about three hours. Do you feel up to meeting with her? I could tell her your medical condition is worse than I thought."

Kirk shook his head. "I knew we'd have to face this sooner or later. We all did. I just didn't think it would be so soon." He straightened up. Certain situations had a way of repeating themselves. No time to consider odds, devise strategies, or change the rules. "Where is she?"

"Conference Room Eight. Do you want me to at least go with you?"

FEDERATION

"Did she ask for you?"
"No."
Kirk smiled, trying to make it easier for McCoy. "It could be nothing, Bones. Leave it to me." Kirk headed for the door to the corridor. He stopped when McCoy called after him.
"Don't get any ideas about taking all the blame on your own. We all agreed. The three of us are in this together. And if you don't tell her that, I will."
Kirk wasn't in the mood to argue with McCoy. He was the captain. He didn't have to. "Understood, Doctor. Tell the admiral I'll be with her in ten minutes." Kirk left.
He was back in his quarters within five minutes, back in uniform in another two. He paused for a moment by his door, looking at his bed. It was very inviting. Despite his complaints to McCoy these past two days, he had to admit to himself that he had appreciated the chance to rest. It wasn't often that the *Enterprise*'s mission was so straightforward as transporting diplomats within a well-protected region of space. It had almost been like a vacation, a chance to get away from it all.
But I'm no Zefram Cochrane, Kirk thought, then turned his back on his bed and left his quarters. There was a limit as to how far away he wanted to get from the rest of the universe, and for how long.
Kirk thought of Cochrane the entire way to Conference Room Eight. Zefram Cochrane. Of Alpha Centauri. The giant who had invented warp drive for humanity and led the way to the stars.
History recorded that Cochrane had disappeared in space in 2117, at the age of eighty-seven.
But six months ago, Kirk, Spock, and McCoy had found him, still alive, a young man again, on a planetoid in the Gamma Canaris region, accompanied only by an energy-based life-form, which Cochrane called "the Companion."
It had not been a pleasant meeting at first. War was threatening to break out on Epsilon Canaris III. Federation Commissioner Nancy Hedford was that world's only chance for achieving a negotiated peace. But she had been stricken with Sakuro's disease, forced to return to the *Enterprise* for treatment. It had been on that trip that the *Galileo* shuttlecraft had been pulled from its

53

course by the Companion. Kirk, Spock, McCoy, and Hedford had been kidnapped to provide company for Cochrane. The four of them had been a gift from the Companion to Cochrane, because the Companion had fallen in love with him.

All that had happened had happened because of that simple, universal emotion. That revelation had not surprised Kirk then, and it did not now. Empires had been forged and destroyed, entire worlds conquered and laid waste for no less a reason. Even Spock had seen no reason to question what had transpired. The fact that to him humans were irrational was explanation enough.

In the end, things had worked out. After a fashion. Moments before Hedford had succumbed to her affliction, the Companion had somehow joined with her, combining to form a single entity that shared both Hedford's and the Companion's memories and personalities. Cochrane had finally comprehended the nature of his relation with the Companion. And because the Companion could not survive being away from the planetoid for more than a handful of days, and even though her powers could no longer be used to arrest Cochrane's aging process, Cochrane had decided to remain with her on the planetoid.

"There's a whole galaxy out there waiting to honor you," Kirk had told Cochrane.

But after gazing into the Companion's new human eyes, Cochrane had said that he had honors enough. When Kirk had asked him if he was sure, Cochrane had sidestepped the question with the skill of a Vulcan.

"There's plenty of water here," the father of warp physics had said. "The climate's good for growing things. I might even try and plant a fig tree. A man's entitled to that, isn't he?"

Kirk hadn't been sure what Cochrane's allusion to a fig tree had meant, but he understood the conviction in the man's voice and in his eyes. After 237 years of life, Kirk supposed, a man was entitled to just about anything.

Then, just before the *Enterprise* was to beam her crew home, Cochrane had said something that did surprise Kirk. "Don't tell them about me."

If it had been anyone else, anywhere else, Kirk would have

argued. But after all that he had seen on the planetoid, he understood Cochrane's request without agreeing with it. "Not a word, Mr. Cochrane," Kirk had promised, immediately sensing the objections of McCoy and Spock.

Those objections had been strong and well thought out, not the least being what should be said about Nancy Hedford's fate, to her family and the Federation.

Kirk, Spock, and McCoy had spent several long nights in McCoy's quarters, debating the possibilities, and the extent of their duty to Starfleet and to history. Between Spock's unassailable logic and McCoy's unalloyed passion, it was Kirk who had come up with a compromise which was acceptable to all and that still respected Cochrane's wish.

Kirk stood before the door to Conference Room Eight. Like all compromises, he had known that the course of action he had taken after returning from Cochrane's planetoid exposed him to some risk. He just hadn't thought he would be exposed this quickly, or at such a high level.

He stepped forward. The doors parted before him. Admiral Quarlo Kabreigny sat at the end of the long table, a cup of coffee beside her. She was a thin woman, her dark skin deeply lined after a lifetime of service, her snow-white hair drawn back tightly into a coiled bun, her admiral's uniform loose on her spare frame.

"I'm sorry to have kept you waiting, Admiral," Kirk began diffidently.

But the admiral was in no mood for pleasantries or politeness. She told Kirk to sit down and pay attention. Then she slid a data wafer into a player at her side. The table's central viewer came to life. It displayed a passenger liner with three warp nacelles, an ungainly design that provided a much smaller increase in speed than the math suggested it would. Twin nacelles was still the most efficient design for warp travel.

"The *City of Utopia Planitia*," Kabreigny stated, identifying the liner. "Mars registry. Crew complement of fifteen. Passenger manifest as of stardate 3825.2: eighty-seven." The viewer flickered to show a Fleet chart of the Gamma Canaris region. A solid line indicated the liner's course. It ended midscreen.

It had happened before, Kirk thought. It could happen again. He tried to get straight to the point. "Admiral, I think there's a possibility the liner was not destroyed."

Kabreigny's smile was cold. "Oh, you do, do you? Are you going to tell me it was drawn off course, the way your shuttlecraft was six months ago?"

"A possibility," Kirk said, hearing the controlled anger in the admiral's words.

"Are you further going to report that you encountered a threat to navigation and *neglected* to include it in your logs, putting civilian shipping in harm's way?"

Kirk realized he would have to move carefully. Kabreigny was not the type of officer of whom it was wise to make an enemy. "As my log recorded, I believe we hit a random energy field that affected the *Galileo*'s guidance controls. I had absolutely no indication that it was a repeatable phenomenon." *Why should it be?* Kirk thought. The Companion had provided company for Cochrane. Now she was content with him and he with her. Besides, what reason would she have to go after an entire liner? And she had said she no longer had the power to control spacecraft.

"Let me put it this way, Kirk, in simple language I think even you will understand: I don't believe you."

Coming from an admiral, that was a serious charge. Kirk placed his hands on the table. He had given his word to Cochrane. He would not betray that. But he had no idea how he could escape the admiral's accusation.

"May I ask the admiral why?" Kirk said evenly.

"The liner hasn't vanished completely. One week ago, while I was in transit, we picked up an emergency subspace transmission from the liner's last known general location. Unfortunately, we couldn't lock on to its origin point, but there's nothing else in the region that could be transmitting." The admiral touched a control on the player. The viewer changed again. This time it showed a frozen, blurry image of a woman, human, her dark hair in disarray, her skin smudged with what looked like dirt or blood. But still the face was recognizable. The woman was Nancy Hedford.

"Recognize her?" Kabreigny asked.

"Yes," Kirk answered warily, "I do."

Kabreigny adjusted the control. Hedford's image came to life, broken by static.

". . . trying to contact Captain Kirk of the *Starship Enterprise*. Please answer. The man is lost. We cannot continue. We need your help again." The image completely broke up into static and then began again from the first. The admiral cut the sound.

"That was received Starfleet Command, stardate 3812." The admiral's eyes bore into Kirk's. "Care to work out the math?"

Kirk shook his head. It was obvious what the admiral was going to say next.

"In other words," she continued, "that message, to *you*, was sent almost five months *after* you informed Command that Commissioner Hedford had died of Sakuro's disease." The viewer displayed a certificate of death. Kirk could recognize McCoy's illegible signature. "We even have this, sworn and attested to by Leonard McCoy as the attending physician."

Kirk leaned back in his chair. It was going to be a long night. "What do you want to know?" he asked.

Admiral Kabreigny nodded with clinical acceptance. She popped the data wafer from the player and slipped in a second one. Kirk saw her hit the controls for Record.

"I want you to start at the beginning, Captain, and explain quite carefully why it is you're receiving messages from a dead woman." She leaned forward, eyes glinting. "And if you ever want to command a starship again, you'd better make your story a damned good one."

THREE

Picard knew the inevitable could be avoided no longer. Odds had nothing to do with it. Strategies were no longer applicable. The rules were firm.

His opponent continued to look downward, his thoughts unreadable. All Picard could hear was the faint hum of the environmental system's fans in his ready room, the steady mechanical pulse of the *Enterprise*'s life-support systems at normal operation, on standard orbit of Legara IV. Picard revealed no emotion in his voice as he leaned forward to rest his hands on the table.

"I'm afraid it's quite hopeless, Mr. Data. Stalemate in four."

The android sitting across from Picard blinked his artificial eyes as he finally looked up from the three-dimensional chessboard in the center of the captain's desk. "I find it most remarkable," he said. "That is the third stalemate you have forced on me in the past forty-seven minutes. I am aware of no other human with the ability to do that. Even Grandmaster Parnel of the—"

"That's quite all right, Mr. Data." Picard tried to smile at his operations manager to show he had no real objections to a three-dimensional-chess history lesson, but the expression felt forced, as if he had forgotten how to move those particular facial muscles. In a sense, he supposed he had. "This has not been a test of *my* abilities."

Data reset the board with the efficiency of an automated construction drone. "I understand, Captain. You believe your proficiency in three-dimensional chess is a result of your recent mind-meld with Ambassador Sarek, who is, himself, a grandmaster many times over." As quickly as that, all the pieces were restored to their starting positions. "Though the intrinsically unpredictable nature of probability theory, or 'dumb luck,' as it is called, tends to put me on a more equal footing in games of chance, such as poker, I would look forward to a fourth round of chess with you. The opportunity to play a challenging game of logic with a human is one I am not often presented with." Data patiently waited a few moments for his captain's reply. "I mean no disrespect by that."

Picard gazed at the multilevel chessboard. Without conscious thought, a flood of opening strategies swept through his mind as if the logic of the game were instinctual to him.

"Sir? Is something wrong?"

Picard jerked his head up. "Poker?" he said. Had Data mentioned something about poker?

The android was most solicitous. "It is a card game, sir. I play each Thursday night with my fellow officers. If you recall, we have often invited you to join us."

The captain looked up to the ceiling of his ready room, trying to remember something about poker. Picard rubbed at the side of his face. He could still feel Ambassador Sarek's fingers there, on the *katra* points of his nervous system. The effects of the mind-meld still trembled within him, though the maelstrom of emotions that had raged through him yesterday had now dwindled to slight, recurring eddies. But still his mind dealt with disturbing flashes of detailed knowledge of the ambassador's life. *A Vulcan would know how to deal with this,* Picard told himself. *A lifetime of training in mind-control techniques would permit the easy setting aside of information obtained from other minds.* And there *were* other minds. Sarek had mind-melded with hundreds of different beings in his more than two centuries of life, and the echoes of the psychic force of all their collective experiences now also reverberated within Picard.

"Captain Picard?" Data said more emphatically. "Shall I call Dr. Crusher?"

Data's familiar voice brought a moment of clarity. Picard shook off a sudden visual image of the red-tinged mountains of Sarek's walled estate—not his. The only property in which Picard had an ownership interest was located in France. Picard tugged at his uniform to smooth nonexistent wrinkles.

"No, Mr. Data, I'll be fine. It's just that . . . from time to time I find myself overwhelmed by an unexpected memory from Ambassador Sarek's past."

Data observed Picard carefully. Picard understood his purposeful gaze.

"But the memories are lessening in both strength and frequency," Picard said firmly. "Both the ambassador's wife and Dr. Crusher have agreed that there will be no long-term, detrimental effects."

"I hope that that is true," Data said. "It has been my observation that emotions can be confusing and dangerous when allowed to develop out of control."

Picard smiled at Data, and this time the expression came naturally. "And yet you still wish to experience them."

Data took on a thoughtful expression, one of his subroutines, Picard knew, designed to help the android relate to humans by providing subtle body-language cues to his thought processes. "It is, as the ambassador would say, a most illogical goal, but one to which I aspire, nonetheless."

"You sound as if you're halfway there already," Picard said with amusement, mixed with a sudden burst of friendship for his officer, a feeling he shared to some extent with almost all of his command staff, but which, like Sarek, he too often allowed to remain hidden. Since he had first taken command of the *Enterprise,* almost three years earlier, Picard had enjoyed watching Data's growth as a . . . person. There was no other word for it. To watch that complex intellect wrestle with ideas and ideals that most humans took for granted helped Picard see the universe through fresh eyes, innocent eyes. At the age of sixty-one, he realized he needed that rejuvenating experience more often. It was a law of nature that when growth stopped, stagnation set in. For now, the *Enterprise* helped Picard keep that law at bay. But it was always out there, circling, like predatory *norsehlat*s worrying a herd of *vral,* waiting to pick off the old and infirm.

Picard blinked, momentarily distracted. "Mr. Data, would you happen to know what a *norsehlat* is?"

Data responded without hesitation. "A nonsentient predator native to the southern, high-mountain deserts of Vulcan, filling a similar ecological niche to that of the Terran wolf."

"I see. And a *vral?*"

"In context with *norsehlat,* I would presume the word *vral* is a plural form of *vralt,* which is a nonsentient herbivore, similar to a Terran mountain goat, again indigenous to the same areas of Vulcan as is the *norsehlat,* and thus its prey." Data cocked his head. "Are you experiencing another of Ambassador Sarek's memories?"

"No, not a memory, really. An allusion. Referring to animals of which I have no personal knowledge." Picard found that innocuous aftereffect much easier to deal with than the torrent of anguish that had stricken him in the first hours after his mindmeld. "It is a . . . most fascinating experience."

"Indeed," Data commented.

Picard stared at his operations manager for a moment, experiencing a strong feeling of déjà vu. Something about the conversation, something about seeing Data on the other side of a three-dimensional chessboard . . . Picard could almost put his finger on it . . . almost grasp that memory . . . almost—

His communicator chirped. Picard tapped it. "Picard."

Riker's voice emerged from the tiny device. "Sorry to disturb you, sir, but Ambassador Sarek's party is ready to beam to the *Merrimac.*"

Picard stood. "On my way, Number One. I'll meet you in the transporter room. Mr. Data, please relieve the commander."

Data left the ready room as Picard opened the storage compart-

JUDITH AND GARFIELD REEVES-STEVENS

ment in which a folded dress uniform lay ready. Three days ago, when Ambassador Sarek had beamed aboard, Picard had had such hopes for their meeting. More than any being now living, Sarek had shaped the Federation, guiding it in its transition. Under his direction, it had evolved over the past century from an expansionist cobbling-together of idealistic, often unrealistic worlds eager to forge an unprecedented alliance without a clear idea of how that could be accomplished, to a mature and stable institution for which each new admission was a further infusion of strength for the integrated whole.

In standard English, the Vulcans called that basic precept IDIC, one of the most profound philosophical cores of the United Federation of Planets. The acronym meant Infinite Diversity in Infinite Combinations. Simply put, it was a celebration of how simplicity could arise from complexity.

In physics, the matching term was "the self-organizing principle," perhaps the most basic condition underlying the universe's existence. Simply put, it was the tendency for replicating systems to arise from the chaotic conditions of the fractal boundaries that separated domains of high and low energy.

In high-energy domains, physical bonds could not form. In low-energy domains, physical bonds once formed could not be broken. But somewhere between the two extremes, in the flux of the Second Law of Thermodynamics, there existed domains where a balance could be achieved. And it was the same in the Federation, thought Picard with a sense of satisfaction, both in the institution and the role he played in maintaining it.

In the universe at large, between those domains of high and low energy, galaxies had coalesced like jewels on the cosmic strings formed in the first instants of the universe's birth. In those galaxies, stars had condensed, then burst into life, shedding energy on their planets, creating pockets of still more boundary domains, neither too hot nor too cold.

In *those* domains, molecules had formed that could survive the more minor fluctuations of local conditions. Among those molecules that were good at surviving, some could replicate duplicates of themselves. Not perfectly, for that would lead to stagnation, but *im*perfectly. For in imperfection, Picard believed, as did the Federation's scientists, there was room for improvement; room for improvement inevitably brought change; and what was life *but* change—the constant shuffling of attributes and abilities to insure that life would continue, even to the extent that life on a planetary scale would evolve the capacity to affect the planetary environment such that it remained a suitable habitat.

Thus on a planetary scale, there was no distinction between life and habitat. Life itself and life's home were like space and time—they could not be thought of as independent entities, only as different reflections of each other.

More and more, Picard knew, the restrictive use of the phrase "on a planetary scale" was being questioned by Federation scientists. Even "systemwide scale" was not broad enough for them. "Galactic scale" was better, for as life begat intelligence and intelligence begat technology, life spread forth from its origin points to propagate into more domains, creating more habitats.

But as Picard had discussed with Will Riker, in one of their frequent philosophical debates, even thinking of life and its influence on a galactic scale was increasingly viewed in some quarters as missing the point. As in all things in the science of cosmology, at some point the study of the very large inevitably led back to the study of the very small, just as the analysis of the very complex uncovered the very simple principles from which complexity emerged.

Derived from that research, Picard had learned, there was a realization that was slowly spreading through the worlds of the Federation. He found he was almost ready to grasp it himself, like searching for a single misplaced memory a hairsbreadth out of reach. It was the notion that the self-organizing principle, the most simple principle in nature, which had led to all the forms and structures of the universe, also had its mirror in the affairs of intelligent beings.

Infinite Diversity in Infinite Combinations. In sociology and politics as it was in physics. From the simple came the complex. From the complex came stability.

Picard believed the founders of the Federation had understood this intuitively. The horror of the Romulan War had truly been the last lesson in valuing life, in all its disturbing complexity, that humanity had needed to learn.

Those who had inherited the founders' Federation had struggled to keep intact what had been forged at such cost. The first contact with the Klingon Empire in 2218, only fifty-seven years after the Federation's birth, had been a trial by fire. But in that trial, what had been created in the Earth city of Paris in 2161 revealed its true strength. Through all the dark years of conflict with the Klingons that followed, until the rapprochement of the Khitomer Conference of 2293, all-out war did not break out between the Empire and the Federation.

The Federation had entered a new phase. It no longer reacted simply by learning from its *mistakes,* it took action, truly going where no one had gone before, by learning from its *triumphs.*

Picard, who had not been born until 2305, twelve years after Khitomer, was a child of the new century, the era the poets had called "Technology Unchained," when *quality of life* became paramount for *all* beings, not just an elite.

He had grown up in LaBarre, a small Earth city a short distance from Paris where the president of the Federation Council kept his official offices. Paris was a city continually enlivened by the constant stream of alien diplomatic missions. The Federation had been as much a part of young Picard's early life as had the pastoral charms of his home's vineyard and winery, each an unquestioned condition of life which, to the child's mind, had always existed, indistinguishable from the constancy of the sun or a parent's love.

Those two images of sun and parents played in Picard's mind as he felt the turbolift carry him to Deck 6 and the transporter room Sarek's party would use. The sun: a force of nature, blind and unthinking. Love: a force of sentience, but equally primal.

Even in Sarek Picard had felt the unity that had arisen from the acknowledgment of emotion as essential to life—the same unity that linked the Federation to the universe it inhabited until, like space and time, like life and habitat, the two were inseparable.

Picard stepped through the sliding doors of the transporter room with a revelation in his mind, created from the images of the sun and the Federation of his childhood—two extremes: the logic of Vulcans, the passion of humans. Perhaps neither one could ever have achieved alone what they had achieved together. Humans a domain of high energy, where structure could never form. Vulcans a domain of low energy, where structure once formed could never change. But together, on the boundaries of their separate domains, from the fractal chaos of their meeting and desire to work together, a new system had come into being.

Riker was already waiting in the transporter room and Picard could see him give his captain a curious look. He realized that the excitement of his thoughts must be showing on his face. Real excitement. Because what had just come to mind was not the result of his own thought processes—it had arisen from that part of Sarek that was still within him. What Picard knew now, all Vulcans knew. The exchange was exhilarating. He made a mental note to add these thoughts to his next discussion with Will.

"Captain?" Riker said. He stood in the center of the room, even more imposing than usual in his long dress coat. The rest of his question about the captain's well-being went unasked. No doubt because of the presence of Transporter Chief O'Brien and Lieutenant Patrick standing off to the side.

"I am having a most . . . unusual day," Picard explained to his first officer. "Impressions from Sarek's mind are still . . . making themselves known to me." Picard saw in Riker's expression the same concern Data had voiced in his ready room. "But it is not a distraction from my duties," Picard reassured his first officer.

Riker marginally relaxed. He gave Picard a quick, sardonic smile. "Be careful what you wish for, sir."

It took Picard a moment, but then he understood Riker's comment. Just after Sarek had beamed aboard, Picard had told Riker and Counselor Troi that he had looked forward to sharing Sarek's thoughts and memories, his unique understanding of the history the legendary Vulcan had made.

At the time he had stated his expectations, he was feeling disappointed. Sarek's aides had preceded him—Sakkath, a tall and characteristically dour Vulcan, and Ki Mendrossen, a human and senior member of the Vulcan diplomatic corps.

The aides had explained that Sarek's age would prevent the

ambassador from undertaking any social functions that would normally be part of the honors given a visitor of his rank. The negotiations Sarek would be concluding with the Legarans—after ninety-six years of patient effort on the ambassador's part—were too vital to the Federation. Picard had understood, but had been disappointed that he would not have a chance to renew his acquaintance with the ambassador, whom he had met years earlier at the wedding of Sarek's son.

But in the days that followed, Picard learned the truth behind the aides' concern for their ambassador. Sarek was suffering from Bendii Syndrome, a rare affliction that occasionally struck Vulcans over two hundred years of age. He was losing his ability to control his emotions. Although Sarek was surreptitiously buttressed in his attempts by the telepathic powers of Sakkath, the end result was that the ambassador's confused emotions bled out to the crew of the *Enterprise,* leading to a series of altercations, fistfights, and even acts of insubordination.

With the meeting with the Legarans absolutely unable to be changed, the only chance Sarek had had to maintain his self-control had been put forward by his human wife, Perrin. She had come to Picard's quarters to suggest the captain share a mind-meld with Sarek. Picard had agreed and the elder Vulcan then, for a few hours, had made use of Picard's self-discipline and iron will—vital tools for this final stage of negotiations to be conducted on board the *Enterprise* herself.

But Picard, in turn, had been left with Sarek's emotions unchecked—the pent-up rage and regrets of centuries, the unspoken love, unvoiced anguish, the soul-crushing despair of approaching, inevitable death. There had been good reason why the Vulcans of millennia past had chosen to suppress their emotions—they were too powerful. The strength of them, even filtered through a mind-meld, had crippled Picard for most of a day, leaving him racked with tears, shaken by fear and anger.

Yet without question the exchange had been worthwhile. Sarek had successfully concluded his negotiations with the Legarans, and the benefits of that achievement would be incalculable to the Federation.

In the end, as Riker's smile had suggested, Picard had also received all he had hoped for from the voyage from Vulcan to Legara IV, but not in the manner he had anticipated.

Picard reflexively smoothed his coat and turned to watch the door expectantly. "They're almost here," he said. "Remarkable. It's as if I'm still in some kind of telepathic contact with him."

"Perhaps you should talk to Deanna about your experiences," Riker suggested, facing the closed doors with his captain.

"I intend to, Number One. As soon—"

Picard stopped talking as the doors slid open. But it was the ambassador's aides who entered, accompanied only by two duty officers. Neither Sarek nor Perrin was with them.

Riker stepped forward with a hint of unease that only Picard could detect. "Will the ambassador be joining you?"

But Picard put him at ease as he suddenly understood the reason for Sarek's absence. "It's all right, Will. The ambassador is letting us say our good-byes first, as he has noticed that his presence at such times can prevent people from speaking freely."

Riker considered that. "Quite gracious," he conceded.

"I hope your journey aboard the *Merrimac* will be uneventful," Picard said to the ambassador's aides.

Sakkath, in deference to what a human would expect to hear, stated the obvious in reply. "With all the pressures of the conference behind him, I believe I can help him maintain his control until we return to Vulcan."

"What will happen to him then?" Riker asked.

Mendrossen, though human, answered with Vulcan control. "The effects of Bendii Syndrome are irreversible." Then, in an afterthought that belied his emotions, he added hopefully, "Medical research is always continuing."

There was nothing more to be said. Riker told O'Brien to stand by for transport. It was then that Perrin entered, tranquil and composed, her placid expression the legacy of a life on Vulcan. But there was nothing Vulcan about the warm smile she gave to Picard as she thanked him for what he had done for her husband.

For a moment, as Picard took her hand in his, he was once again caught between two minds, seeing Perrin as he had known her—a charming guest aboard his ship—and as Sarek had known her—his lifemate, his lover. Picard fought with the confusion, trying to express to the woman who had lost her heart to a Vulcan what that Vulcan could never say, would never say.

"He loves you," Picard told her. So simple, yet so profound. "Very much." The words came nowhere near expressing the richness of the emotions he was experiencing.

But Perrin regarded him as if she understood what he was feeling, what he was trying to say, and at that moment, like a sudden flash of sunlight through the trees of a forest, Picard had a glimpse of Perrin's mind. She had melded with Sarek. An essence of her remained in Sarek's mind and was now in Picard's. Without knowing how, without seeing details, Picard saw that Perrin truly understood, and was content.

"I know," she answered Picard. "I have always known."

And Picard knew without question that she spoke the truth.

With that final farewell between humans, Sarek entered, serene, implacable, a force of nature not by the strength and purpose that enveloped him, but by the unquestionable sense that he could not be stopped in anything he chose to do.

Except for the matters of your heart, Picard thought. The image of a young Vulcan boy came to mind, a scrape of green blood on his cheek, sullen, a forbidden tear forming in his eye. Picard felt afresh the warring desires to instruct the boy in his Vulcan heritage and to hold him in his arms, to keep him safe from harm, to tell him his tears were permissible. The boy was Spock, Picard realized, and from just a quick flutter of Sarek's eyes, Picard knew that the ambassador had shared that memory, which had passed between them as a spark. Though it would never be acknowledged.

Sarek spoke first. "I will take my leave of you now, Captain." Each word perfect. Even so simple a statement vested with unshakable authority. "I do not think we shall meet again."

"I hope you are wrong, Ambassador." Picard, at least, was able to say what Sarek could not. Earlier, Perrin had told him that the ambassador had taken an interest in his career, that he had found Picard's record "satisfactory." Picard had been gratified by that verdict, the highest of praise in Vulcan terms. And he saw now in what he shared with Sarek that Sarek, too, had hoped for more time with Picard, and hoped, too, that this would not be the last time they met.

Sarek's eyes stared knowingly into Picard's. "We shall always retain the best of the other, inside us."

Picard already knew that to be true. "I believe I have the better part of that bargain, Ambassador." He held up his hand, parting his third and fourth fingers. "Peace and long life," he said.

Sarek nodded, almost imperceptibly, and returned the traditional Vulcan gesture. "Live long and prosper."

Sarek joined his party on the transporter pad. A moment before he departed, he took Perrin's hand in his, as couples often did before a shuttlecraft took off, or when any journey together began.

Then the giant of the Federation dissolved into the quantum mist of the transporter effect, and except for one small part of him still in Picard's mind, was gone.

"*Merrimac* confirms transport," O'Brien announced from his console.

"Very good," Picard answered. He looked at Riker, Riker at him. They both glanced down at each other's long coat.

"Time to get out of these monkey suits?" Riker asked.

Picard appreciated the sentiment. "But we'll need them again on Betazed." Counselor Troi's planet of birth was their next port of call, in conjunction with the biennial Trade Agreements Conference. Picard was actually looking forward to the mission —it promised to be dull. Despite his need for rejuvenating experiences, just for now he could use a few days of restful routine. He suddenly felt weary.

Riker followed Picard into the corridor. "The conference is ten days away, sir. I thought until then we might trade the dress uniforms in for some natty, wide-lapeled suits, loud ties, and a couple of gats, if you know what I mean."

Picard was tempted. The Dixon Hill programs in the holodeck were getting better all the time, and he was intrigued by the notion of matching wits with a criminal genius like Cyrus Redblock while his mind still retained some of Sarek's impressive logic. If he could force Data into three stalemates, who knew what he'd be able to accomplish against the *Enterprise*'s computer in 1930s San Francisco?

But another wave of fatigue swept over him. A cup of Earl Grey in the quiet of his quarters seemed to be what he needed most.

"Not right now, Will. Maybe in a few days."

Riker upped the stakes with an almost conspiratorial come-on. "Are you sure? Geordi's been adding some refinements to a new scenario. A lady in red . . . a mysterious black bird . . . it should be a real challenge."

They came to the turbolift. "Tempting, but I think I'm going to call it a day. Have Data take us out on our course to Betazed."

The doors swept open. Riker hung back. "It's going to be a long ten days without something to break it up," he said in a final attempt to have the captain change his mind. "Even Dr. Crusher said—"

Riker stopped as Picard's eyebrows lifted in feigned suspicion. "Oh, I see. You've been discussing this with Dr. Crusher."

Riker put his hand out to stop the turbolift door from shutting. "A deep Vulcan mind-meld can be a terrible strain, sir. Dr. Crusher suggested you could use some R-and-R to help recuperate."

But Picard shook his head. "I appreciate your concern. But as the ambassador said, it is the best parts of each other we shall retain. A few days of quiet rest is all I need, and a direct course to Betazed is the best way to get it."

Riker knew when he had been overruled, and he took it well. "Understood, sir." He stepped back from the doors. "Let me know when you get bored. We could even discuss philosophy, if you feel up to it."

Picard smiled. "I look forward to that."

The doors began to shut. And just in time for Picard and Riker to catch an instant of surprise in each other's eyes before the doors closed completely, it was then that the corridor filled with the sirens of a Red Alert.

The *Enterprise* was being called to battle.

FOUR

LONDON, OPTIMAL REPUBLIC OF GREAT BRITAIN, EARTH
Earth Standard: June 21, 2078

London was in flames. Not even the drug-controlled soldiers of the Optimum could contain the riots any longer. Zefram Cochrane had no trouble admitting that his return to the planet of his birth had been a mistake.

His companion in the backseat of the stately Rolls limousine tapped the silver handle of his cane against the viewscreen that angled out from the seat back before them. The windows of the limousine were set to maximum opacity and the external scanners were the only way to see what was going on in the streets they traveled.

"Look at them," Sir John Burke said in disgust. "Worse than bloody Cromwell and his lot." The elder scientist was a shrunken man, frail, in his seventies, with transparent skin, a dusting of wispy gray hair, and a thin mustache. Once he had been chief astronomer for the Royal Astronomical Society. But that had been before the Optimum Movement had triumphed in the general elections of 2075. Now the word "Royal" was banned from this island nation, Queen Mary was in Highgate Prison, and most of the rest of the Royal Family had gone into hiding in what had become the Republic of Great Britain, or cowering in exile in

71

the United States. And who knew what was happening over there anymore, with the Constitution suspended and only the fifteen states with Optimal majorities permitted to send representatives to Washington.

Everything Micah Brack had said to Cochrane on Titan, seventeen years ago, had come to pass. It was no longer a question of *if* there would be a third world war, but *when* it would start. As for *where,* between the splintering of the Optimum Movement, Colonel Green's atrocities, the collapse of the New United Nations, and a dozen other nightmarish escalations of global tension, there was no end of places where the first shot could be fired, or the first atomic charge detonated.

What his friend Micah Brack thought of these developments, Cochrane could not be certain. Eight years earlier, after three Optimum assassination attempts against him in as many months, the industrialist had intentionally disappeared. Rumors placed him on Mars, helping draft the Fundamental Declarations of the Martian Colonies; on Altair IV, excavating the ruins of an alien civilization; or still on Earth, leading any one of a number of resistance cells in regions ruled by the Optimum. Cochrane didn't know which stories to believe. Perhaps each of them was true to some extent. All he knew was that the bulk of Brack's fortune had been given to the Cochrane Foundation for the Study of Multiphysics, and that Brack himself had vanished so completely and so thoroughly that Cochrane couldn't help but suspect his friend had had considerable experience in the process.

Cochrane glanced at the viewscreen beneath Sir John's cane. The limo was approaching a checkpoint near the Thorsen Central Hub, once known as Victoria Station. The data agencies were reporting that some maglevs to Heathrow were still running. From there, an orbital transfer plane to any platform would be enough to get Cochrane off planet.

But Cochrane wasn't hopeful. On the viewscreen he saw the ominous gray hulks of zombies—the name the public had given to the Fourth World mercenaries the Optimum employed—lining civilians up against a wall. Some zombies stood with inhaler tubes from their self-medication kits pressed to one nostril, then the other. Cochrane had been told the drugs took away all fear, and all moral compunction.

And I wanted to take this species to the stars, he thought with repugnance. He was forty-eight years old but felt far older because of what he believed might be his complicity in what was happening on Earth—nothing less than its destruction.

What sense of reason existed among the humans of this system in the late twenty-first century was exclusive to the burgeoning colonies on the moon and Mars, those orbiting Saturn, and those newly established in myriad other sites around the sun. Those colonies, Earth's children, had rightly declined to become involved in their parent's self-mutilation.

Cochrane wondered if that ready indifference would exist if the solar colonies were still dependent on Earth for critical supplies and technology. With the extrasolar colonies now, on average, no more than four months away from the home system— about the same time it took to travel across the system in the first decades of the century—the solar colonies for the first time could turn to other worlds. Already manufacturing specialties were emerging in many extrasolar communities: biochemical engineering in Bradbury's Landing, molecular computer farms in Wolf 359's Stapledon Center, and continuum-distortion generator design and manufacture on Cochrane's own Centauri B II.

Brack had been right when he had told Cochrane that every airtight freighter in the system would become an interplanetary vessel when retrofitted superimpellors became readily and inexpensively available. But the ensuing grand, faster-than-light, second wave of human exploration had developed far more swiftly than even Brack had anticipated. Still, the result, also as Brack had intended, was undeniable: Earth was no longer critical to the survival of the human race. And all because of Zefram Cochrane.

Cochrane watched Optimum's mercenaries on the screen with dismay, and wondered if it might be best if he *didn't* escape tonight, if he could somehow find a way to atone for what he had caused to be.

But then he recalled Brack's voice from so many years ago:

"The genie is out of the bottle and will never go back in." True enough, once again more rapidly than the industrialist had predicted, there were now thirty-three self-sufficient human colonies on ten extrasolar, class-M planets, and the Optimum had been unable to influence them. It took so much time and effort to restrict the free flow of information and resources on Earth that its leaders could not extend their repressive reach the necessary dozens of light-years. Everything had unfolded exactly as Brack had said it would, because people remained people no matter what new technological advances came their way.

Micah Brack's successful prediction and analysis of the consequences of the human condition, however, gave Cochrane no cause for happiness. He still couldn't help but feel responsible. And guilty.

Cochrane and Sir John shifted against the deep upholstery of the Rolls's passenger compartment as it dropped gently from inertial-dampened, urban-flight mode to its wheeled configuration, slowing as it approached the checkpoint. On the viewscreen, one of the civilians against the wall they were passing turned to flail wildly at the mercenaries. One of the impassive brutes, bulky in radiation armor, swung up a fistgun. But its threat did nothing to halt the civilian's outraged tirade.

Cochrane saw a stuttering blue pulse of plasma fire erupt from the fistgun and looked away as the civilian's body crumpled to the ground, all protests at an end. Cochrane, miserable, wondered again why he had ever decided to return to Earth. The Multidimensional Physics Conference he had attended on the moon last week, the first he had ever attended off Centauri B II, was as close as he should have come.

But he, too, was only human. And just as the leaders of Earth had been unable to believe that the followers of the Optimum could be as dangerous and as destructive as the past two decades had proven, he, like most others of his species, had found it hard to believe that something bad could happen personally to *him.* Whether that was a result of self-delusional blindness or transcendent optimism, Cochrane didn't know. But it was a weakness of all humans, and Cochrane felt sickeningly certain he was about to pay for his naïveté.

The compartment speaker clicked on and Cochrane heard the chauffeur's clear young voice, calm and composed. "Checkpoint ahead, gentlemen. You'll need your cards."

Sir John grumbled as he reached inside his jacket and removed his identification card. Cochrane had never put his away since it had been given to him back at Sir John's town house and its forged contents described to him. The slender strip of flexible glass, sparkling with quantum-interference inscriptions, falsely identified him as an American businessman from one of the Optimum-controlled states. Sir John's network had further established an elaborate scenario to preserve Cochrane's real identity. In the trunk were two suitcases with American-made clothes in Cochrane's size, as well as suitable business records and doctored family photos.

The need for such subterfuge had been prompted by the leader of this region's Optimum Movement, Colonel Adrik Thorsen himself. Acting as the provisional governor of the British Republic, Thorsen had appeared on data-agency uploads, proclaiming Cochrane to be an enemy of the Greater Good. At first, Cochrane had hoped Thorsen's motivation had only been the result of the long-ago insult to his pride when he had arrived at Titan to meet Cochrane and found only Brack. At Brack's urging, Cochrane had fled Thorsen then and wished he could do so again, right now. Especially since Sir John's network of contacts in the lower echelons of the movement's headquarters, in what used to be the Parliament Buildings, had revealed that Thorsen's continued obsession with Cochrane appeared to go far beyond any simple redress for personal insult. The Optimum had apparently concluded that Cochrane's superimpellor *did* have military uses, and that Cochrane alone held the key to unleashing that potentially unconquerable power.

It was a mad hypothesis, Cochrane knew, derived from an incomplete understanding of his work. But despite all that Brack and he had done to spread his work to the broadest possible audience, the Optimum still clung to the belief that Cochrane had held back certain aspects of his research—aspects they obviously now thought they could extract from Cochrane's mind by the most optimal methods.

75

Fortunately, when Sir John had learned of Thorsen's true intent, he had immediately arranged the cancellation of the informal private sessions scheduled between Cochrane and Europe's independent scientific community. Three days after arriving on Earth, two days after visiting his parents' graves and walking past the home where he had grown up, Cochrane was bundled off to a safe house as preparations were made to return him to the stars.

There was a harsh tapping on the window next to Sir John. The elderly astronomer touched the control that cleared the window. A mercenary leaned down, her features swollen by the chemicals flooding her system and distorted by the encircling elastic of her radiation headgear. Her bizarre countenance flashed red then yellow in the harsh glare of the spinning warning lights of the checkpoint barricade. She tapped again, harder, using the upper barrel of her fistgun. From her expression, if she had to tap a third time she'd use that upper barrel to launch an imploder into the Rolls.

Sir John touched another control and the window slid into the doorframe.

"Cards," the zombie said. She slurred the word. Through the open window, Cochrane could smell a sudden onslaught of smoke and other burning things he did not want to think about. A few hundred meters off, a thin voice wailed, inconsolable. He passed his card to Sir John, who gave both to the trooper.

The trooper slid each into the scanner on her shoulder, then read the output on the status screen on her fistgun. She snorted to herself, and without apparent conscious thought pulled the delivery tube from her medication kit and absently inhaled a dose of whatever concoction her duty roster called for. Cochrane watched with distaste as the mercenary's eyelids fluttered.

The zombie threw Sir John's card back at him. "You're *old,*" she mumbled. "Not *optimum.*" Sir John didn't meet her gaze. He looked down at the floor of the compartment. His lips involuntarily trembled out of the mercenary's line of sight.

The trooper leaned forward, her radiation armor scraping against the edge of the window. She stared at Cochrane, then at the status screen. "Yank, huh?"

"That's right," Cochrane said.

"Passport?"

Cochrane nodded at the fistgun. "It's encoded on the card."

The trooper looked back at her status screen with a disbelieving expression. She tapped a control, blearily strained to focus on the screen, then snorted again. She pointed her fistgun at Cochrane. The preignition light on the lower plasma barrel glowed ready. "You wait here. Go anywhere, an' you'll be *contained.*"

The trooper pushed herself back from the car, then lurched away, heavy boots scraping the old asphalt street.

"Contained?" Cochrane asked.

Sir John frowned. "The movement's polite term for murder. As in containing the spread of contagion." He tapped his cane against the privacy shield between the driver and the passenger compartment. "Not optimum," he hissed. "Bloody monsters."

The shield cleared. The chauffeur, a distractingly attractive young woman in a traditional black uniform, looked back at Sir John.

"What's the holdup?" the old astronomer asked.

"They appear to be running your guest's card through an uplink," the chauffeur replied lightly, as if commenting on the weather.

"I see." Sir John slumped heavily back in his section of the passenger bench. Cochrane heard the adjustment motors in the upholstery change their support characteristics to account for his change in position.

"To be candid, Mr. Cochrane, it doesn't look good. Not by a long shot."

Cochrane inhaled slowly. In his all-too-brief forty-eight years, he had already had a life no other human before him could have imagined. He had walked the lands of alien worlds so distant that Earth's sun was only a twinkling point of light. He had seen healthy, happy babies born beneath alien suns, their very existence a promise for a future without limits. He had glimpsed the stars at superluminal velocities through some trick of physics that even he could not yet fully explain. Perhaps that was enough for any one person. Perhaps he had reached the end. He put his finger on the door control.

"I should go," he told Sir John. If he ran, the zombies would use their fistguns on him. He doubted he would feel a thing. "You can say I lied to you. The network will be safe."

"Monica!" Sir John said quickly. "Override!"

Cochrane heard the door lock click beside him. He pressed the control, but nothing happened. "Sir John, I appreciate all you've done for me. But your network is worth more than my life."

The astronomer gazed at Cochrane, then gave him a wink. Once again Cochrane thought how impossible it was to tell what an English person ever really felt. There was no hint in Sir John that he thought he might be facing death, or optimal interrogation, within minutes.

"This isn't the end of the ride, young fellow." He sat up straighter and squared his shoulders. "You forget you're dealing with a Fellow of the Royal Astronomical Society."

"With respect, sir. That's not quite the same as dealing with an agent of UN Intelligence." Two of those dedicated professionals had met with Cochrane between sessions on the moon. They had strongly suggested he avoid traveling to Earth, and had sought his advice about whom to contact in order to make arrangements for the transfer of provisional New United Nations headquarters to Alpha Centauri. Cochrane had not taken that as an encouraging sign. Nor, however, had he listened to their warnings.

Sir John leaned forward. "I shall take your comment as a challenge, sir." He tapped on the privacy shield. "Plan B, if you please, Monica. Drive on."

"Done," the chauffeur replied.

An instant later, Cochrane felt himself slammed down into the passenger bench as the Rolls seemed to explode beneath him. His first thought was that an imploder had hit the car. But a moment later he saw city lights and the fires of Buckingham Palace through the window beside him as the limousine banked sharply, leaving the checkpoint far behind.

"Inertial control!" Sir John boomed out delightedly, tapping his cane on the floor. "I still say it's impossible, but, by God, it's exceedingly useful."

Another moment passed, and any sense of acceleration vanished as the internal inertial compensators caught up with the fields propelling the car. The fanjets, which had been designed to make a one-tonne vehicle hover a meter off the ground, were now being used to control a car with an inertially adjusted mass of no more than ten kilos. The city flew by.

"We'll never make it past the coastal defenses," Cochrane said, marveling at the abrupt change in their situation. However, the rest of Europe might as well be light-years away. Even with inertial damping, he doubted the Rolls had enough fuel to reach North America. The Rolls was a sleek-looking vehicle, but its aerodynamics were designed for surface travel, not atmospheric flight.

"Give us credit for having half a brain between us," Sir John said. "We brought you to Earth under the Optimum's nose and we'll bloody well see to it that you get back where you belong."

Cochrane judged their progress by watching the city pass by below. Whole grids of London were blacked out, small fires from the riots flickering like stars in oceans of darkness. For all their vaunted efficiency, the Optimum couldn't even keep the country's fusion reactors on-line. Then, it seemed to Cochrane, after less than a minute's flight time, the limousine began to descend into one of those pits of blackness.

"What, exactly, is Plan B?" Cochrane asked, beginning, in spite of himself and their situation, to feel the stirrings of excitement as the whistle of air around the Rolls diminished. The car had leveled out and was now dropping straight down. What seemed to be a large curved wall, unlit, blocked out the lights in the next powered grid, about a kilometer distant. Cochrane felt as if they were descending into an enormous well.

"Controlled panic," Sir John said briskly. "Since we can't get you out by regular means, we shall resort to something a bit more, shall we say, unorthodox."

The inertial field around the car winked out as it came within a meter of the ground. Cochrane rocked once, then felt the limo bounce as the wheels made contact.

Sir John checked his watch, a golden Piaget from which a small pattern of red bars was holographically projected. It was an astronomer's watch, at least half a century old, from a time when stargazers worked in the dark, actually peering through telescopes with their own eyes, instead of letting computers reconstruct images. The pale red bars would not interfere with any observer's night vision.

"Just about now," Sir John said, "those drug-addled zombies will have gotten word to their commanders about our escape. But when they check for air traffic, we won't be there." Sir John gestured with his cane. "Well, get out, young fellow, we're here."

Cochrane pressed the Open control and this time the door swung up without being overridden by the chauffeur. The oppressive humid heat of London in June enveloped him and made it difficult to breathe. Humidity, thankfully, was not a problem on Centauri B II, where most water came from underground reservoirs and there was only a single ocean, the Welcoming Sea, which was no more than ten percent of the planet's surface. Cochrane thought wistfully of the cool, dry air of his home.

"And where, exactly, is 'here'?" Cochrane asked as he looked around. They were ringed by a tall circular structure. Looking up at the dull orange glow of the low clouds reflecting the fires and streetlights of London, he could see that they had entered the structure through a large, irregular hole in its roof, at least a hundred meters overhead. But with the limo's running lights extinguished, there was not enough illumination to see what kind of a structure it was.

"As I recall from an interview you once gave to the *Times,*" Sir John said as he walked around the Rolls to join Cochrane, "you've been here several times before. As a child, I believe."

The chauffeur stepped out of the limo, being careful to keep the interior lights switched off. Cochrane looked around again, his eyes slowly adjusting to the lack of light. It came back to him in a flash of recognition.

"Battersea Stadium," he said with a long-forgotten sense of wonder. He heard his mother's voice complete the timeworn phrase, "Home of the London Kings."

"Nail on the head," Sir John said approvingly. "Ghastly game though. Can't say I'm sorry to see it go."

Cochrane peered into the darkness, wishing he could see more. Back in the thirties, his mother had brought him here to watch baseball games. Sitting in these stands, eating roasted peanuts and battered fish and cold greasy chips, and staring at the men and women in white who were running around in incomprehensible patterns on the artificial grass were some of his earliest memories. Knowing what had happened to baseball, he guessed the stadium had been shut down for years, even before the Optimum had imposed restrictions on public events.

"Mr. Cochrane," the chauffeur asked, "do they have baseball on Alpha Centauri?"

Cochrane looked at her closely for the first time. She was surprisingly young, glossy brown hair sleeked under her cap, expression serious. She reminded him of someone he had met long ago. But there was something about the set of her large, dark eyes, even in the gloom, that also reminded him of Sir John.

"Lacrosse, mostly," Cochrane said as he held out his hand. "Call me Zefram, Ms. . . . ?"

She shook his hand politely. "Monica, please. Monica Burke."

"Granddaughter," Sir John confirmed. "A year away from graduating medical school when the bloody Optimum closed the universities."

"There's a wonderful medical college in Copernicus City," Cochrane said. "I toured it when I was on the moon. Very inspiring."

Monica Burke frowned. "Can't get travel papers." She took off her cap and ran her hand across her thick, coiled braids. "And besides, Grandfather and his friends need an errand girl from time to time."

"And a doctor," Sir John added, standing next to his grand-daughter. " 'From time to time,' the network has run-ins with the Optimum, and all weapons injuries must be reported to the movement's headquarters."

Cochrane sighed. It was like living in a war zone down here. But as Brack would say, when had it been any other way? "May I ask what we're waiting for?"

Cochrane could hear the smile in Sir John's voice, even if he couldn't see it on his face. "A slightly more direct route back home."

"An orbital transfer plane?" Cochrane said in disbelief. "Landing here?"

Sir John put his arm around his granddaughter. The smile was still in his voice. "Not quite, but you've got the right idea. You just wait."

Then, shockingly, for the first time in thirty-six years, since the playing of the final game of the last World Series before a solemn crowd of only three hundred die-hard fans, the night-lights of Battersea Stadium flared on, bathing the stained and tattered artificial playing field with harsh blue light.

Cochrane, Monica, and Sir John threw up their hands to shield their suddenly blinded eyes.

"The fools!" Sir John breathed. "They don't need lights to land!"

Cochrane tried to scan the opening in the torn fabric of the stadium's roof, but it was hidden in darkness by the contrast with the blazing lights that ringed the stands.

"*We* didn't wire this place," Monica said in matching alarm. She moved in front of Sir John. "Get into the car, Grandfather. We'll have to—"

A precise line of baseball-sized explosions stitched across the field at the front of the Rolls, ripping across the gleaming black hood over the engine compartment, shattering the Flying Lady hood ornament, and continuing on to the ground on the other side. Coolant vapor vented explosively from the punctured metal. A shrill grinding noise rose sharply as the kinetic-storage flywheel tore free from its severed moorings.

Years spent in space had honed Cochrane's reflexes to emergency situations and instantly he grabbed Monica and Sir John and shoved them behind him.

Then the stadium's announcement system blared into life, and on three sides gigantic viewscreens flickered with the first image they had carried for decades. Despite the failure of a quarter of the pixels on the screens, the striking face of the man who looked down from them was unmistakable.

Colonel Adrik Thorsen.

"Attention on the field," Thorsen said, his hoarse voice booming from all directions at once. "Under the provisions of the Emergency Measures Act of 2076, you are under arrest. Those who resist will be contained. Those who cooperate will be dealt with under optimal conditions."

"Monster," Sir John shouted, shaking with anger or fear, Cochrane could not tell which. But Cochrane agreed with the assessment, and at that moment, Cochrane saw his future clearly: he would never leave Earth again.

FIVE

☆

U.S.S. ENTERPRISE NCC-1701
IN TRANSIT TO BABEL
Stardate 3850.1
Earth Standard: ≈ November 2267

For Kirk, there was no mistaking the disapproval in Spock's tone. "Captain, there is a fine line between withholding the truth and lying. It may well be that that line has been crossed."

Though under strict doctor's orders not to undertake strenuous activity, Spock was in uniform again. McCoy had hurriedly discharged him from sickbay while Kirk had met with Admiral Kabreigny. It was ship's morning now, and Kirk, Spock, and McCoy had gathered in the relative privacy of the captain's quarters. Kirk's meeting with the admiral—confrontation, really —had not gone well, as he had just recounted for his friends. *And, according to the admiral,* he thought, *fellow conspirators.*

"I would *never* lie to Command," Kirk said coldly. The tension between the captain and his first officer had been slowly escalating through their discussion. They had had differences of opinion in the past, and their friendship, in part, grew from the understanding that addressing those differences often led to a new course of thought or action, becoming a learning experience for two minds dedicated to the pursuit of the best of which they were capable. But Kirk's handling of their unexpected discovery of Zefram

84

Cochrane was threatening to become a real division between them, offering no hope of conciliation.

For once, though, McCoy was the peacemaker. "We know you'd never lie, Jim. But what we all agreed to six months ago just doesn't seem to apply anymore."

Kirk made a fist and went to pound the bookshelf beside his desk. But he stopped the action at the last instant so that he gently tapped it instead, barely disturbing the antique books and statuary arranged on it. This was not the time to lose control, no matter how badly the wearing off of the tri-ox compound was affecting him. He felt as if he needed to sleep for a week, but he was the only one still standing in the room and he was determined to keep it that way. These men were his friends, but at times like these, his command of this ship must always take precedence.

"I gave Cochrane my word that I wouldn't tell anyone we had found him," Kirk stated flatly. "And I won't."

McCoy was getting tired of the argument. "But you already did, Jim. Your personal log. You set it all out there . . . finding Cochrane . . . what happened to the commissioner . . . everything."

"That log is for the historians," Kirk said. "It's sealed in the Starfleet Archives. Not to be opened for a century." It had seemed such an elegant solution at the time, Kirk remembered. Even Spock had approved, if reluctantly.

Under Starfleet regulations, log officers were required to record all details of activities relating to their duties. But Kirk had argued to McCoy and Spock that their meeting with Cochrane did not fall under those standing orders.

Clearly, their mission of stardate 3219 had been to transport Commissioner Hedford to the *Enterprise,* treat her for Sakuro's disease, then return her to Epsilon Canaris III. Clearly, they had failed in their mission, but through no fault of their own. Kirk's report to Command had described the conditions that had led to that failure, without falsehood.

Kirk had reported that while en route to the *Enterprise,* the shuttlecraft carrying himself, Spock, McCoy, and Hedford had encountered an unknown energy field that affected guidance controls and resulted in a forced landing on a planetoid in the

Gamma Canaris region. By the time the *Enterprise* had located the missing shuttle, Nancy Hedford had succumbed to her affliction. In the interim, the energy field had dissipated, so there was no reason to think that any other vessel in the area would ever run afoul of that particular navigational hazard again. It was the truth and nothing but the truth. Just not *all* of the truth.

Kirk had placed his name on the report without misgivings. McCoy had signed a death certificate for the commissioner in good conscience, not because her body had died, but because Nancy Hedford no longer existed in the strict sense of the word. At least, not as she used to exist.

With his duty to Starfleet discharged, Kirk had then turned himself to fulfilling his duty to history in a way that Starfleet officially encouraged.

Starship captains had a way of being on hand when history was made, and some aspects of important events were best left unreported for a time. History might record that a peace treaty was signed on a particular date at a particular place, but for the participants, it was best if some years passed before the starship captain in attendance made public any personal observations about those people involved. Let the moment of glory be celebrated before details about a diplomat's marital problems, or a general's predilection for Antarean brandy, became public knowledge.

To insure discretion, but to encourage the preservation of historical facts, Starfleet maintained a system of sealed, personal logs. Officers were free to record their unique, non-duty-related observations and opinions, then deposit those records in the Starfleet Archives on Earth's moon with a note indicating how long they should remain sealed—a century was usual if only because humans were so long-lived these days.

It was in such a log that James T. Kirk had recorded every detail of his encounter with Zefram Cochrane. For now, the brilliant scientist's remaining years would be undisturbed, and his fate would remain a mystery, just as he had wished and Kirk had promised. But a century on, when Kirk's record was released, to the delight of historians the mystery would be solved. Any resulting mission to Cochrane's planetoid would uncover only a simple shelter cannibalized from an antique ship, an overgrown garden gone to seed, and the skeletons of two people who had lived out their lives together, untroubled and bound by love.

"Acceptable," Spock had declared six months ago when the captain had laid out his compromise. Even McCoy had said it sounded almost logical, grimacing as he did so.

But as of now, upon hearing what Admiral Kabreigny had related to Kirk, Spock had changed his mind. "I submit that the point of such secrecy is moot," he said. He sat with folded arms on the other side of the desk from the captain. McCoy sat beside him, his medical kit on the desk beside the viewer. "We agreed to withhold purely personal, nonessential facts from Starfleet Command, based on the assumption that what the Companion did to the *Galileo,* and to Commissioner Hedford, would never be repeated. However, with the disappearance of the *City of Utopia Planitia* under similar circumstances in the same region of space, logic compels us to consider the possibility that the Companion is once again a threat."

"She was *never* a threat," Kirk insisted. "What she did was without malice. She loved Cochrane. Cochrane was lonely. So she brought him visitors. The Companion didn't know about Sakuro's disease."

"On Vulcan, *norsehlat* also have no conception of right or wrong, yet we do not allow them to eat our citizens."

"What's a *norsehlat?"* McCoy asked.

"A type of Vulcan wolf," Kirk answered. But he kept his attention on Spock. "I don't give a damn what logic compels us to do in this case. When the Companion . . . merged, or whatever she did with the commissioner, she lost her powers. She couldn't keep us on the planetoid anymore. So how can she be responsible for the liner's disappearance?"

"The Companion is an energy-based life-form unlike any ever encountered. It is improbable that we know the full extent of her powers given the short time we had to study her."

Kirk and Spock stared at each other, neither willing to move from their position. Kirk knew the only way to break the impasse was to pull rank and issue an order. But McCoy stepped into the fray again.

"Jim's right, Spock. I certainly got the impression that her bonding with the commissioner was permanent. What was that she said . . . ?" McCoy looked up to the ceiling of the small room. " 'Now we are human. We will know the change of the days. We will know death.' That sounds awfully permanent to me."

Kirk was thankful the argument would not escalate further. He gave his science officer a conciliatory smile. "Two to one, Mr. Spock."

But Spock was unimpressed. "I doubt Admiral Kabreigny will embrace the notion of command by democratic vote."

McCoy added, "How *did* you leave it with her, Jim?"

Kirk tried to think of the simplest way to put it. He had spent two and a half hours with the admiral, going over his original report, word by word. Kabreigny had acted as if she believed some information was being withheld, but Kirk had been able to answer all her objections in detail. "Let's call it a bluff," he decided. He directed his attention to his science officer again. "I know as well as you do that if there is *any* indication that the Companion is once again capable of threatening space vessels, that I can withhold *nothing* from Command. No matter what I promised to Cochrane. But for now, there's no evidence—" Kirk saw Spock about to protest and qualified his terms. "—not *enough* evidence to convince me that's what's happened." He took a deep breath as a sudden wave of fatigue rushed through him. "I managed to convince the admiral that there was a slight possibility that a second energy field similar to the one we encountered has manifested in the Gamma Canaris region, and because of our previous experience with it, the *Enterprise* is the ship to investigate."

"And how did you explain the message from a 'dead woman'?" Spock added, with so little inflection that the irony was readily apparent.

"I didn't," Kirk said simply. "Because I can't. Obviously the Companion's using the subspace transmitter we beamed down with the other supplies before we left. But since it's a secure unit—so Cochrane could use it without giving away his location —there's no way Command can track the signal from a distance."

"The admiral must have asked for *some* kind of theory,"

McCoy insisted. Kirk could see the doctor wasn't comfortable with the idea of patients he had certified dead turning up in a subspace transmission. Kirk doubted Starfleet's Medical Branch would be impressed, either.

But there were larger issues to be worried about here. "I told the admiral that before the Commissioner's death, she was badly affected by her encounter with the energy field. What we're seeing might be another manifestation of that field, re-creating an essence of the commissioner."

McCoy frowned skeptically. "You think she believed you?"

"Not a hope in hell," Kirk confessed. "But I wasn't expecting her to."

"You were just buying time," Spock commented.

Kirk leaned against the edge of the bookshelf, too tired to stand. "Spock, there's nothing wrong with buying time at this point. I think the admiral is just playing out the line, hoping to reel me in when whatever scheme she thinks I'm involved in explodes in my face."

McCoy stood up and moved around the desk to the captain, medical scanner in hand. "Did she say what kind of a scheme she thought that would be?"

Kirk leaned his head back against the bulkhead as if the artificial gravity in his quarters had been turned up to three g's. "Something 'worthy of a starship captain,' she told me. It seems the good admiral is not all that taken with the officers in charge of what she feels should be the cutting edge of scientific exploration."

Spock remained seated. "Admiral Kabreigny *was* instrumental in having the *Intrepid* placed under the auspices of the Vulcan Science Academy."

McCoy kept his eyes on his scanner as he moved it over Kirk's chest. "That's the ship with the completely Vulcan crew, isn't it?"

"Correct, Doctor. I believe the Vulcan approach to scientific investigation is closer to the admiral's view of how Starfleet should be run. 'Any military operation is automatically a failure.'" Spock had quoted an old Starfleet adage.

"And 'The most expensive army in the world is the one that's second best,'" Kirk countered. It was an old debate in Starfleet and would likely remain so. There was little chance that Kirk and Spock would settle it here and now. "Spock, we don't need to have this argument. You know as well as I do the balancing act Starfleet has to put on between its military and scientific missions. So far, I think it's working."

"Captain, for Starfleet to have success in any of its missions, each member must act consistently in the manner laid out by Command."

Kirk stared at Spock, knowing what had to come next. It did.

Spock said, "I believe you should tell the admiral the complete details of our encounter with the Companion and Mr. Cochrane."

Kirk didn't think he was going to last much longer, and McCoy was making no move to get another miracle from his medical kit. Kirk knew he'd have to recuperate from the tri-ox on his own. He struggled to keep his mind focused. "I've already said that telling the admiral everything was an *option,* Spock. *When* circumstances warrant. Instead of sticking so blindly to what *you* think is the most logical course of events, why not give *me* the benefit of the doubt for a few hours?"

"I do not see what that would accomplish. In a few hours, we will have arrived at the site of the Babel Conference. Once the diplomats and dignitaries have been accommodated there, I presume we will go directly to the Gamma Canaris region."

"Exactly. Whatever I tell the admiral, we're going to end up at Gamma Canaris anyway. So why say anything I don't have to?"

McCoy agreed. "Put your damned logic to use, Spock. Assume for the moment that the captain is right—that the Companion is still merged with Commissioner Hedford and no longer has the power to divert space vessels. Now tell us, under those conditions, what happened to the liner?"

Spock took on the manner of a stern Academy lecturer. "Logic is not a poker game, Doctor. We cannot change initial conditions with a new deal of the cards. Whatever happened to the liner must be connected to the Companion's message to Captain Kirk. She said, 'The man is lost.' The Companion called Cochrane 'the man.' If he is lost, then it is logical to assume that she is looking for him. To look for him, she might require a space vessel."

Kirk felt his head begin to pound with the effort of remaining upright. "What if the connection goes the other way?" he asked. "What if the liner's disappearance is linked to *Cochrane* being 'lost,' and not to anything the Companion might have done?"

Spock raised both eyebrows to indicate how preposterous the idea was. "Cochrane had no way to leave the planetoid. He could not have interfered with the liner."

"What about the other way around?" McCoy said. "Somebody got the liner, and used it to go after Cochrane."

Spock looked away. "That would presuppose that your hypothetical 'somebody' knew Cochrane was on the planetoid. And no one has that information except the three of us."

"Not necessarily," Kirk said. He could hear his voice fading as quickly as his strength. "The information is in my private log."

"The *Enterprise*'s computers are quite secure," Spock said. He had customized most of the starship's computer programs, and it would be a point of personal, if emotional, pride to him that no unauthorized access to restricted files could occur.

But that wasn't what Kirk had meant. "What about Starfleet Archives?"

Spock's serene demeanor faltered for a moment, an indication of his surprise.

Kirk pressed on with his sudden revelation. "Is there any way you can check on the security of the archives *without* doing anything that would arouse Kabreigny's suspicions that additional information might be found there?"

Spock considered the request. "Informally, I believe there are one or two avenues open to me."

"How long?" Kirk asked.

"Since it would not be advisable to transmit my requests as priority messages, I estimate that responses to initial inquiries will take several hours." Kirk saw Spock become aware of McCoy staring at him expectantly. "Seven point two hours, to be precise," Spock said, regarding McCoy with detached curiosity.

McCoy smiled. "I knew you couldn't leave it at 'several hours.'"

"Really, Doctor. I hardly—"

Kirk wouldn't let them get started. "Do it, Spock." If the ship had been under attack by Klingons, Kirk knew he could keep his eyes open for a few minutes longer. McCoy might even risk another shot of tri-ox. But there was no immediate crisis here. It would be safe to let his body start to heal itself. He began to relax his concentration. "How long till we reach Babel?"

"Eight point—" Spock looked at McCoy. "Approximately eight hours," he said. Then he added, "More or less."

Kirk saw McCoy's expression of consternation. He hoped his two officers wouldn't do anything foolish while he was indisposed. "Let me know as soon as you learn anything about the archives, Spock. And, Doctor, somehow I have to be in condition to speak to the delegates before they leave."

McCoy nodded. "A few hours' sleep will work wonders. If Spock doesn't get word from the archives first, I'll look in on you before we reach Babel."

"Fair enough," Kirk said. "We'll reconvene then." Then he waited until Spock and McCoy had left his quarters before he allowed himself to walk around the room divider to his bed, lie back, and close his eyes.

As he let his mind drift, Kirk thought of Cochrane. Spending four months alone in a converted interplanetary scoutship, making the first faster-than-light voyage to Alpha Centauri. Without subspace sensors or communications, the scientist had been forced to drop out of warp every five days to fix his location and adjust his course. Without dilithium crystals he had run his warp-field generators at less than fifty percent efficiency. Without Starfleet behind him or a Federation to cheer him on, he had journeyed to the stars.

Cochrane was a real *hero,* Kirk thought, and Kirk could never think of himself that way. Not with the power and grace of the *Enterprise* to carry him through the void. Not with the dedication of a crew of 430, committed to following his every order. What was heroic about that? Where was the *real* excitement of interstellar exploration today?

Gone, Kirk thought. *Those days of true adventure are a hundred years in the past, when everything was new.* He had an image of himself as a small speck riding the expanding surface of an impossibly thin bubble. The stars rushed past him, but it was the bubble that was doing all the work. He remembered a long summer's afternoon as a child, lying under a tree with his brother, Sam, waving a wand dipped in soap, watching the glistening spheres they made ride the sun-warmed currents, floating into the sky of Iowa, so overwhelming, so enveloping.

But those days were long behind him, Kirk knew. Childhood. Bubbles. Cochrane. All his thoughts arranged in chaos, he fell asleep—

—and awoke what seemed an instant later as the computer told him Spock was outside, waiting to come in.

Kirk asked the computer the time and it told him. He had been sleeping for just under six hours. He got up, told the computer to switch on the lights, told it to open the doors.

Spock entered, as direct as a Klingon, not even inquiring about the captain's condition. "Twenty-seven days ago, an explosion interrupted main and auxiliary power at the Starfleet Archives at Aldrin City. All security systems were down for forty-two minutes. Several storage areas were exposed to vacuum when pressure locks failed."

"Including the storage area containing my personal log," Kirk concluded.

"The storage cylinder containing your personal log was out of place upon the restoration of power. Several others were as well. Whether any of them were the main target of what appears to have been an attempt to breach the security of the archives is unknown."

"It sounds as if the 'attempt' succeeded," Kirk said. "Do they know what caused the explosion?"

"My sources do not know," Spock said. "Though Starfleet Security's investigation is ongoing with the cooperation of the Lunar Police."

"Conclusion, Mr. Spock?"

The science officer looked uncomfortable. "There is a possibility that a person or persons unknown have read the contents of your personal log and learned of the continued existence of Zefram Cochrane."

"And went after him," Kirk said.

"Captain, I can think of no reason why. Despite his genius, his original work has been eclipsed many times over by the scientists and engineers who followed in his footsteps."

"Just because *we* can't think of a reason, Spock, that doesn't mean someone else can't."

Kirk was wide awake and alert. The knife wound still ached in his back, but the aftereffects of the tri-ox were gone. He had a new mission. He felt it was time to start living again.

Someone else had learned the whereabouts of Zefram Cochrane and gone after him, most probably not for good reasons.

And Kirk couldn't shake the feeling that he himself was to blame.

SIX

U.S.S. ENTERPRISE NCC-1701-D
STANDARD ORBIT LEGARA IV
Stardate 43920.6
Earth Standard: ≈ May 2366

The Romulan Warbird filled the main viewscreen, its sweeping curves and lines giving it the look of a predator about to spring forth from the distant cloud bands of Legara IV. The wavering optical haze of the ship's cloaking device still clung to it as Picard and Riker rushed onto the bridge. Picard thought it odd that the ship was still decloaking, given the time it had taken him to reach the bridge, but it wasn't the time to stop to question what he saw.

Data jumped from the captain's chair, relinquishing command. Red Alert warning lights flashed silently. "As soon as sensors perceived a decloaking pattern I ordered Red Alert," he reported. "Our shields are at maximum. The Romulan is not responding to our hails."

"Weapons report on the Warbird," Riker called as he swung his command console into its ready position.

"Romulan weapons are not on-line," Worf growled from his tactical station directly behind and above the command chairs. The powerfully built Klingon moved his fingers over his consoles with the grace of a concert pianist. "We have not even been scanned, Commander."

Picard and Riker exchanged a quick glance. "That's not a standard Romulan procedure," Riker said.

Picard stepped up behind Ops. Ensign McKnight could handle that station during Red Alert, so Data wasn't needed at his usual post. But a replacement *was* needed for navigation. "Mr. Data, take the conn." In an instant, Acting Ensign Wesley Crusher slipped out of his chair to be replaced by Data. The look of relief on the teenager's face was evident. Piloting the *Enterprise* in standard orbit was one thing, but facing a potentially hostile vessel with the same responsibility was another. Picard kept his attention on the screen as his crew responded smoothly and efficiently around him. "Ops, magnify the Warbird. Keep our weapons off-line, as well, Mr. Worf."

"But, Captain, this could be a Romulan trick to—"

Picard held up his hand to silence his security officer. On the viewscreen, the image of the Warbird wavered; then a full third of it expanded to the edges of the screen. But the image still rippled and would not come into sharp focus.

"Is there a problem with the viewer?" Picard asked.

At her Ops station, Ensign McKnight reset the optical enhancers on the ship's main sensors. "Main viewscreen is within operational tolerances, Captain."

Data spoke quickly before Picard could ask another question. "Captain, I believe we are detecting residual cloaking bleed from the Romulan vessel."

Picard wrinkled his brow. "'Residual cloaking bleed'? I've never heard of it."

"Until now, it has only been detected in high-speed, optical sensor scans of decloaking vessels. Usually, it appears for only a few tenths of a second when the cloaking field is switched off."

"Is the ship damaged?" Riker asked.

"I do not know, sir. However, it would appear that some part of its cloaking device is not operating correctly."

Picard stepped back to confer with Riker. "What do you make of this?"

Riker's expression indicated he was neither impressed nor concerned. "It's not answering our hails. It's not making any demands. If it were any other kind of ship, I'd scan it for life signs, but the Romulans might mistake that as preparation for locking our weapons. Then again, as long as its cloaking device is operational, it can't fire its weapons."

"Captain Picard," Data said. "The Warbird is cloaking."

On the viewscreen, the ominous green ship began to ripple as if seen through water. But it didn't disappear entirely. After a few seconds, the rippling effect lessened again.

"My mistake, sir," Data amended. "It appears to have been a power surge in its defensive systems."

Picard turned as Counselor Troi hurried onto the bridge. She wore a shimmering blue Parrises Squares uniform and her face was flushed. The Red Alert had obviously caught her at practice on the holodeck. She stared at the bizarre image on the screen as the Warbird faded out of and into view again.

"Are they in trouble?" she asked.

"I was hoping you could tell me, Counselor," Picard answered.

Troi took a deep breath and her face fell into an expression of concentration. "Without a screen image to focus on, it's difficult reading anything at this distance." Her eyes focused on something beyond the confines of the bridge. "I'm sensing . . . that's odd." She looked at Picard with an apologetic frown. "I'm not sensing anything from the Romulan ship, Captain. I'm only picking up the crew of the *Enterprise.*"

Picard frowned. "Is it possible the whole Romulan crew is incapacitated?" He turned to Worf, waiting impatiently at his console at the back of the bridge. "Mr. Worf, I think we're going to have to risk a sensor scan. Make it as low-power and as brief as you can. But I want to know about the general health of the crew aboard—"

"Just a minute," Riker interrupted. He reached down beside McKnight at Ops and tapped the viewscreen's enhancement controls. "Those aren't *Romulan* markings. . . ."

Picard stared at the viewscreen as it went into its enhancement mode, freezing pixels of clear optical information in each refresh cycle until a still picture of the Warbird, free of residual cloaking bleed, began to fill in.

"They're *Ferengi*," Riker said.

Picard didn't bother to hide his surprise; the evidence was there before him. Instead of the blocky, vertical calligraphy of the Romulans, emblazoned on the Warbird's hull were the branching, hard-angled, bidirectional ideograms of the Ferengi Alliance. "Can you read it, Will?" Picard knew his first officer had taken advanced courses in the language and engineering philosophies of nonaligned worlds. If he ever found himself on a Ferengi ship, he could most likely pilot it.

Riker squinted at the screen as the image became sharper. "I believe it says, 'The *62nd Rule.*'"

"Commander Riker is correct," Data said.

"Any idea what that might mean?" Picard asked.

Data's eyes momentarily flashed to the side as he exhausted his onboard data banks and accessed the *Enterprise*'s main computer. "None at all, sir. Perhaps it has a mythical connotation."

"Unlikely for a Ferengi name," Riker said. "And what the hell is it doing on the side of a Romulan Warbird?"

"Captain," Data announced, "the residual cloaking bleed is diminishing. It appears they have their cloaking system under control."

"Go to main viewer," Picard said.

"Shall we go to Yellow Alert?" Riker asked.

Picard shook his head. He knew that the Ferengi were officially considered to be less of a threat than the Romulans. Romulans were known to shoot first and ask questions later. The Ferengi, though, often tried to beguile or outbargain their victims first, then shoot.

But Picard still remembered the incident at the Maxia Zeta Star System, which the Ferengi insisted on calling the Battle of Maxia. Eleven years earlier Picard had lost his ship, the *Stargazer,* after an unprovoked attack by a Ferengi Marauder-class vessel. Picard had managed to destroy the attacker before being forced to abandon ship, but the shocking savagery of the unexpected encounter would forever color his dealings with the Ferengi.

"We'll stay on Red Alert until we find out what they're up to," Picard said.

FEDERATION

Worf announced that the Warbird was finally responding to his hail.

The captain pointed to the main viewscreen. "Put it onscreen, Mr. Worf."

The Warbird image was replaced by the grinning face of a Ferengi DaiMon, obviously if surprisingly the commander of the Romulan vessel. He was male—spacegoing Ferengi were *always* male, as they never allowed their females to leave the homeworld —and his enlarged cranial lobes glistened with sweat as the hand-sized ears framing his pinched face dripped with rivulets of the same.

Picard did not need Troi to tell him the Ferengi was agitated about something. Which was just as well. Betazoids could not form empathic or telepathic impressions of Ferengi, which suggested that the Romulan ship had a completely Ferengi crew. Why, or even *how,* such a thing could be possible, Picard did not venture a guess. He hoped the Ferengi would tell him. "This is Captain Jean-Luc Picard of the *Starship Enterprise.* Are you in need of assistance?"

The Ferengi drew himself up, as imperiously as a Ferengi could manage, and through twisted teeth said, "What makes you think I am in need of *hew-man* assistance, Captain Jean-Luc P—"

The image of the DaiMon dissolved in a burst of static and was instantly replaced by the forward view of the Warbird.

"We have lost their signal," Worf reported. "They no longer appear to be transmitting."

Riker smiled, a mischievous glint in his eye. "What do you want to bet they stole it?"

Picard considered the possibility for a moment, but rejected it. "Not even the Ferengi could be so brazen." He sat down in his chair. Danger seemed less imminent each moment, but he still wasn't ready to step down from Red Alert.

But Troi was apparently not convinced by the captain's certainty. "Though I can't read the DaiMon's emotional state, I heard no sense of guilt in his voice, Captain." She sat down in her chair to the captain's left.

Riker took his own position to the right. "Deanna, a Ferengi wouldn't feel guilt about stealing a starship from a Romulan. I doubt a Ferengi would feel guilt about stealing a crust of bread from his starving mother. If they have mothers."

Picard spoke over his shoulder. "Can we pick up anything at all, Mr. Worf? Perhaps intercept their intraship communications? Under the circumstances, I think we can risk a more powerful sensor scan. If we keep it brief."

Worf sounded perplexed. "I am detecting no intraship communications in use, Captain." There was a flash from the screen and when Picard looked back at it, every interior and running light on the Warbird had gone out, followed a moment later by the slow fading of its green propulsion generators. "In fact," Worf continued, "I am now detecting no power usage at all."

Riker reacted with urgency. "Full sensor scan, Mr. Worf. I want to know if they've lost containment of their warp core. All transporter rooms stand by for emergency evacuation of the Romulan vessel."

Data interjected, "Excuse me, Commander, but it is not known if the D'deridex-class vessels employ warp cores."

"Then find out if they've lost containment on *anything*," Riker amended.

But by the time he had finished speaking, the Warbird's running and interior lights were back, and its propulsion glow intensified.

"Warbird power back on-line," Worf said. "We have reacquired their signal."

"Riker to transporter rooms: Stand by."

The viewscreen image changed again as the *Enterprise* resumed communication with the Romulan ship. The Ferengi DaiMon was caught hissing at someone out of the visual scanner's range, off to his side. He instantly recovered as he realized Picard was watching, and a patently false smile grew over his face.

"I repeat," Picard said, making no attempt to hide his own smile, "are you in need of assistance?"

The DaiMon leered into the scanner. "We have not come to ask assistance, Captain Pee-card. We have come to offer it."

Picard looked from Riker to Troi in an unspoken poll of their opinions.

Riker leaned forward in his chair. "Whom do we have the pleasure of addressing?"

The Ferengi's tiny eyes narrowed suspiciously. "I am Pol, DaiMon of this vessel."

"And how do you come to be in possession of a Romulan military vessel, DaiMon Pol?" Riker's gaze was riveted on the Ferengi's image. Picard did the same. Something was definitely not right here.

The Ferengi's lips drew back from his pointed teeth. "By the most fundamental law of the universe, *hew-man:* Everything has a price."

Picard heard a beep from the tactical console behind him, indicating that the audio portion of their signal to the Warbird had been cut.

Worf spoke: "Captain, I recommend a full sensor sweep of the Warbird. This could be an unprecedented opportunity to study Romulan technical capabilities."

Picard nodded. The Warbird was obviously stolen and it appeared likely that its Ferengi crew had neither the training nor the experience to use it to launch a realistic attack on the *Enterprise.* "Make it so," he said to Worf. To Riker he added, "And let's try to keep the DaiMon busy while the scan's underway."

The tactical console beeped again as audio was restored.

"DaiMon Pol," Riker began. "The *Enterprise* is in no need of any form of assistance. You have nothing which we would like to or need to buy."

Picard's face tightened in alarm. He stood up, looked at Worf, and drew his fingers quickly across his neck, signaling for the audio to be cut again. Then he spoke to Riker with his back to the screen.

"I said keep him busy, not break off negotiations."

Riker looked hurt. "I *am* negotiating, Captain. In the Ferengi tradition."

Picard had had better things to do in his career than to study the economic traditions of the Ferengi. But as long as his first officer felt he knew what he was doing, though it seemed rash this time, Picard was still inclined to trust him. He cleared his throat.

"Very well, Number One. By all means continue." He nodded at Worf to restore audio once again.

"—and what you say might very well be true," DaiMon Pol said, finishing his reply to Riker's opening volley. "But the assistance we have to offer is something which *will* have great value to *some* motivated buyer. If not the Federation, then perhaps the . . . Romulan Empire?"

Picard saw the look that flashed over Riker's face. A game of negotiation was all well and good if it involved just a small matter of one ship dealing with another. But the Ferengi had invoked the name of the Federation, suggesting the stakes might be higher than Picard had first thought.

"Let me take this," Picard told Riker. He stood up and approached the screen. Behind him, Worf muttered softly that the sensor scan was underway.

"I am curious, DaiMon Pol," Picard began. "What could the Ferengi Alliance have that might be of any assistance to the entire Federation?"

"This is not an Alliance matter," the DaiMon hissed angrily. He suddenly looked off to the side, blinked in consternation, then barked out another command in his own language.

"The Warbird's shields are up," Worf said more loudly. "Full power. Our sensors can barely penetrate them."

DaiMon Pol dropped any pretense of being a friendly trader. "I did not come here to be insulted, Pee-card. If you wish to know the secrets of this vessel, you will have to pay for them like any respectful buyer. But you are fools indeed if you do not realize that there are other, greater concerns facing your Federation than the weapons of the Romulan Empire."

Riker stepped up behind Picard and spoke in a whisper. "He seems to be in a hurry to make a deal. Too much of a hurry."

Picard understood what Riker meant. If the Warbird *were* stolen, the Ferengi could not very well make an offer to sell whatever he had to the Romulans, without risking automatic execution for piracy. Picard turned back to Riker so his face was hidden from the screen, and whispered in return. "Perhaps we have a motivated *seller.*"

Picard faced the inexplicably nervous Ferengi again. It was

time to find out how much of what the DaiMon was saying was hyperbole, and how much was truth.

"What do you believe is of more concern to the Federation than the weapons of the Romulan Empire?" Picard asked.

DaiMon Pol hesitated a moment. A sly smile began to grow. But then he shook off the expression in anger and snapped his fingers at someone offscreen.

A second display area on the screen appeared beside the Ferengi, displaying an image of a mechanical object.

Picard had a sudden flash of recognition. And of fear.

The object on the screen was an artifact—a dark and twisted assemblage of power conduits, junction boxes, weapon nodes, and hull metal laid out in a perverse system of maniacally redundant engineering. Picard had first seen its style of construction more than a year ago, at System J-25, seven thousand light-years from the Federation's boundaries.

Whatever the object on the screen was, there was no doubt as to its origins. It had been created by the greatest threat the Federation had ever faced. A threat that even now was moving forward through space toward the Federation's borders as Starfleet undertook the largest defensive buildup in the history of Earth and a thousand other worlds.

That threat was the Borg.

No member of the Federation had ever managed to lay hands on any sizable artifact of the Borg's alien manufacture. The object on the screen might just hold the secrets of how to defeat them and save the Federation from assimilation into the Borg Collective.

Picard knew that whatever the price, he had to acquire that artifact.

And judging from the smirk on DaiMon Pol's pinched face, the Ferengi knew it, too.

SEVEN

LONDON, OPTIMAL REPUBLIC OF
GREAT BRITAIN, EARTH
Earth Standard: June 21, 2078

Colonel Adrik Thorsen held out his hand to Zefram Cochrane with a friendly, cheery smile. "Mr. Cochrane, as you must know," he said affably, "I *have* been looking forward to the pleasure of this meeting for a long time."

But Cochrane remained seated, his hands on the arms of the old wooden chair. He only stared at Thorsen, seeing the pale, handsome face he had seen a thousand times on update transmissions, fiche, and the networks—icy blue eyes, sleek blond hair, short in a military style, all the attributes of a demigod, a deranged fiend.

Thorsen slowly lowered his hand with a self-deprecating grin of good humor. If he felt slighted by Cochrane's rejection, he didn't show it. "I think we have a great deal to talk about" was all he said, in the slightly raspy voice that invariably made people strain to listen carefully, lest they miss anything, creating the impression that everything he said was worth hearing. Then he sat down on the desk behind him and made an offhand gesture to the guard behind Cochrane to step out into the hallway.

"Where's Sir John?" Cochrane demanded. "And his driver?"

"They're simply waiting in another office," Thorsen said easily.

"And believe me, I'm not comfortable holding them. But, I have to tell you, by avoiding that checkpoint . . . I don't know, Zefram. The mood of the citizens today. They don't want to think that the rich and the privileged are above the law." He grinned obscenely, it seemed to Cochrane, as if he were speaking as one equal to another. "And who can blame them, hmm?"

Cochrane remembered the citizens he had seen lined against a wall by the Fourth World mercenaries. "What's the penalty for avoiding a checkpoint?"

For the first time, Cochrane saw a glimmer of the real Thorsen. The man's face became expressionless, just for an instant, as if its mask had slid aside. But the practiced smile, perfected for the interviewers and the public, returned just as quickly. "Hard to say. I'm no expert on these matters. It all depends on mitigating circumstances, doesn't it?" Thorsen stood up again, glanced away, adding, "If there are any, of course."

Cochrane stared at Thorsen as he in turn studied the posters on the wall. The office was in an underground section of the Battersea Stadium. Flat photographs of old baseball players with their bats and gloves were faded behind dust-streaked glass. Newson, Jein, Delgado, Bokai . . . the names again stirred memories from Cochrane's youth. A youth that increasingly seemed centuries past, not merely decades.

"It is a pity we're not meeting under more favorable circumstances," Thorsen said. He reached out to straighten a crooked team photograph of the Manchester Druids. "I've been getting the impression—surely unintended—that you've been trying to avoid me."

"I have been."

Thorsen paused to regard Cochrane, then walked slowly, menacingly, around him, returning to sit down behind the desk of some nameless administrator, long retired, along with the sport he had served. He folded his graceful, beautifully shaped hands before him on the writing surface. The office was lit with retrofitted emergency fixtures and the strong light from overhead cast dark shadows across his finely featured face. When he spoke, it was as if the words came from a death's-head.

105

"Yet here you are at at last."

"Only because six of your zombies held fistguns on me."

"These are dangerous times, Mr. Cochrane. It would not serve the Republic well if it was learned that a noted visitor such as yourself had come to harm here."

Cochrane didn't understand the game Thorsen was playing. Nor did he care to learn what it was. "So now that I'm safe, am I free to go?"

Thorsen opened his hands. "Of course you're free to go. Any time."

To test the theory, Cochrane stood.

Thorsen remained seated. "Of course, I would appreciate a few moments to talk with you, but . . ."

"But what?"

"Nothing. I have work to do, too, Mr. Cochrane. These are busy times for the Republic. For the whole planet for that matter. And you _were_ just a passenger in the limousine." Thorsen sighed, as if with the burden of his office—an office which he had taken, not been given. "Of course, at some point, Sir John and his . . . 'driver' will have to be interrogated. And my troopers can sometimes get . . . carried away in their zealous pursuit of perfection." Thorsen's mask slipped again. "Shall I call for an escort so you can be on your way?"

Cochrane remained standing. "I want to leave _with_ Sir John and his driver."

Thorsen's voice slowly colored with a terrible, restrained fury. "And I would like to talk with you, sir. As I have wanted to talk with you for the past seventeen years. You at least owe me that much common courtesy if you expect me to show the same toward your friends."

Cochrane sat down.

Thorsen's calm returned. "Better," he said.

"What do you want to talk about?"

" 'The time has come, the walrus said,' hmm?" Thorsen replied playfully. His anger seemed to have vanished as quickly as it had appeared. "And what I want to talk about is . . . you and me. But I know we're both busy men. In fact, I know a great deal about you." Thorsen pursed his lips and stared down at his folded hands as if checking unseen notes. "To begin, you were born in what used to be the United States."

"The last I heard it was still there," Cochrane said with a slight edge to his own voice. This man was dangerous, but Cochrane had difficulty accepting that Earth now allowed such arrogance as Thorsen's to so routinely threaten others' well-being.

"Things change, Mr. Cochrane. Like your life. Raised in Hawaii, in London, India, Seoul—your parents were teachers, weren't they, traveling the world? Then education at MIT." Thorsen glanced up to give Cochrane a significant look. "Left after three years, no degree. Genius is seldom appreciated, as I well know. Then to Kashishowa Station on the moon, thanks to a grant from Brack Interplanetary. And finally swallowed up by useless, self-indulgent, private industry."

Cochrane locked eyes with Thorsen. "I go where my work takes me."

"Does that include Centauri B II?" Thorsen smiled horribly. Cochrane did not look away although he wanted to, desperately.

"Alpha Centauri is my home," Cochrane stated with an inward shudder at the thought of this man's beliefs ever invading his world. It had taken four years to establish a self-sufficient farming community there that could support a fully equipped continuum-distortion research facility, and now the small colony was thriving. Cochrane was perhaps the first human to have ever said that another world was his home, but it was true.

"I am so sorry to hear that, especially from you." Thorsen frowned slightly in disapproval. "I'm sure you're aware that the sentiment here on *my* home is that anyone who leaves Earth in these turbulent, troubled times is a coward, if not an outright traitor, for abandoning one's birthplace at the time of her greatest need."

Cochrane knew the argument all too well. Years ago, when he had finally decided to accept Micah Brack's offer and establish a fully equipped facility on Alpha Centauri, he had taken part in the same debate a dozen times over, arguing from the other side, Thorsen's side. In the end, Brack had convinced him otherwise. And for the right reasons. Modern technology had made Earth too small. For humanity to survive, it was imperative that it leave its cradle and establish itself on other worlds around other suns. That way, Brack had finally persuaded Cochrane, even the destruction of an entire planet, by nature or by folly, would not doom the species.

"It is tragically wrong to believe that the advancement of humanity must proceed at the pace of its slowest members," Cochrane said forcefully, thinking how ironic Brack would find this moment.

Thorsen looked troubled. He cracked his knuckles and the sudden noise in the tense, silent room startled Cochrane. "Are you suggesting that because I *care* about my home, because I *care* about saving the planet instead of abandoning it, that I am somehow holding back the species?"

Cochrane was tiring of Thorsen's game and the wretched restraint it required of him. "I am suggesting that your Optimum Movement has brought Earth to the brink of destruction and that because there are functioning, independent colonies on other planets, the species will survive despite your insanity."

The corner of Thorsen's mouth twitched. "Because of my deep and abiding respect for your work, sir, I will overlook such treasonous slander. But I do suggest you choose your next words more carefully. As a friend of Sir John's, anything you say will be held against him. *And* his driver. With most unpleasant consequences."

Cochrane resisted the impulse to strike the sneer from Thorsen's handsome face. But this tyranny had to end. Someone had to take a stand.

"Just what is it you want from me?"

Thorsen stared intently at Cochrane, as if to bend the scientist to his will by the force of his obsession. "I want you to help your real home, Mr. Cochrane. I want you to contribute to Earth instead of sucking it dry and abandoning it."

"I have helped Earth. There's an interstellar community growing. New economic possibilities for mutual expansion. A whole new—"

Thorsen suddenly slammed his palm against the desktop, making Cochrane jump. "A whole new mentality that says because Earth is no longer unique, it is permissible for it to be destroyed!"

"It's your Optimum Movement that's doing that," Cochrane snapped.

"On the contrary, sir—it is *your* greed and selfishness that is at fault."

Cochrane gripped the arms of his chair in frustration and rage. This man was stupid as well as venal. "Then what do you want me to do?! Go out and ask everyone to give back their super-impellors? Tell the colonists there's been a mistake and would they all like to come back to Earth now?"

"Don't be infantile," Thorsen said coldly. There was more open threat in his manner now than there ever had been.

Cochrane forced himself to calmly try again. There had to be something he could do to help Sir John and Monica, and everyone else this lunatic held hostage. "You say you want me to contribute . . . then tell me how."

"I want, quite simply, the secret of the continuum-distortion generator."

Cochrane stared at Thorsen, not understanding the request. "Complete information on the superimpellor is available in any library. Through the Cochrane Foundation, you can download plans for fifty different models at no charge. You can buy parts or fully assembled units or even complete spacecraft from a hundred different companies. Hell, man, if you've got fifty thousand Eurodollars for parts and two graduate students, you can build one for yourself in a week. Is that what all this is about?"

Thorsen's reply was slow and measured. "You misunderstand me again, Mr. Cochrane. It's becoming a bit of a habit with you, isn't it?" Cochrane felt the hair on his arms bristle. He saw insanity in Thorsen's empty blue eyes.

"I am not interested in escaping from Earth. Your fluctuating superimpellor holds no interest for me as a mode of transporta-tion. But the continuum-distortion generator at the heart of it does."

Cochrane knew he had to be extremely careful. For Sir John's and Monica's sake, he couldn't risk raising his voice again, not the way Thorsen was looking at him now. "Again, sir—the plans for my generator are available from any library, or from my Foundation, free of charge."

"I have been patient for seventeen years, Mr. Cochrane. Please, *please,* don't make me lose patience with you now."

Cochrane continued with as much composure as he could. It was obvious that Thorsen was about to reach some kind of decision point. "Then with respect, Colonel Thorsen, allow me to say that I do not understand your request. What exactly is it that you want?"

Thorsen stood up, leaned forward on his knuckles, his face completely hidden in shadow.

"I want the secret of the warp bomb, Mr. Cochrane. And if you expect yourself and your friends to live to see the dawn, you will give it to me now."

Of all the emotions Cochrane felt at that moment, the most powerful was relief. He knew how precarious his position was, but at least he finally knew *why* Thorsen had pursued him with such obsession. And that obsession had been for nothing.

Cochrane looked at the madman with a steady gaze. "There is no such thing as a 'warp bomb,'" he said. "Listen to me carefully: That's an old, senseless rumor without a particle of truth to it."

But Adrik Thorsen shook his head. "On August 8, 2053, a pressurized dome one hundred kilometers from Kashishowa Station literally . . . disappeared from the face of the moon."

Cochrane sighed. It seemed that old tale would haunt him forever. Shortly after that event, he had appeared at a hearing of the Lunar Safety Board. His testimony had lasted for three days. Weapons research was not allowed on the moon, which is how the rumors had presumably begun. His residency permit was threatened with suspension. But he had been able to convince the board that his work was not weapons-related. In fact, the explosion was proof that the continuum-distortion generator he was trying to perfect as a precursor to the superimpellor had no possible military application.

"I'll say it again, Colonel Thorsen: The destruction of that test facility was the result of the failure of the lithium converter and the resulting uncontrolled mixing of matter and antimatter. The instability of lithium under these conditions is probably the single biggest problem we've still to overcome in regulating the intense energy flow we need."

Thorsen stared fiercely, uncomprehendingly, at Cochrane, and the scientist could see that the soldier was not willing to let go of his dream so easily. "Yet your own testimony at the hearings confirmed the total *absence* of radiation traces. You are a scientist, sir: How is it that matter and antimatter can annihilate each other *without* the creation of prodigious amounts of ionizing radiation?"

Cochrane struggled to maintain control. Not just for himself but for Sir John and his granddaughter. "If you had reviewed *all* of my testimony before the board, you would know the answer to that. An engineering failure created a runaway continuum distortion that made everything within it vanish from normal space-time—*including* the radiation."

Cochrane leaned forward, drawing the outline of the asymmetrical distortion field with his hands, as if he were back in the lab talking to students. "It's a simple concept," he said frantically, trying to reduce physics only a handful of people truly understood to something Thorsen would grasp. "The radiation created by the matter-antimatter reaction traveled outward from the point of annihilation at the speed of light. However, the momentary surge in power to the continuum-distortion bubble, in the two femtoseconds the generator remained intact, propagated at one *point six* times the speed of light—faster than the radiation. When the bubble was pulled out of normal space-time by the proximity of the sun's gravitational distortion, *everything* within it was pulled out of space-time, too. Including the generator, the explosion, and *all radiation* released by the explosion."

Thorsen narrowed his eyes. "Leaving behind a perfect, hemispherical crater in the lunar surface with a diameter of eighteen meters, beyond which *nothing* was disturbed." Thorsen rose slowly and walked around to the front of the desk again. "You do understand that you created the perfect weapon, don't you?" Even the dim emergency lights were enough to reveal the cruelty in his eyes. "Complete destruction of the target, with no radiation fallout, no blast effects. The ultimate surgical strike guaranteed not to produce unwanted civilian casualties."

"You're not listening," Cochrane pleaded. "It doesn't matter how big a generator you build, or how powerful you make it, all you will ever get out of it is a bubble of displaced space-time eighteen meters in diameter. This close to the sun, that's as large as the continuum-distortion bubble can grow before it no longer exists in space-time."

Thorsen gazed steadily at Cochrane, as if willing him to change what he knew to be true. "I never thought you would be a fool who suffered from a lack of imagination, Mr. Cochrane. Your superimpellors regularly travel at what velocity now? Sixty-four times the speed of light? Earth to Alpha Centauri in a little less than a month? What kind of hole would you have left on the moon if your distortion bubble had propagated at that speed? I'll tell you: half a kilometer. If you boost it by another of your time multiplier factors: three-quarters of a kilometer. And by another factor: almost a kilometer and a half of complete destruction. With *no* collateral damage!"

"What you are suggesting is impossible," Cochrane stated firmly, though his heart sank as he realized why he had become so important to Thorsen's demented vision of Earth's future. "I haven't been able to prove it yet, but I suspect it's because the sun's gravity creates wormholes when continuum-distortion fields are formed too close. Empirical experiments show that near Earth, the distortion field can only *ever* be eighteen meters in diameter no matter how fast it propagates. On Mercury, it would be no more than six meters across. Out by Neptune, perhaps one hundred meters. Any farther out, and you have continuum-distortion propulsion. The sun's gravity is the limiting factor. Not technology."

Thorsen loomed over Cochrane, casting his shadow across him. "I *have* read your research, sir! I know for a *fact* you are working to control the size of the field. I know for a *fact* you *can* control the size of the field!"

"To make it *smaller,*" Cochrane insisted. "So superimpellors can operate more closely to a star. So we can use it planet to planet

FEDERATION

instead of system to system. Someday we might even be able to launch from the surface of a planet with them.

"The whole trick is to *shape* the region of distortion around the spacecraft. I *can* increase the efficiency and the operational range of the superimpellor within a gravity well. All I need to do is create an alternating series of overlapping fields. Each field helps shape the other at finer resolutions. Look at the designs of most of the ships—two generators balanced like a tuning fork offset to either side of the center of transitional mass. *I* have nothing at all to do with that. My engineers have nothing to do with that. It's the nature of the continuum."

Thorsen stepped back to lean against his desk again. He regarded Cochrane thoughtfully. "As I have said, I have read your papers. I have studied your work and your life. I even admire your mind. I consider your accomplishments to be the hallmark of what the Optimum Movement is striving to become—what it *must* become if this world, if humanity, is to survive." He rubbed the bridge of his nose as if he had gone too long without sleep. "But the Optimum has enemies, sir. Ignorant cowards who would have us huddling by fires in caves, afraid of what lies outside, and of each other." He looked away, seemingly lost in remembrance of some secret regret. "Those enemies attack us even now. They rally against us across the globe. No matter how hard I try to bring enlightenment and a new order to the world, *they* want to stop me, throw away everything I have achieved."

Thorsen looked at Cochrane as if inviting him to reply, to offer encouragement. But Cochrane restrained himself from saying anything. He knew who the Optimum's enemies were: decent women and men who had the courage to stand up to fanatics, who believed that order could never come out of any group that governed by exclusion, prejudice, hatred, and genocide.

"A warp bomb could save us, Mr. Cochrane. With such a weapon, purely for self-defense, no one would dare attack us. War would at last become unthinkable."

Cochrane stared at Thorsen with incredulity, hearing the man say exactly what Micah Brack had predicted would be said, though under different circumstances.

"Colonel Thorsen," Cochrane said slowly, "even if a warp

113

bomb were possible, if it were the only thing that would keep the Optimum Movement in power, I would rather die than build it for you."

Thorsen reached into the breast pocket of his blood-red jump-suit and withdrew a local net phone from his pocket—a slender, pen-shaped object with a tip that glowed green when he twisted it on. He glanced at Cochrane and his mouth flickered up into a ghastly approximation of a smile. "Even if you resist me, Mr. Cochrane, you are too valuable to die. For now. But, fortunately, there are many other nonoptimal people available to take your place."

"This is Colonel Thorsen," he said into his net phone, as if with great reluctance. "Mr. Cochrane and I appear to have reached a deadlock which must be broken. Bring in the old man. And his driver."

EIGHT
☆

U.S.S. ENTERPRISE NCC-1701
STANDARD ORBIT BABEL PLANETOID
Stardate 3850.7
Earth Standard: ≈ November 2267

As he entered the transporter room, Ambassador Sarek's face was tinged with a greenish cast, the perfect picture of Vulcan health, completely recovered from McCoy's surgery. At the ambassador's side, Amanda, his human wife, walked with a placid smile. The other delegates given passage on the *Enterprise* had already beamed down or had been taken by shuttle to the Babel planetoid. Only Sarek and Amanda remained.

Kirk, uncomfortable in his dress uniform, had been looking forward to a final meeting with the ambassador. But the presence of Admiral Kabreigny had forced him to scale back his expectations. The admiral was impatient to get under way for the Gamma Canaris region and there would be little time for Kirk and Sarek to converse. The presence of the transporter technician behind the console would also constrain what could be said.

"Ambassador Sarek," Kirk said formally, "though I wish the circumstances had been less trying, it has been a pleasure having you aboard."

Sarek nodded his head respectfully. "The voyage has been most interesting," he allowed. Then he looked tellingly at Spock, standing at Kirk's side, between the captain and McCoy. "And most productive."

Spock and Sarek regarded each other impassively, but Amanda beamed. "I would take that as a supreme compliment, Captain."

"I'm pleased to have contributed in any way to . . . what has transpired," Kirk said. In deference to his science officer he tried not to match Amanda's emotional display. Prior to this voyage, Spock and his father had not spoken in eighteen years, and Amanda was clearly delighted that the impasse between her husband and son was at an end.

Kirk became aware of Admiral Kabreigny looking at Sarek in agitation. Kirk realized the admiral had no idea what the ambassador and his wife were talking about. That suited Kirk. He decided to add to her confusion.

"And I look forward to having you aboard again," Kirk continued, "especially so I can have a chance to win back some of Dr. McCoy's tongue depressors."

With an air of complete detachment, Sarek said, "You can try, Captain."

Kirk kept track of the admiral's look of extreme confusion. As far as he was concerned, Sarek had just made a joke.

With the same unchanging expression, Sarek addressed McCoy. "Dr. McCoy, I find your surgical skills to be satisfactory."

Kirk watched as McCoy's grin faded. "Satisfactory" was not the accolade he apparently had been expecting to hear from a patient whose life he had saved under exceptionally trying circumstances. But before he could register his *dis*satisfaction, Spock quickly addressed him. "I will explain later, Doctor."

Then it was Spock's turn to say farewell to his parents. "Father, I wish you success at the conference."

"That is not logical, Spock. Your wishes will not affect the outcome."

"But as someone who respects the Federation and your position on the question of the Coridan Admission, it is logical for me to have those wishes."

"Undoubtedly. But why do you find it necessary to share them with me when they can have no part in what I must do?"

116

"I do not find it necessary. I merely state them so you may know your logic is supported by independent analysis."

"I see. It is a logical position."

Amanda sighed with a happy smile. "Just like the old days. Thank you, Captain. And Dr. McCoy—" She stepped up to the doctor and gave him a hug, leaving him with a large Southern smile of his own. "—thank you for all you've done for Sarek." She glanced back at her unsmiling husband. "We are both deeply appreciative."

Then Amanda stood in front of Spock, and Kirk could see the internal struggle she underwent, forcing herself not to hug her son as well. "I do hope you'll come home the next time you're on leave. There's so much to catch up on."

"I do write as often as I can, Mother."

Amanda smiled at her son, a smile warm enough for both of them. "That's not the same and I know you know it."

Sarek held out his hand, extending only his first two fingers. "My wife, attend me." With an expression of peace, Amanda joined her fingers with her husband's in the traditional way for a married Vulcan couple to physically interact in public. Sarek held up his other hand, parting his middle fingers in the familiar salute. "Live long and prosper, my son."

Spock returned the salute, and in a tone equally devoid of emotion, replied, "Peace and long life, Father."

"Dr. McCoy has seen to that," the ambassador replied; then he stepped up on the transporter platform, Amanda at his side.

Kirk and McCoy gave their own versions of the salute—McCoy still couldn't get his fingers to behave—and Kirk gave the order to energize.

When Sarek and Amanda had departed, Spock turned to McCoy and raised an eyebrow. "Doctor, I have never seen my father so full of gratitude."

McCoy's own face screwed up in confusion. "That was gratitude?"

"Of profound depth. In addition, I have never seen him behave in such an emotional manner in public."

"Emotional?"

Spock held his hands behind his back. "For whatever reason, my father seems to have become quite taken by you."

McCoy turned to Kirk. "This is a joke, right?"

But it was Admiral Kabreigny who answered. "Vulcans don't joke, Doctor."

Kirk was surprised to hear the admiral say that. She obviously didn't know Vulcans the way he did. Vulcans might not understand human humor, but they had their own version of it, Kirk was sure.

The admiral glared at Kirk. "And now that this . . . family reunion or whatever it was is over, your duties at Babel are completed, Captain."

Kirk went to the intercom panel by the door and called the bridge. Sulu answered. "Lay in a course for the Gamma Canaris region," Kirk said. "Proceed when ready, warp factor seven."

Sulu acknowledged, and by the time Kirk had rejoined the admiral, he could already hear the distant thrum of the Cochrane generators begin to resonate through his ship. Warp factor seven would be a strain, and undoubtedly Mr. Scott would complain after a few days, but the speed would bring the *Enterprise* to her destination in less than a week.

But Kabreigny said, "Warp factor seven isn't good enough, Captain. There are one hundred and two crew and passengers on the *Planitia.*"

Starfleet admiral or not, Kirk did not take kindly to officers attempting to give him orders on his own ship. "I'm certain that if Command thought their lives were in real danger, then other ships would have gone to the region before now, instead of waiting for the *Enterprise.*"

Kabreigny pursed her lips in stern disapproval and a network of fine wrinkles formed around them. "Since when is it your job to guess what Command thinks?"

Kirk replied with equal forcefulness. "Since I took command of this ship, Admiral, and was given standing orders to interpret the laws and regulations of the Federation and Starfleet whenever I am outside the range of timely communication with both—which is just about *all* the time."

Kabreigny stepped closer to Kirk, staring up at him furiously.

"*I* am Starfleet Command on this ship, Captain. And we *are* in communication. The *Enterprise* isn't a private yacht for your own amusement—for . . . games with tongue depressors."

Kirk made one of the hardest command decisions he had made in months: he kept his mouth shut.

"Warp factor *eight,* Captain. Unless you've let standards on board the *Enterprise* drop so low you don't think she can maintain it."

"Is that an order, Admiral?" The ship could manage warp eight for brief periods of time, but it strained all systems, as well as the ship's structure.

"You're damned right it is."

"Then we'll go to warp factor eight at my chief engineer's discretion. And I shall also log my objection to the unnecessary risk to which your order has exposed this ship and crew."

Unexpectedly, Kabreigny almost grinned. She was clearly an officer who thrived on confrontation. "Noted, Captain. I will look forward to any board of inquiry you care to call." Then, before Kirk could try to get the last word, Kabreigny turned her back on him and left the transporter room.

Kirk stared at the doors as they slid shut behind her. McCoy came to stand by his side.

"How's your back, Captain?" He obviously thought there was more to Kirk's foul mood than the provocation of the admiral's curt manner.

But Kirk ignored the question, just as he ignored the constant low-level pain around the knife wound. He thought McCoy was on the right track, but from the wrong side. "There's something more to Admiral Kabreigny's presence on this ship than that missing liner, isn't there?" Kirk said.

McCoy didn't reply until Spock had dismissed the transporter technician and the three senior officers were alone.

"The message from Nancy Hedford can't be going down too well at Command, either," the doctor said.

But Kirk shook his head. "No, even more than that. Her whole confrontational manner . . . I know she's got a reputation for being abrasive, single-minded, determined to get her way no matter what the cost . . ."

119

JUDITH AND GARFIELD REEVES-STEVENS

"They let people like that into Starfleet?" McCoy interrupted with an innocent expression.

Kirk narrowed his eyes at the doctor's idea of a joke. He preferred Sarek's dry wit, instead. He turned to his science officer.

"Mr. Spock, those . . . friends of yours who informed you about the explosion at Starfleet Archives, do you think they might be able to shed some light on the admiral?"

"In what sense, Captain?"

Kirk frowned thoughtfully. "Any special projects she might be involved in, special interests . . . anything that might explain what appears to be her overreaction to that liner's disappearance and the message from the commissioner."

McCoy put his hand on Kirk's arm in a cautioning gesture. *"Is it an overreaction?"* he asked.

Kirk was certain. "On the surface, the worst thing I could be guilty of is failing to report a navigational hazard and conspiring with my ship's surgeon to hide the true cause of death for an important passenger. From Command's point of view, those are serious charges. But not as serious as the admiral is making them out to be."

"You don't suppose she knows anything about Cochrane, do you?" McCoy asked.

Kirk shrugged. "What if she does? As Spock said, he's little more than a historical curiosity. His desire for privacy is so he can avoid the onslaught of historians he'd be subjected to." Then Kirk caught sight of Spock's expression, as if he were about to speak. "You don't agree?"

"Could it be possible that Cochrane has another reason for keeping his whereabouts secret?"

McCoy rolled his eyes. "Like what? An ex-wife waiting for . . . what did they call it back then . . . 'alimony,' Mr. Spock?"

Kirk agreed with McCoy's assessment. "As far as anyone else knows, he's been dead for one hundred and fifty years."

"As I recall," Spock continued, "history does not record much detail about the nature of his disappearance."

Kirk didn't like his idea being sidetracked. "He was eighty-seven years old, Spock. He told us himself he was going to die and

120

he wanted to die in space. That sounds like a man who had made a deliberate decision to break off with the details of living. I doubt he had any unfinished business."

Spock studied Kirk and McCoy for a few moments, then appeared to make his own decision. "Nonetheless, I shall investigate both avenues: Admiral Kabreigny's interest in these matters, and the nature of Zefram Cochrane's latter years, prior to his disappearance."

"At warp eight, you've got less than seventy-two hours," Kirk said. "Which reminds me, I should be hearing from Mr. Scott right about—"

The intercom signaled and Chief Engineer Scott's agitated voice said, "Captain Kirk to Engineering."

Kirk went back to the wall panel, hit the Send switch. "Go ahead, Scotty."

"Captain, Admiral Kabreigny was just here—in the engine room, sir. And she says we're t' make warp eight all the way t' Gamma Canaris."

"Is the *Enterprise* up to it, Mr. Scott?"

"Aye, Captain. Warp eight and a wee bit more if you'll be needing it."

"Then what's the problem?" Kirk asked.

"No problem, sir. It's just that . . ." Scott obviously couldn't bring himself to admit the reason for his call.

"I understand, Scotty," Kirk said. "Your orders are confirmed."

Scott quickly replied, "I wasn't looking for confirmation, Captain."

"I know," Kirk said with a smile. "No Starfleet officer would need to check the orders of an admiral."

"Absolutely not, sir."

"But off the record, Mr. Scott, there's good reason to push the engines to warp eight," Kirk said. "The admiral is not taking them for granted."

The relief in Scott's voice was unmistakable. "Off the record, thank ye, sir. Scott out."

"Off the record," McCoy added, "I'd say the admiral is not endearing herself to too many of the crew."

"Off the record," Spock said, "I shall endeavor to find out why."

"And on the record," Kirk said, "I don't believe there *is* good reason to strain this ship. So for the *Enterprise*'s sake, and the admiral's, Mr. Spock, I hope you do come up with something."

"I would prefer not to," Spock said. To Kirk's unvoiced question, he added, "As things stand now, the only logical explanation for the admiral's behavior would be most distressing." But he would not elaborate further, and left Kirk and McCoy in the transporter room, alone to wonder what Spock knew, and when they would learn it.

NINE

U.S.S. ENTERPRISE NCC-1701-D
STANDARD ORBIT LEGARA IV
Stardate 43920.6
Earth Standard: ≈ May 2366

Picard touched the communicator at his chest and called for Engineering. Lieutenant Commander Geordi La Forge responded immediately.

"Mr. La Forge, I want your opinion of the artifact being displayed on the main viewscreen."

"Calling it up now, Captain."

The chief engineer's disembodied voice was the single one heard in the silence of the bridge. The only other sound was the pervasive background whisper of the *Enterprise*'s many systems. Everyone else had recognized the provenance of the artifact the Ferengi had displayed and which now filled the entire viewscreen, but Picard knew his crew remained silent in order not to interfere with their captain's negotiations with DaiMon Pol.

La Forge whistled. "I know what it looks like, Captain. Part of a Borg ship. Any idea what scale we're dealing with?"

Picard spoke to the empty air. "DaiMon Pol—"

As quickly as that the Ferengi was back on the main screen.

"You have our attention," Picard admitted. "Can you provide any details as to the size, location, and operational status of the object you have shown us?"

The Ferengi settled back in his own version of a captain's chair. Unfortunately, it was designed for the larger frame of a Romulan and gave the impression of a child in a grown-up's seat. Picard could imagine the Ferengi's feet swinging back and forth above the deck.

"Because I like you, Pee-card, I will *give* you some information, even though this generous offer on my part cannot profit me in any way." The grin had returned. The DaiMon obviously felt he had regained control of the negotiations. "The object's mass is forty-five point three five kilotonnes. And it has *no* operational status, though it does have a functioning power supply. The location, alas, is something I, as a poor though honest trader, must keep to myself. At least, for now." The Ferengi's grin broadened for a moment, then became an insincere frown. "But, if you are not interested, you are not interested. Such is the woeful lot of a trader. However, if there is anything else I might be able to provide for you or your crew . . . Romulan ale, Deltan holochips . . . anything at all, please do not hesitate to call upon me. I shall remain in orbit of Legara IV for, let us say, one standard hour." DaiMon Pol's image winked out, replaced by a forward view of the Warbird. It was crisp and steady. Whatever had earlier been wrong with its cloaking device had apparently been rectified.

Picard turned to face his crew. "Lieutenant Worf: Send a priority message to Admiral J. P. Hanson, Starbase 324. Inform the admiral that a Ferengi trader has offered us the opportunity to 'purchase' what appears to be a sizable and inactive section of a Borg vessel. Transmit the visual image DaiMon Pol showed us." Picard tugged on the bottom of his tunic. "Senior officers, to the observation lounge." He had an hour. It was time to plan strategy.

In the observation lounge, Legara IV moved slowly past the windows and the image of the Borg artifact was displayed on the main wall viewer. But everyone's attention was on the captain.

"At this distance from Starbase 324, we will not hear back from Admiral Hanson before DaiMon Pol's time limit is up," Picard said. "Which is a shame, because the admiral is leading the effort to prepare the Fleet for the inevitable arrival of the Borg."

"I think we can assume that the admiral will want that artifact, whatever the price," Riker added thoughtfully.

"Oh, I agree, Number One. But don't let DaiMon Pol hear those words, 'at any price,' because that's exactly what he'll charge."

"Not necessarily," Riker replied. Picard and the other officers at the conference table waited expectantly. La Forge had arrived from Engineering, Dr. Crusher from sickbay, and Worf from his tactical console. Counselor Troi was still in her Parrises Squares uniform, but her face had returned to its usual, less florid color. Data sat beside her.

"Please. Continue," Picard said.

Riker did. "I agree with your assessment of DaiMon Pol's chances of conducting business with the Romulans. That ship is obviously stolen and the Ferengi are having a hard time operating her. There's no doubt that the Romulans have had their own run-ins with the Borg, and would dearly love to get hold of that Borg artifact. But they'd dearly love to get hold of DaiMon Pol as well, so we might well be his only customer."

"Which will put us in a powerful negotiating position," Troi concluded.

"However," Data added, "if there is even the slightest possibility of DaiMon Pol selling the artifact to the Romulans, I suggest we do all that we can to prevent their acquisition of it. If the Federation obtains the artifact and learns from it a suitable defense against the Borg, then the Federation will share that information with the Romulans and, indeed, with all the non-aligned systems. If the Romulans do the same, their past record indicates that they will not be as forthcoming."

Worf looked troubled. "Why should the Ferengi want to sell the artifact? Why not examine it themselves, come up with defensive strategies, and sell those instead?"

Data responded. "The sum of known Ferengi science and technology is basically an elaborate collection of devices and knowledge which they have acquired from other cultures. They have no strong research and development capability of their own."

"So," Riker continued, "it's to their advantage to sell it to us because we stand a better chance of unlocking the Borg's secrets before anyone else." He smiled at the captain. "Our position is looking better all the time."

But La Forge raised an objection. "There is another possibility, Commander. What if the Ferengi have already examined the artifact and found out it's just junk? Instead of throwing it away, they're trying to cheat us."

"Or," Dr. Crusher added, giving Picard a skeptical look from beneath her vibrant red hair, "the Ferengi are attempting to sell the same artifact to a number of different buyers at the same time."

Troi looked surprised. "I wouldn't have thought of that."

"You're not as devious as the doctor," Riker said with a grin.

"But the Ferengi are," Picard stated. Then he saw his officers' amused expressions. "Um, sorry, Dr. Crusher. Not quite what I meant."

"In any case," Troi suggested, trying not to smile, "I recommend we ask DaiMon Pol to let us see the artifact for ourselves. To be certain no one else has made off with it."

"And," La Forge added, "to be sure it's something more worthwhile than a twisted hunk of old Borg plumbing."

Picard looked around the table. Each of his senior officers had stated his or her view, and he sorted them now to determine the best course of action. He had found that that was generally the one course which did the least to limit future options.

"Very well," Picard concluded. "We shall ask DaiMon Pol to take us to the location of the artifact so we can examine it prior to making our offer."

"And if he refuses?" Riker asked.

Troi answered. "Then I would tell him that we interpret his refusal as an indication that the artifact is no longer in his possession, or is a fraud, or contains nothing of value. If it *is* any of those things, the DaiMon will continue to refuse, and we will have lost nothing. If it *is* a legitimate Borg artifact of scientific interest and the DaiMon *does* take us to it, then we will have cost him time. And the longer he remains in that stolen ship, the more anxious he will be to sell."

"I agree," Picard said. "And since we're not due at Betazed for at least two more weeks, we have some time to pursue this negotiation." The captain folded his hands on the table before him. "So . . . now that we know what we're going to do, all we need is a negotiating stance to get us the best possible deal. Any suggestions?" he asked.

As he expected, everyone spoke at once.

"Impossible!" DaiMon Pol exclaimed. "If we tell you where the item is, you will steal it!"

Riker leaned close to Picard and whispered, "What he means is, in our position, the Ferengi would steal it."

The DaiMon obviously overheard Riker's comment and appeared shocked. "It would not be stealing, *hew-man*. It would simply be exploiting a negotiating advantage. There is no crime in that."

Picard remained seated in his chair at the center of the bridge. Troi, now in her Starfleet uniform, and Riker were in their usual command positions, Dr. Crusher was to the side, and all three officers also remained seated. Riker had suggested that standing up to address the Ferengi might indicate an unseemly eagerness to close the deal.

"We have stated our concerns, DaiMon," Picard said flatly. He covered his mouth as he yawned, one of Troi's contributions to their negotiation tactics. "We do have an interest in acquiring the artifact you have shown us, primarily to see if it might be a smaller part of the other pieces of Borg technology already in the Federation's possession." That had been Dr. Crusher's suggestion, implying that the Ferengi's offer to sell the artifact did not represent an all-or-nothing opportunity for the Federation.

DaiMon Pol narrowed his tiny eyes skeptically. "If the Federation has other pieces of Borg technology, then why has the Alliance not heard about it?"

Picard saw Riker lean forward with a wide smile and let him take the rejoinder. "Perhaps because the Federation pays Ferengi spies more than the Ferengi do," he said.

DaiMon Pol clamped his mouth shut, outraged by Riker's suggestion.

"I repeat, DaiMon Pol," Picard said. "We are willing to buy the artifact. And we are authorized to act on behalf of the Federation in this matter. But we must examine it—*ourselves*—in order to be certain it is what you represent it to be."

"I am crushed, Captain Pee-card, that there is so little trust in you."

"And I am in a hurry, DaiMon Pol. Do you wish to sell to us or not?" Picard made a show of turning around and saying, "Mr. Worf, alert Engineering to prepare the warp engines. We'll be on our way soon." Picard could see it took Worf a moment to realize the odd request was part of the negotiating tactics. Except during scheduled maintenance, the *Enterprise*'s warp engines were always on standby mode. And Mr. La Forge was sitting almost directly behind Worf at the propulsion station.

"Aye-aye, Captain Picard," Worf replied heartily. "I shall certainly inform Engineering that the engines must be ready for immediate departure at once. I will do so now."

Picard frowned at the Klingon's overacting, but decided it would do no harm. He turned back to the screen.

"This is not a question of trust," Picard explained to the Ferengi commander. "It is a question of timing. The *Enterprise* has a schedule to keep and unless we become involved in serious negotiations, we must keep it. However, in the interests of fairness and better relations between the Federation and the Ferengi Alliance, we can make arrangements for another Federation starship to rendezvous with you, in say . . ." Picard glanced at Riker. "Four weeks, would you say, Number One?" The time delay had been Mr. La Forge's contribution. He said the DaiMon would froth at the mouth to see a deal slip through his fingers because of a scheduling conflict.

"More like five weeks," Riker said seriously.

Picard nodded, as if disappointed. "Five weeks it is, Number One." He looked expectantly at the screen. "If that would be convenient?"

Apparently, it wouldn't be. "Very well, very well," the DaiMon complained. "I shall escort you to the artifact's location. But there will be conditions."

"How can there be conditions if we haven't even begun to negotiate?" Riker said in surprise. He turned to Picard. "Captain, we really should leave this to a Federation commercial negotiating team. Besides, they've been trained on Vulcan so they'd probably be able to get a better deal than we ever would." Mr. Data had come up with that particular addition to the overall strategy. Why should the DaiMon want to wait for experts if he might be able to get a more generous price right now?

"Conditions? Did I say conditions?" DaiMon Pol said quickly. He laughed quickly, insincerely. "I meant to say *suggestions*. Just a few suggestions to make things go . . . more smoothly. Faster, even."

Picard gave the Ferengi a cheery smile. "Ah, splendid. And what suggestions might those be?"

DaiMon Pol looked pained. "Um, so I can be sure there is no . . . ill intent on your part, you will not use your ship's main sensors to examine the artifact. After all," he added quickly, "that could tell you everything you need to know and then where would I be?"

Picard frowned. "DaiMon, really—the whole point of this exercise is that we must examine the artifact before we buy it."

"And you shall," the Ferengi said hurriedly. "But with handheld tricorders. Optical sensors, even. You can crawl all over it if you wish to. But if you *don't* buy it, you . . . will have to give the tricorder records back to us."

Picard looked at Troi and Riker. Though no one else would be able to read the subtle signals, both officers agreed.

"Very well," Picard said. "We accept your 'suggestions.' "

The Ferengi emitted a large sigh for such a small being. "That wasn't so difficult, was it?" he asked, almost plaintively.

"Not for us," Riker said quietly through unmoving lips.

"Now," Picard said, "how far away is this artifact?"

DaiMon Pol waved a finger at someone offscreen. "Transmitting coordinates now, Captain Pee-card."

Data spoke up from the conn. "We have received coordinates for a point approximately three light-years distant, sir. It appears to be deep space. No astronomical bodies of note have been charted there."

"DaiMon," Picard asked, "is this the location where you found the artifact, or where you have hidden it?"

The Ferengi grinned as for the first time in an hour he clearly realized he was truly back in control. "When you have completed your purchase, Captain, I shall of course be more than happy to answer all your questions. But for now, I 'suggest' you follow me."

The transmission ended.

Picard stood up and stretched his back. "How did we do?" he asked his officers.

"I believe the threat of a Vulcan-trained negotiating team strengthened our position considerably," Data offered.

"I'd say it was the time-constraint issue that really got a rise out of him," La Forge suggested.

"I was watching him carefully," Dr. Crusher said. "When he heard that the Federation had other pieces of Borg technology, *that's* when he started to fold."

Picard eyed his officers, each having given credit to her or his own tactic. "And what is your opinion, Mr. Worf?" The Klingon's suggestion had been to send a boarding party to the stolen Romulan vessel, capture the Ferengi crew, then offer them immunity from extradition to the Romulan Empire in return for the artifact's location. In the meantime, the Romulan ship could be taken back to the Utopia Planitia Fleet Yards for reverse engineering. He had offered to lead the boarding party personally.

Unfortunately, Picard had told him, Starfleet tended to frown on acts of piracy, even when they were committed against pirates.

"My opinion," Worf answered, "is that we are being led into a trap."

Troi looked up at the Klingon. "Worf, you think that about everything."

"It is my job to be prepared," Worf conceded. "But why should the Ferengi leave a potentially valuable artifact unguarded in deep space?"

"We don't know that it's unguarded," Riker said.

Worf gave him a withering stare. "*I* know it is unguarded. I have scanned the coordinates the Ferengi provided. There are no vessels of appreciable size anywhere near them."

"Can you detect an artifact there, Mr. Worf?" Picard asked.

"If it is of the mass DaiMon Pol told us, it would not register at this distance."

"Then how can it be a trap?" Riker asked.

Worf frowned grimly. "The Ferengi are an exceptionally tricky species."

"Does anyone have any other interpretations of events?" Picard asked. Sometimes when his senior officers went after each other like this, he felt more like the captain of a debating team than a starship. But their quest for excellence could not be faulted, and they were always supportive.

"I'd say it's a test," La Forge said.

"A test?" Riker repeated.

"Makes sense," the engineer continued. "The *Enterprise* is at least two factors faster than a D'deridex-class Warbird. If we wanted to, we could get to those coordinates a good five hours before DaiMon Pol, and he's got to know it."

Picard had to admit that assessment did make sense. "So you're suggesting that he's just giving us what is no more than a rendezvous point. To see if our intentions are pure."

La Forge nodded, then patted Worf on the shoulder. "Either that or it's a trap."

Captain Picard surveyed his officers with appreciation. "I am in awe of your ability to think devious thoughts, every one of you," he told them. "You must have brutal poker games."

"Always room for a fresh victim," Riker said charmingly, "if you'd ever care to join us."

Picard opened his mouth to answer, then stopped. There was something in the sudden juxtaposition of thoughts of poker and a victim . . . he had seen a deck of cards . . . a knife held high. He put his hand to his eyes, shook his head. Counselor Troi was beside him in an instant, looking up at him with concern.

"Captain, I've never felt you react like that. Are you all right, sir?"

Picard allowed himself to be helped to his chair, still overcome. "It must be an aftereffect of my mind-meld with Ambassador Sarek," he said. "Some memory not my own." He looked into Troi's questioning dark eyes. "But what a memory. Something to do with a poker game and a knife . . . it makes no sense."

"There are no known games extant on Vulcan involving both playing cards and cutting weapons," Data said helpfully, turning

131

around in his chair at the conn. "However, among the Ecklarians, there is a ritual form of recreational surgery which is played with—"

"That will be all, Mr. Data," Picard said. "Thank you."

Data fell silent, blinking innocently in a behavior that told those who knew him well that his programming had been interrupted for no reason which he understood.

Picard knocked his hand in the air, as if beating time for an imaginary orchestra. "I think the ambassador once played a poker game with someone who . . . who had been injured by a knife . . . a victim? I think that's the connection. The ambassador was quite impressed with the way the victim conducted himself. Most satisfactory."

"Any idea who it was?" Riker asked.

Picard tried to call up a picture from the memory but nothing came to mind. The impressions were fading as quickly as they had come. "There's something about an Andorian," he said. "But that's all." He sighed. "The ambassador has been in contact with many minds in his career. Many different beings."

"Captain," Data announced, "the Warbird is preparing to leave orbit."

"Give it a comfortable lead, Mr. Data. Just in case they press the wrong control on their intervalve."

"A wise precaution," Data agreed. A moment later he said, "They have gone to warp."

"Are they still in one piece?" Riker asked cynically.

"And continuing to accelerate," Data confirmed. "Holding at warp seven."

Picard shook his head again. The flashback incident had passed. "Mr. Worf," he said, "send a follow-up message to Starbase 324 and advise Admiral Hanson of our intentions. Be sure to give him our destination coordinates."

Troi sat back down by the captain. "Do you think there's a chance this *is* just some plot to draw us into a trap?"

Picard didn't have a straightforward answer for the counselor. "All I know is that whatever's waiting for us out there, it involves the Romulans, the Ferengi, and quite possibly the Borg." He settled back in his chair. "Therefore, I believe it is incumbent upon us to be ready for anything." Picard glanced up to the side. "Would you agree, Mr. Worf?"

"A wise decision, Captain."

"Number One?" Picard asked.

"Without question, sir."

Picard smiled. Whenever Worf and Riker agreed on the same course of action, then he could be certain he had achieved consensus on his bridge.

"Mr. Data," Picard said, "take us out of orbit and match course and speed with the Warbird."

"Should I hold a course slightly offset from theirs, sir? So we don't run into them in case they come to a sudden stop?"

"Make it so," Picard agreed.

Then he settled back into his chair and did the hardest thing it was for any starship captain to do—he waited.

And despite what any of his officers predicted was going to happen, Picard felt certain that whatever the *Enterprise* discovered at the coordinates the Ferengi had provided, it was going to be unexpected.

The universe, Picard had found, generally tended to work like that. And he wouldn't have it any other way.

TEN

LONDON, OPTIMAL REPUBLIC OF GREAT BRITAIN, EARTH
Earth Standard: June 21, 2078

Cochrane lunged at Thorsen, both hands outstretched, aimed for his throat.

But he never reached the madman. Instead, Thorsen seemed to blur, to shift, sidestepping easily even as a rigid hand scooped up to strike Cochrane beneath his sternum, changing his angle of attack just enough to carry him past Thorsen and into the desk behind.

Cochrane saw stars of a different kind explode before him as the edge of the desk slammed into his stomach, knocking his breath from him in a wrenching gasp. Before he could even think to try to breathe again, the side of Thorsen's open hand slammed into the back of his head, smashing his face onto the writing surface.

The pain was unlike anything he had felt before, fiery needles shooting up through his nose, behind his eyes, into the back of his head.

He tried to moan, but his lungs were off-line. He tried to push himself up, but Thorsen's boot crunched into his side and with a crack he felt more than heard, Cochrane rolled from the desk to the floor.

Thorsen stood over him. His face was in darkness against the

134

overhead light. Cochrane tasted blood in his mouth. He couldn't catch his breath. He felt he was smothering, enveloped in pain.

The door to the office was open again. Two zombies stood inside it, vacuous, drug-puffed faces staring at him with dull indifference, fistguns pointing at him.

"You are only a scientist," Thorsen said. "I am a leader of men. I trust the lesson will not have to be taught again."

He reached down to Cochrane, grabbed his hand, pulled him up as if he were without mass.

Cochrane found his breath and his voice as he screamed with the agony of the broken ribs where Thorsen had kicked him.

Thorsen flung him back into the wooden chair like old garbage. The rigid chair legs squealed against the floor as the chair slid into one of the mercenaries. The butt of a rifle pushed Cochrane forward again.

Thorsen squatted down in front of the scientist so Cochrane wouldn't have to look up again. Cochrane doubted he could. He shook with spasms of wordless torment. His nose, his head, his ribs. Thorsen handed him a white cloth from another pocket.

"What you must always remember, Mr. Cochrane, is that people such as you exist only because people such as I allow it. You and your kind are a luxury in this world. The food you consume could be given to my soldiers. The ideas you spread can disrupt the public order. And the public, *my* public, will not stand for that."

Cochrane took the cloth, and even that simple movement shot pain across his back. He tried to use the cloth to wipe the blood from his nose, but he couldn't bear the pressure of the fabric anywhere on his face.

He opened his mouth, gasping as he felt cold air strike a broken tooth.

"You're nothing more than a thug," he said with extreme difficulty.

Thorsen looked amused. "Mr. Cochrane, really. *I* was discussing physics. *You* attacked *me.*" He stood up again.

Dimly, through his pain, Cochrane heard footsteps behind him. Sir John and his granddaughter were pushed roughly into the office. Cochrane was thankful to see that neither of them looked the way he felt. They hadn't been harmed. Yet.

"See here," Sir John exclaimed in shock as he saw Cochrane. "There is no call for this." He rapped his cane on the floor for emphasis. "This man was only a passenger. I instructed my driver to leave the checkpoint in order to get to Heathrow on—"

"Please, Mr. Burke," Thorsen said in a tone of supreme aggravation. The old astronomer's royal honors would not be acknowledged by the Optimum. "We're not playing games any longer. I know this passenger is Zefram Cochrane. I know you are part of some ill-considered, futile resistance organization. And I know your driver is your granddaughter. My time is short so, please, let's not waste it."

Sir John smoothed down his wispy, flyaway hair. Monica stood ramrod straight at his side, her dark chauffeur's uniform giving her the look of a soldier as well.

"To get to the point," Thorsen said, "I have asked Mr. Cochrane for information which he does not wish to provide. Therefore, I am hoping that one of you might persuade him to change his mind." He stood too close to Monica. "Ms. Burke? Is there anything you'd care to say to Mr. Cochrane which could convince him of the, shall we say, precariousness of his position?"

Monica spit on Thorsen's gleaming black boots, never breaking contact with his eyes. Cochrane admired her defiance and her aim. It was good to know there were still humans on Earth who could and would fight oppressors.

Thorsen didn't move. "Very good, Ms. Burke. But hardly wise." And then his fist shot out and caught Sir John in the stomach, making the old man grunt and stumble backward into a mercenary. The mercenary jabbed him in the back with the barrel of his fistgun, knocking him jarringly to his knees, making his cane fly from his grip to clatter on the floor. Even before Sir John had come to a rest, Thorsen's hand had caught Monica Burke by the throat as she attempted to strike him.

"Do you know what my soldiers do to people like you?" Thorsen asked her silkily, his voice barely betraying the tension in the muscles of his arm. Then he released her and she dropped to her knees by her grandfather, who wheezed to catch his breath.

136

Cochrane had had enough. He struggled to his feet. The pain in his side was unbearable but he knew what he had to do.

Thorsen watched him, seemingly puzzled. "What drives you people? You're supposed to be scientists. You're supposed to be smart. Can't you see the inevitable?"

"If I *had* accepted the inevitable," Cochrane said thickly, "we'd still be traveling slower than light." He reached out his hand. "A pen, something."

Thorsen looked intrigued. He slipped Cochrane a pen from a side pocket on his jumpsuit. "You're not going to try to kill me with that, are you, Mr. Cochrane?"

Cochrane shuffled to the desk. There was an old paper calendar on the writing surface, showing a month at a time. It hadn't been changed for more than thirty years. With uncertain movements, he ripped off the top sheet and turned it over. Dust flew. "Here," he said weakly. "Look."

Thorsen moved around the desk to see what Cochrane would do. Cochrane squeezed the pen and its ready light came on. He tapped it twice for a broad nib and the tip of it changed shape. Then he drew a star shape. He had given this presentation a thousand times to his students and he no longer even had to think about it. The standard asymmetric energy-curve comparison diagram told the whole story to anyone who would bother to look at it and understand. It was the fundamental basis of all he had done to create faster-than-light physics; as important, he believed, as pi or *e.*

"This is it," he began, tapping the pen on the topmost tip of the star for emphasis. "Right here. The Holy Grail. The speed of light. The absolute fastest, ultimate speed anything can move in this universe."

"Very pretty," Thorsen said dryly.

"You know what happens when you try to reach the speed of light?"

"Enlighten me, Mr. Cochrane."

"Einstein happens. Plain, old-fashioned, hundred-and-fifty-year-old relativistic effects. Like time dilation. I know you've heard of time dilation. The faster you go, the more your subjective time flow decreases. And at the same time, your mass *increases.* It's a straightforward ratio: the faster you go, the more massive you become, and therefore the more energy you need to continue to increase your speed." With some difficulty, he brought the pen to the paper again. "So look what happens." He drew an energy expenditure curve over the star.

With the pen tip, he moved again up the curve's left-hand side for emphasis. "See? The closer you get to light-speed, the more your mass and energy requirement increases, until at the very speed of light"—he tapped the curve's topmost point, *above* the star that represented absolute speed—"your mass becomes infinite so you need infinite energy. Now, once you get past light-speed . . ." Cochrane's voice gained in strength as he continued. ". . . over here to the right, sure, the Clarke corollary shows that power consumption will drop off dramatically. But you can't get *past* light-speed without getting to light-speed first. And that's up here, Thorsen. Off the scale. Beyond the infinite. Can't be reached. Can't. Be. Done."

"Yet you do it, Mr. Cochrane."

"Exactly," Cochrane agreed, hoping Thorsen would listen to him, that somewhere in the soldier's military training he had had some introduction to basic physics. "Because I do not exceed the speed of light in normal space-time. I change the rules. I distort the continuum to change a small volume of it into something else where the restrictions of normal space-time no longer apply. And look what happens."

He brought pen to paper again and sketched a rough approximation of the asymmetric peristaltic field-manipulation function, this time below the star representing the speed of light, where it belonged, where it made all things possible.

"Look at it, Thorsen. This is the literal, bottom-line energy expenditure for my superimpellor. It's well below infinity, easily obtainable from a basic matter-antimatter reaction. But look how it's *offset*—separated—from the standard energy expenditure of normal space-time." He tapped the pen to the top of the bottom curve, where it reached its peak to the right of light-speed. "Don't you see? *Because* the field is asymmetric, because it *doesn't* reach peak power until after it's *outside* normal space-time, you can *never* have a warp reaction cause a destructive release of energy that's anywhere near as great as matter-antimatter annihilation. As soon as you get into that range, you're going faster than light in a different continuum. There can be no interaction. It cannot function as a bomb. Period."

Cochrane threw down the pen. "It's a law of nature, Thorsen. No matter how big you build it, no matter how powerful you make it, the only thing a warp bomb could ever possibly do is to destroy itself. And a few grams of antimatter will do the same, far more cheaply, far more efficiently."

Thorsen took the pen, switched it off, then slipped it back into his side pocket, all the while looking at the diagram Cochrane had drawn. He lifted the sheet of paper. He folded it in half, in half again, and again, so it made a small booklet in his hand. Then he stared at Cochrane and crushed that booklet into a ball, dropping it back to the desk.

"Corporal. Take the old man outside and kill him."

"No!" Cochrane gasped. He saw two mercenaries grab Sir John by his coat and haul him to his feet. Monica tore desperately at one of the zombies, ripping away his inhaler hose. But the mercenary swung his fistgun up into her face and sent her slight form crashing to the wall, then the floor.

"You can't do this!" Cochrane said. Forgetting his own injuries, he grabbed Thorsen's arm, and was grabbed fiercely in return.

"You're the only one who can change my mind, Mr. Cochrane."

In Thorsen's implacable grip, Cochrane craned to look at Sir John.

"It's all right, young fellow," the astronomer said, and Cochrane was amazed by the aura of calm around him. "It seems that every once in a while, history requires that the monsters win." The old man glared undefeated at Thorsen. "So that when they are utterly defeated, future generations may count their blessings."

"No, Thorsen," Cochrane said urgently. "Maybe there's some other way I can—"

"Don't," Monica implored him.

Cochrane acted as if he ignored her. There was no way he could explain to her his motives. He was willing to promise *anything* just to buy time. "But the warp bomb is still impossible."

Thorsen shrugged. "Then none of you is worth anything and you've lived seventeen years too long." He nodded at the mercenaries holding Sir John. "Record that one's death, then take the body to Sandringham and feed it to my dogs. Record that, too. For his naïve friends in the resistance."

"What about 'er?" one of the zombies asked, unconscious of the small trickle of drool that ran from his mouth. He nodded at Monica. She was on her feet, barely, blood dripping from a ragged gash on her cheek.

"What about her, Mr. Cochrane?" Thorsen asked.

"Do nothing for him," Monica warned. "Nothing."

Cochrane's gaze met her dark eyes. Saw the passion there. The thrilling intensity of her determination to stop Thorsen. Cochrane realized that saving Monica Burke by capitulation would be no favor to her or to those like her. Every lesson Micah Brack had taught him about history came back to him now. The genie was out of the bottle. No matter what Thorsen and the others like him did to Earth, humanity would survive.

Cochrane faced Thorsen squarely. "You've got it wrong again, Thorsen. People like *you* exist because of people like *me*. Because we're smarter than you, more aware than you'll ever be, so in your jealousy, you try to destroy everything we stand for—rationality, humanity, common decency and respect."

Thorsen's face tightened.

"You're everything that's base in humanity," Cochrane continued. "Drawing up strict, senseless rules for the sole reason of putting you at the top and excluding anyone you say doesn't belong or fit in, for no other reason than just because you say so." He turned to the mercenaries holding Sir John. "What's your leader going to do when he's killed all of *us?* He can only survive if there's someone he can crush. When we're gone, are you his next enemy?"

One of the zombies burped loudly. Both laughed, the sound ugly, disturbed.

"Finished?" Thorsen asked, then he addressed the mercenaries. "Transport the girl to Highgate for interrogation." He looked back at Cochrane. "There are specialists there, Mr. Cochrane. Some of them even used to be doctors of a sort. Now they're interface experts. Have you ever seen what happens to human nervous tissue after the insertion of Josephson probes into the brain?" He stroked the bridge of his nose with a thin finger. "Well, you will."

Thorsen snapped his fingers at his mercenaries. "Make the old fool suffer. I'll want close-ups for the uploads."

They started to pull Sir John to the door.

"You dare call yourself a soldier?!" the astronomer called out.

"I am *the* soldier," Thorsen corrected.

141

"Then at least give me the dignity of walking to my fate under my own power, sir."

Thorsen sighed. He looked around, saw Sir John's cane, reached down and brought it to the old man.

"Let him walk to his fate," Thorsen told the mercenaries. He looked down at Sir John. "I'll put your head on this when they're finished with you." He slapped the cane into Sir John's hands.

Sir John shook himself loose from the mercenaries, tapped his cane on the floor as if to see if it still worked, smoothed his coat, then nodded his head at Cochrane. "Accept my apologies, sir. On behalf of the planet." He looked over at his granddaughter. "Monica," he said, "you were always the light of my life."

"I understand," Monica said. And that was all. Cochrane found the whole subdued exchange excruciatingly British, though there had almost been something to the way Sir John had said "light" that made Cochrane wonder if the astronomer had been passing on a hidden message.

Then Sir John turned his back on Thorsen and the office and walked ahead of the mercenaries, out the door. The mercenaries plodded after him, indifferent to their destination.

Thorsen crossed his arms and faced Cochrane. "I'm thinking of making Centauri B II the first example of what happens to colonies who don't contribute to Earth. What do you think, Mr. Cochrane? Superimpellors with antimatter bombs? Are they any match for your warp bombs?"

"If you come out of a distortion field within half a parsec of my planet, you'll have asteroid interceptors locked on to you two weeks before you get within a million kilometers," Cochrane said fiercely. Every colony world had the same defense because no extrasolar system had been studied in enough detail for asteroid impacts to be predictable. The result was that superimpellors, which could not operate close to a sun, were not a viable military threat.

"Still," Thorsen replied, "it might be worth a—"

A hideous shriek echoed down the corridor outside the office. Cochrane felt sick.

"How surprising," Thorsen said as he studied Monica's reaction. "I thought he would be the stiff-upper-lip type. 'So sorry to bleed on your carpet.' That sort of—"

A second scream echoed. It was not made by the same person who first had cried out.

Cochrane felt electrified with hope. Thorsen reached for his net phone. Monica, for some reason Cochrane didn't understand, immediately leaned over and ripped at the heel of her boot.

"This is Thorsen," the colonel barked into his slender phone. "Get me—"

And then Sir John was in the doorway again, cheeks flushed, the few strands of hair he had standing straight out to the side, and he was aiming his cane at Thorsen as if it were a rifle.

"Put it down, Colonel," Sir John commanded, only a bit out of breath.

"Get me Operations!" Thorsen shouted.

A spike of red light lanced out from the tip of Sir John's cane and swept across Thorsen's chest. The red fabric of his jumpsuit was unharmed but the interlinked triangles of the Optimum Movement he wore on his chest exploded in a spray of molten metal, his net phone burst into blue-white flames, and white smoke burst from the back of his hand as Cochrane heard the sizzle of burnt flesh.

Thorsen grunted in pain but made no other sound. He clutched his injured hand to his stomach. "You will never survive," he panted. "You are unfit."

Then Monica was at him, the black plastic of her heel in her hand. She jammed it against Thorsen's arm as he tried to avoid her and this time he did scream.

His swinging fist sent Monica back. He started for her, snarling something incomprehensible. Cochrane could hear a capacitor whine from Sir John's cane. Whatever system powered its laser wasn't ready to fire. Someone had to act.

"Thorsen!" Cochrane yelled in challenge.

Thorsen spun around, his arm still raised to strike Monica. His narrow face was twisted in animalistic fury.

Cochrane matched it.

The scientist charged the soldier, ignoring the pain of his own

143

nose and ribs. He heard the alarming sound of grinding bones below his lungs, but he would not let Thorsen win. No matter what it took.

Cochrane slammed his head into Thorsen's chest and howled in pain as the shock of impact tore through his own chest. Thorsen's fist crashed down on his back but the counterblow was too late.

The two men flew back into a wall, shattering the glass over an old baseball photograph, then slid to the floor. Cochrane pushed himself off Thorsen, feeling shards of glass dig into his hand. Thorsen kicked at him, tried to get up, then shivered, arms stiff at his side. His heavy boots thumped at the floor for a moment, then were still.

Cochrane caught his breath, staring at Thorsen lying on the floor. The madman wasn't unconscious. His pale blue eyes remained wide with hatred and still bored into him. Then Monica was at Cochrane's side, holding out her hand. In the other, she still carried the heel of her boot.

"We have to hurry," she told Cochrane as she helped him to his feet. She smiled at him as if he were an old friend, a trusted ally. Cochrane felt an unexpected warmth in his chest. He hoped it didn't mean he was bleeding to death from internal injuries.

"What happened to him?" Cochrane asked. Thorsen still stared unblinking at him.

Monica held up her boot heel. Cochrane could see three silver needles arranged in it, stained by blood. "Selective neural inhibitor," she explained. "Shuts down the section of the brain responsible for physical movement. Same process that keeps us motionless when we dream we're moving." She tugged on his arm and Cochrane winced. "Sorry, but there're more zombies at his Rover. We have to leave."

Cochrane looked back at Thorsen's hate-filled stare. "Why not kill him?"

"Tempting," Monica said. "But then we'd become him, wouldn't we?"

Cochrane saw something in Monica's eyes that brought the warmth back to his chest again. Perhaps he wasn't mortally wounded after all.

"Come along, you two, our ride will be waiting," Sir John urged.

Cochrane turned away from Thorsen. "Nice shooting, by the way," he said.

"Optics are optics," Sir John answered with satisfaction. "Though I must say they never went into this at Cambridge." He tapped his cane against the floor. It was buzzing now with a constantly resetting capacitor hum, ready to fire at any time.

The three of them headed for the corridor. Cochrane found he had to limp to keep his ribs from grating. In the office doorway, he stopped, then turned back to Thorsen's fallen form as he suddenly thought of a way to get the final word.

"Don't you even think of leaving Earth," Cochrane told him. "The colonies are the future of humanity and people like you have no place in it."

Cochrane noted with appreciation the way Thorsen's whitened face began to redden.

"And if you do come after me," he added, unable to resist doing so, "I'll use my warp bomb on you."

At that, Thorsen groaned, mouth half opening. Whatever was in him was wearing off. The scientist turned his back on his pursuer and stepped out of the office.

Cochrane, Sir John, and Monica moved through the dimly lit corridor three levels below the playing surface of the Battersea Stadium. Sir John moved slowly with the cane that was just as necessary for his support as it was for their defense. Monica stumbled along awkwardly because of the missing heel of her boot. Cochrane could only shuffle because of his breath-stealing injuries. They were in sorry shape. But they had won. So far.

"*Is* there such a thing as a warp bomb?" Monica asked in a low voice as they began to ascend a pedestrian ramp. The sliding pathway beside it had long since ceased to function. Old advertising posters for beer and suborbital airlines studded the drab walls.

"Utterly impossible," Cochrane said.

"So you just said that about the bomb to annoy him?" Monica asked.

"I had to do *something* to him." Cochrane was surprised at the

145

vehemence he heard in his own voice. But he loathed people like Thorsen, the strong preying on the weak with no other reason than that they could.

"I, uh, I liked what you said back there," Monica told him, still whispering as they came to the last level of the ramp. "About people like Thorsen being created by people like, well, like you and my grandfather. Not on purpose, of course, but as . . . a sort of by-product."

Cochrane didn't have the strength to get caught up in a philosophical discussion, but he felt gratified by the fact that she had paid attention. He had taught students like Monica Burke on Alpha Centauri, thoughtful, capable, and he had always enjoyed doing so. But for now, all he said was "I liked what you *did* back there. Sometimes I worry I don't do enough."

"You're joking," Monica said. She spoke aloud.

Sir John turned around and shushed her. "This isn't over, you two. Adrik Thorsen does not travel alone." His old voice shook with exhaustion.

Cochrane whispered to Monica. "Should I go ahead of Sir John? I mean, your grandfather's been through a lot."

"You should take a look at yourself," Monica said. She gingerly touched the gash on her cheek. "We've all been through the stamper." She looked ahead. Sir John had reached the top of the ramp where it exited into a main lobby. All the lights were out, creating a cavern of darkness, but a white glare streamed in through the large entrances leading to the lower level seats around the playing field. The astronomer motioned to his granddaughter and Cochrane to stay where they were.

"Grandfather's been through things like this before," Monica said softly. "After the elections, when the Optimum dissolved the Royal Academies, it was all we could do to keep him from flying his car into Parliament."

"We?" Cochrane asked. He suddenly wondered if Monica was married, or at least involved with someone. Whoever the lucky person was, Cochrane was surprised to discover he was envious. Confused by his new and unexpected emotion, he kept his eyes on Sir John, who looked carefully around ahead.

But Monica said, "My father and I."

Cochrane heard it in her tone, in her hesitation. Monica's father, Sir John's son or son-in-law, was no longer alive.

Monica confirmed his guess. "The Cambridge Riots," she said. "When the Optimum sent zombies in to close it down. Father was a botanical engineer. He knew nothing of politics. He was part of the group who sat down on the commons, expecting to be arrested and get carried off."

"I'm sorry," Cochrane said. The news of the shredderbomb assaults on England's universities had made it to Alpha Centauri.

"Come along, come along," Sir John whispered loudly to them.

As Cochrane and Monica joined him at the top of the ramp, Cochrane could hear the stuttering pops of distant plasma pulses. There was a firefight somewhere near. Probably out on the playing field.

"It doesn't sound like we should go out there," he said.

"On the contrary," Sir John said. "That's what we've been waiting for. We have some associates clearing the landing site."

The astronomer stumped off toward the entrance to the lower level seats. Monica followed. Cochrane followed also. He didn't have much choice.

The playing field was still brightly lit from the banks of light channels that ringed the stadium. Sir John's Rolls-Royce was parked out past second base, and Cochrane could see the dark form of a Fourth World mercenary stretched out on the artificial turf beside it. For a moment, he thought the zombie was staying low for cover, but then he saw the dull metal of a fistgun lying a meter away from the zombie's hand. He had been shot. But by whom?

"Stay low, children," Sir John said. He handed his cane back to Cochrane. "The trigger's under the cap," he explained. "There're only two more discharges left. You know what energy density is like for these contraptions."

"Aren't we staying together?" Cochrane asked. He wouldn't allow the old astronomer to sacrifice himself for them.

"Of course we are," Sir John answered. "But when we're crawling between the seats, I'm afraid this old back won't let me pop up with the abandon of my youth. It will be up to you to cover our withdrawal, as it were."

147

Cochrane hefted the cane in his hands, trying not to jar his chest with sudden movement. "Withdrawal to where?"

Sir John pointed up toward the ragged hole in the roof of the stadium. The dull orange glow of low clouds over London shone through it. "You're going home, young fellow. Just as we promised."

They were a few meters from the entrance. Sir John motioned them to the side, then down to their knees. "Heads down, follow me."

Plasma fire continued to echo in the stadium, but it seemed far enough away not to be directed at them. Sir John crawled behind a row of seats, and Cochrane followed, awkwardly keeping the cane in front of him, with Monica close behind.

Suddenly, a bright flare flickered around them, followed a second later by a thunderclap. After that, there was no more plasma fire.

"Keep down," Sir John called back to them. "It's just a temporary respite."

They came to the end of the row and Sir John started down a wide aisle. Cochrane got to his feet, remaining crouched over. "Where are we headed?"

"Home plate," Monica said, squeezing his hand. "Almost there."

Now she ran directly after her grandfather, head ducked. Cochrane did the same. He began to hear a strange pulsing in the air. Not gunfire, but something else.

A distant voice yelled out through the stadium. *"Mr. Bond! Casino Royale!"*

Sir John waved Cochrane and Monica to a stop by the next to last row before the low wall separating the seats from the field. "Our associates," he wheezed. "Right on schedule."

"Who's Mr. Bond?" Cochrane asked.

Monica smiled fondly as she patted her grandfather's shoulders. "Grandfather is a devotee of twentieth-century literature. For some reason known only to him, his code name is 'Mr. Bond.'"

"And we only have two minutes to wait," Sir John added, apparently explaining the rest of the enigmatic message.

"Code name?" Cochrane asked.

Monica had a serious expression as she stared up at the opening in the roof. "No matter what Thorsen thinks of it, the resistance is quite real, Mr. Cochrane. And quite well organized."

"Her Majesty's Royal Resistance Force," Sir John said proudly.

Before Cochrane could ask any additional questions, the pulsing that he had heard intensified to the point where he would have to shout to say anything. The sound was coming from overhead.

Then a blinding flash of light shone through the roof opening. Reflexively, Cochrane looked away, covering his eyes with his arm. When he squinted back at the playing field, a craft had landed, but what kind, he couldn't tell. It was circular, a flattened disk shape with a gently elevated center, top and bottom, with no obvious markings or registry numbers. No landing legs had extended from it, yet there was no sign of a fan effect on the turf beneath it, either. It was, however, the source of the pulsing sound he heard.

"Move along," Sir John said urgently. "Move along."

Monica pushed ahead to the low wall, straddled it, then held out her hand to Cochrane. Gingerly, Cochrane sat on the wall, moved one leg over, then the other, and dropped the five feet to the turf, losing his grip on the cane. Dark spots sparkled in his vision with the pain of the landing. He coughed and tasted blood again. He felt and heard gurgling with each breath he took and knew a lung had been perforated.

A moment later, Sir John dropped beside him, but landed far more professionally, rolling from his feet to his knees to his side, absorbing the force of impact along the entire length of his body. Sir John blinked up at Cochrane with delight. "Just like in the bloody paratroopers," he said. Then he awkwardly got to his hands and knees as Monica leapt lightly down beside them. Cochrane retrieved the cane. It was still humming and resetting itself. He doubted the batteries or whatever it used could last much longer even if it wasn't discharged.

In the center of the field, not far from Sir John's Rolls, the circular craft waited; two brilliant searchlights were deployed from its far edge and swept the distant stadium seats in a search pattern.

149

"What is that thing?" Cochrane asked, though he had a good idea. He just couldn't believe it.

Monica stared at it, as if waiting for a signal.

"Plan B," she said. "A lunar transport disk. Inertial gravity drive."

Cochrane decided he'd believe it when he saw it take off. Inertial gravity drive couldn't take anything from the earth to the moon in any reasonable length of time. Maybe someday it could be used to generate artificial gravity fields, but as a propulsion method, it had proved inefficient except for landing and surface maneuvers.

A blue strobe light on the forward edge of the disk suddenly flashed three times.

"Clear!" Monica shouted. "Run!"

Sir John took off with surprising speed and Cochrane, after a moment of startled hesitation, followed, trying not to pump his arms as he ran. He heard Monica right behind him.

Then a new sound swept through the stadium, so powerfully that Cochrane couldn't tell where it came from.

"Down!" Monica shouted behind him.

He felt her arms hit his legs as she dove onto him from behind, pushing him to the ground with an explosion of pain that cut through him like red lightning.

He couldn't talk, felt only the harsh spikes of the artificial turf pressing into his cheek. Monica was lying beside him, one arm across his back. "Sorry, sorry," she said into his ear.

"Sir John?" Cochrane suddenly gasped.

"He's all right," Monica answered, but there was worry in her eyes and voice.

Cochrane looked ahead. Another vehicle had entered the playing field, floating forward from a players' entrance, fanjets flattening the turf below it.

He recognized it as an armored troop carrier, with a plasma cannon mounted at its back.

The carrier's headlight strip blazed across the turf, turning it from green to white, catching the disk on its side.

The carrier's cannon flared, and the stadium rocked with

thunder as the plasma explosion hurled a projectile forward at supersonic velocity.

But the projectile exploded a heartbeat later in the far stands, as if it had ricocheted from the disk.

"What's that disk made of?" Cochrane said faintly. He didn't think he could keep talking much longer.

"The shell never hit the disk," Monica said. "It's generating an EM shield. Nothing physical can touch it."

Cochrane felt the stadium melting and twisting around him in time to his thundering pulse. "Then how can we get on board? Is it a selective frequency?" Even facing death, the drive for knowledge in him was still never far from the surface.

"Shh," Monica said, sensing and soothing his confusion. "Almost home."

Cochrane stared back at her. From that angle, he couldn't see the wound on her other cheek. He tried to touch her face. She looked at him, surprised, but not troubled.

"Thank you," he said, and he knew his words were almost inaudible, drifting off.

"For what?" she asked.

"Paying attention," Cochrane mumbled. He wasn't sure what it meant, but he did mean it.

Another flare of blinding light hit them. Wearily, Cochrane struggled to turn his head to see the light's source.

There was an enormous gout of flame shooting up from the field from the point Sir John's Rolls had been parked. The car was gone.

"Betsy!" Sir John moaned as if he had lost an old family friend.

The fanjet carrier sped for the disk. When it had disappeared behind its bulk, Monica pulled Cochrane to his feet. He felt as if he were floating, losing touch with his body. He decided there was too much pain for his brain to deal with. He was disassociating. He fought against the temptation of unconsciousness. But it was a difficult battle, so much easier to give up.

Abruptly, he realized he was heading toward the disk, Monica supporting him, Sir John beside her. There was another explosion somewhere else, perhaps on the other side of the disk. He saw

flickerings on the overhead roof. Monica told him the disk had hit
the carrier. But to Cochrane, everything seemed to be happening
to someone else. He was no longer in his body. He was no longer
on Earth. He thought he saw Micah Brack before him, floating in
microgravity, out by Neptune.

"This is the way it always goes," Brack told him. "Fire and
destruction."

"No," Cochrane whispered to his absent friend. "No more.
We'll change that. Can't we?"

Monica asked him what he had said.

Cochrane couldn't remember.

And then he heard his name, blaring, echoing, coming at him
from every surface in the stadium as if the gods themselves were
calling for him.

They were almost at the disk, a gangplank was extended, but
Cochrane stumbled, looked up to the side.

The giant visage of Adrik Thorsen looked down upon him.

"You will not leave!" Thorsen screamed. His enraged face was
repeated on the display boards ringing the stadium, blotched by
imperfect pixels, incomplete, flickering. His cruelly commanding
voice echoed from everywhere all at once. "Air defense will
destroy you a hundred meters from the ground."

"Don't listen to him," Monica shouted. She pulled on
Cochrane's arm. He cried in turn with pain.

"You are the dead!" Thorsen thundered.

The gangplank was almost before them. And then it disappeared in an eruption of fire.

Sir John whirled in a circle like a mad ballerina, a dozen small
fires at work on his coat. He fell to the turf even as Monica
doubled over atop him.

Cochrane staggered to a stop. He thought he heard plasma
pulses, or were they just the echoes?

"You will never escape the Optimum!" Thorsen shouted. "You
will never escape your destiny!"

Dimly, terrifyingly, Cochrane became aware that Thorsen's last
words had not come from the displays. They had come from
behind him. He turned.

Thorsen stood on the wall by home plate. He had a fistgun. It was aimed directly at Cochrane.

"Earth will be your graveyard," Thorsen said. "Unless you join me, Zefram Cochrane. Only I can unchain your science."

Cochrane listened, thought, considered. He half-convinced himself he was asleep on the *John Cabal,* that this was all a dream, a nightmare, deep within the crew quarters of the old ice freighter.

He leaned on Sir John's cane to keep a semblance of his balance. His body shook as a sharp cough brought up bright red blood to spatter on the green turf. He realized he wasn't dreaming. He realized he was going to die soon.

Thorsen jumped from the wall and began walking forward, fistgun held ready.

"Cochrane—think—your only possible future lies with me." One of Thorsen's hands held death. The other was outstretched in friendship. "Give me the warp bomb. Let me celebrate your genius. You need not die when that ship is shot down."

Cochrane heard the cane cycle up and reset itself.

He heard Monica moan. Smoke drifted up from Sir John's still body.

Cochrane realized he could kill Thorsen.

In his mind, he heard Monica's voice, telling him that by killing he would only become Thorsen.

Cochrane closed his eyes. This was all happening to someone else, anyway. Besides, he had made Thorsen. "I am Thorsen," he said.

"Did you say something?" Thorsen called out. He was only fifty meters distant.

"You exist because of *me!"* Cochrane heard himself shout. He saw blood spray from his mouth in the brilliant blue light of the stadium, a halo of blood around him.

"You're delirious, my friend," Thorsen said. "Let me help you."

Cochrane raised the cane, aimed it at Thorsen from the hip.

Thorsen stopped moving forward. He turned sideways, decreasing the size of the target he offered. He raised the fistgun, keeping the barrel pointed up.

"There are still secrets to be discovered, Mr. Cochrane. Don't let your work end here. Don't let your life mean nothing."

Cochrane put his finger on the trigger stud. Suddenly, he realized he didn't care about his work anymore, he didn't care about secrets. He only cared about what he had done with his life. And he was certain he had not done enough. Had not shared enough.

"You hurt Monica," Cochrane said.

The capacitor in the cane built up to discharge level.

"What does the life of one person matter?" Thorsen called back. He began to lower the barrel of the fistgun, taking aim.

"Everyone matters," Cochrane said, his voice so weak he knew he could no longer speak loudly enough for Thorsen to hear him.

"This is your last chance!" Thorsen screamed.

"I know," Cochrane said.

He fired the cane, and even as the red laser hit Thorsen's fistgun, Cochrane realized that as fast as that beam was, Thorsen had been faster.

The fistgun fired, then exploded.

Something burned past Cochrane's cheek.

Thorsen's scream pierced the air.

Cochrane felt hands grab him from behind. The sudden movement brought such intense pain that he dropped the cane, dropped from his body, became only an observer in his mind.

He felt himself carried up the gangplank into the disk. Somewhere, Monica's voice still murmured. That meant she was still alive. That meant she would continue. Even without him. The knowledge made him feel better, somehow.

Gentle hands strapped him into a reclining chair, a blast couch, a display screen above it. Nearby, he thought he heard Monica call out her grandfather's name. He thought he heard other people asking about Thorsen. But they had the name wrong, he could see that now.

"His name is Ozymandias," Cochrane muttered. He remembered his mother reading that poem to him. It had made him think of history. Micah Brack could recite it as readily as if the industrialist had written it himself. " 'Look on my works, ye mighty,' " Cochrane said.

No one heard him.

An artificial voice ordered everyone to prepare for orbital insertion. Cochrane wished he could say good-bye to Monica. He wanted her to have a happy life. She deserved that. He wished he could give it to her.

The blast couch shook beneath him. On the screen above, he saw the stadium grow smaller. Then it disappeared in a gout of blue plasma, in waves of explosions.

In a far-off corner of his still lucid mind, Cochrane understood that was how the disk traveled from the earth to the moon. Inertial gravity generators for landing and surface maneuvers, but an impulse drive for propulsion.

The fusion flames of the disk's departure bathed whatever had been below it. He pictured Battersea Stadium melting as if a small sun had ignited within it. Baseball really was dead, he decided. And so was Thorsen . . . or Ozymandias . . . whatever his name was. All would soon be incandescent. Back to the stuff of stars.

Cochrane felt a hand grip his. He looked through blurring, closing eyes to see Monica at his side. He heard the hiss of a spray hypo, but felt nothing.

"I wanted to do more," he said to her. He knew she would understand.

She smiled at him. Her smile was beautiful. She would make someone very happy someday, he decided, and he tried to tell her so. Then he realized that he could not last until they cleared the atmosphere. Darkness rolled up for him like the clouds of Titan, bringing on the night. "The stars," he said to her. "I wanted to see the stars again." He could see her lips move as she said something back to him, but he could no longer hear.

Then Zefram Cochrane slowly closed his eyes and waited peacefully for death and history to claim him.

But history wasn't finished with him yet.

ELEVEN

☆

U.S.S. ENTERPRISE NCC-1701
GAMMA CANARIS REGION, PLANETOID 527
Stardate 3853.2
Earth Standard: ≈ November 2267

Kirk, Spock, and McCoy resolved from the transporter beam and set foot once again on Cochrane's world. Without question, as sensors had indicated, things had changed.

The air, once a pleasant and constant 22°C, was cold. Frost covered the ground. Wispy clouds stretched like a web across the sky, dark now, almost as if it were dusk, though the planetoid's sun was directly above at local high noon.

Kirk could guess what had happened, but he waited for Spock to confirm it with tricorder readings.

"Gravity is at eighty-two percent of what it was six months ago," Spock announced, reading from the device's tiny screen.

"Resulting in loss of atmosphere," Kirk stated, not surprised.

"And heat," Spock added. The energy once held by the dense air of the planetoid had evaporated into space with the atmosphere.

"Any indication of what caused the change?" Kirk asked.

Spock moved the tricorder in an arc about them, watching it intently. "The tricorder detects no underlying cause."

"What about *you*, Spock? Any theories?"

Spock looked at McCoy. "Doctor, have you detected any life signs?"

156

McCoy studied the screen of his own medical tricorder, which Spock had adjusted so it would pick up life signs from the Companion as well. But the doctor shook his head. "Nothing, Mr. Spock. No sign of Cochrane or the Companion."

Mr. Scott had beamed them down to the precise location where the *Galileo* shuttlecraft had been brought to a landing when the Companion had controlled it. Admiral Kabreigny had remained on the *Enterprise,* though she had approved the landing site as a reasonable place to begin an investigation. But Kirk knew something the admiral did not, that around the ridge to the west, Cochrane's small shelter waited. He didn't want to think what they'd find there. Especially given what Spock had uncovered about Cochrane's final days on Centauri B II.

"Could it have been a symbiotic relationship between the Companion and this place?" Kirk asked as he reached for his communicator.

"Intriguing," Spock said. "And possible."

The Companion had told them she was unable to leave the planetoid for more than a tiny march of days, that she drew her life from this place. Perhaps the planetoid's unusual gravity and climate had also been the result of the Companion's presence as well, as if conditions here could no longer exist without her, as if life and habitat were one. So much about that type of energy-based creature was unknown.

Kirk flipped open his communicator. "Kirk to *Enterprise.*"

"Kabreigny here."

Kirk frowned at that response, thankful that Starfleet consistently rejected requests to include standard optical sensors on communicators. He didn't want to see her sitting in his chair on the bridge, and he certainly didn't want her to see his expression as he spoke with her. "We're at the *Galileo* landing site," Kirk reported. "No energy readings of any kind."

But Kabreigny wasn't going to give up easily. "What about the wreckage that sensors are showing about a kilometer to the west?" she asked.

Kirk had known the admiral would see the sensor readings of Cochrane's shelter, and so had prepared her for them by stating that they had previously discovered the crash site of an antique ship, apparently drawn off course the same way the shuttlecraft had been. For Kabreigny, the presence of the wreck was further indication that Kirk should have noted there was a chance that a permanent navigational hazard existed. But Kirk knew that if he had done so, within a year Starfleet would have dispatched a mapping and survey expedition to the area to determine the extent of the hazard, and they would inevitably have discovered Cochrane.

"We're proceeding to the wreckage now," Kirk said. "I'll report when we get there. Kirk out."

"She seems to be taking it well," McCoy said as he switched off his tricorder and let it hang at his side.

"She has no choice," Spock reminded him. "She does not yet have all the pieces of the puzzle she is assembling."

"Gentlemen." Kirk waved toward the ridge and began walking in that direction. He heard McCoy and Spock fall into step behind him. Unfortunately, they didn't have all the pieces of the puzzle either. Though they had more than the admiral did.

Kirk, Spock, and McCoy had met earlier that morning, as the *Enterprise* continued on her way to Cochrane's planetoid. McCoy's office in sickbay was deemed to be secure from Admiral Kabreigny's sudden intrusion. In any case, the admiral was more concerned with remaining on the bridge and observing the sensor sweeps firsthand than she seemed to be with the captain's activities, or those of his senior crew.

Just the same, McCoy had instructed the computer to lock the sickbay doors so they could talk in peace, unless any crew member required medical attention.

As Spock related them, the events of Cochrane's final days were as Kirk had remembered them—history recorded few details. That paucity of information could be explained by the fact that following his historic accomplishment, Cochrane had developed a reputation for being a private, reclusive individual. Historically, Kirk knew that that had been the response of Neil Armstrong to personal historic achievement—the first human to set foot on another world had virtually disappeared from public view for the remainder of his life, at great cost to history and undeniably affecting public support of the fledgling space exploration programs of the time. Yoshikawa had also behaved in a similar fashion, though by his remaining on the moon, his life of seclusion was more understandable to many. How Daar would have chosen to live following her own unique success would forever be a mystery, since her life had been cut short by the tragedy that had befallen her during her return from Mars.

But Spock had suggested there was more to the lack of information about Cochrane's final years than could be explained by mere human eccentricity and a desire for privacy. Spock's informal communications with the Cochrane Foundation of Alpha Centauri revealed that many of the contemporary accounts of Cochrane's friends and coworkers, and Cochrane's own journals, remained sealed, though for what reason, no one at the Foundation seemed able or willing to say. Even the journal of Cochrane's wife, the granddaughter of celebrated astronomer Sir John Burke, was not available to the public. Most intriguingly, there was apparently no indication as to how long those records would remain sealed. The Foundation had simply reported that any potential release date was subject to ongoing review.

Spock had concluded that such an arrangement indicated that someone within the Foundation was indeed aware of the contents of the sealed journals and associated files, and was only then waiting until certain conditions were met before allowing them to be released. But what those certain conditions could possibly be after a century and a half, not even Spock would hazard a theory.

In short, all that was available to be known about Cochrane's final years was all that had already been known since the date of his disappearance. At the age of forty-eight, he had attended a scientific conference on the moon, during which he had met Monica Burke, the woman who became his wife. They had returned to Alpha Centauri together, shortly before World War III devastated Earth.

During the reconstruction period, when all Earth colonies had strained themselves to their limits to aid the home planet, Cochrane had devoted himself to further refining his warp drive and had traveled among the many worlds to insure that each colony had the scientific and engineering capability to support its own warp drive industry. Recordings of the talks he gave showed how he stressed again and again that for his invention to truly benefit humanity, no one world or group of worlds should ever be able to develop a monopoly on it.

Several years before his disappearance, Cochrane's desire to share the fruits of his labor drove him to take part in one of the first diplomatic missions to a colony world established by a race then known as the Vulcanians, from Vulcanis, a more accurate phonetic version of the Vulcan name for their world. In a daring move vehemently protested by conservative human organizations at the time, Cochrane turned over *all* his research on warp drive technology, without conditions. The Vulcans, of course, had independently created their own version of the drive, but the explosion of scientific advancement that resulted from Cochrane's unprecedented gift was quickly reciprocated by the enigmatic Vulcans. Far from weakening Earth, Cochrane's gift, in fact, had led to a long-term and unshakable alliance between humans and Vulcans in which, many historians said, the first seeds of what would become the Federation were sown.

Thus did a shy and reclusive scientist live to see his invention forever change the shape and history of humanity. It was even widely accepted that Cochrane had made it possible for the species to survive atomic devastation; had made it possible for war-torn Earth to be rebuilt in decades, not centuries or millennia as had happened on some worlds; and had lived, too, to witness many more first contacts between humans and spacefaring alien cultures.

When Cochrane was eighty-seven, his wife, Monica, had died, apparently in a vehicle accident near the Cochrane ranch on Centauri B II—Cochrane, ever modest, had objected to any efforts to rename the world after him during his lifetime. The details of her accident were not available, either because no account survived, or because no account had been released.

Shortly after, Cochrane had revised his will, leaving his surprisingly small estate to the foundation that bore his name. He then filed a flight plan to Stapledon Center and disappeared.

The search that followed had been massive by contemporary standards. But the invention of subspace radio and subspace sensors remained several decades in the future, and ships that vanished while in warp were typically never seen again, as no faster-than-light method existed for communicating with or detecting them. A year after his failure to arrive at Stapledon Center, Cochrane was declared dead and the human worlds officially mourned his loss.

The story Spock told was the same as the one Kirk remembered studying in school as a child. But it was McCoy who detected the anomaly. He tapped his fingers on his desk in a sign of his agitation.

"Cochrane told us he was dying, Jim," McCoy said after Spock's report. "Isn't that an odd coincidence? His wife dies in an accident just as he's dying of . . . of whatever he was dying from."

Spock seized on McCoy's recollection of their conversation with Cochrane. "Contemporary accounts do indicate Cochrane's health was excellent," he said. "Moreover, colonists in those days generally lived longer and healthier lives than did their counterparts on Earth, owing to an absence of environmental toxins, though of course they had a higher death rate from accidents involving heavy machinery, as Monica Cochrane's death would illustrate."

"Perhaps he wasn't dying when he left Alpha Centauri," Kirk countered. "He told us the Companion had brought his *disabled* ship to the planetoid. Maybe something happened to him on board his ship."

"Another accident?" McCoy asked skeptically. "That's even more of a coincidence."

When given a choice, Kirk tended to favor the simplest solution to a problem—a predilection Spock proclaimed eminently logical. So he wasn't enthralled by McCoy's suggestions that Cochrane's disappearance and his wife's death might not have been accidental.

But Spock's second report, concerning Admiral Kabreigny's intense interest in the *Enterprise*'s previous visit to the Gamma Canaris region, seemed to go in that direction as well.

"This is what Starfleet knows," Spock began. "Six months ago, the *Galileo* encountered navigational difficulties in the Gamma Canaris region and was delayed in making its rendezvous with the *Enterprise*. As a result of that delay, Federation Commissioner Nancy Hedford died of Sakuro's disease. Within twenty-four hours of his return to the *Enterprise,* Captain Kirk filed a detailed log describing those events. Those events, while regrettable, are not uncommon occurrences during starship exploration on the Federation's boundaries.

"However," Spock continued, "Starfleet is also aware that within five days of the captain's return to the *Enterprise,* he shipped, by message pouch, an item for deposit in Starfleet Archives: a personal log to be sealed for one hundred years. Again, this in itself is not an unusual action for a starship captain to take. The archive review board informally concluded that his personal log contained specific details of the death of Commissioner Hedford, withheld, perhaps, to spare her family any unwarranted grief."

Kirk could feel Spock building to a substantial "but." He wasn't disappointed.

"But since then, the archive review board, in conjunction with Starfleet Security and the Lunar Police, have decided that whatever the nature of the information in the captain's sealed log, it was the reason for the recent break-in."

Kirk was shocked. "That's not possible."

Spock's expression of concern told Kirk it was more than possible. "Captain, what I am about to say is considered classified by Starfleet Command. I regret to inform you that I have obtained this information by other than official channels and it would be best if you did not inquire as to my methods. I would like to point out, however, that given the precariousness of our situation in regard to Admiral Kabreigny, and in light of the admiral's interest in these events, it is my opinion that I have been justified in pursuing this course of investigation in a nonregulation manner. I am, of course, willing to make that case before any Starfleet board of inquiry and submit myself to its judgment."

McCoy had had quite enough. "For heaven's sake, Spock, just get on with it."

"By sharing this information with you, Doctor, I am making both you and Captain Kirk subject to disciplinary proceedings at least, and I want you to be so informed."

"We're informed, Spock," Kirk said. "What have you found out?"

"The Starfleet central computer system on Earth's moon has been compromised."

"That's impossible," McCoy sputtered.

"Apparently no longer," Spock replied calmly. "Starfleet Security has learned of unauthorized data-retrieval worm programs that have somehow been inserted into the system. How or why this has been done is unknown. However, it *is* known that one of the triggers for a particular program was the reference 'Gamma Canaris.'" Spock paused and looked at Kirk.

Kirk understood the significance of Spock's information. "I included that on the filing data for the personal log."

"Precisely," Spock said. "And though the actual contents of your log were not uploaded to the system, its filing data were, giving the source of the item, the time and place of its creation, and—"

"Its location within the archives storage stacks," Kirk concluded grimly. "And since the information it contained was not available in the computer itself, someone needed to physically break in to obtain the log."

"But you said the log wasn't missing," McCoy objected.

Spock regarded McCoy with extreme forbearance. "Doctor, the log was in the form of a standard, unencrypted data wafer. A simple tricorder could record its data in seconds without leaving any trace of the process."

Kirk was deeply troubled by Spock's revelation. "Why would anyone be so interested in the Gamma Canaris region, Spock? And who would have the technical ability to compromise Starfleet's central computer?"

Spock appeared almost apologetic. "I have been able to arrive at only one, extremely tenuous connection between Gamma Canaris and current events," he said. "According to celestial navigation charts as they were used one hundred and fifty years ago, the Gamma Canaris region is almost directly opposite the course that would be set at the time between Centauri B II and the colony of Stapledon Center at Wolf 359."

Kirk understood instantly. "If Zefram Cochrane had been intending to . . . throw off anyone who might be following him, for whatever reason, what better way to gain some distance and some time than by heading off in the opposite direction from the one anyone would suspect?"

"Without subspace sensors," the science officer agreed, "the possible volume of space Cochrane might be found in would grow exponentially with each passing second."

"You're saying Cochrane was *running* from someone?" McCoy asked, clearly astounded at this sudden expansion of his foul-play theory.

Spock crossed his arms, clearly not eager for a debate. "I said it was only a tenuous connection, Doctor. If it is real, I do not pretend to understand its significance."

But the events of one hundred and fifty years ago weren't Kirk's immediate concern. "What about Starfleet's computer system, Spock? Who has the capability to enter it without detection? Klingons? Romulans?"

"It is inconceivable that any hostile force could get operatives close enough to the system's programming units. Such a force would have to infiltrate key input stations on Earth's moon in order to upload the sophisticated worm programs Starfleet has detected," Spock said.

"Then who?"

"Only someone working *within* Starfleet would have both the opportunity and the capability to circumvent existing security protocols."

The logical outcome of Spock's reasoning hit Kirk like a phaser blast. There *was* no other explanation.

McCoy leaned forward, his voice an urgent whisper. "Do you know what you're saying, Spock?"

164

"I am well aware of the conclusions that can be drawn from the information I have uncovered, Doctor."

Kirk stated those conclusions out loud, as repugnant as they were. "There is a possibility that Admiral Kabreigny herself is involved in a conspiracy at the highest levels of Starfleet, and that that conspiracy has something to do with Zefram Cochrane."

McCoy was incensed. "That's madness. Next thing you'll be saying that it's up to us to find the conspirators on our own because we can't trust anybody!"

Spock nodded. "Indeed, Doctor, you have anticipated me. I suggest we proceed with utmost caution, pursuing these affairs outside of normal channels, as I have already begun. By acting against Admiral Kabreigny, it is possible that we are helping to preserve the stability of Starfleet and the Federation itself."

"But," Kirk warned, "if there is no conspiracy, it is just as possible that we're engaging in treason."

On that encouraging note, Kirk recalled uneasily, the meeting had ended.

As Kirk, Spock, and McCoy rounded the ridge to the west, they didn't need their tricorders to tell them what had happened to Cochrane's home.

The jewel-shaped prefab shelter had been torn apart by phaser blasts. Half of it had fallen in on itself and the remnants were streaked with soot from a long-extinguished fire. Two standing wall sections were partially melted, and the ripples of solidified metal that had formed around the beam blasts bore the unmistakable glitter of phasered metal.

"Good Lord," McCoy whispered.

"We didn't give them any weapons," Kirk said with bitter regret. Before leaving orbit six months earlier, he had personally beamed down two pallets of supplies, with seeds, farming implements, a computer reader, a library of data wafers, even a subspace radio in case Cochrane changed his mind about communicating with the galaxy. But he had included no phasers.

Spock checked his tricorder. "Judging from the ferocity of the attack, Captain, hand phasers would not have offered much in the way of defense." He pointed to a rise in the distance. "Note the

165

disturbance in the soil on that small hill." Kirk saw it. "I surmise a craft of some kind landed there. Most likely armed with a phaser cannon."

Kirk felt sick. Is this how the twenty-third century had welcomed Cochrane? Is this what Kirk had done to him?

Spock squinted at his tricorder screen. "Doctor, are you still detecting no life signs?"

McCoy broke out his medical tricorder. "I . . . I don't know." He looked at Spock. "The Companion?"

"Captain, there appears to be something in the wreckage of the shelter which is alive. Barely."

Kirk was scrambling through the loose, sandy soil before Spock and McCoy had shut off their equipment. *"Cochrane?!"* he shouted. *"Companion?!"*

He looked down as he sprinted toward the shelter. There were dozens of bootprints in the soil, overlapping, many switching directions, all the signs of a fight. Most were softened by the wind, but no more than a few weeks old.

Kirk came to the melted doorway of the shelter. There was no way in. He called out again.

There was an answer: a moan from the back.

Kirk swung around to the left. Spock and McCoy went to the right. One fallen wall panel had been propped up like a lean-to against an empty supply pallet from the *Enterprise*. Empty water packs were strewn around it along with wrappings from Starfleet emergency rations.

"Cochrane?" Kirk asked of the shadows beneath the wall panel. Someone—something—moved within the darkness. A thin, white hand fell out. There was another moan. Spock and McCoy ran up from the other side as Kirk dropped to his knees and reached in to gather the small figure in his arms.

"Companion," he said gently. "I heard your message. I've come for you."

Kirk stood up with the limp form of Federation Commissioner Nancy Hedford in his arms. She was dressed in a torn, pale orange jumpsuit similar to the one Cochrane had worn. Her face was smudged with dirt, dried blood at the corner of her mouth and under her nose. On one side of her head, her dark hair was caked with blood. On the other side, it was little more than singed bristle, with angry red blisters visible on her scalp. She was also at least five kilos lighter than she had been when Kirk had seen her last, on a frame that could not remain healthy with that loss.

McCoy held a scanner delicately to her temple, ran it above her chest, adjusting the device's sensitivity to block out Kirk's readings.

"Companion, what happened?" Kirk asked. "Where's Zefram?"

The Companion's eyes fluttered open at the name. The white of one eye was dark red with broken capillaries. She had been hit by a strong phaser blast, Kirk realized; probably left for dead by whoever did this.

"Zefram . . ." the Companion whispered. Her voice was dry, weak, but there was still the faint, haunting overlay of two voices speaking at once—the energy being and Nancy Hedford combined as one.

Kirk glanced at McCoy. McCoy shook his head grimly. He pulled a hypospray from his medical kit and held it to the Companion's arm. It hissed softly.

"They took him," the Companion said weakly. "They took the man and he is gone." Then whatever McCoy had injected her with took hold. For a moment, awareness blossomed in her eyes and she looked directly at Kirk.

"We are alone," the Companion cried out in anguish. Tears cut furrows through the smudges on her cheeks. Kirk felt her frail body tremble in his arms. "How do you bear it? How . . . ?" Her body shuddered, then went limp. Kirk looked at McCoy in alarm.

"I can't tell you why she's still alive, but she is," McCoy said. "Extreme symptoms of exposure bordering on hypothermia. Dehydration. Starvation. Massive phaser damage to the central nervous system. Jim, she was hit by a beam set to kill."

Kirk looked at his officers and made his decision. "We can't keep this to ourselves any longer."

"No," McCoy agreed. "She must be treated on the *Enterprise.*"

Spock disagreed. "She draws her life from this place, Doctor. She cannot remain apart from it."

"Damn it, Spock—if I can't stabilize her, it won't matter where she is. Besides, look around you. Whatever it is she draws from this planetoid, somehow it must be getting something from her in return. And the way she is now, she's in no condition to keep it functioning. It's all going to blazes." McCoy turned to Kirk. "Jim, if I keep her in isolation, we can probably avoid Admiral Kabreigny hearing any mention of Cochrane, but I've got to treat her up on the *Enterprise.*"

"The admiral can't be our main concern now," Kirk said. "But keeping her in isolation is worth a try. Call for a beam-up, Doctor. Medical emergency. Mr. Spock, I want a full security detail down here. I want to know what kind of phasers were used, what landed on that hill, and how many attackers were involved. I also want a full orbital scan, looking for any ionization traces of a ship that might have left here in the past four to five weeks."

"I shall remain here to coordinate," Spock said.

McCoy spoke into his communicator. *"Enterprise,* three to beam up at these coordinates. Mr. Spock is staying on the surface. Alert sickbay we have a medical emergency. The patient is . . . human."

Kirk shifted his grip on the Companion's unconscious form. She felt so fragile he was afraid she might break in his grasp.

Spock stepped away from Kirk and McCoy to give the transporter technician on the *Enterprise* an easier fix. "Good luck, Captain," he said.

Kirk regarded his friend with a slight smile. "That's not very logical, Spock."

"Perhaps," Spock agreed. "But I have found there are times in human affairs where logic does not apply. This, unfortunately, may be one of them."

"They came for him," the Companion said, her voice twinned in eerie harmony with Nancy Hedford's. "At night, a ship landed, not far, on the hill. Zefram was so happy, so excited." She looked over at Kirk with a bittersweet smile. "He thought it might be you, Captain Kirk."

Kirk squeezed the Companion's gaunt hand. Her pulse as amplified by the life-sign monitor above the medical bed was regular, though weak. She had been cleansed of blood and dirt, and McCoy had worked his magic so that there was color in her face again, but the glittering bandage around her forehead and over her phaser-damaged eye still attested to the seriousness of her condition.

However, McCoy was certain she would pull through, if only because the effect of the Companion on Nancy Hedford's human body had a cumulative, restoring influence, no doubt the same process by which Sakuro's disease had been vanquished. But Kirk didn't know if the Companion would maintain the will to survive. The security detail on the planetoid's surface had found no trace of Zefram Cochrane. Only indications of wanton destruction, as if whoever had come for the scientist had wanted to leave no trace of his presence there.

"Do you know who they were?" Kirk asked, keeping his hand closed over the Companion's, trying to help her fight the desperate aloneness he knew she must be experiencing.

"Part of us does not," the double voices sighed, "but part of us says . . . 'Orions.'"

Kirk tried to stay calm. McCoy was by his side and had been firm in his insistence that Kirk not alarm or tire his patient. "Did they have green skin?" Kirk asked.

The Companion nodded. "And they came with phasers . . . phasers . . ." She closed her one exposed eye. "Such a hateful thing it is. The man ran to them, he welcomed them to our home, and they used energy against him, made him fall. We heard his thoughts cease. We were so alone. . . ."

Kirk wasn't sure what she meant by hearing Cochrane's thoughts cease. "Was Zefram alive?" he asked. "Did he . . . continue?"

The Companion looked up to the ceiling of sickbay. "The man continues," she said. "We can feel him still. But he is so far away."

"How far?" Kirk asked.

The Companion opened and closed her mouth as if trying to answer. "Part of us knows, but the other part cannot say." She sighed again. "We will not feel him for long. He is that far away."

"Could you take us to him?" Kirk said.

JUDITH AND GARFIELD REEVES-STEVENS

But that was crossing McCoy's line. "Jim! You know she can't leave the planetoid."

"Companion," Kirk said, leaning closer to her, "how long can you remain away from your home?"

"Without us there to tend it, care for it, our home is dying," she said wistfully. "We will know death. Without the man, how can we have a home? How can we live?"

McCoy took over. "Companion, listen to me. I'm your doctor. Part of you has to know what that means. And as your doctor, I guarantee you you're *not* dying. You're strong, getting stronger. You'll be able to continue. But what I need to know is, how soon must you return to the surface?"

"A tiny march of days," the Companion said. "Less than a year, less than a month. You have so many names for what is the same thing, this passage of time. How do you keep it all in your mind, worrying about such things?"

"Less than a week?" Kirk asked. "Can you stay off your home for no more than a single week? Two weeks?"

"We do not know."

"Try," Kirk implored her. "Both parts of you must work together if you ever want to see the man again. Do you understand me? Nancy Hedford must *listen* to the Companion, translate her thoughts into terms we can understand."

The Companion stared straight up in silence. At last she spoke. "Six days," she said. "If we do not return in six days, we will not continue."

"And how far away is the man?" Kirk said. "Ask the Nancy Hedford part to remember what she knows about starships. Can we reach the man and return with him here in less than six days?" Kirk felt McCoy's hand on his shoulder, silently warning him not to continue this pressure on the woman much longer.

"It is so confusing," the Companion said. "Zefram would help us when this happened."

"Can I help?" Kirk said urgently, knowing that McCoy would act to stop him soon. "Is there anything I can do to make this easier?"

"He is close," the Companion wept. "He is in such pain."

"How close?" Kirk demanded.

"Captain! You can't push her like this," McCoy finally snapped.

Kirk ignored the doctor. "Companion, talk to Nancy Hedford again. Wherever the man is, can this ship go to him and return here in six days?"

"Yes," the Companion whispered after a moment. "At your fastest speed."

"Can you tell us where to go?" Kirk asked, excited to finally be getting somewhere.

"We do not have the words," the Companion replied. "No part of us has the words."

Kirk squeezed her hand. "That's all right. We'll teach you the words." He looked at McCoy. "Do whatever you have to to get her to the Auxiliary Control Center."

"What?!"

"I'll have Sulu meet us there. He can go over the charts with her, work out some sort of mutually understandable coordinate system we can feed into navigation without being on the bridge."

Refusal was in McCoy's eyes. "She won't be able to take the strain."

"She loves him, Bones. She'll be able to take the strain. Or neither of them will continue."

"This is insane," McCoy said. But as Kirk had known he would, the doctor was weakening at the mention of the power of romantic love.

"Only for six days. Then . . . it won't matter."

"And what will you tell the admiral? I can't keep saying that Commissioner Hedford is in a coma."

"We'll tell the admiral we're searching for the missing liner. And we will be. It has to be connected with this." The heartbeat from the medical board began to slow. Kirk felt the Companion's fingers loosen in his.

McCoy checked the board. His tone was stern, filled with medical authority no captain could override. "She's sleeping again. It would be advantageous if she were allowed to continue to do so."

171

Kirk thought it over. "Spock needs another hour on the surface. But then I want her working with Sulu."

McCoy nodded though it was clear he wasn't pleased. Then he took on a different expression, troubled, wondering. "Who do you think has him, Jim?"

Kirk shrugged. "Orion pirates? Smugglers? They were behind the attempt to derail the Babel Conference."

"But if Spock's right about the Gamma Canaris connection to Cochrane, then this has been going on for longer than we've even known about Coridan. Longer than there's even been a Federation."

"I can't answer that, Bones, because I don't know." Kirk wasn't happy with the answer but it was the best he could do. "What matters is that someone has Cochrane, and they have him because of *my* log. Why they were even looking for him in the first place, I don't know. Why Admiral Kabreigny is interested in all this, I don't know. But what I do know is that we're going to find Cochrane, we're going to free him, and then we can look into the other questions." Kirk paused for a moment. "Besides, chances are that Cochrane's the one who can answer all of them for us."

McCoy shook his head as if trying to clear it. "What can possibly last a hundred and fifty years?" he asked.

Kirk looked down at the sleeping form of the Companion. "Love," he said.

Kirk stepped out of the turbolift and onto the bridge of the *Enterprise*. At once he was rewarded with the pulse of the great ship, the constant background sounds of her computers, the lowered voices of her crew, speaking quickly, competently, keeping her on her course. But he felt punished, too. His chair wasn't empty. Admiral Kabreigny still sat in it, a cup of coffee in her hand, speaking with Uhura.

Kirk stood by his chair but the admiral made no move to relinquish her position of command. Kirk could see unease flicker across Uhura's face. He wasn't the only one to think that only one person had the right to that chair.

"How's the patient?" Kabreigny asked. "Still in a coma?" The way she asked the question left Kirk no doubt that she did not believe McCoy's diagnosis. But still, the admiral had made no attempt to see Nancy Hedford herself.

"The doctor thinks she'll recover," Kirk said.

"She's already come back from the dead once, Captain." The admiral smiled tightly. "I have no doubt she'll be able to throw off the effects of exposure just as easily."

"With respect, Admiral: The patient in sickbay is not, strictly speaking, Nancy Hedford. She is a . . . blending of two life-forms into one. The energy anomaly that drew the *Galileo* off course has—"

But the admiral was not in the mood for Kirk's story. "Spare me, Captain. Commissioner Hedford is not why I'm out here."

Kirk waited for her to continue. In the meantime, the urge he felt, the *need,* to sit in the command chair was almost physical.

"I've been reviewing the commissioner's first transmission with your communications officer," the admiral said.

Uhura glanced at Kirk as if to ask if it was all right for her to have worked with the admiral. Like Mr. Scott, she was seeking confirmation for orders, though none was necessary. Kirk nodded, certain that Kabreigny had caught the exchange.

"And what have you found?" Kirk asked.

Kabreigny leaned back in the chair, making a show of how comfortable she found it. "Because of the smeared carrier wave which prevented anyone getting a fix on its source, Command originally presumed it had come from the missing liner. However, I noticed among the sensor scans of the 'wreckage' Mr. Spock is investigating on the surface that there is a Starfleet secure transmitter down there."

"That's correct," Kirk said. He and McCoy and Spock had already prepared the next level of revelation for the admiral— telling the whole story of what had happened six months earlier, only leaving out the parts about Cochrane. "I left it for the Hedford being in case she ever wished to change her mind about her desire for privacy."

Kabreigny checked a list on the writing padd in her lap. "Along with farming supplies, emergency rations, computer equipment, library wafers, et cetera, et cetera?"

"From the stores we carry specifically for the support of

colonies," Kirk said. His standing orders made ample provision for the *Enterprise* to provide help of any kind for beleaguered colonies. He had done nothing wrong in leaving supplies for Cochrane and the Companion.

"Of course, of course," Kabreigny agreed offhandedly. "I was just checking through the titles of the computer journals and books you left behind for the . . . the 'Hedford being.'"

Kirk prepared himself. He and Spock had picked out most of those titles together. He knew what they were and what the admiral had found.

"It seems," Kabreigny said, "that the Hedford being has made quite a hobby out of multiphysics and warp-drive theory."

"As an energy being, she was capable of moving at warp velocities on her own," Kirk said unconvincingly. "We thought—"

"Captain Kirk," the admiral interrupted sharply. "Join me." She indicated the turbolift, handed her coffee cup to Uhura, who didn't know what to do with it, then rose majestically to her feet, leaving the command chair.

Kirk let her lead the way. Chekov took over the chair behind them. That didn't bother Kirk. As part of the crew of this ship, Chekov belonged there in the established chain of command during nonemergency duty. It was only the admiral's presence that rankled him.

The turbolift doors shut. Kabreigny stood facing forward, hands behind her back. "Take this car out of service," she said.

The computer replied, "This car is not experiencing any mechanical difficulty."

Kabreigny's lips thinned. "Is everyone on this ship going to question my orders?"

"Computer," Kirk said, "take this car out of service."

Instantly the lift car began to drop through the ship several levels, before shunting to the side and parking near a turbolift service bay.

When the car came to a stop, Kabreigny faced the captain. "You know what it means when you get to be my age, Kirk?"

Kirk shook his head, steeling himself to endure whatever it was the admiral felt she must say to him. All he wanted to do was save

Cochrane. Keeping the admiral mollified might help him accomplish that.

"It means you don't have much time left, so you're not inclined to waste it. So I won't." She fixed him with a penetrating stare. Her bright eyes displayed no hint of the age of the rest of her. "Zefram Cochrane was down there, wasn't he?"

Kirk had already made up his mind not to be surprised by anything the admiral might say, but that hadn't prepared him for this. There was only one possible explanation.

"It appears that personal logs aren't that personal after all," he said.

Kabreigny's stare became fierce with displeasure. "The archive personnel take their jobs seriously, Captain. I didn't read your log. But from your comment, am I to assume your log contains a *full* account of what transpired here six months ago?"

"It does."

"Well, that's one consolation, at least. You weren't completely derelict in your duty."

Kabreigny might as well have slapped Kirk for the response her comment drew from him.

"Does the admiral wish to bring formal charges against me?" he asked coldly, barely restraining his own anger.

"At ease, Captain. This conversation is off the record."

Kirk held his derisive laughter with some difficulty. So far, it seemed, this whole mission was off the record. "Then may I ask why you think Zefram Cochrane was present on this planetoid?"

Kabreigny patted the back of her head, without disturbing the tightly coiled bun of white hair.

"You can ask, Captain. But I'm not inclined to answer. However, what I intend to know is: Do *you* know where Cochrane is now?"

"You do realize Zefram Cochrane was born on Earth in the year 2030," Kirk said. If the admiral wasn't going to give up information, he didn't see why he should, either. He still had no indication that what she was doing was under authority of Starfleet. "If he's anywhere, he would be two hundred and thirty-seven years old."

"Mere calendar age is becoming less and less of an issue these days, Captain. Cryonic suspension, Einsteinian time dilation from high-velocity impulse-powered flights . . . there're lots of opportunities to slow down the clock, as I know you know from your run-in with Khan." Kabreigny's eyes narrowed as she regarded Kirk with suspicion. "Now, Captain, I am *ordering* you to tell me: Was Zefram Cochrane present on the planetoid six months ago, and, if so, where is he now?"

The inevitable had arrived. One option was for Kirk to refuse to obey the admiral's orders and have her placed under arrest until he could determine the reason for her involvement in the search for Cochrane. If Spock was correct in implying that the admiral was somehow connected to a conspiracy within Starfleet, then Kirk would be acting within the bounds of the Starfleet charter. However, if the admiral was not part of a conspiracy, if she was involved in a classified program of which Kirk had no knowledge, then he faced charges ranging from insubordination to mutiny.

But Kirk had long ago determined that when faced with an impossible decision, the best choice was to change the playing field. In this case, the playing field was the *Enterprise*. And Kirk held absolute control over it. His decision became much simpler. He would acquiesce to the admiral's demands, secure in the knowledge that she would not be permitted to send one message from this ship without Kirk's knowing about it and approving it.

He felt the hum of the *Enterprise* through the floor of the turbolift. It was as if his ship were urging him on, a part of him. For a fleeting instant, Kirk wondered if this was how Nancy Hedford had felt when she had merged with the Companion—two life-forms becoming one.

"On stardate 3219.8, Mr. Spock, Dr. McCoy, Commissioner Nancy Hedford, and I met Zefram Cochrane on the planetoid we're orbiting."

Kabreigny folded her arms and leaned back against the wall of the turbolift, an expression of intense interest on her face. "A wise decision, Captain. Now, what was his condition?"

"Excellent. Mr. Cochrane related to us that he had set off into space at the age of eighty-seven, that his ship was diverted by the energy being who lives on the planetoid—"

Kabreigny's eyes widened. "There *is* an energy being?"

Kirk nodded. "The name Cochrane gave her is 'the Companion.' She somehow rejuvenated him, bringing him back to the general health and appearance of a human in his thirties, and maintained him at that level for the next century and a half."

Kabreigny unconsciously touched her own wrinkled face. "Rejuvenated him? Brought back his youth?"

Kirk continued. "The Companion subsequently merged with Commissioner Hedford, moments before Sakuro's disease claimed her. They have since become a single life-form."

Kabreigny spoke slowly, deliberately. "To be candid, Kirk, I thought you were making up all that crap."

"We were simply trying to respect Mr. Cochrane's wishes not to be disturbed."

"Unfortunately, Mr. Cochrane no longer has that luxury. Do you know where he is now?"

"No," Kirk said, "but the Companion does."

"Can she take us to him?"

"Possibly." Kirk decided to test the new relationship he seemed to have with the admiral. "By all indications below, it appears that someone . . . unfriendly . . . learned of Cochrane's presence on this planetoid by reading my personal log, then came after him and . . . kidnapped him."

"That's a fair assessment," Kabreigny agreed.

"Do you know who that might be?"

"Possibly." The admiral did not elaborate.

"Klingons?" Kirk prodded, trying to provoke a response from her. Anything to provide him more clues to work with.

But Kabreigny shook her head. "If only it were that easy." Then she continued before Kirk could say anything else. "And any suspicions I might have are classified, Captain. I'm sorry," she added, as if she really were trying to sound apologetic, "but you're going to have to trust me just a bit longer."

Kirk thought that was an odd thing for her to say, considering he was finding it increasingly difficult to conceal that he didn't trust her at all.

"Now get this lift back in service and get the Companion up on the bridge. At this moment, Zefram Cochrane holds the future of Starfleet in his hands. And I want him before . . . anyone else gets to him. Do I make myself clear, Captain?"

"Not really," Kirk said. "But the *Enterprise* is at your disposal."

Kabreigny looked thoughtful. "I appreciate your cooperation," she said. "I wasn't sure I'd get it so quickly."

Kirk smiled noncommittally. He had no intention of being cooperative with someone who might be out to tear down Starfleet and destroy the Federation. But there was no need to tell the admiral that.

Until it was time to stop her, of course.

TWELVE

U.S.S. ENTERPRISE NCC-1701-D
DEEP SPACE
Stardate 43921.4
Earth Standard: ≈ May 2366

"Coming up on Ferengi coordinates," Acting Ensign Crusher reported from the conn.

Beside him, back at his regular position at Ops, Data confirmed what Picard and his officers had suspected. "No sign of any object with a mass of forty-five point three five kilotonnes, Captain. In fact, sensors detect no sign of any object other than the Romulan Warbird within range."

Picard glanced at Riker. "What did they use to call this, Number One? A 'wild-goose chase'?"

Riker smiled appreciatively.

But Data added, "Perhaps I should clarify that, sir. Other than the Ferengi crew, sensors also report no life-forms of any kind in the surrounding region, including representatives of the class *aves.*"

"It was just a colloquial expression, Data," Picard explained.

Data blinked, assimilating his misinterpretation. "I see. Then should I file 'wild-goose chase' under the same classification as the 'snipe hunt' Commander Riker had me engage in while we were at Starbase Twelve?"

Picard hadn't heard about that incident. He had been otherwise engaged with Vash when the *Enterprise* had been at Starbase 12 a few months earlier. But Mr. Data's snipe hunt must have gone well, because he saw Riker cover his mouth in order to stifle a laugh.

"That would probably be a good idea," Picard agreed.

"Have you ever attempted to capture snipe, Captain Picard?"

Picard concentrated on keeping his voice neutral. "In my Academy days, Mr. Data. I believe it is an activity all cadets become familiar with."

"I see," Data said reflectively. "I was not successful, though I did hold the bag and call for the snipe exactly as Commander Riker had instructed me. Snipe appear to be exceptionally well evolved for remaining unseen. Even the ship's computer has no record of—"

Riker couldn't contain himself any longer. He laughed. Data looked back at him, then at Picard. "Captain?"

"I'm sorry, Data. It's just that, well, there are no such things as snipe."

"What?" Wesley Crusher said.

Data looked across at him in commiseration. "Have you also hunted snipe, Wesley?"

The acting ensign's face tightened. "Geordi told me—"

But Riker interrupted. "Eyes on the board, Mr. Crusher!"

"Aye, sir." The acting ensign went back to his duties, as did Data.

"At least that would explain why no one has ever seen one," Data said.

Picard and Riker exchanged a smile.

"Dropping to sublight," Mr. Crusher announced. "And full stop."

The Ferengi-operated Warbird appeared in the center of the main viewscreen.

"Full sensor sweep," Picard ordered.

"We are the only two objects within range," Data responded.

Picard made a gesture toward the screen. "Hail the Romulan—uh, Ferengi vessel, Mr. Worf."

"Onscreen, Captain."

DaiMon Pol appeared. "Greetings, Captain Pee-card. I am—"

"I do not wish to engage in additional small talk," Picard said, full of bluster, trying to keep the Ferengi on his toes. "Where is the artifact?"

DaiMon Pol appeared hurt by Picard's attitude. "Negotiations should be a time of social interaction, Captain Pee-card. There is no need—"

"Look," Picard said more forcefully. "You have given us coordinates that were supposed to have been those of an object you wished to sell us. There is no object here. Now explain yourself or we will withdraw." Picard turned to Troi. She gave him a nod. He was carrying out his role perfectly.

DaiMon Pol shook his head sorrowfully. "I will never understand *hew-mans.* You have no sense of the joy of commerce in your souls." DaiMon Pol pointed a finger offscreen. "When next we talk, Pee-card, you will make your offer or *I* will withdraw." Then DaiMon Pol vanished from the viewscreen, replaced by an image of his ship a kilometer distant.

Riker looked at Picard. "What was all that about?"

"I'm not sure," Troi answered with concern. "He's acting as if he does not expect to talk with us again."

"Captain," Data stated calmly. "A second Warbird is decloaking."

Picard stood as, in front of DaiMon Pol's ship, an optical wavering began. "Red Alert, Mr. Worf. Maximum shields."

"I knew it!" Worf exclaimed, even as the sirens began and the warning lights flashed. "All phaser banks on standby. Photon torpedoes armed and ready."

The second Warbird finished its materialization, becoming solid before them.

"Battle readout on the second ship," Riker said.

"Its shields are down, Commander," Data replied. "In addition, none of its weapons systems are on-line."

"Full magnification on the Warbird's markings," Picard said. He looked over at Riker. "Do you think the Ferengi are bold enough to have stolen *two* Romulan ships?"

The viewscreen image jumped to a close-up of the second ship's hull, clearly showing Romulan script on its side.

"Maybe they haven't had a chance to repaint it," Riker suggested sarcastically.

"The second ship is hailing us," Worf reported.

Picard sighed. He was getting exactly what he had anticipated —the unexpected. "Onscreen, Mr. Worf. And switch off those alarms, please."

The alarms ended as the viewscreen image changed, once again showing the interior of a Romulan bridge. But, for a change, a Romulan was present. She wore a standard military uniform and her black hair was pulled back tightly to her skull in a warrior's queue, making her vulcanoid ears more pronounced. Her heavy, angular brow threw dark shadows across her eyes, but Picard could tell that unlike most Romulans he had encountered, she was not attempting to hide anything. She was clearly anxious, though about what, he did not know.

"Captain Picard," the Romulan began. "I am Tarl, commander of this vessel. I apologize for the subterfuge that was used to bring you here."

Picard was aware of Troi standing behind him, out of sight of the optical sensors that were relaying his image to the Romulan ship. "I'm picking up worry, Captain."

Picard turned to face Troi, his back to the screen. *"Is* this a trap?" he whispered.

Troi shook her head. "I do not sense she means us harm. Only that she fears others wish to do *her* harm."

"I see," Picard said. He turned back to the screen.

"Commander Tarl, I must ask for an explanation of this subterfuge. Am I to take it that there is no Borg artifact?"

"Oh, but there is, Captain," the Romulan said. "Though it does not belong to the Ferengi."

Picard waited expectantly. "Please. Continue."

The Romulan lifted her chin defiantly.

"This is difficult for her, Captain," Troi said softly behind him.

"I have stolen the artifact from my people," the Romulan said. "I wish to give it to the Federation in exchange for a ship and supplies for myself and my supporters."

"She's hiding something," Troi whispered.

182

"May I ask why?" Picard said.

The Romulan appeared deadly serious. "I am not a traitor, Captain. But I know the threat the Borg represent to my people. And I know that the politics of the central command preclude any chance of understanding the nature of the artifact before the Borg reach our borders." She sighed. Even Picard could tell that what she said *was* painful for her. "I want your Federation scientists to study the artifact, to devise some kind of defense against those creatures, and to share it with us. Otherwise, the Romulan Star Empire will not survive."

"Then why go through all this to sell the artifact to us?" Picard asked. "And why involve the Ferengi? Why not just *give* it to us?"

The Romulan's face darkened in anger. "Understand my situation! I have stolen from the Empire! There is no escape for me except what you can provide. A ship, supplies, a chance for my crew and me to survive, in exchange for a chance for your people and mine to survive. The Ferengi are my brokers, Captain, no more than that. I needed them to seek you out and entice you here in a way that would not alert your Betazoid counselor. DaiMon Pol has received a Warbird in partial payment for his services. When you give me a new ship, he will have this one as well." She clasped her hands before her, a most human gesture of supplication. "I am not bargaining with you, Captain. The artifact is yours without conditions. I only ask recognition that I have not acted against the best wishes of the Empire, and a chance to live."

Picard chose his next words carefully. "Your proposition is extremely compelling, Commander. But I must confer with my staff before giving you what you have asked for."

"Then be quick about it," the Romulan said. "The compliance divisions are searching for me even now."

She disappeared from the screen. Two green Warbirds hung against the stars. Picard went to Data.

"Well, Mr. Data, it appears your analysis of the Federation's generosity was not only correct, it is shared by the Romulan commander," Picard told the android.

Data turned to Troi. "I would be interested to know if the counselor feels Tarl was telling the truth."

183

Troi looked thoughtful. "For the most part, yes, I believe she is. But she *is* holding back something."

"Something harmful?" Picard asked.

Troi shook her head. "I don't think so, Captain. But she *is* afraid of what will happen to her if her mission fails."

Riker stepped up beside Picard and Troi. "It would be nice to know exactly what that mission is."

Worf added his opinion. "I see no need to try and second-guess a Romulan. She has said that there is an artifact. Let us demand to see it. There is still the possibility that this is nothing but an elaborate hoax."

"That seems most reasonable," Picard said. Riker and Troi agreed. "Put the Romulan commander back onscreen, Mr. Worf."

When Tarl had appeared again, Picard laid out his conditions. "So you see," he concluded, "it is imperative that we examine the artifact in order to know how to proceed past this point."

Tarl looked impatient. "I do not understand how people so cautious have accomplished all that you have. If you had been Romulan, this business would have been completed within a minute of our meeting."

"If we had been Romulan," Picard observed, "you would already have been executed for treason, and the Borg would still threaten your Empire. Now, where may we find the artifact?"

"Assemble a scientific team, then beam them to my hangar deck. The artifact is there."

"On your *ship?*" Picard asked.

The Romulan's lip curled in a sneer. "I have already answered that." She made a curt gesture and the transmission ceased again.

Picard turned to Riker and Troi. "Well, this should be most interesting. I have never seen the hangar deck of a Warbird."

"And you're not going to see it today," Riker said with an edge to his voice. "With all respect, sir, there is no way I'm allowing you to beam over to a hostile vessel."

"That is not a hostile vessel, Number One. Commander Tarl is no longer part of the Romulan Empire."

But Riker remained unconvinced. "We'll transmit images of

the artifact as we examine it," he said. "Data, Worf, you're with me." He touched his communicator. "Mr. La Forge, report to Transporter Room Four. Bring a field engineering diagnostic kit."

Riker headed toward the aft turbolift. Data and Worf were already falling into step behind him as La Forge acknowledged.

"Will," Picard said just before the lift door closed. "Be careful over there."

Riker smiled at his captain. "That's my job, sir." Then he was gone.

Picard was left on the bridge, feeling removed from the action once again. That was the problem in dealing with the unexpected, he decided. It never worked out the way he hoped.

The Romulan D'deridex-class Warbird was almost twice the length of the Federation Galaxy-class starship, and her hangar deck was at least three times the volume of the *Enterprise*'s main shuttlebay. Even on the bridge viewscreen, the structure was impressive to Picard, and he couldn't help wondering what it would feel like to walk its green metal deckplates himself.

The image Picard and Troi watched from their command chairs was being transmitted by a small optical sensor carried by Data. For the moment, the android was using it to scan the entire hangar deck. Picard lost track of the number of smaller Romulan craft he saw, some ready for launching, others stacked in metal grillwork on the distant walls. He was hopeful that no matter what information they recovered about the artifact, these interior views of the Warbird would be useful to Starfleet Intelligence.

Data's voice came over the bridge communication system. "Are you receiving the images clearly, Captain?"

"We are," Picard answered. "Is the artifact nearby?"

The image on the screen began to shift as Data pointed his sensor in a new direction. "Commander Tarl is directing us to it now. Can you see it?"

Picard felt his heart rate quicken. The artifact was there, at least the size of three Federation runabouts crushed together, encased in green metal scaffolding and ringed by portable lights. It grew larger on the screen with each step Data took toward it. From time to time, the backs of La Forge, Riker, and two Romulans intruded on the scene, but that did nothing to lessen the visual impact of the object.

Troi smiled at Picard. "I can sense your excitement without even trying, Captain."

Picard nodded. He was not embarrassed to admit it. What could be more exciting than discovering something that could save the Federation? "The survival of the Federation might be about to be dropped in our laps," he said. "This could be a pivotal moment in our history."

"In the galaxy's history as well," Troi agreed.

"Captain," Data transmitted, "Commander Tarl is permitting us to examine the artifact now. Initial scans confirm its composition closely matches that of the Borg vessel we encountered at System J-25."

"Wonderful," Picard said under his breath, hoping his excitement was not as apparent to Tarl as it was to his counselor. "May I speak with the commander?"

The viewscreen image swung to the side until Tarl appeared. She looked into the optical sensor. "Yes, Captain?"

"Commander, can you tell me where you obtained this specimen?"

The Romulan looked grim. *"I obtained it when I took command of this vessel with a small group of supporters. As for where the Empire obtained it, I am too much of a patriot to reveal all the details. Suffice it to say a Borg vessel attacked one of our most distant outposts. In the ensuing battle, a fleet of twenty ships was lost, five of them Warbirds. At the height of the battle, a freighter managed to collide with the Borg ship and some debris was knocked free. This artifact is part of that debris, removed by mechanical force and not energy weapons. That is all I can tell you."*

"That is enough," Picard said compassionately. "I have no wish for you to compromise the security of the Empire."

"Thank you, Captain." Commander Tarl stepped away and Data returned the optical sensor to a view of the artifact. Then the image jiggled beyond the capability of the ship's computer to steady it.

"Captain Picard," Data said, "I am going to mount the optical sensor on a light stand so that you may monitor our activities. I will be more useful working on the artifact myself."

"Carry on, Mr. Data," Picard approved.

Data's back appeared on the screen as he walked toward the Borg monstrosity. Riker, La Forge, and Worf were already on the scaffolding, scanning the artifact intently with tricorders. Picard turned to Troi. "Was there much equivocation in the commander's story about the origin of this artifact?" he asked.

"Some," Troi said. "But mostly she was hesitant about revealing the location of the outpost. Also, she was feeling a great deal of frustration over the number of ships that had been lost in the attack."

"Twenty," Picard repeated. "And five Warbirds. A significant loss. But I do have to wonder why such an armada was available for the defense of one of the Empire's farthest outposts."

"Perhaps they had some warning that the attack was imminent?"

"If they do have some way of detecting the Borg at great distances, perhaps the commander can be persuaded to share that secret with us as well."

La Forge's voice came over the communications system. "Captain, this chunk of machinery is in better shape than it looks. The outside is pretty banged up, but the interior structure seems to be intact. And I *am* picking up a low-level energy reading."

Picard grew anxious. "You're certain there are no defensive systems in the artifact which you might inadvertently trigger?"

"Fairly certain, Captain. If the Romulans have been poking around this thing as much as this scaffolding suggests and they haven't run into anything, we're not going to either."

"Just the same, monitor that energy reading continuously and withdraw if it starts to increase."

"Understood, Captain. I'm going to try to squeeze in between two conduits here and take a look inside. But I'm almost positive that this *is* a legitimate piece of Borg technology."

"Thank you, Mr. La Forge. Carry on." Picard looked over at the counselor.

"I agree," she said, responding to his emotional state.

For the next few minutes, little happened. Picard overheard some of the conversation among his away team, mostly exhortations to hold something still, or to shine a light in a different direction, but what exactly they were doing was impossible to see from the optical sensor's angle. Commander Tarl contacted Picard once to ask that the process be accelerated. But Picard politely declined to interfere with his people. La Forge had said he was "almost positive" about the artifact's origin. When he said he was *absolutely certain,* that was when Picard would act.

More silent minutes passed, until Troi commented on the fact that they had heard nothing for quite a length of time.

Picard frowned. *"Enterprise* to Commander Riker. Status report, please."

Uncharacteristically, Riker replied, "Just a moment, Captain. We're in the middle of a . . . tricky measurement."

"That was, without question, a lie," Troi said.

But Picard knew Riker would never lie to him. "Are they in danger?"

Troi shook her head. "On the contrary, sir. They seem to be giving absolutely no thought to the fact they're on a Romulan vessel inside a piece of potentially deadly technology." The Betazoid counselor looked perplexed as she struggled to understand the impressions she received. "If anything, sir, they're even more excited now than they were when they first saw the artifact."

"More excited?" Picard said.

As if in answer, Riker finally replied to Picard. "Sorry for the delay, Captain. Commander Tarl is here beside me and I think we should go ahead and make our deal with her. But I also think you should probably take a look at the artifact yourself, just to confirm its . . . condition."

Picard looked to Troi. "He's concealing something, Captain. Extremely powerful emotions of . . . discovery."

"But no sense of danger?"

"Absolutely none."

"Commander Riker," Picard said, "could you move into range of the optical sensor?"

"Certainly, sir."

As Picard asked his next question, he saw Riker, La Forge, Worf, and Data step in front of the artifact. Tarl was with them. Two other Romulans were at the side.

"Lieutenant Worf," Picard began, "as security officer, have you any objections to my coming aboard the Romulan vessel?"

Tarl frowned in disgust at the question. But Worf stepped forward.

"Absolutely none, Captain. The vessel is secure."

Troi confirmed the Klingon's statement. "He is convinced there is no threat, sir. I pick up no sense of coercion or mind control of any kind. However, I do get the impression that they have obtained some knowledge which they do not wish to share with Commander Tarl."

Picard stood up and tugged at his tunic. "How extraordinary. What do you suppose they've found over there?"

Troi smiled at her captain indulgently. "There's only one way to find out, sir."

Picard understood the amused expression she wore. It was just that for all the wonders the *Enterprise* encountered, he sometimes felt a prisoner upon her, his well-being so fervently guarded by Riker and the rest of the crew. But now, to be free to go aboard a Romulan vessel, to take part in something of obviously great import, he felt such elation that he really was embarrassed to consider what his counselor might think of him if she sensed the depth of his emotional response. He wondered if she knew how frustrated he so often felt to merely be an observer and advisor during his colleagues' adventures.

"No need to be embarrassed," Troi said, proving his point. "I think you should do what Will suggests and go over to the vessel."

"I look forward to it, Counselor, very much. Alert the transporter room. You have the bridge."

"Very good, sir."

Then Jean-Luc Picard walked up the ramp to the aft turbolift, trying to imagine what could intrigue his crew even more than a piece of Borg technology. As he did so, he had a sudden wave of misgiving, even of danger. Yet, upon reflection, he could discover no reason for it, other than some deep-seated feeling of distrust for the Romulans, a distrust which he was suddenly surprised to find was not his own.

Then Picard smiled in the privacy of the turbolift as he realized the source of the unease he felt. Somewhere deep inside of him, a small part of Ambassador Sarek, the best part, he hoped, was giving him warning.

The Romulans were not to be trusted.

THIRTEEN

LAZY EIGHT RANCH,
MICAH TOWNSHIP, CENTAURI B II
Earth Standard: ≈ Early April 2117

Zefram Cochrane removed the woven hat from his head and let the early evening breezes of the secondary winter dry the moisture there. His scalp was bare, darkened from the suns, spotted with age, ringed by shaggy gray locks. Monica had teased him about the look, said it had made him seem quite the authentic gentleman farmer. But Cochrane knew the style reminded her of her grandfather, Sir John, gone these many, many years.

So much had gone with him, then and now.

"Mr. Cochrane, sir?" Cochrane recognized the voice. Montcalm Daystrom had arrived from the Foundation. The youth was Cochrane's personal assistant, a promising student, part of the family. But he was twenty Earth years old, seventeen Centauri, and like all the first children of this world, treated Cochrane with a respect and deference that made the old scientist cringe and wonder when he had stopped being a person. Instead, somewhere in the past decades, he had somehow become an icon, a symbol for this brave new era of humanity.

Cochrane could hear Micah Brack laughing at that label, even as he thought it. No era of humanity was new, according to Brack. Simply a succession of new skins for old ceremonies. Cochrane missed his friend. No word of his fate had ever come back to him, though he doubted a man of Brack's age would still be alive.

Looking at Montcalm's far too solicitous smile made Cochrane also think that the first children of Centauri could stuff it, and he told Montcalm so.

But Montcalm only smiled and stepped closer to Cochrane. He was used to the fabled scientist and his ways, both in the lab, where the young man excelled, and in Cochrane's private life, where more and more he needed an extra pair of arms. Together, student and teacher, they stood on the crest of a rich purple-green hill from where the Landing Plains stretched out to the edge of the Welcoming Sea. At this point midway in the planet's bizarre orbit in the ternary system, Centauri B was setting even as Centauri A rose. Centauri C, as always, was nothing more than a bright star, lost among the alien constellations, and the sea shimmered on the horizon with light of two different hues coming from two different directions.

Monica had loved this view. So had Cochrane. But now that its splendor continued without her, he begrudged each day it renewed itself, each day that it increased his time alone.

"The guests have arrived, sir," Montcalm said.

"Guests," Cochrane muttered. Was there no other name for those who had come to attend a funeral? Why not mourners? Why not victims?

"May I assist you?" Montcalm asked. He held out a powerfully muscled black arm. Growing up under high gravity had produced a generation of weight lifters here. The medical facilities in Micah Town worked round the clock to develop the technologies and treatments these children invariably required as they reached their fortieth Earth birthday and their strained hearts began to rebel against Centauri B II's gravity. But the answers were locked in their cells, needing only a slight medical coaxing to come out and protect them, so their lives were safe. As Cochrane had thought fifty-six years ago, when he had first set foot on this world and done the unthinkable by removing his breathing mask to taste alien air without ill effect, humanity *was* meant to go to other worlds unencumbered—though his sinuses still troubled him each primary winter, when the planet was exposed to the light of a single sun and the plains exploded with temperate vegetation and a convulsion of flowers.

Standing before that view, Cochrane didn't move away from Montcalm. He knew the young man meant well, though Cochrane would be damned if he'd admit it. Here on this world, his home, Cochrane had come to accept his age and his infirmities, mostly through Monica's good humor and patience, and it was with that humor and acceptance that he took Montcalm's arm and began the long walk back to the farmhouse. That welcoming white building, trimmed in green, had been Monica's delight as well. Its façade was real wood, shipped from Earth at a horrendous cost no one would ever reveal, a gift from the newly formed world government to the man who had created the conditions for Earth's dramatic recovery from World War III, though that recovery continued still.

Natural wood remained a luxury on Centauri B II, a world where rigid trees had not evolved. Engineered forests of Earth pines had been planted for fuel and cellulose production, but it would be decades still before there was a sustainable forest system which would allow the harvesting of trees for decorative purposes. Monica had understood the rarity of the gift Cochrane had been given. She had sketched the clapboard design for their house herself, overseen its installation, even sanded and painted sections of it on her own, to make it perfect for him.

And she *had* made it perfect. Everything she had done for him had been perfect.

Cochrane felt tears slip down his cheeks. How could she be gone from this world when so much of it reminded him of her? How could her youth have fled before he himself had died, almost thirty years her senior?

What had drawn him to her at first, Cochrane still didn't know. Love, he supposed, though he didn't really understand that emotion any better now than when he had been young. They had survived Battersea together. They had escaped the Optimum and found safety on the moon. Sir John had recovered there, in Copernicus City. The scar on Monica's face had faded. Cochrane's shattered ribs and punctured lungs had been made whole.

They had shared so much, Cochrane and Monica, that by the time their wounds had healed he supposed it had been inevitable they would feel themselves bound together. She had returned to Alpha Centauri with him, to finish her medical training at the colony's first and only medical facility. She had been granted her degree here, one of this world's first. Sir John had given her away at their wedding and had become an astronomer again, establishing the colony's first observational outpost in his final, most productive years.

As those years and more had passed, Monica had always set aside time in her own life to listen to Cochrane, and to pay attention to him as no other had before her, and late at night as he dreamt of his role in the horror that had unfolded on Earth, thirty-seven million people dead in a war that had consumed the world like no other, she had held him and told him that he *had* done enough, that it had not been his fault.

Whatever he had meant to her, and he had never really understood why she had chosen to share her life with him, she had let him carry on. The superimpellors grew faster, sleeker, more efficient, the result of a thousand minds at work on the secrets of continuum distortion. While Monica had pursued her medical career on Alpha Centauri, Cochrane had ridden those new engines to other worlds, met other intelligent creatures, marveled at the similarity of their DNA and suspected, like half the scientists he knew, that some deeper pattern was afoot in the universe, or at least in this section of the galaxy.

And Monica had always been waiting for him when he returned, keeping him focused, understanding, paying attention.

Until two days ago.

Cochrane's feet dragged along the dusty path leading from the ridge to the farmhouse. He could see the vehicles of the guests parked near the barn. Wheels had become passé on Earth, where energy had passed into a golden age of fusion reactors and sarium krellide batteries with virtually limitless energy density. But here in the colonies, cars and trucks and carriers still rolled and bounced along the unpaved roads on spring tires. Monica had said that in a hundred years, the entertainments of Alpha Centauri's frontier days would depict wheeled vehicles in the same way the old flat movies of the American West depended on horses and wagons to show how times had changed.

She had always been looking to the future, the future she said Cochrane had created.

For that devotion to him, he had accepted her love, for though he had never understood why she loved him, never had he ever doubted her enthusiasm. In return, he hoped he had at least given her adventure, at least fulfillment. She had wept the night she had met the Vulcanians with him. She had thanked him for that, for including her in a moment in history when everything had changed because of what Cochrane had done. The Vulcanians, though some called them Vulcans, even now were negotiating closer ties with Earth, and Cochrane knew his gift of superimpellor research to those aliens had in part convinced them of what they would call the logic of the situation.

And now both Sir John and Monica were gone from his life. The dust of Earth to the dust of Alpha Centauri. It had happened before, Cochrane knew, and would happen again, this merging of the worlds through death. But once again he felt the sting of self-doubt without his wife, and feared he had been selfish once more—taking more from her than he could possibly have given. Never had he ever felt he had done enough. Never.

"They're gathered out back," Montcalm said as they passed the parked vehicles.

Cochrane knew why his guests were there, and not inside. He had planted fig trees in the back. Legend said it was under a fig tree that the Buddha had sat when he had received enlightenment. Cochrane liked the story and understood why Brack had told him about the trees. Newton had had his apple. Cochrane some nameless oak or elm in a suburb of London. And now, who knew who else would sit under trees on a hundred different worlds in the future, thinking new thoughts, receiving new enlightenment? Because of Buddah, Micah Brack, and Zefram Cochrane, there were fig trees on Alpha Centauri waiting just for that moment.

They passed a carrier whose flywheel hummed deep within it, the linear motors over its wheels still ticking as they cooled. It had a symbol of the scales of justice crookedly affixed to the door. The Centauri B II police force had arrived.

Cochrane remembered the way Monica had laughed at Sergei's vehicle—the whole colony's police force dependent on a single, used farm vehicle. Cochrane actually enjoyed that dependence, the fact that the whole colony *could* depend on just a single officer of the law in a single, slow-moving vehicle. Sergei spent more time working at the power station than he did as a police officer. There was no real need for police here. The lack of crime on the colony worlds had once given Cochrane hope that perhaps there were some parts of human nature that had been left forever in the past, burned in the fires with the ashes of the Optimum.

Sergei waited for them in the doorway of the farmhouse, hat in hand, looking glum through his immense walrus mustache. He approached Cochrane and Montcalm, hand extended, mouthing his sorrow and his regret and speaking of his respect for Cochrane's wife. Cochrane didn't hear a word. He still could not believe Monica was no longer with him, that she wasn't just on her way back from the clinic, smelling of antiseptic, anxious to slip out of her whites and share with him the adventures of her day and his. Surely these words Sergei said were meant for someone else to hear.

Cochrane knew that in his younger days, full of energy, full of his questing spirit, he had always wanted to be alone, always appreciated solitude, yet now in these latter years, when he had been granted his wish, he knew he was no longer desirous of solitude. He wanted to hear Monica's soft voice again. He wanted to—

"—wasn't an accident, sir."

The last four words exploded in Cochrane's mind. He blinked at the colony's lawman. "What did you say?" he asked.

Sergei looked pained. "I took the wreck to the recycling depot," Sergei said loudly, speaking too slowly and too precisely, as if talking to a child, or someone over eighty. Cochrane hated that kind of treatment. "To see if anything could be reclaimed."

"Of course you did," Cochrane said, wishing the young man— Sergei was fifty—would get to the point. "Of course you did. SOP."

"And Crombie—he's the tech on duty when I went there—

Crombie takes one look at the engine hood and says some of those holes in it, well, sir, some of those holes aren't from the flywheel fragments busting out. They're from something else busting *in.*"

Cochrane stared at the lawman who was really a power station technician, trying to comprehend what he was saying.

Monica had been driving their carrier back to the farm from Micah Town. The flywheel had slipped out of its capsule and ripped apart the engine compartment, sending shrapnel into the passenger area. It had been a tragedy. But tragedies still happened. Every once in a while, things just broke.

The carrier had been ripped in half. The electrical system had ignited the fuel tanks. The storage batteries had exploded.

At the hospital, the medical team had not allowed Cochrane to view the body.

"I don't understand," Cochrane said. His heart fluttered in his chest.

"What I mean, sir, is that I think someone deliberately shot at your wife's carrier."

"Shot?" Cochrane repeated. He felt Montcalm's powerful arm move around him as his legs weakened.

"I had Crombie cut out those hood sections—you know, entry holes—took them to the metallurgical department at the Foundation. Ionized gas residue, sir. All around the metal."

Cochrane shook his head. This had no meaning for him.

"Whatever projectiles hit your car, they were propelled by a plasma burst."

The memories flooded back to Cochrane. "You mean, a fist-gun?"

Sergei shrugged, out of his league. "A military weapon of some sort, sir. But not a beam weapon. Projectiles absolutely. The Foundation's going to go through the wreck again, see if they can find projectile fragments."

Cochrane gaped at the man without speaking. His pulse hammered in his eardrums, the roar of a distant dark wave sweeping forward, unstoppable, consuming all.

Sergei had wrung his hat into a cloth tube. "Sir, I've never handled a homicide case before. I mean, this whole entire colony's never had a homicide case before. I'd like . . . I'd like to turn it over to the Orbital Defense Bureau. They're the closest thing to military we've got around here. Maybe they can send a pouch to Earth. Get some lab there to identify the weapon."

Cochrane felt his chest continue to constrict. Could it be true? Could someone have *taken* Monica from him? Deliberately?

"Is . . . is that all right, sir?" Sergei asked.

Cochrane nodded. Of course it was all right. Whoever did this must be found, must be punished, must be . . . He heard Monica's words come back to him from so long ago, even as he was consumed by the desire for revenge. *Tempting,* she said, her voice so young, so sure, *but then we would become him.*

"Please do . . . whatever you must," Cochrane choked out.

Sergei nodded grimly. He started to walk off. Then he stopped, turned back, one finger lifted. "Uh, sir, just one more thing. I know they're going to ask me. I . . ." He looked embarrassed. "Sir? Do you have any enemies? You know, someone who might have wished you harm?"

"Enemies," Cochrane said, thinking of ashes. "Let me bury my wife, Sergei. Then we can talk."

"Thank you, sir." Sergei walked back to his carrier, smoothing his hat.

Montcalm escorted Cochrane around the house, toward the fig trees, where the guests were assembled by a simple grave. Sir John was buried nearby, out of the shade, so he could always be beneath the stars.

Throughout the service, Cochrane continued to feel as if each moment were happening to someone else. Just as he had felt that night on Earth, thirty-nine years ago, fleeing across the artificial turf of Battersea Stadium, the Optimum in its death throes all around him. The world hurtling toward the atomic horror. London in flames.

He heard another, less welcome voice from his past, echoing from long-vanished stadium seats and walls, a face repeated an infinite number of times around him.

You will never escape the Optimum! that voice screamed. *You will never escape your destiny!*

Throughout the service, hearing nothing, Cochrane stared up at the fluttering leaves of the fig trees. But there was no enlightenment for him that day. Only his destiny, bleak and inescapable as it had always seemed to him.

Later that day, that night, it was difficult to tell under the lighting conditions of midpoint, Cochrane sat in his study, listening to patient young voices, and he knew it would take a lifetime to explain the truth behind what their words described.

Sergei was there, and Montcalm. Melanie Ark from the Foundation's metallurgical department, quiet and intense. Sirah Chulski of Orbital Defense, massive enough to block an asteroid on her own.

Montcalm had put down a plate of sandwiches left over from the food the guests had brought. Cochrane wasn't hungry. Doubted he would be hungry ever again. But Ark went through them, one at a time, as methodically as she constructed superimpellor shielding, one molecular layer after another.

"There can be no doubt," Chulski said. "It *was* a murder, Mr. Cochrane."

Cochrane sat behind his desk and fingered a small metal medallion one of the Vulcans had given him years ago. It was a circle in which an off-center jewel served as the origin point of a triangle. The translation of what it represented had not been perfect. The linguists felt it would be many years still before communications were effortless. But the disk had held great meaning for the somber, pointed-ear aliens. Everyone fit within it, they had told him. But it was more than just a symbol of the universe; it meant behavior as well, as if they meant that all beliefs fit within it, too.

Cochrane decided the planet Vulcanis had never given birth to its own Optimum Movement.

He had no doubt that that was who had been behind the murder of his wife.

He just didn't know if he could tell these young people the truth, without them discounting him because they thought that age had finally moved to claim his mind.

"But for us to be able to solve a murder," Chulski said, "we need to know a motive."

Sergei looked more sorrowful than even Cochrane felt. "Who would want to kill Dr. Burke?" he asked.

Cochrane sighed. "I don't think whoever did it cared whether or not Monica lived or died." All eyes were on him. "They wanted to hurt *me.*"

Chulski leaned forward. "Who did, sir?"

Cochrane couldn't bring himself to say it. But he had no other choice. In the end, what did it matter if anyone believed him or not?

"The Optimum," Cochrane answered, and from the reaction of the people in the room, he might as well have said Jack the Ripper, as if that monster from old Earth could possibly be resurrected on another world.

"Sir," Chulski said far too politely. "The Optimum Movement died a long time ago. And it was strictly an Earth-based aberration."

"I'm from Earth," Cochrane said, carefully putting the Vulcanian medallion down on the desk. "I had run-ins with the Optimum before the war. Colonel Adrik Thorsen in particular."

"Colonel Thorsen's dead, sir. So's Colonel Green. The whole cadre."

"'The evil that men do lives after them,'" Cochrane said.

Ark took another sandwich from the plate on the small table beside her. She looked at it intently, as if wondering what an atomic reading might reveal about its contents. "I have heard stories of Optimum cells still functioning," she admitted. "There have been so many rumors of war criminals escaping Earth to live under assumed names in the colonies . . . maybe some of them are true."

Sergei looked unconvinced. "You're saying we have an Optimum cell on Alpha Centauri? C'mon, Melanie. They'd be reported so fast we'd be shipping them home before they had a second meeting."

Ark popped the sandwich into her mouth and chewed it methodically.

"Maybe someone just arrived?" Montcalm suggested hesitantly. "You know, there's a cell somewhere else, and they sent someone here to . . . to you know."

Chulski shifted her impressive bulk in her chair, managing as always to make the others seem less significant. "We could check with immigration. Find out who's come here in the past six months or so, and from where." She glanced back at Cochrane. "You sure there's no one else you can think of, Mr. Cochrane?"

"Of course there's not," Montcalm said, too forcefully. "He created the interstellar community single-handed. We owe our existence to him. Who could possibly want him dead?"

The light bar on the desk communicator flashed. Cochrane watched it. The farmhouse system would pick it up in a moment. But he nodded at Montcalm to answer.

The young man lifted the handset. The viewscreen remained dark. "Mr. Cochrane's office," he said. His eyes widened. He looked at Cochrane. "There's been an accident, sir. At the Foundation." He passed the handset to Sergei. "The fabrication crew is . . . dead, sir. All of them."

Cochrane slumped back in his chair. The students on the fabrication team were the ones who engineered the latest theories, hand-wrapped the coils. They were the Foundation's best. The brightest. Already Cochrane knew that whatever happened, this, too, had been no accident.

Sergei listened to the details. The others stood in agitation. Cochrane alone remained seated.

Sergei confirmed it. "It was a matter-antimatter blast," he said.

Montcalm was confused. "They never have fuel in the fabrication facility."

Sergei looked to Cochrane for confirmation. "He's right," Cochrane said. He closed his eyes and saw the faces of the fabrication team. Saw their parents' faces. Their children's. Was Micah Brack right? *Did* evil *never* die? Was the battle never over?

The communicator flashed again. Sergei grabbed it, identified himself. After a moment, he passed the handset to Cochrane. The viewscreen was still blank. Cochrane wondered bitterly who had died now.

"Cochrane here," he said.

"You know what I want," Adrik Thorsen answered. It had been thirty-nine years, but the voice, the tone, the cruelty were unmistakable. "You promised you'd use it against me if I came after you. And I *am* coming after you."

Cochrane wanted to drop the handset but his body was paralyzed with shock. "You're dead," he said, his voice sounding older than even his years.

"You're confused," Thorsen said. "It's your wife who's dead. It's your students who are dead. But you and I, we're still alive."

Cochrane was aware of the others in the room watching him. Sergei went to a home system panel and inserted his police ID card, punching numbers furiously into the keypad, trying to override the privacy circuits.

"One by one," Thorsen said. "One by one, I promise you they'll fall—until I have your attention."

"You've got my attention!" Cochrane said to stop that terrible voice.

"Then give me what I want."

"It doesn't exist! It never has!"

"I don't believe you, Mr. Cochrane. But I'll make certain that *you* believe *me.*"

Cochrane stared at the handset. This couldn't be happening again. It had ended in Battersea. In a blast of fusion fire. "You can't . . ." he said, already knowing that if anyone could, it would be Thorsen.

"You're weak, Mr. Cochrane. Weakness is not optimal. Perhaps I was weak to ever have admired you. But in—"

Sergei ripped the handset from Cochrane's rigid hand. "Who is this?!" he shouted into it.

But from Sergei's expression, Cochrane could see that Thorsen had already broken the circuit.

"Mr. Cochrane?" Sergei demanded. "Do you know who that was?"

"Could you leave, please," Cochrane said. He felt exhausted.

But Sergei didn't let go of the handset. "Does your home system automatically record calls?"

It didn't. Monica hadn't thought that was right. Few systems on

202

Alpha Centauri were set for automatic record. But Cochrane didn't say that. What was the point? "Leave," he told his visitors. "Except you." He pointed a shaking finger at Montcalm.

No one made a move to the door. Cochrane grabbed the handset from Sergei and slammed it down on his desk. The Vulcanian medallion bounced up and rolled off onto the floor, where it spun and clattered on the tile.

Sergei motioned to the others. Chulski and Ark followed him out, though both seemed uncertain it was the right thing to do.

Montcalm stood in front of Cochrane's desk. The young man was tense, muscles bunched, ready to strike wherever his teacher directed. "Will you tell me who it was, sir?"

Cochrane wondered what it would be like to have youth again. He wondered what it would be like to have second chances. He wanted Montcalm to have a better life on Alpha Centauri. This horror pursuing him was something from the past. His past. It shouldn't concern Montcalm or anyone here. "It was someone who . . . just wants me," Cochrane said.

"There're only two million people on this planet," Montcalm answered earnestly. "We can find him. We can find anyone."

But Cochrane shook his head. The truth was that his own arrogance had caught up with him.

Arrogance, he thought with sorrow. That final word he had felt compelled to have with Thorsen in the stadium, thirty-nine years ago. Turning back in the doorway to say that he would use his warp bomb if Thorsen ever came after him. Just to torment him, to hurt him, to be *better* than Thorsen ever could be. Monica had been right. He had become Thorsen. And that transformation had cost him her life and others, just beginning their journey.

Cochrane felt so weary. Here he had hoped that his invention might someday let humanity leave the worst of its inner nature behind, yet he himself was a repository for it. *The cursed* need *to be better.* He wondered if the Vulcans included that in their medallion.

"I want you to prep my ship," Cochrane told Montcalm.

"You don't have to run, sir. I can protect you. This whole world can protect you."

Cochrane shook his head, tried to smile reassuringly. No need to disturb another life. "I'm not running. I want to go to . . . Stapledon Center. They have a good fabrication shop there. We're going to need new staff."

Montcalm studied Cochrane carefully. "Are you sure? What about that call? Aren't you going to do anything about it?"

"Life has to go on," Cochrane lied. Monica had always told him that. He hadn't believed her then, he didn't believe her now. But it was important to the safety of everyone he cared for on this world that Montcalm believe him at this moment. "Send a message pouch to Stapledon. Let them know I'm coming."

"When do you want to go?"

"Right away," Cochrane said. "Look after it for me?"

Montcalm nodded slowly, anxious to do something, anything, for his teacher. "Do you want to keep the trip a secret, sir? I mean, if there *is* someone after you . . ."

"I have nothing to hide," Cochrane said. "That call . . . it was just a crank." He looked around his study, all the books, the fiche, the computer cards, the building blocks of his mind, no longer with purpose. "I'll feel better helping the Foundation. Really."

"Can I at least post some guards around the house? I know they keep some old rifles out at the landing facilities."

"That's not necessary," Cochrane said. "Increase security at the Foundation, that's all. So there won't be any more . . . accidents."

Cochrane was relieved to see that whatever Montcalm believed about his real motives, he headed dutifully for the door.

"And, Montcalm?"

"Yes, sir?"

"Thank you. For everything."

Montcalm studied Cochrane carefully. "You're not thinking of doing something stupid, are you, sir?"

Now Cochrane smiled. "You know me better than that."

Montcalm tried to smile back but his effort lacked sincerity. Then he was gone.

Cochrane remained at his desk for some time, staring into the years, remembering all the times Monica had come in here to tell him he had been working too long, too late. And all that time,

Thorsen had been somewhere else in the galaxy, doing . . . what? Plotting what?

Why had it taken so long for his return? Cochrane wasn't hiding out on Alpha Centauri. Everyone knew it was his home. But where had Thorsen's home been since Battersea, since the world war? And why had he come here now, wanting a technology that, even if it did exist, could no longer give him the power he had craved? In the end, Cochrane decided, the madman's motives were merely an abstraction—a mystery Cochrane would never comprehend in his lifetime, just another question to be placed aside, abandoned, with so many other unanswerable questions of youth.

Cochrane pressed the control that made his computer rise up from his desktop. He asked it to display his will. It would be remiss of him not to at least give some thought to the future, the future Monica had seen, and he had been blind to.

Then, with the changes made, leaving all that he had to the Foundation Micah Brack had established, Cochrane's thoughts of the future came to an end.

Instead he remembered back to a time when he had wanted to take on the universe. He thought of that first night back in his home system, under the dome at Titan. So many possibilities, so much to do.

But now he was only tired. And alone.

He wanted to see the stars once more, then die.

He wondered if this feeling was something built into the human species, the sense that when death was inevitable, it must be accepted, embraced.

Or was it just his way of making certain someone like Adrik Thorsen could never win?

Cochrane had no answer. As much as it sickened him to admit it, the war that had begun on Earth so long ago still continued, and he was to blame.

He had given humanity the stars, and then he had defiled them.

But now, finally, that intrusion would end. For no matter how his friend Micah Brack might argue if he were here to do so, Zefram Cochrane believed there was still hope for humanity. That things could change.

For only a moment, he felt a brief twinge of regret that he would not live to see those changes. But his time was over. Alpha Centauri was no longer his home.

The stars would have to beckon to someone else.

He remembered another old, old poem his mother had read to him. It seemed to fit the moment.

Deep space was his dwelling place, and death his destination.

There was never any escape from that. Not for anyone.

FOURTEEN

U.S.S. ENTERPRISE NCC-1701
LEAVING THE GAMMA CANARIS REGION
Stardate 3854.7
Earth Standard: ≈ November 2267

The *Enterprise* blazed through space so that the stars were rainbow smears of light around her. Kirk watched them pass on the main bridge viewscreen, knowing they had been a sight at first unknown to Zefram Cochrane in his early voyages.

The key to being able to perceive anything of normal space-time while in warp was directly related to the characteristics of the warp field itself. Cochrane had quickly learned that for warp propulsion to be efficient, a minimum of two fields must be generated, so that one overlapped the other, offset at oscillations on the order of the Planck interval—the smallest possible unit of measurable time. Unfortunately, when the two warp fields were of sufficiently different sizes, any photons from normal space-time that impinged on the outermost field generally were absorbed by what was, to them, a perfect radiation sink—the gap between the fields.

In the beginning, Cochrane had accepted this state of affairs because it neatly explained why Einsteinian notions of time dilation did not apply inside the warp field—with no possibility for the exchange of meaningful information, there was no conflict with established physics. The existence of information-free, faster-than-light phenomena such as this was well known, dating back to experimental confirmation of the Einstein-Podolsky-Rosen Paradox in the mid-1900s.

Thus, Cochrane's first faster-than-light voyages had left him literally in the dark. Once he entered warp space, he lost all communication with the normal universe. Eventually, as his system became more efficient and the warp fields became more tightly focused and layered, photons were able to penetrate into the warp bubble, bringing with them the breathtaking image so dear to Kirk of stars passing by so quickly that they became little more than streaks of light. And, once scientists were able to exploit subspace as a medium in which they could propagate electromagnetic signals at speeds in excess of 190,000 times the speed of light, standard computer enhancement techniques created hyperreal images from subspace sensor scans, much the way old-fashioned radar systems on old Earth had created echoes of distant objects in centuries past.

Though science had not been Kirk's first love in school, he could understand how scientists had arrived at these breakthrough innovations. Like Cochrane, they had not wasted their time running headlong into the solid walls of accepted theories. Instead, they had chosen to broaden their arena, change the rules, and step outside accepted boundaries. Kirk knew the approach well.

His ship was proof that the approach worked in physics. The fact that he commanded her was proof it worked in the world of human affairs as well.

But the fact that it was Admiral Kabreigny who still occupied the *Enterprise*'s command chair told Kirk that he still had some lessons to learn in applying the approach.

For now, Kirk stood at the admiral's side, eyes fixed on the screen. The Companion, wearing a standard blue technician's jumpsuit, sat behind him on the upper level, in the chair at Spock's science station, guiding the *Enterprise*'s course by her mysterious contact with Cochrane, which Sulu had managed to translate to navigational charts. Spock was with her and McCoy was nearby with a fully stocked medical kit. So far, more than a day out from her home planetoid, the Companion's stamina had not yet failed her. But McCoy wanted to be prepared for anything, and was.

"Keptin," Chekov announced. "I mean, Admiral, I am picking up a wessel in the indicated flight path."

"Onscreen," Kabreigny ordered. "Full magnification."

Sulu adjusted a control and the stars rippled as the viewer's image expanded to include a tiny spot of light, clearly not a star. "She's at the limit of our sensor range," Sulu said.

Kirk glanced back at the Companion and Spock. The Companion held her hands to her face. She whispered something Kirk couldn't hear. Spock nodded.

"That could be it," Kirk said. He fought the urge to give the next orders as he reluctantly deferred to the admiral. Like most women in Starfleet's upper echelons, Kabreigny had earned her rank in the science and support branches, meaning she had no frontline command experience. But that rank technically did allow her to take over the *Enterprise,* and after a day of seeing her in his chair, Kirk was getting better at remembering that state of affairs. Though he had no intention of getting used to it.

"Target vessel's speed?" Kabreigny asked.

"Cruising at warp factor three," Chekov said. "No indication that she's seen us."

"If it is the *Planitia,* her sensors won't be effective at this range," Kirk said.

"Zefram!" the Companion suddenly gasped. "The man is closer . . . so alone . . ."

Kabreigny leaned forward in the chair. "Navigator, I want you to slowly drop speed and match course with the target vessel. Come up behind like a sensor echo. It's just a civilian ship so it shouldn't be difficult."

"Aye-aye, Admiral." Sulu went to work on his board. The stars shifted as the *Enterprise* changed course.

Kirk watched the admiral closely, trying to fathom the reason for her order. "A luxury liner has no defenses or weapons that can stand up to the *Enterprise,* Admiral. Why the caution?"

"It's not the liner I'm worried about," Kabreigny said, not

bothering to explain further. Without looking at Kirk, she added, "I presume you have a transporter team experienced in high-velocity transport."

"I'll put my chief engineer on it."

But Kabreigny put her hand on Kirk's arm before he could activate the chair's intercom panel. "Leave Mr. Scott right where he is. We might need better than warp eight in a few minutes. Who's your next choice?"

Kirk understood that for whatever reason, Kabreigny was preparing for a fast flyby and transporter retrieval of Cochrane. She didn't want to risk a showdown. "Mr. Spock," Kirk said.

"Will you be able to handle the Companion?"

"The Companion can handle herself quite well."

Kabreigny ignored Kirk's insubordinate tone. "Have Mr. Spock stand by in the transporter room and wait for my signal."

Kirk did not acknowledge the order, but he went to Spock, explained what the admiral was preparing for, and took the science officer's place at the Companion's side. Spock left the bridge.

"We have matched course," Sulu announced.

"Come up on her slowly, Navigator," the admiral said sharply. "I want to see her onscreen as soon as we have her in range."

Long moments passed. Kirk was aware only of the Companion's erratic breathing. McCoy had earlier suggested it was the result of the connection she felt with Zefram Cochrane. It was Zefram Cochrane who was in bad enough shape that he was having difficulty breathing, wherever he was. The Companion's health, so far, was fine.

"Wessel coming into range," Chekov called out. "Onscreen."

The target vessel was a civilian liner—an elongated ovoid about half the length of the *Enterprise,* with three nacelles in the same configuration as the missing *City of Utopia Planitia.*

"Are you receiving any identification signals?" Kabreigny asked.

Chekov answered without taking his eyes from his side of the command console. "Negative, Admiral. The liner is powered-down. No communications. But sensors confirm her warp signature as the *Planitia.*"

"Shield status?" the admiral asked.

Sulu answered. "I'm reading navigational shields only."

Kabreigny spoke rapidly over her shoulder to Uhura. "Communications: Relay that to Mr. Spock. I want him able to hear everything on this bridge from now on."

Uhura contacted Spock in the transporter room. Kirk knew as long as the liner was using only her forward navigational deflectors, deployed solely for sweeping debris out of her flight path, the *Enterprise* would be able to come up from behind and transport Cochrane without difficulty. But only as long as the crew of the liner—presumably Cochrane's kidnappers—didn't realize the *Enterprise* was closing on them.

Uhura looked up from her board after talking with Spock. "Open channel established, Admiral."

"Distance to target?" Kabreigny asked, intent on the screen.

Sulu read from his board. "One hundred thousand kilometers."

"Take us into transporter range, Navigator. Mr. Spock, stand by for emergency transport. Lock on to human life signs on the target vessel."

Spock's voice answered from the bridge speakers. "What if there are multiple human life-sign readings?"

"Transport them all, Mr. Spock. We'll sort them out later."

Kirk couldn't stand it any longer. Kabreigny was going by the book, but it wasn't enough. "With respect, Admiral, if you're planning on transporting hostiles aboard the *Enterprise*—"

Kabreigny cut him off. "Security detail to the transporter room. Phasers set to stun."

Kirk relaxed, but only a bit. "May I make another suggestion, Admiral?"

"Coming up on transporter range," Sulu announced. "Still no indication that they've spotted us."

Kabreigny looked at Kirk. "Say what you have to, Captain."

"If the liner is in the hands of Orion pirates, where's their original ship?"

Kabreigny tightened her grip on the arms of the chair. "The craft that landed by Cochrane's shelter on the planetoid was small, Captain. I presume it's docked on the liner's hangar deck."

Kirk could feel nervous energy roiling up inside him. "The pad marks on the planetoid were from a *landing* craft, Admiral. Something that small couldn't have taken over a liner."

"Then they took it over from within," Kabreigny said, but for the first time Kirk could hear uncertainty in her voice.

So did McCoy. "For God's sake, Admiral—what liner is going to let *Orions* book passage without packing them in freeze tubes?"

"Do you have a recommendation?" Kabreigny asked in annoyance.

"Full sensor sweep of the surrounding area," Kirk said, stepping down from the operations section to the command-chair level.

"Why not fire a photon torpedo across their bow," Kabreigny snapped, "and really let them know we're here?"

"Admiral—you're taking my ship into danger."

Kabreigny pushed herself out of the chair, towering over Kirk because of the chair's raised platform. "Captain, you are attempting to warn the enemy."

"What?!" McCoy said. "Since when are Orion pirates the enemy? They're criminals, annoyances . . . but enemies?"

"Dr. McCoy," the admiral ordered, "you will leave the bridge."

But McCoy had no intention of following that order. "I will not leave my patient."

Kirk shot a glance at the Companion. Her face was still buried in her hands. Alarmingly, her breathing was coming in shorter and shorter gasps.

Kabreigny pointed at McCoy. "I have given you an order, Doctor."

McCoy bristled with indignation. "You are outside your authority, Admiral."

Kabreigny matched him, bristle for bristle. "Very well. You force me to relieve you of duty."

"You cannot relieve me of my medical obligations to my patient."

"We are in transporter range," Sulu said, his voice carefully neutral.

Kirk watched the admiral intently, ready to step in the instant she made a mistake that would stand up to review. His fists opened and closed in frustration at his sides.

Spock's cool voice came from the speakers again. "I have detected eighty-three humans aboard the liner, Admiral. Do you wish me to transport them all?"

"Eighty-three?" Kabreigny said, momentarily distracted.

"What did you expect? It's a *passenger* liner!" Kirk shouted. "One hundred and two crew and passengers!"

Kabreigny looked confused. "But they kill their prisoners."

"Who are you talking about?" Kirk demanded. "Tell my people what to do or step down, Admiral!"

"I am awaiting orders," Spock said.

The Companion moaned.

"Keptin, warp signature approaching, dead ahead. It is the same configuration as we encountered en route to Babel, sir."

"Admiral! Give me command!" Kirk demanded.

"Shields!" Kabreigny ordered, ignoring Kirk. "Go to Red Alert!"

Chekov confirmed shields up. Warning lights flashed and sirens pulsed.

"Liner has raised her shields," Chekov said. "She's coming about."

"Unidentified warp vessel closing," Sulu reported. "Her weapons are preparing to fire."

"Evasive maneuvers!" Kabreigny ordered.

"What?!" Kirk sputtered. "What about Cochrane?"

The deck pitched as the inertial dampeners lagged behind the sudden change of course Sulu initiated.

"Wessel firing!" Chekov shouted. "Torpedo impact in ten seconds."

Kabreigny leaned back in the command chair. "Warp seven. Take us out of here."

The Cochrane generators whined as they surged with power.

"Enterprise is moving out of range," Chekov confirmed. "But enemy wessel is pursuing." Chekov paused, then looked over his shoulder. "Awaiting orders, Admiral."

"We're going to outrun them, mister," Kabreigny said stoutly.

"We *can't* outrun them," Kirk countered, his voice rigid with suppressed rage. "They've tied all their power into their warp drive. It's a suicide configuration for a one-way mission."

"Enemy wessel closing."

Kabreigny eyed Kirk suspiciously. "You seem to know an awful lot about our adversary, Captain."

"We faced a ship just like it last week."

"How convenient."

"Are you implying that I'm somehow in league with our attackers?"

McCoy stepped up to the other side of the command chair. "Careful, Captain."

"No," Kabreigny said. "By all means, *Captain* Kirk, continue."

"Enemy wessel has fired," Chekov said. "Impact in eight seconds."

"Come about," Kabreigny ordered. "Concentrate power in forward shields."

Sulu glanced over his shoulder in alarm. Kirk reached his limit.

"Belay that order! Drop to impulse on my mark! And cut those blasted sirens!"

The Red Alert lights remained but the sirens instantly cut out. Sulu smiled as he turned back to the console. "Aye-aye, sir!"

"Captain Kirk, you are relieved of duty!" Kabreigny barked. "Leave the bridge."

"Impact in four seconds, three . . . two . . ."

Kirk hammered his fist in empty air. *"Mark!"*

Sulu slammed his hands over his controls and the ship lurched as it dropped to sublight the instant the enemy's phaser fire hit.

But the energies of that blast were dissipated, half in warp velocity, half in normal space, as the *Enterprise* threw off her warp fields. The ship rumbled, shook, but Kirk could tell from the way she absorbed the blow that she had resisted damage.

The admiral hit the intercom switch on the chair arm. "Security to the bridge," she commanded.

"Admiral, I'd advise you to consider your next move very carefully," Kirk warned.

"Enemy vessel coming about," Sulu said.

"Prepare photon torpedoes," Kirk ordered. He moved in close to Kabreigny. "If we had taken that blast with full power to our forward shields, shield capability would have dropped fifty percent for the next round. The case could be made that you were deliberately trying to sabotage the *Enterprise*'s defenses."

"That's ridiculous! I was putting us in position to return point-blank fire."

"Enemy wessel in range."

"Fire one, three, and five," Kirk said swiftly.

The capacitor hum of the torpedoes' linear induction launching tubes echoed on the bridge.

"You were the one who gave us away," Kabreigny accused Kirk. "You already know what's on that liner."

"I'm in the dark, Admiral." Kirk shielded his eyes as the first of the torpedoes detonated, sending a flare of orange light into the bridge.

"Enemy wessel breaking off attack."

"Pursue!" Kirk said. "Maximum warp! Don't give it time to come about. Ready phasers!"

Sulu's voice was filled with tension. "Closing on enemy . . . it's changing course again . . . it's running, Captain! Warp factor seven . . . seven point five . . ."

Kirk jammed his finger against the chair intercom. "Kirk to Engineering—Scotty, give me everything you've got, just for a minute."

The engineer didn't waste time replying. Kirk felt the *Enterprise* lurch again. Her engines whined.

"Range?" Kirk asked.

"Twenty thousand kilometers," Sulu answered. "They're climbing to warp eight. Sir . . . we're at eight point three!"

Kirk grinned. That was almost four percent greater than the ship's fastest possible speed. He had no idea how Scott was managing it. Kirk could almost feel the wind in his hair, hear the flap of the sails, smell the smoke from the cannons as the seas raged all around him. "Thatta boy, Scotty . . ." he whispered. The enemy ship began to grow on the screen. It could outrun the *Enterprise,* Kirk knew, but it would take a few moments to accelerate to faster than warp eight point three. And Kirk wasn't going to give it those moments. . . .

"In range, sir!"

"Fire phasers! All banks!"

Twin strands of glowing blue energy erupted through space, converging toward the glowing orange light of the enemy.

The orange light blossomed into a shimmering white flower.

"Direct hit!" Chekov exclaimed, fist in the air.

A second explosion silently filled the screen, more violent than the first. Kirk held his hand to his eyes before the screen compensated for the increased level of optical radiation.

"That was her antimatter containment field," Sulu said. "Reading only fine debris, sir. The target is completely destroyed."

"Resume heading back to the liner," Kirk said. "Warp factor seven." He hit the intercom again. "Scotty, you're a miracle worker."

"Aye," the chief engineer replied with exhaustion over the speaker, "that's what I keep telling ye."

Then Kirk released the Send button and stepped back from the chair. "Now that my ship is safe, Admiral, where were we?"

"You and Dr. McCoy were leaving the bridge."

The turbolift opened and two security officers sprang out, phasers drawn.

"At ease," Kirk told them. He stepped in close to the admiral and dropped his voice. "There's no need to make this harder than it already is. Remember, everything we say, everything we do on this bridge, goes directly into the flight recorder. Command's not going to have any trouble seeing that I stepped in to save the ship when you endangered her."

McCoy joined them, also whispering. "The captain's done everything regulations require to accommodate you, Admiral. But if he should decide that *you* should be relieved of command, as chief medical officer I will support him."

Kabreigny's face twisted in anger. She stared at McCoy in outrage. "Do you know what you're saying, Doctor?"

But McCoy didn't escalate the confrontation. His reply was kind. "It's not what you think, Admiral. But what I am saying is that your expertise is in other areas than the command chair of a starship. And that at your age your health might not be up to the challenge of command under fire."

Kabreigny's lips thinned.

"I saved the ship," Kirk said. "Now let me save Cochrane."

Kabreigny drew in a ragged breath and Kirk could see her struggle to remain calm. "How can I know that's what you intend to do?" she asked.

McCoy brought up a medical scanner and waved it by the admiral.

"I don't understand," Kirk said. "Why wouldn't I want to save Cochrane?"

"You could be involved in this whole business," Kabreigny said.

"Keptin, we are coming up on the liner."

McCoy checked the reading on his scanner. "Admiral, if you do not relinquish command now, I will have you relieved for medical reasons. Your heart's beating like a blasted trip-hammer."

"Involved in what?" Kirk asked.

"The conspiracy," Kabreigny said. Her voice was raspy. Her dark face was becoming ashen.

The *Enterprise* creaked as sparkles of light flared across her viewscreen.

"The liner is firing her navigational phasers at us," Sulu reported. "No damage to shields."

"What conspiracy?" Kirk demanded.

Kabreigny stared him in the eyes. "You're either telling the truth, or you're even better than Starfleet thinks you are." She stood up. "Captain Kirk, I am ordering you to bring Zefram Cochrane safely aboard this ship. I now turn over command of the *Enterprise* to you." Head held impressively high, she stepped down from the chair.

In seconds, McCoy had pressed a hypospray to her arm, telling her it would lower her heart rate.

Kirk took the chair. It was like coming home. The liner's navigational phasers struck again and he felt like laughing as the *Enterprise* effortlessly rode out their attack. Nothing could stop him now, nothing could stop *them*.

"Mr. Chekov," Kirk announced.

"Standing by, Keptin." There was almost joy in Chekov's voice.

Kirk leaned back in his chair as if his ship embraced him. "Take

217

us in to five hundred meters. I want pinpoint hits on the liner's navigational phaser emitters. Low power. No damage to the interior."

Chekov liked the sound of that. No ship should be able to fire at the *Enterprise* and expect to get away with it.

"Uhura, opening hailing frequencies. Tell the *City of Utopia Planitia* to prepare to receive a boarding party."

But as Uhura transmitted her message and the *Enterprise* moved in, Sulu said, "Captain, I am picking up venting of interior atmosphere. Someone has opened an airlock on the liner."

"Onscreen," Kirk said.

The side of the liner sprang up into full magnification. Kirk instantly saw what had happened. The writhing form of a human drifted away from an open airlock. "Spock! They've thrown someone out through an airlock. Get a fix and beam him in!"

"Animals," McCoy gasped.

Spock's reply over the speakers was calm, but not encouraging. "Whoever has been ejected from the ship is within the navigational shields. The transporter cannot save him."

The figure floating at the side of the liner ceased its struggles. Kirk knew there were only seconds remaining to save a life. "Chekov! Target the liner's shield generators! Fire at will!"

"Aye-aye, sir." Chekov's fingers flew over his controls. But then he paused. "Keptin—I am picking up multiple life-sign readings around the liner's shield generators."

Kirk couldn't take his eyes off the drifting figure. Someone's life had been sacrificed to make a point. And now more hostages were assembled by the shield generators to make another.

Uhura broke the silence of the bridge. "Captain Kirk, the liner is responding."

"Onscreen."

As quickly as that the face of the enemy appeared on the main screen.

And the enemy was Klingon.

FIFTEEN

ROMULAN VESSEL *TEARS OF ALGERON*
DEEP SPACE
Stardate 43921.5
Earth Standard: ≈ May 2366

The Romulan ship smelled damp.

That was Picard's first impression of the Warbird as the transporter effect faded around him and he gazed into the vessel's cavernous hangar deck in person for the first time. Damp, and hot, and with an unsettling blend of spices and alien sweat.

He found it invigorating.

Commander Tarl stood before him, impressive in her battle uniform. She was taller than he by almost half a meter, and in person she looked strained. But then, Picard considered, how would he appear if he had stolen the *Enterprise* in order to deliver stolen property to the Romulans? The Romulan commander had taken a difficult path. Picard felt obligated to honor her.

"Request permission to come aboard," Picard asked formally.

Tarl narrowed her eyes at him. "You are aboard. This way." She turned her back to him and began to walk toward the scaffolding twenty meters away. All in all, Picard decided his reception lacked a certain grace. He breathed deeply, committing the scent of the vessel to his memory, realizing that in Sarek's memories the scent was already there and known.

Picard smiled as he approached his away team. He felt like an

219

explorer, and the exotic expanse of stars seen through the open hangar doors, obscured only by the slight flickering of the forcefield retaining the ship's atmosphere, enhanced that feeling for him.

The artifact, though partially hidden behind the green scaffolding and in the glaring halos of the encircling lights, was just as impressive as the stars. It was at least five meters tall, ten meters long, and who knew how many meters deep. The angular arrangements of conduits and pipes along its one flat side were certainly reminiscent of the Borg approach to engineering, and when Picard looked more closely, he saw that the exposed surfaces were pitted with small impact craters, most no larger than a fingertip.

"Is this part of the Borg vessel exterior?" Picard asked.

"Judging from the scarring," Riker said, "the consensus is yes."

Picard smiled at his number one. "I appreciate the chance to come aboard and see this firsthand, Will, but it's so obviously of Borg manufacture, I'm surprised you found it necessary for me to be here."

Riker responded with a matching smile, though Picard could see it was patently false, assumedly only for the benefit of Tarl and the two stern Romulans who accompanied her. "It's the interior we think you should see, Captain. There are some . . . unusual Borg components there."

"I do not see the reason for this delay," Tarl said impatiently. "The artifact is yours. I need a ship for my crew."

"Commander, please, a few minutes more," Riker said. "We have strict protocols we must follow. I'm sure your command structure is no different from our admiralty."

Tarl frowned. "Deliver me from subpraetors with their computer screens and regulations," she muttered.

Riker nodded and sighed in agreement. "They're everywhere."

Tarl gestured for them to continue. "A few minutes then."

As Picard moved around the side of the artifact and saw it extended another ten meters, he gave Riker a puzzled glance. "The protocols we must follow in a matter like this are very straightforward, Will. It's all at the captain's discretion."

"We needed an excuse to bring you over," Riker said in a suddenly lowered voice. "Data, where are you?"

Picard was startled by the android's head suddenly poking out from among some tightly woven conduits on the surface of the artifact. He was already inside it.

"Allow me, Captain," Data said. His body emerged just enough to allow him to push aside some strands of metal, bending them back until a narrow entry hole had been opened. "There is a corridor inside which is more or less undamaged. If you could come this way."

Then Data disappeared back inside the mass of the artifact. Picard didn't hesitate. This was thrilling. He climbed in after Data.

Picard's uniform snagged a few times on rough pieces of metal or wiring, he couldn't tell which, but after gingerly edging through a two-meter-thick section of the artifact, he found himself inside a large, well-defined passageway, whose appearance suggested that it had been sliced clean out of the interior of a Borg ship. As he stood up, Picard grew even more intrigued. If Starfleet could determine what kind of weaponry had been used to penetrate Borg defenses to cause such physical damage to their ship, the Federation would have nothing to fear when the Borg finally arrived at its borders.

"I am very encouraged by this," Picard said. He looked around at the complex construction all around him. Starfleet engineers would be ecstatic.

"Just around this corner, sir." Riker led the way now, Data hanging back. The internal passageway was lit by the small palm torches the away team carried, sending bars of light and shadow rippling through the mesh and interwoven conduits. La Forge handed his torch to Picard as he came to the corner where Riker stood. Picard was aware of how quiet everything seemed, as if the passageway were lined with a perfect acoustical shield.

"Do you notice the flattened quality of the sound in here?" Picard asked. He wondered if it had any significance.

Then La Forge held up a tricorder. "That's because I've set up an acoustical baffle, sir. So we can talk without being overheard."

"Talk about what?" Picard asked.

Riker glanced at the rest of the away team, then looked the captain in the eye. "We know the Borg assimilate the technology of whatever race they come in contact with."

"Yes . . ." Picard said, not knowing where this was leading.

"Around this corner is another artifact, sir. An object which was obviously incorporated into the original Borg ship. It is our conclusion that neither the Borg nor Commander Tarl has realized what it is. We can't be certain ourselves, but with your archaeological expertise, we think you should be able to confirm our suspicions."

"I must say you have piqued my interest, Number One. But why not link up your tricorder to the *Enterprise*'s history computer?"

"If the Romulans are monitoring our communications, which they should be, we didn't want to reveal what we suspect." Riker extended his hand to the hidden passageway. "Take a look for yourself, sir. You be the judge."

Picard tightened his grip on the palm torch and with a thrill of excitement, walked around the corner.

He found himself in a blind alley.

"What, exactly, am I looking for?" he asked as he moved the beam of the torch over the heavily textured walls. The moisture in the air gave the beam shape, making it glow as a blue cone against the dark Borg machinery.

"At the end, sir. The silver panel," Riker said from behind him.

Picard shone his torch straight ahead. Sure enough, a patch of silver gleamed back at him. He could see where a metal panel had been pulled back to expose more of it, about a square meter in all. He moved closer to it. There was something engraved on the silver surface.

"This panel here?" he asked. "With what appears to be inscriptions?"

"Yes, sir," Riker said.

Picard was aware of Data, and Worf, and Mr. La Forge all standing behind Riker at the open end of the passageway, watching the captain's every move.

"And it's more than a panel," La Forge added. "My scans show

222

it's the surface of a discrete object about two meters by three meters by five meters."

Picard touched the silver panel. It was cold. Moisture had condensed on it.

"The object is also the source of the power readings for the entire artifact," Data said. "Because there appears to have been no effort to remove the object from the artifact, we assume that the Romulans have decided it is a power supply of some kind."

"But you don't believe that's what it is," Picard said. He rubbed at the gleaming silver surface, smearing the water droplets, feeling the depth of the inscriptions. They were an odd combination of delicate cuneiform wedges, broken up by simplistic, almost geometrical drawings of circles and squares and dotted lines. He could see why his away team had asked for him. The markings did look familiar.

"You're certain we can't risk even a brief contact with the *Enterprise?*" Picard asked. The ship's computer would be able to identify these markings within seconds.

"That's up to you, sir," Riker said.

Picard turned his head sideways, seeing if that would make the inscription more recognizable. "I don't know if I appreciate all this mystery, Number One. Perhaps my archaeological acumen leaves something to be desired when compared to Mr. Da—"

The pattern jumped out at him like lightning.

"*Sacré merde,*" Picard whispered.

He *had* seen inscriptions like this before. Just never so many of them at once. In Professor Galen's study at the Academy. Reproductions of engravings from a hundred different worlds, so controversial that the professor would not even show them in class. Only to a select few students in whom he believed rested the future of exoarchaeology.

Picard realized he had stopped breathing. "What—" He had to clear his throat before he could make any recognizable sound. "Mr. Data . . . what is the age of this . . . object?"

"Overall, the age of the rest of the Borg artifact in which the object rests is approximately four centuries. However, the object itself is, at minimum, three point five billion years old."

Picard's mouth was open. He held his hand reverentially to the silver surface, feeling the textures that had been placed there by thinking beings when life on Earth was still primordial soup.

"And its power supply *still* functions?"

"That is correct, sir."

Riker was beside the captain. "Have you recognized it, Captain?"

"Without question." Picard almost felt as if the passageway were spinning around him, leaving him motionless in its well of silence. He looked at his first officer, and realized that the next words he spoke he would remember for the rest of his life. "This object was made by . . . *the Preservers.*"

It was not known what the Preservers had called themselves. Some Federation scientists still doubted that they had in fact existed. Others maintained that the relics and legends attributed to the Preservers were actually the work of a dozen different races over a broad range of time, blended only by the passage of eons. Still others believed that the ancient race, whether one species or many, was little more than a myth, similar to a hundred others common to almost all sentient, spacefaring species—the much-desired promise that somewhere in the void the answers to all questions were waiting to be found, if only the seekers were worthy.

It was a powerful belief, the fuel of uncounted religions and space-exploration programs. Privately, Picard was of the mind that it was far better to discover things than to be given them. But the secrets the Preservers represented were so profound that he sometimes doubted there would be much difference between discovery and revelation in their case, should they actually be fact and not fiction.

Among humans, what would eventually become the Preserver legend had begun at the same time as the exploration of space, reflecting more a change in the way of thinking about humanity's place in the universe than any response to the discovery of evidence of extraterrestrial visitation of Earth. But as humanity ventured to other planets and met other spacefarers, tantalizing fragments of evidence did accumulate. It was clear that life was everywhere. It was clear that just as there were cultures on the brink of space travel, and cultures that had traveled among the stars for centuries, there were also advanced cultures that had arisen thousands, if not millions, if not billions, of years earlier. The ruins of their cities and accomplishments could be found throughout the galaxy. Picard had seen his share of them, including those of the Tkon and the Iconians.

But which among these ancient civilizations had given birth to the Preservers was still unknown. The most recent and probable sign of their hand had been discovered on an Earth-like planet to which a group of humans from the North American plains civilization had been transported almost six hundred years earlier. The largest known artifact attributed to the Preservers, a powerful graviton-beam generator contained in a metal obelisk also marked with inscriptions, had been discovered there, and was still being studied, as it had no apparent source of power.

In the decades since that artifact's discovery, other examples of the mysterious writing on it had been uncovered at archaeological sites throughout the galaxy, including the inscriptions on a handful of metallic shards dating back more than a billion years. With that discovery, still controversial, made by Professor Richard Galen, arguably the greatest living archaeologist of the day, excitement had spread through the Federation. It was unheard of that any culture had survived with its written language unchanged for more than a few millennia at best. Yet Galen insisted that the similarities between the inscriptions on his shards and the so-called Preserver obelisk proved that an astoundingly stable culture, dedicated to the preservation of life, still existed today, unseen.

Galen's critics, citing Hodgkins's much-maligned Law of Parallel Planet Development, pointed out that given the enormous number of civilizations that had arisen in the galaxy, it was statistically inevitable that some forms of writing had been developed that were similar, and saw Galen's claims of a single, founding culture only as an inescapable coincidence.

In response, Picard had read, Professor Galen had since gone on to a more scientific mode of exploration, analyzing the similarities of the DNA structure among many of the galaxy's sentient life-forms, searching for other, more irrefutable signs of a Preserver-like race. But there were others in the Federation who pressed ahead to extend Galen's early work at an archaeological level, searching for physical evidence of a culture that might have seeded the galaxy with life at the beginning of time, preserved it from destruction in the ages that followed, and somewhere unknown kept watch even now, for reasons unfathomable but endlessly compelling.

In the instant he had recognized the inscriptions, Picard understood that the object in the Borg artifact might be that one telling piece of evidence which had been sought on thousands of worlds. No mere handful of shards, but an actual, functioning device, richly detailed with Preserver-style writing, perhaps holding the key to understanding the origin of life.

And its ultimate purpose.

Picard had good reason to feel magically isolated while his world spun around him. Within his grasp could be the absolute answer to the ultimate question of existence.

And why else was there a Starfleet but to discover exactly that?

"I will make the following arrangements," Picard said to Commander Tarl. He hoped that in the past few minutes he had recovered enough from the staggering discovery within the Borg artifact that his voice sounded normal and unremarkable. So far, at least, Tarl and the others of her crew seemed to suspect nothing. He continued reading the points he had entered on the small padd Riker had given him. La Forge, Worf, and Data remained by the Borg artifact, running a structural load analysis to devise a method to take it to the *Enterprise.*

"To begin: Immediate transport, under cover, for yourself and your crew to Starbase 718," Picard said.

Riker added, "I've already requested four high-speed transports to rendezvous with us back at Legara IV, for your journey."

Tarl regarded the captain and his first officer without expression, arms crossed.

"At Starbase 718," Picard continued, "you will be provided with a Nautilus-class colony ship, fully equipped for the auto-

226

mated construction of a self-sustaining, class-M-world, farming and mining community, with a range of two thousand light-years at warp six before refueling. That should take you far beyond the Federation's boundaries, and the Empire's."

Tarl stared at the deckplates. "Farmers and miners." She shook her head as if she could imagine nothing worse.

"Other options are available," Picard reminded her. "But they would require you to remain within the Federation. In time, should the Empire discover what you have done, we might be asked to extradite you for charges of piracy and . . . treason."

Tarl unfolded her arms. "The Empire already knows what I have done, Captain. Your assistance is . . . acceptable." She didn't sound convinced, but Picard knew she had no other choice.

"Your assistance is most appreciated," Picard replied. "And when the time comes, I shall personally see to it that you receive the honor that is due you."

Tarl looked as if she hadn't understood a single word. "When what time comes?"

"When the Federation enjoys the same relationship with the Romulan Empire as it does today with the Klingon Empire."

Tarl reacted with amazement. "You actually believe that will come to pass?"

"Of course," Picard said. "It is inevitable."

Tarl stepped closer to Picard, making him look up at her. "The Federation will *never* conquer my people."

Very calmly, Picard replied, "The Federation does not conquer, Commander. It invites. There is a considerable difference. And someday, when your rulers are convinced that the Federation's ideals are their own, shared by thousands of worlds and cultures, they will *ask* to join and the invitation will be extended to them as it has been extended to so many others for more than two hundred years."

Tarl stared down at Picard for long moments. Then she said, "You humans truly are the most arrogant life-form the galaxy has ever seen."

"Humans are not the only species in the Federation, Commander. Therefore, your argument is not logical."

"Logical," Tarl sneered. "The corrupt Vulcan influence is everywhere." She then strode away, her boot heels clicking loudly on the deckplates.

"'Not logical'? I take it Ambassador Sarek is still with you," Riker said.

Picard sighed. "From time to time." He regarded Commander Tarl's diminishing form. "She doesn't seem happy, does she, even though we're giving her all that she's asked for. Even more."

"Who understands the Romulan mind?" Riker said. "I know she thinks she's actually helping the Empire by turning over the Borg artifact to us, but still, for a Romulan to *not* think that her system and science and technology are the best . . ." Riker shrugged. "But she *is* doing the right thing."

"You mean," Picard said, "according to *us*. In our . . . 'arrogant' viewpoint."

Riker eyed his captain with interest. There was little the two men could hide from each other. "Are you having second thoughts about this transaction?"

For the first time, Picard wondered if he was. Or was it just an echo of Sarek's long-held doubts about the Romulans that was affecting him?

"You don't suppose it's gone too easily, do you?" Picard asked.

"You mean: Are we being set up?"

Picard nodded.

Riker laughed. "Now you sound like you're recovering from a mind-meld with *Worf.*" Riker saw that Picard was not returning his laughter and he responded to the question seriously. "If it *is* a setup, you have to admit it's fantastically elaborate."

"It all depends on what the purpose of the setup is," Picard said.

"Any theories?" Riker asked.

Picard had been asking himself the same question. "Perhaps their intention is to mislead us about the nature of the Borg. Therefore, they have given us this artifact to study, to base our defenses on, only for us to discover in battle that it's not true Borg technology at all and that all our efforts have been wasted."

Riker shook his head. "Our defeat under those conditions would leave the Romulans facing a Borg Collective which had assimilated all the technology and firepower of the Federation. I doubt even they could be so shortsighted."

That had been Picard's only plausible theory and he was glad that Riker had pointed out its obvious flaw. He supposed there was a possibility that the Borg artifact contained a bomb of some sort. But any explosive device powerful enough to damage the *Enterprise* would have been easily detected by the away team. And if the Romulans were that intent on destroying a Federation starship, then there were other, more direct and efficient ways to go about it.

"Do you suppose they know about the Preserver object within the artifact?" Picard asked.

"It's apparent that Commander Tarl doesn't. No matter what she thinks about the Empire's scientific capabilities, she would have to be a fool to give away something with a power source that's still functioning after three and a half billion years. I can only think of a few devices like that that have ever been discovered, and so far they've given up none of their secrets."

Picard agreed. The Preserver object about to come into his possession was on the order of the Guardian of Forever in terms of age. And that device had defied all attempts to understand it over the century it had been studied.

"So the only question remaining," Picard said, "is how to get the artifact aboard the *Enterprise.*"

"Geordi is mapping out the tractor-beam support points in its structure," Riker said. "At close range, we could probably handle it with our cargo transporters, but Geordi and Data are both concerned about whether or not the artifact's power supply will remain functioning after transport."

Picard understood. There was an entire class of molecules, substances, and devices that could not be transported without having their structure subtly altered. Until his engineer knew exactly what was powering the device, it made good sense to treat it cautiously.

"Then if Mr. La Forge is considering towing the artifact to our shuttlebay," Picard said, keeping caution in mind, "I'd recommend using two tractor beams from two shuttlecraft, just so we have the extra factor of safety."

"I'm sure Geordi is already planning on that," Riker said. "But there is one other problem we have to address. Commander Tarl has a 'skeleton' crew of three hundred and twelve personnel on board. She's insisting on turning over this vessel to DaiMon Pol as soon as the artifact is off-loaded, so we'll have to make arrangements for taking all those Romulans back to Legara IV."

"For one day we have ample room for that many passengers. I'm sure Mr. Worf can handle the security arrangements. Anything else?"

Riker looked serious. "Only that we not send word of the Preserver object to Starfleet until after we're back in friendly waters. Once word gets out about this, I have a feeling a lot of people are going to come looking for it."

"If," Picard emphasized, "it is what we think it is."

Riker angled his head questioningly. "Is that Ambassador Sarek speaking again?"

"Only Jean-Luc Picard," the captain replied with a shake of his head. "With so much at stake, I prefer to take the conservative approach."

Though his excursion to the Romulan ship had been exhilarating, and a welcome change, Picard had no doubt that his proper place was on the bridge of the *Enterprise*. He sat in his command chair, perfectly at ease, as the great ship pulsed with its own inner life around him. He was glad to be part of it. He felt at home. Here he could deal with any problem the universe presented him, and that included 312 Romulans and what might be the greatest archaeological find of human history.

La Forge's voice came over the bridge communications system. "Captain Picard, the *Gould* and the *Cochrane* have established tractor-beam linkup with the artifact. We're ready to bring it aboard."

"On visual," Picard requested. At his Ops station beside Ensign McKnight, Data changed the main screen image. Instead of the two Warbirds, Picard now viewed the interior of Tarl's hangar deck as seen from the optical sensor Mr. La Forge carried with him there. The presence of two of the *Enterprise*'s sleek, type-7 shuttlecraft, hovering among the predatory designs of the

Romulan Warbird's parked fighters and shuttles, was incongruous to say the least. But perhaps it was a harbinger of things to come. There would be peace between the Federation and the Romulans one day, Picard was certain. Perhaps this exchange would someday be seen as its starting point.

"Picard to main shuttlebay," the captain said. "Are you prepared to receive the artifact?"

Riker acknowledged.

"We're standing by, Mr. La Forge," Picard confirmed. "Proceed when ready."

On the viewscreen, the two Federation shuttlecraft began to lift even higher off the hangar deck, and the angle of the sensor changed so that Picard could see the Borg artifact, now clear of scaffolding and lights, begin to rise, bathed in the shimmering blue glow of twin tractor beams.

"We are registering no stress on the artifact," La Forge reported. "Taking it out."

The *Gould* and the *Cochrane* and the Borg artifact began to move slowly forward, until they escaped the Warbird's bright interior lights and were framed by the wide hangar doors.

"Switch to external viewers," Picard said.

The viewscreen image changed again. Gracefully, the two shuttlecraft emerged from the hollow void between the Warbird's dorsal and ventral planes. The artifact, four to five times the size of each shuttle, trailed easily fifty meters behind them.

"We're clear, Captain," La Forge announced. "I'm beaming back to our main shuttlebay."

"Well done, Mr. La Forge," Picard said.

"Registering no change in the artifact's power load," Data said.

"After all that artifact has been through," Picard observed, "I'd be surprised if it reacted at all to this gentle ride."

"Captain—La Forge here. I'm back on the *Enterprise.* Shuttlecraft pilots advise two minutes to landing."

Picard felt pleased with himself. Everything was proceeding perfectly, exactly as planned. Sometimes he suspected the *Enterprise* actually ran herself.

"Mr. Data," he said, "once the artifact is stowed, begin the transportation of Commander Tarl's crew to Shuttlebays Two and

Three." Dr. Crusher had set up the standard refugee-processing centers in those bays. Picard was almost certain the treatment the Romulan crew would receive there would be better than they received in their own quarters on Tarl's Warbird.

Data acknowledged the order, then added. "Captain, I am picking up an increased neutrino flux."

Picard leaned forward. "Is it coming from the artifact?"

"Negative, sir. It seems to be emanating from the Ferengi Warbird. The signature is as if the ship were decloaking. But since it already is decloaked, I am at a loss to explain the reading."

Picard sat back. "Perhaps the Ferengi have found something else to break on their new ship. Mr. Worf, hail DaiMon Pol."

"Coming onscreen, Captain."

Picard forced himself to smile as the image of the Ferengi-run, Romulan bridge appeared on the main viewer. "DaiMon Pol," he began, about to inquire if there was any assistance the *Enterprise* could once again supply.

But DaiMon Pol was not in the command chair. Instead, Picard saw two Ferengi rush past behind it. He heard Romulan warning sirens, Ferengi shouts of alarm.

"DaiMon Pol!" Picard said, getting to his feet. "What is the status of your ship? Mr. Data: Full scan of the *62nd Rule.*"

Then DaiMon Pol lurched into the range of the viewscreen. *"They've cheated us!"* he squealed, high-pitched, full of anger. "None of it works! They've—"

In a burst of static, DaiMon Pol and the Romulan bridge disappeared from the screen, to be replaced by a forward view in which Commander Tarl's vessel still maintained position on the right, but where DaiMon Pol's vessel had been to the left was nothing more than a rapidly expanding ball of plasma, studded with spinning hullplates.

"Data . . ." Picard said in alarm. "What happened? Did they self-destruct somehow . . . ?"

But before Data could reply, Picard saw the answer to his question for himself.

A *third* Warbird flew through the cloud of destruction that had been the *62nd Rule.*

All phasers blazing, it flew for the *Enterprise.*

232

Part Two

METAMORPHOSIS

THORSEN

Some of them had been doctors once.

But the Optimum had closed the universities. The Optimum had believed in the survival of the fittest, and medical care was considered a luxury. To the Optimum, those who were too old, unhealthy, incomplete, were little different from those of the wrong color, the wrong religion, the wrong political beliefs. Doctors were unnecessary because those who were nonoptimal would be cleansed from the Earth by the raging fire of change, of purification, of rebirth.

But the fire had come to Adrik Thorsen first.

In the long weeks of his recovery, he remembered little of how that last night in Battersea had ended. He remembered Cochrane, of course. He remembered how the scientist had mocked him, had lied to him, had dared to touch him.

He remembered how the scientist had raised his laser, rejecting Thorsen, rejecting the future.

Cochrane's light had cut across Thorsen's face, seared his eye, so that in all the years ever after, whenever he was in darkness, the scintillation of that laser still echoed in what remained of his optic nerve. A flickering shadow, a shimmering souvenir of his first and

235

only meeting with the one man who could have guaranteed a new life for the Earth. The one man who, through his refusal of the Optimum, had brought about all that had followed in the vacuum of the Optimum's collapse.

Thorsen had crawled along the turf of Battersea, the laser afterimage burning in his eye, his brain. He had screamed Cochrane's name as he had crawled, tasting blood, feeling pain, seeking darkness and coolness and relief.

He had crawled onto concrete, down rough stairs, to a place where cameras had once been installed, when the Battersea Stadium had meant something.

Then the night had caught fire and he remembered nothing else until they woke him up to scrub the dead skin from his body with wire bristles that found each nerve on his shiny new skin.

Eventually, the worst of the pain faded, except for the light that would shine forever in his missing eye, and the ache that would haunt his arms and legs.

Although those who had been doctors explained that he had no arms and legs.

Adrik Thorsen had been cleansed by fire.

And been left incomplete.

Nonoptimal.

As he lay helpless in his sterile bed, what had happened to Thorsen happened also to his dreams of salvation.

The mistakes of Khan had been avoided. But new mistakes had been made. The Optimum collapsed. Pilloried by those who had no vision.

From his sterile bed, Adrik Thorsen called for doctors to make him whole, so he could escape with the others of the cadre. Go into hiding. Learn from their mistakes and try again.

But those who answered his call were no longer doctors. He had helped see to that. They were interface experts now. And Adrik Thorsen learned firsthand what happened to human nervous tissue when Josephson probes were inserted into the brain.

When they were through with him, Thorsen was whole, after a fashion. He could walk, he could pick up and manipulate objects, after a fashion. But his new limbs ran on batteries, and every nerve

236

impulse intended to cause movement also triggered intense pain through the crude interface of the Josephson probes.

Nonoptimal.

In return for information about those in the cadre who had abandoned him, certain fanatics eager to replace him gave Thorsen passage from the Earth, forcing him to become what he despised most—someone who deserted the homeworld.

The night he left, another fire ignited round the globe, and when the ashes fell and Earth's sun shone through the smoke again, and the postatomic horror had exhausted itself and the planet, thirty-seven million corpses shamed those who had survived.

The inevitable cry went out: This must not happen again.

And this time, on the colony worlds, that cry was finally heard.

Something changed in humanity with that last war, because for the first time it was clear even to the masses that no human conflict, even one that could consume a world, could ever be allowed to overshadow or assume more importance than the human race itself.

There was a universe waiting, and with the infinite possibilities it offered, there came a generation that had no time or need for bigotry, intolerance, and greed.

Even as enemy soldiers turned to one another to share water on the battlefield once the guns had fallen silent, humanity finally abandoned the old ways and learned the new.

But Adrik Thorsen was not of that generation. He would always be a creature of Earth's past, and in time he fled even the system of his birth, to hide on distant colonies, using his artificial nerve pathways to control machinery and spaceships, finding safety in the oblivion of mindless work.

And during all his struggles to survive, he seethed with the knowledge that each ship he rode was powered by the genius of Zefram Cochrane.

He still woke at night screaming Cochrane's name.

The laser beam still burned hellishly in what was left of his optic nerve.

The same energy that had fueled the Optimum now fueled Thorsen and his obsession.

JUDITH AND GARFIELD REEVES-STEVENS

Hatred.

He dreamed of revenge. He dreamed of forcing Cochrane to build a warp bomb so powerful whole systems would fall before it. Before him. He knew it could be done. He wore out pens in his mechanical fingers and wrote out the figures and diagrams on endless sheets of paper, on endless display screens, on walls, on sheets, on whatever surface he could find.

In time, other geniuses created machines into which he could plug his stumps with their artificial pathways to see his work appear on screens as fast as he could think.

His dreams came alive then, no longer bound by nonoptimal flesh. He only feared that he would die before he had a chance to complete his work. To make Cochrane finally do what he should have done so many years ago. To bow down and submit to his master.

But the universe held many possibilities.

And one of them was an alien race called the Grigari.

Thorsen saw in them his future.

He was eighty years old now, but flesh itself, he had come to realize, was nonoptimal.

And the Grigari did not deal in flesh.

Thorsen paid their price and he was renewed.

From his exile, he journeyed to Alpha Centauri.

He set in motion his challenge to Zefram Cochrane—one that would take from the scientist everything he had held dear, just as Cochrane had taken from him.

His plan was perfect. Cochrane would suffer. And then, because he would be left with no other choice, the scientist would at last be forced to give Thorsen the secret. The warp bomb.

It did not matter that Thorsen no longer had the armies to use that secret. It only mattered that Thorsen win.

It would be him against Zefram Cochrane, just as it was meant to be, as if they had met on Titan as history had demanded.

The challenge began. Cochrane's wife died at Thorsen's hand. Cochrane's students were consumed by fire.

But then Cochrane the scientist did the unthinkable—what Thorsen the warrior had never considered.

238

FEDERATION

Cochrane ran.

Thorsen was stunned. Cochrane was supposed to be a genius. A genius would have known. There was no escape from the Optimum.

Thorsen had not escaped it.

And neither would Zefram Cochrane.

ONE

BONAVENTURE II
OUTWARD BOUND
Earth Standard: ≈ April 2117

It was over, and Cochrane was glad of it.

Alpha Centauri was light-years behind him. Stapledon Center, where he was expected in the next month, light-years farther still. And his past life, farthest away of all.

His small ship hummed along at time-warp factor four. In his first voyages, half a century ago, he had had to drop back to normal space every few days, in order to check his bearings. But now the continuum-distortion fields were so tightly focused that he could see the stars slip past the viewports, and a navigation computer could constantly adjust his course.

Which was good, because he had no intention of ever again leaving the continuum he had discovered. He would die here, for no other reason than that he had nothing more to do except bring pain to others.

The ship, a personal yacht with one hundred square meters of living space, luxurious by the standards of the day, was filled with music, a symphony by Brahms. For years he had been haunted by the melody he had heard that first night back at Christopher's Landing. At the time he had thought that it had sounded like Brahms. But he had never been able to find it again, in any collection of recordings. Almost as if Brahms had dropped into the twenty-first century and written one final piece.

But even this music was just background noise now. He had given up his search. He had given up everything.

His Monica lay in the soil of Centauri B II. His staff and students were at risk. Colonel Adrik Thorsen had returned from the dead. And all because of him. Cochrane no longer felt like fighting. Science and the thrill of discovery had been his life and they had brought him nothing.

Fame, yes. There were planets named after him.

Fortune, as much as he wanted, though when actually given the choice, he had realized he wanted very little.

Admiration. An unconscionable amount.

The ears of the powerful, the beds of the beautiful, the eyes of the media on a hundred worlds.

Zefram Cochrane knew that by anyone's measure, he had been given everything.

But he had nothing.

And he didn't know why.

What he did know was that the action he took now wasn't killing himself. He was simply returning to his natural state.

One of nothing.

He welcomed oblivion.

To be free of the selfish loneliness left by Monica's death, of the unreasoning implacability of Thorsen's hate, of all the useless regret and self-doubt that had plagued him all his life.

He watched the stars slipping past him. But it wasn't the stars that drew him now. It was the void between them.

Perhaps this was why he had invented the superimpellor. Not to take humanity to other worlds, but so that he could cast himself into nothingness.

After an unchanging week of travel, sitting passively in his pilot's web, venturing out only to use the head, Cochrane believed he was beginning to think less often of his past. He found the tedium blessedly healing. Numbing.

The stars slipped by. Forever.

The same music recordings played for the twentieth cycle. The fiftieth cycle.

He didn't move. His beard grew shaggy. His fingernails ragged.

He wondered idly how long it would take for his body to just stop.

He could open the airlock, he knew. At his age, in ten seconds it would be over.

He could jump out the airlock and be the first human to experience continuum-distortion propulsion without benefit of a spaceship. For about one nanosecond.

He could plot a course to a star and be drawn into its endless gravity well, or drop to impulse and drive into it at half the speed of light, creating a nova that all the human worlds would see.

But all those deaths required willful action. And he who had never believed that life would run out of challenges to inspire him, was spent, without the will even to die.

It seemed to Zefram Cochrane that he had faced life's challenges, but life had won.

He was old, he was sick, he was ready to die.

And life's final challenge to him was that it would not let him go.

Five weeks passed.

He knew they would be searching for him now. But the knowledge meant nothing to him. Not only had he succeeded in blanking his mind to his past, he was beginning to hallucinate, to create new images for his future.

In spite of himself, he found this development wildly funny. Deprived of stimuli, the brain created its own diversions.

He wondered when his fantastic mirages would begin talking to him.

They began at the end of the fifth week.

He awoke, distraught that he still lived, his body clamoring for sustenance, stinging from the sores on his skin where restraining straps kept him from floating in the cabin. His mouth was parched. His lips cracked and dry. A squeeze bottle of water was hooked to his chair, but he merely watched it swing back and forth on its tether, the water thick weightless globs within it.

The aurora was back.

He had seen it before. Three times now. Maybe four.

Gold-flecked and shimmering, it would rush up beside his ship, swirl around it, then rush away.

The first time he had seen it, it had reminded him strongly of dolphins following the wake of a ship, playing and splashing in the free ride.

The second time he had seen it, he had wondered how a phenomenon like it could travel at faster-than-light velocities.

The third and fourth times, he had decided it was a hallucination like all the others.

Except he liked this one.

It was pretty.

Now, instead of swirling all around his ship, the glowing cloud hung on the viewports, obscuring the streaking stars beyond. Its shifting, shining patterns pressed against the transparent aluminum panels, and through some trick of the lighting or his failing eyesight, Cochrane was almost convinced that he saw tendrils of the thing push through the window to reach inside the cabin.

He tried to speak. To say, Careful there, you'll make a breeze if you open the window. But he had not spoken for many weeks and no sound came from him.

Yet the tendril withdrew. Or it seemed to, at least. And the cloud remained against the viewport, as if it were looking in. As if it wanted something.

Wanted something.

Cochrane squinted, trying to see it more clearly. The absurd question expanded in his mind. What could an energy cloud capable of traveling faster than light want?

His thoughts seemed to clear as he focused on the cloud. It was interesting to have a problem again.

After an hour or so, he figured it out.

He forced his stiff fingers to reach out and grab the floating water bottle, then close around it. *You're thirsty, aren't you?* he asked, though he couldn't speak the words, only think them.

He was fairly certain the answer had been, Yes.

He studied the problem even longer. Then he pulled out the straw and slipped it between his raw lips. He drank for the first time in days.

How's that? he asked, still without words.

The answer seemed to be that drinking water had been exactly the right thing to do.

But the cloud didn't leave.

Cochrane almost smiled. *You want more, do you?*

Shimmering reflections danced in the viewports, answering again.

Okay, Cochrane said in his mind. *Okay, I get you.*

He fumbled with the seat webs until he floated free and pushed himself back to the food dispenser. He hung there, exhausted, until he could ask another wordless question. *Soup?* he asked, and soup it was.

Then he set up the shower tube and washed himself.

His scalp felt strange when he used the shampoo. As if there were hair growing on the top of his head again. In his dreams.

He dried off, rubbed ointment on his strap sores, put on a fresh jumpsuit, then strapped himself loosely to his seat and slept.

When he awoke, he was disappointed to discover that the cloud wasn't at the window anymore. It had been an interesting game he had played with the hallucination.

Then Cochrane realized the stars were no longer streaking by. They were still. He was traveling at sublight. But the impulse engines were switched off. He had disabled them himself.

He peered through the viewports. A string of glowing dots were laid out before him. Planetoids, he guessed. Too many of them to be planets. Too big to be asteroids.

He found himself hoping he wouldn't crash into one of the planetoids, for then the cloud would come looking for him and wouldn't be able to find him. He wondered if not finding him would upset the cloud, if it would miss him. He didn't like that thought.

But that was exactly what was going to happen, he realized about an hour later, when he saw a planetoid looming before him.

Sorry, he said to the cloud wherever it was. *I won't be here to feed and water you.*

The window sparkled at him.

Cochrane released his straps, and his fingers moved so quickly and so easily that he looked down at them in surprise.

There were no age spots on the back of his hands. His fingers weren't gaunt as they had been. They were strong, well fleshed. But he couldn't stop to think about that now. He pushed himself to the window. He put his hand to it.

From the other side, a tendril of the glowing cloud pushed through and wrapped gently around his fingers.

Cochrane had spent forty days alone in space preparing to die. The sensation of the cloud's touch felt like the most natural thing of all.

He wiggled his hand inside the cloud, as if he were scratching the ear of a dog. *You don't like it up here, do you?* he said. *You want to find a home.*

Cochrane knew he had figured it out. *Poor thing,* he said. *How about that planetoid right down there?*

The cloud let him know that was a magnificent idea.

He went through a list of questions for the cloud, finding out all the things it would need to be content on the planetoid—the right kind of shelter, the temperature range, the force of gravity, food and water.

Amazingly, what the cloud needed was exactly what was conducive to human health and growth. And it could all be found on the planetoid beneath them.

Cochrane landed his ship without touching the controls or using the engines. After forty days in space, why not?

He stepped outside and breathed the air. It tasted just as he remembered the air had been on Centauri B II. He was also surprised by how deeply he could inhale without coughing. He was surprised by how his legs didn't ache. How he felt he could run right around the planetoid if he wanted to. It was almost as if he were young again. If only that could be true.

The cloud, he decided, was fortunate to have found such a perfect place for itself.

The cloud, right beside him, agreed. He liked the way it swept around him, carefully, tentatively, not enveloping him all at once.

Poor thing, Cochrane said. *All alone down here. You need a friend, don't you?*

The cloud needed a friend.

Do you want me to take care of you? Cochrane asked.

The cloud thought that would be fine.

Well, I don't seem to have anything on my agenda, Cochrane said. *Why don't you let me stay here and help you?*

The cloud thought it over for about half a second. The cloud thought it was the best idea ever in the history of the universe.

Cochrane spent the next few weeks using the supplies from his ship to build a shelter for the cloud, plant some seeds, and make things right. During that time, as he threw off the mental lethargy of the past forty days, he figured out what the cloud had done. It was more than just a dolphin or a lonely dog looking for company. It had been quite shrewd. Its agenda had included him.

At another time in his life, Cochrane might have resented the manipulation. But that life was over. He had left so much that was old and unnecessary behind.

The planetoid seemed like an interesting place. The cloud was an interesting companion. And it felt good to have someone—or something—to care for. It was as if he had never felt that way before.

Because for all that the cloud took care of him, Cochrane had no illusions about what he was doing when the cloud embraced him.

He was taking care of the cloud, as well.

It seemed a fair bargain.

He decided his life might have room for one more challenge. Once again, Zefram Cochrane realized he was looking forward to finding out what would happen next.

TWO

U.S.S. ENTERPRISE NCC-1701
RENDEZVOUS WITH THE CITY OF UTOPIA PLANITIA
Stardate 3854.8
Earth Standard: ≈ November 2267

On the main viewer, the Klingon's dark face was distorted by his forced smile. It twisted his stringy beard into an unnatural angle.

"Greetings, Captain Kirk of the *U.S.S. Enterprise.*"

"Save it," Kirk shot back. "Drop your shields and let us beam in the poor bastard you blew out the airlock."

The Klingon widened his eyes insincerely. "Ah, you noticed that, did you?"

"Drop your shields now!"

"And put myself at your fabled terran 'mercy'? Come now, Captain. I may be Klingon, but that doesn't make me stupid. We have other matters to discuss."

Kirk stood up from his chair. As far as he was concerned, there was only one thing Klingons understood, and the *Enterprise* was the ship to deliver it. "Drop your shields *now! Then* we can discuss anything you want."

The Klingon turned to the side and spat out some commands in his own guttural language.

"Keptin, their shields are weakening by the open airlock."

The Klingon smiled broadly. "You have five seconds, Captain Kirk. Any treachery will result in the deaths of even more of—"

"Spock! Now!" Kirk shouted.

Over the bridge speakers, Spock acknowledged from the transporter room. "Transporter locked, and energizing."

Chekov confirmed that the body had vanished from the side of the liner. A moment later Spock announced recovery and called for a medical team.

"Shields restored," Chekov said.

"Spock here. The recovered human is dead, Captain. From his uniform, he was one of the crew members of the *Planitia.*"

Kirk was enraged. "You killed him!"

But the Klingon on the screen shook his head. "Not I, Captain Kirk. *Au contraire,* it was *your* unfortunate and unprovoked attack which caused such . . . unpleasantness."

"Your hijacked liner is no match for this ship," Kirk said.

"But my hostages are more than a match for your conscience, Captain Kirk." The Klingon settled back into his own command chair, an ornate, high-backed style popular on human civilian ships. "Now, I believe you said that once I dropped my shields to allow recovery of the body of the man you killed, we could talk. And I would like to talk, Captain Kirk. About so many things."

Kirk had never run across a Klingon who liked to talk. "Shut him down, Uhura." The screen jumped back to a view of the liner.

"Aren't you going to negotiate with him?" The question came from Admiral Kabreigny. McCoy had positioned her at an unused navigation station on the upper level. Her color was better and she appeared to have recovered her composure. Just in case, McCoy hovered close by, a medical kit at his side. At Spock's science station, the Companion sat hunched over, silent and still, face in her hands, breathing almost back to normal. The two security officers remained at ease by the turbolift doors.

"Klingons don't negotiate," Kirk said. "He's just stalling for time."

"Why?" Kabreigny asked. The bridge crew braced themselves for a repeat of the earlier clash of wills.

But Kirk found it easier to answer, now that the command chair was his again. "He'd never make it back to the Empire in that liner. He must be heading for a rendezvous point."

"No Klingon ship could get this far into Federation territory to meet him."

Kirk tapped his fingers against the arm of his chair, working out his options. "Admiral, he doesn't need to rendezvous with a Klingon ship. The ship that attacked us was an Orion. It was fast enough to get him back home in a month and not even the *Enterprise* could have caught him."

McCoy leaned forward on the rail circling the upper level. "Do you think that ship we destroyed *was* his ride home?"

"Possibly," Kirk said. "But he's bound to have a backup plan. The question is, when does it go into effect?" He turned his chair around to face the Companion. "Companion, is the man near?"

She sighed and spoke into her hands. "The man continues." She looked up. Her one, unbandaged eye was full of pain. "Part of us wishes to tell you he is in the ship before us."

"Can you tell us where in the ship he is?" Kirk asked.

But the Companion shook her head. "We cannot," she said sadly. "We only know that he is near."

Kirk stared at the liner on the screen. A clock was ticking. He had no idea what schedule it was on, but sooner or later another ship would be arriving to rendezvous with the *Planitia.* Cochrane had been kidnapped by Orions, but then brought to a hijacked liner under the command of a Klingon. Kirk wouldn't put it past the Orions to work with the Klingons—they specialized in playing both ends against the middle in any conflict. But what did the Klingon Empire want with Zefram Cochrane? Their level of warp technology was at least the equal of the Federation's. Cochrane would be a century and a half behind the times in the Empire, as well.

Then there was the matter of Admiral Kabreigny's conspiracy. What or who it involved, Kirk didn't know. Only that Kabreigny still thought that he might be part of it, just as Kirk was still worried that she was a part of another conspiracy. He bounced his fist on the arm of his chair. The only connection to all of this was Cochrane. Whatever else was going to happen, Zefram Cochrane had to come first.

But how could Kirk save one person from a ship filled with hostages and a bloodthirsty Klingon who wouldn't balk at killing everyone? Kirk didn't need Spock to tell him that the answer was that it couldn't be done. Which meant, Kirk knew, he had to find another approach, he had to come up with a different question. One that did have an answer.

Change the rules. Do the unthinkable.

The question came to him. The answer was outrageous. As outrageous as a commercial liner armed only with navigational phasers being able to keep a Constitution-class starship at bay.

"Admiral Kabreigny," Kirk said as pleasantly as he could as he stepped down from his chair, "do you feel up to negotiating with a Klingon?"

Kabreigny eyed him warily. "I thought you said Klingons don't negotiate."

"They don't," Kirk agreed. "But then, you won't be negotiating either. You'll just be buying time."

"For what?"

"So I can follow my orders and rescue Mr. Cochrane." Kirk looked over at Uhura. "Lieutenant, cancel Red Alert. All hands stand down."

McCoy put his hands behind his back. "This is going to be good, isn't it?"

Kirk shrugged. Spectacular was a better word. Good or bad, win or lose, what he was planning was definitely going to be spectacular.

"Admiral, I'd like you to take the chair again. I'd like you to identify yourself to the Klingon and tell him that you have relieved me of duty because . . . I wanted to blow the liner out of space." He guided the perplexed admiral to the chair. "Play it straight with him. You want to get those hostages back. But don't let on in any way that you know about Cochrane. Give him that edge. It will make him feel in control."

Kabreigny settled back in the command chair. "And what will you be doing during all this?"

"I'll be in the Auxiliary Control Center." He turned to the command console. "Mr. Chekov, Mr. Sulu, report to me there as soon as your replacements arrive."

The helmsman and navigator acknowledged their orders.

"Dr. McCoy, Companion, please accompany me." Then Kirk

ducked down to Uhura and whispered. "Lieutenant, monitor every word the admiral and the Klingon say. If you detect any hint of a code, or if the admiral says anything that could endanger the ship, close the channel and contact me at once."

Uhura nodded. "Aye-aye, Captain."

Kirk ushered the Companion and McCoy onto the turbolift. "Admiral Kabreigny, you have the conn."

The doors swept closed and the lift began to descend. McCoy studied Kirk closely. "*Now* can you tell me what you're planning?"

"Spock and Scott had better hear it, too," Kirk said. If he was going to have all of his senior officers think he was crazy, he wanted to get it over with at once.

Buried deep within the decks of the *Enterprise,* the Auxiliary Command Center was the ship's backup command facility. From it, all basic command functions could be controlled in the event the main bridge was damaged or lost. But in this case, the main bridge was serving as the backdrop of a diversion carried out for the Klingon commander of the hijacked liner. As the Klingon conducted his negotiations with Kabreigny, Kirk and his officers prepared behind the scenes for the moment they would take control of the situation.

Just over an hour after Kirk had left the bridge, he was minutes away from enacting his plan. Spock gave it a thirty-three percent chance of success, much higher than Mr. Scott allowed. McCoy thought it was just plain impossible. But Kirk knew his crew and his ship. He was confident, and that confidence was contagious.

At the smaller command console in the cramped control center, Sulu and Chekov ran one final simulation. They reported a twelve-percent casualty rate.

"Not acceptable," Kirk told them. But he knew there was no more time to rehearse. Whatever help the Klingon commander was obviously expecting could arrive at any moment. The *Planitia* was a soft target. There was no guarantee that what was coming to rendezvous with the liner would be as simple to overcome.

Kirk checked the readouts on the command console, scanning Mr. Scott's data from the engine room. The warp-eight-point-three chase had cracked one of the dilithium crystals in the matter-antimatter converters and engine efficiency had dropped dramatically. The chief engineer couldn't promise speed, but he did promise that all the power the captain's plan needed would be available on demand.

McCoy was standing by in the main transporter room. Ten other emergency medical teams were at their positions throughout the ship. Everything had been arranged by runners. Kirk had not permitted any of the detailed planning stages to be transmitted over the ship's intercom system. He presumed the Klingon's crew would be attempting to monitor the *Enterprise*'s internal communications. He didn't know if the liner had the capability for that, but they were close enough to each other that he didn't wish to take the chance.

Kirk checked behind him. The Companion sat quietly, focusing all of her attention on her heart's desire, less than a kilometer away through the void. "We'll get him back," he promised her. Then at Kirk's signal, Spock and the transporter chiefs confirmed their readiness by code.

Kirk took a breath, preparing himself. He knew he'd feel better if Spock had been able to verify that anything like this had been tried before. But the procedure books had nothing like it. As McCoy had dryly noted, it wasn't as if trying something new was unusual for this ship.

Kirk touched a communications control so he could listen in to the admiral's conversation with the Klingon.

". . . escort back to the Empire," she said, "but the *City of Utopia Planitia* is private property and must be returned to us at the border."

"Alas," the Klingon replied, "that cuts to the core of any possibility of friendship between our two peoples. By transporting known Orion pirates, this liner has been used in crimes against the Empire, and we must have it for justice to be served."

Kirk rolled his eyes. It was all nonsense and obfuscation. The Klingon was claiming some cover story about the *Planitia* having been used to smuggle Orion criminals convicted in the Klingon Empire to safety in the Federation. At least Kabreigny was playing along, and the Klingon did seem to be delighted to be negotiating with a fleet admiral. Kirk decided the Klingon thought he'd be able to kidnap her as well. He frowned and turned down the volume of the negotiations, reducing them to a background whisper.

"One minute, gentlemen," Kirk announced. The command chair in this facility was smaller and less comfortable than the one on the bridge, but it filled him with the same power.

"Science officer?" he asked. It was an innocuous request that would mean nothing to any unwanted listener.

"Spock here," Spock replied over the intercom. The simple announcement meant all transporter circuits were on-line— every single one of them.

"Engineer?"

"Scott here." The ship's power plant was ready for what would be demanded of it.

"Medical?"

"McCoy here. But I still say—"

"Thank you, Doctor," Kirk said, quickly cutting off McCoy's objections.

"Mr. Sulu," Kirk asked his navigator, "are you ready with the tractor beams?"

Sulu didn't take his eyes off the board. "Target sites located, Captain."

"Mr. Chekov?"

His hands were poised over his controls, ready for action. "Torpedoes armed. Phasers ready for cold start."

Kirk leaned forward to better see the image of the *Planitia* on the reduced-size viewscreen in front of the command console. The instant he put this in motion, the lives of everyone on board the liner *Planitia* would rest with the skill of the *Enterprise* crew. In fifty seconds, the operation would be successful, or more than one hundred innocent people would be dead. But Kirk would not accept that possibility, and neither would his crew. "Let's make this one for the history books," he said. "Mr. Spock, you may begin."

"Energizing," Spock replied from the transporter room. There

JUDITH AND GARFIELD REEVES-STEVENS

was no longer any need for communications security. One way or another, the Klingon would know what was happening within seconds.

On the screen, a hundred meters out from the forward tip of the *Planitia,* Kirk saw a tiny, twinkling dot of transporter energy just ahead of the liner's invisible shield boundary. A second later, the image disappeared in a flare of orange light as the transported photon torpedo detonated. Four seconds had passed.

With the liner's shields at full force, Kirk knew the explosion would not harm it, but those shields—intended to prevent impact with space debris—would be disrupted and thrown into timing disarray, which was all that Kirk required.

"Energizing," Spock said again. A moment later, a second transported torpedo detonated at the liner's stern. Kirk saw flickering arcs of energy ripple across the vessel's normally invisible shields as they tried to compensate for the power overload the torpedoes caused at opposite ends of the protective field. Eight seconds.

"Reading multiple airlock openings," Sulu announced tensely.

Kirk felt his fingernails dig into his palms. The Klingon was repeating himself, exactly as Kirk had gambled. If he had decided to shoot hostages at the first sign of Kirk's treachery, rather than eject them into space, the plan wouldn't have worked, even this far.

Kirk could hear the Klingon's harsh voice on the open channel. Kabreigny was silent, obviously as surprised as the Klingon was.

"Here they come," Sulu said. Ten seconds.

Kirk saw them—dark figures twisting in the vacuum. More hostages tossed out to their deaths. But Kirk would not allow that.

"Mr. Chekov—*now!*" Kirk ordered.

At precisely twelve seconds, a broad beam of cool blue phaser energy spread over the liner, completely encompassing this side of its shields, making the usually invisible forcefields glow in kind. Spread out to its widest beam width, the energy per square meter from the prolonged phaser burst would not be enough to harm anyone caught in it, but by hitting the liner's shields equally over half their area at once, after the disruption caused by the torpedoes exploding at opposite ends—

254

The blue glow winked out like a light being shut off.

"Shields down!" Chekov exclaimed. "Total failure!"

Fifteen seconds.

Kirk allowed himself half a second to breathe. If the shields hadn't failed, the hostages would have been lost. But they *had* failed, exactly as he had anticipated and Spock had confirmed. Now, according to the computer's analysis of the liner's backup systems, Kirk's team had fifteen seconds before the shields could be brought back on-line.

"Next phase," Kirk said. Then he did what was hardest for any commander—he waited.

At exactly seventeen seconds into the operation, multiple dots of transporter energy sparkled around the liner's airlocks as the hostages cast adrift were retrieved only ten seconds after being exposed to the vacuum of space. The *Enterprise* had four main operational transporter rooms, each capable of transporting six people at a time, two cycles per minute. In addition, there were five emergency personnel transporters, each capable of moving twenty-two people at a time, one cycle per minute in their safest, most redundant signal mode.

As long as sensors could find targets—and at a distance of only a few hundred meters that was assured—the *Enterprise* could beam aboard every living being on the liner within thirty seconds, well within the safety limits of vacuum exposure. According to sensor scans, those living things included eighty-three humans, four Klingons, six Orions, one Andorian, two dogs, five cats, and twelve small avians, which appeared to be part of a display in the liner's bar. The Klingons, Orions, and Andorian would be beamed to a single emergency transporter ringed by security officers with drawn phasers. Kirk wished he could be there to see their faces, especially the Klingon commander's. But he still had one important task before him.

After disabling the shields in order to start the process, success for the daring operation lay in making certain that the shields could not be reestablished, while at the same time insuring that the captors would not begin indiscriminately shooting their hostages when they realized the ones in space had been rescued.

So Kirk had come up with the ultimate distraction.

Now, at twenty-one seconds into the operation, he deployed it. As the transporter flares vanished around the liner, nine seconds before the liner's shields could come back on-line, narrow phaser beams shot out from the *Enterprise* under Chekov's expert aim. The beams were directed not at the shield generators, where hostages had been gathered to prevent such a direct attack, but at key superstructure support beams. In six seconds, the pattern the beams scorched into the hull took on the pattern of an orange being sectioned. But none of the beams penetrated the hull. They only weakened it so that no passenger would be harmed. Frightened, certainly, by the roar of coruscating energy blazing across the hull metal around them. But not harmed.

When the scorch pattern was complete, Kirk issued the last order. "Final phase, Mr. Sulu." They were twenty-seven seconds into the operation, two seconds from the liner's shields being raised. This was the point at which Spock had said the odds grew worse. Two seconds was not enough of a safety margin.

But it *was* a margin, Kirk had said.

Instantly, the phasers were replaced by tractor beams. Kirk imagined he could almost hear the *Planitia* creak and groan as the tractor beams took hold, applying carefully calculated stress to key areas. Suddenly, just as the liner's shields should have come on again, all running lights winked out at once. Interior lights followed and every window went dark. Only thirty seconds had passed since the first torpedo had detonated and Kirk was certain that even the most battle-hardened Klingon warriors on that ship would have better things to do than shoot hostages as the gravity shut off and the ship came apart around them.

The Klingon commander's futile background ranting cut out as communications failed. Spock's voice was clear and calm over the speakers. "Cargo transporters have locked on to the liner's antimatter supply. Wide-beam dispersion astern." Thirty-three seconds.

Kirk tapped his fist against his hand. So far, everything was working perfectly. There wouldn't even be an antimatter explosion from the failure of the liner's magnetic bottles.

The *City of Utopia Planitia* came apart like an eggshell. A sudden cloud of air and crystallizing moisture formed around her, swirling like fog. Sparks and flickerings from small explosions of internal gas mixtures and storage batteries lit up her inner decks as if a thunderstorm raged within her. She was like a computer graphic being torn apart, each deck exposed. Loose furniture, bedcoverings, luggage, cargo modules, constellations of glassware and gambling chips, all spun madly, glittering in the blue tractor beams.

"Spock here, Captain—transporter teams confirm positive lock on all personnel. We have retrieved everyone." Thirty-seven seconds exactly.

Kirk wanted to cheer for his crew but the mission wasn't a success yet. "Medical condition?"

McCoy's answer was harried. Kirk could picture him leaning over patients in the transporter room, treating them expertly as he frantically coordinated the other medical teams by the other transporters.

"No casualties so far. Some youngsters in bad shape. We've got a woman in premature labor . . . *no,* hold that clamp *there,* dammit!"

Kirk stood up. He looked at the Companion. "Is he here?" he asked. "Is the man here?"

A tear welled up in the Companion's uncovered eye. "He is with us," she said with joy. "Oh, Captain, the man is with us."

Kirk could breathe again. He hit the ship's public-address control. On the screen, the liner was no more than eight slowly rotating sections in a cloud of debris, torn apart gently without a single major explosion, without a single destructive use of phasers or torpedoes. And *no* casualties. He'd beaten the odds again. The *Enterprise* had beaten the odds again. Together, they'd won.

"This is the captain to all passengers of the *Planitia.* Will Mr. Cochrane please make himself known to security personnel."

Lieutenant Kyle reported a moment later from emergency transporter three. "Captain Kirk, sir. I have a gentleman here identifying himself as Mr. Cochrane. He looks like he could use medical attention."

"Escort him to sickbay, Mr. Kyle. Tell him . . . the Companion will meet him there."

Sulu called for the captain's attention from the command

console. "Sir, Admiral Kabreigny is demanding to know what just happened."

"Ask the admiral to meet me in sickbay," Kirk said.

"Captain Kirk?" The voice on the intercom was unsteady, but recognizable, and for the first time Kirk allowed himself the luxury of believing that the plan had worked perfectly.

He pressed the Send button on the arm of his chair even as the Companion rushed to Kirk's side. "Welcome aboard the *Enterprise,* Mr. Cochrane," Kirk said.

"Can you . . . can you tell me what's going on?" Cochrane asked. Over the speakers, Kirk could hear the confusion of Mr. Kyle's transporter room. Children were crying. Medical technicians were shouting at each other. To Kirk, the noise sounded like victory. They were all alive and safe.

"Well, sir," Kirk answered, "I was hoping you could tell *me.* It seems—"

The *Enterprise* shuddered as a barrage of explosions echoed through her. Kirk was driven back against his chair. Gouts of flame shot out of the equipment lining the walls. Chekov cried out. Alarms wailed.

Kirk looked up at the flickering viewscreen.

The help the Klingon commander had been expecting had finally arrived.

Three Klingon battle cruisers hung in space beyond the spinning wreckage of the *Planitia.*

And as Kirk watched helplessly, the lead ship fired again.

THREE

U.S.S. ENTERPRISE NCC-1701-D
ENGAGED WITH THE ENEMY
Stardate 43921.8
Earth Standard: ≈ May 2366

"Maximum shields!" Picard ordered.

The bridge shook as the first bolts of Romulan phaser fire splashed against the *Enterprise*'s saucer section. Then the third Warbird shot past the forward sensors and disappeared astern.

Sirens blared. Damage reports flooded the bridge.

"It must have decloaked directly behind the *62nd Rule* so we could not detect it," Data said.

But Picard had no time for the fine points of Romulan tactics. He had two shuttlecraft in transit. "Picard to La Forge—where are those shuttlecraft?!"

"One minute to docking, sir!" the engineer replied from the shuttlebay. "What the hell was that anyway?"

"Another Warbird," Picard said.

"The Warbird is returning, Captain," Data announced.

Picard turned to the tactical station. "Mr. Worf, extend shields around the *Gould* and the *Cochrane*. Transporter control, once the shields are established, beam in the pilots. Commander Riker?"

Riker answered from the shuttlebay.

"You are responsible for bringing the artifact in. Use cargo tractor beams directly on it and abandon the two shuttlecraft if you must, but get it aboard."

Worf acknowledged that the shields had been thrown around the *Gould* and the *Cochrane.* Transporter control acknowledged the pilots were safely aboard.

The third Warbird flashed by the main viewscreen again. But this time it did not fire.

"We are being hailed by the attacking vessel," Worf said.

"Onscreen," Picard snapped. He was furious. He glared at the new Romulan commander who appeared on the viewer, elegant fingers steepled before him as if the wholesale murder of a shipful of Ferengi were only an idle diversion.

"Commander of the Federation vessel," the Romulan said, "you will withdraw or be destroyed."

"You are in Federation space!" Picard shouted, ignoring the commander's order. "You have fired upon a neutral vessel! You will lower your shields and prepare for boarding."

The commander appeared bored with Picard's bluster. "We have destroyed a stolen Romulan vessel in order to prevent military secrets from falling into our enemy's hands. We have no quarrel with you. Withdraw so we may deal with our own affairs in our own way."

"Cargo aboard," Riker announced from the shuttlebay. "We have recovered both shuttlecraft as well."

Picard was surprised by that news. He had expected the Warbird to destroy the shuttlecraft on its return run. Perhaps the commander hadn't wanted to risk destroying the artifact.

"The *Enterprise* will *not* withdraw from any location in Federation space," Picard retorted indignantly. "The Romulan vessel here with us is under our protection. And we will use force to defend it." Picard glanced around as he heard the turbolift doors open. Counselor Troi rushed onto the bridge.

The Romulan commander moved his hands apart in feigned resignation. "To whom am I speaking?"

"Captain Jean-Luc Picard of the *Starship Enterprise.*"

The Romulan's eyelids flickered slightly as he looked to the side, as if that had been the last name he had wanted to hear. "Captain Picard," he said, adopting a more conversational tone.

"I repeat: I have no desire to fight you. But the ship you are misguidedly trying to protect is Romulan property. The commander you are defending is a traitor to the Empire. This is strictly an internal affair. And I know the Federation prides itself on noninterference. In this matter, I am sure you will wish to withdraw before this turns into an incident neither of us desires."

Troi stood beside Picard. "He's telling the truth, Captain. He's not eager for a confrontation. But he will fight if he feels you force him to."

"In this matter, the Romulan Star Empire does not fall within the scope of our Prime Directive," Picard said. "It is you and your presence which are interfering with us, and we have the right to defend ourselves from any such encroachment."

"Captain," Worf announced, "Commander Tarl wishes to speak with you as well."

Picard didn't understand why Tarl hadn't taken the opportunity of his conversation with the new Romulan commander to flee. "Onscreen," he said.

The viewscreen now displayed two images: Tarl to the right, the new commander to the left. Both were on their respective bridges.

"Captain Picard," Tarl said, "I appreciate your offer of asylum. But I have come to understand that it is wrong of me to turn my back on my own people. Please, let me return without further violence. To make amends." She hung her head, as if in shame.

"She's holding something back," Troi said for the captain's ears only.

The new commander gestured with open hands. "Captain Picard, you have heard the traitor speak with her own words. There is no need for you to become involved in this."

The turbolift doors flew open again and Riker sprinted onto the bridge. He saw the two Romulans on the screen and immediately asked, "Are they asking for . . . anything to be returned?"

Picard turned away from the screen and signaled Worf to cut the audio. "The new commander hasn't mentioned the artifact. It's almost as if he doesn't know it's missing."

"Or else he thinks that it's still on board Tarl's ship," Troi suggested.

"No," Picard said, "sensors would let him know where the

261

artifact is within seconds. I think the new commander really has come just to retrieve Tarl and her vessel."

"And she appears to want to go along with that," Troi observed.

"Because she wants us to get away with the artifact," Picard agreed. "But I'm not about to abandon someone who has proven herself so brave, and so farsighted." He faced the viewscreen again and motioned for Worf to restore the transmission.

"To whom do *I* have the honor of speaking?" Picard asked.

The new Romulan commander nodded his head in greeting. For some reason as yet unclear to Picard, the Romulan commander certainly wasn't behaving like the belligerent type of Romulan Picard knew all too well. "I am Traklamek. Will you withdraw, Captain Picard?"

"I would like to propose a compromise," Picard said.

"That is not necessary," Tarl replied, and there seemed to Picard to be a warning in her voice. He looked to Counselor Troi for confirmation that she had sensed it, too. Troi nodded slightly.

"Nor is it acceptable," Traklamek added curtly.

Unperturbed by the lack of both commanders' encouragement, Picard continued. "Commander Traklamek, the Federation has no desire to compromise the safety of the Empire, and we are willing to turn over Commander Tarl's vessel to you. However, we do wish to provide sanctuary to the commander, and however many of her crew wish to join her."

"*Completely* unacceptable," Traklamek stated.

"I do not wish to escape my fate," Tarl said in a tight voice. "As a warrior, Captain Picard, you must understand."

"She's still not being truthful," Troi said softly.

Picard heard the tone which indicated Worf had broken audio transmission again. "Captain," the Klingon announced from behind, "I am reading a considerable volume of subspace communication between the two Romulan vessels."

"Can you intercept?" Picard asked.

"The communications are heavily encrypted."

"Traklamek might be trying to take control of Tarl's computers," Riker suggested.

Picard considered their options. "We were prepared to beam aboard Tarl's crew. Can we do so while under attack?"

Riker said, "We can't beam through shields, but if we were able to get close enough to Tarl's ship so that our shields and hers combine, as we did with the shuttlecraft, it might be possible."

"How long would we have to stay beside her?" Picard asked.

"If we're limited to just our own transporters, maybe fifteen, twenty minutes to get all three hundred plus of her crew."

"And if Tarl uses her transporters as well?"

"Faster, but still no less than ten minutes. Warbirds aren't set up for evacuation."

"Captain Picard," Traklamek's voice resounded from the screen. "I must have your answer *now.*"

Picard addressed his crew, including the navigator who had replaced Wesley Crusher. "Mr. Worf, prepare to launch a wide-burst spread of photon torpedoes. Ensign McKnight, on my mark you will bring us to within five meters of Commander Tarl's forward hull. Resume audio, please."

Picard stepped forward to face the Romulan commanders. "I have already given you my answer," he said defiantly. "You have five seconds to withdraw."

Instantly Traklamek's image disappeared from the screen.

"He has gone to maximum shields," Worf said. "Romulan phasers coming on-line."

"You had your chance to get away!" Tarl exclaimed. "Why didn't you take it?"

"The Federation does not abandon its friends," Picard said.

"Traklamek is firing!" Worf growled.

Picard pointed at the screen just as Tarl's image winked out. "Fire torpedoes! Ensign—*mark!*"

The bridge lurched as more phaser fire burst against the ship, the thunder of its disruption joining the echo of the torpedo launching tubes. Then, just as a wall of photon-torpedo plasma flared around Traklamek's ship, Ensign McKnight's hands swept over the helm controls and the *Enterprise* raced toward Tarl's massive vessel.

"Traklamek must have been expecting an attack, sir!" Worf said with surprise. "He is engaged in evasive maneuvers."

Picard smiled. A fortunate miscalculation on the Romulan's part.

"He'll be mad as hell when he figures out we aren't going after him," Riker said.

"Five meters!" Ensign McKnight announced.

On the screen, Picard could look directly into viewports on Tarl's ship. The *Enterprise*, less than half the length of the Warbird, was now protectively nestled in the curve of the massive ship's main dorsal and ventral hulls leading to the masklike forward bridge.

"Transporter control," Picard said quickly, "commence emergency evacuation of Commander Tarl's—"

The viewscreen image unexpectedly rippled, and then the optical rippling *continued off the viewscreen and across the bridge.*

Picard stared in horror as he saw Ensign McKnight and Data flutter as if they were no more than mirages at a desert's edge. He felt a wave of nausea flood through him as he stared down at his own hands and saw them ripple as well.

Picard spun around as the distortion continued moving through the bridge. He saw the look of shock on Worf's face as it passed through him. And then it was gone.

Riker strode forward, eyes wide. "Data! What the hell was that?!"

Data looked up from his board with the android equivalent of surprise. "It appears Commander Tarl has cloaked her vessel, sir, and that the *Enterprise* is close enough to have been caught in the cloaking effect. The unusual optical effect must be the result of our being on the fringe of that field."

Worf confirmed Picard's hopes. "Captain, Traklamek's ship appears to have lost track of us. He is using broad-beam sensor sweeps to scan the region, but is not receiving any positive feedback. I believe we are cloaked, sir."

Picard approached Riker. He could see in his first officer's eyes that they were thinking the same thing—this was even safer than combining the two ships' shields. "Mr. Data, lock tractor beams on Commander Tarl's ship to maintain close contact. Mr. Worf, maintain communications silence and target Traklamek's—"

La Forge's voice cut through the background noise of the bridge. "Engineering to Captain Picard—we've got an emergency situation down here!"

"Go ahead, Mr. La Forge."

"Captain, some kind of field distortion wave just passed through us—maybe a new Romulan weapon—but whatever it was, it's disrupted the magnetic constriction elements of the warp core. We're going to have to shut everything down or the computer's going to initiate an automatic core ejection."

The last thing Picard needed was to face battle with no power for his warp engines, shields, or phasers. The warp core must not eject itself from the ship. "Shut it down, Mr. La Forge," Picard ordered. "But begin immediate emergency transfer of power from the impulse propulsion reactors to shields and phaser banks."

The bridge lights flickered and dimmed as the ship's main matter-antimatter reactor ceased operations.

"We are now in reduced-power mode," Worf said. "Life support on reserve power. Impulse generation has begun. Full shields, phaser, and transporter capability in fifteen minutes."

"Captain," Data said, "the plasma exhaust vented from our impulse engines will eventually provide Traklamek with the means by which to locate us."

"How long before that happens?" Picard asked.

"Provided we do not use impulse power for propulsion, we may be able to avoid detection for another three and a half minutes."

Picard's mind raced. On the screen, he saw Traklamek's Warbird poised at relative stop, maintaining its original distance from Tarl's last known position. "Are the Warbirds still communicating with each other, Mr. Worf?"

"Negative, sir. Both ships are observing total communications silence."

"Any indication that Tarl is preparing to leave this position?"

Data answered. "None, sir. Warp and impulse engines are in standby mode."

Picard stared at the screen. "I know what Traklamek's waiting for—us. But why is Tarl still here?"

"Perhaps she knows she's protecting us with her cloaking field," Riker suggested.

"That might be it, Number One. But if she's expecting us to help her now, she obviously doesn't know that field knocked out our warp core."

"Two minutes, thirty seconds before detection, sir."

"Two minutes . . ." Picard repeated, staring at the screen in intense concentration. With only impulse engines available to her, the *Enterprise* couldn't run from Traklamek's Warbird and she couldn't fire her phasers for another fifteen minutes. She did have torpedoes but she'd never be able to fire enough of them to penetrate Traklamek's shields before the Romulan commander returned fire. And the *Enterprise* did not have enough power for her shields to withstand more than a single round of phaser fire. The only advantage the *Enterprise* had right now was that she was invisible to Traklamek's sensors. And that advantage would only last another . . .

"Two minutes," Data said.

The bridge was silent, all eyes on the captain.

Picard laughed silently at himself. What was that he had just been thinking? About the ship running herself? As good as she was, it was her crew who made the *Enterprise* work. And the crew that mattered most now was the occupant of the center chair.

"Considering that we can't run," Picard said, "can't fight, and can't remain hidden, and that Traklamek will never accept our surrender now that we've fired upon him, I am open to suggestions."

Riker was the only one who spoke. "Some of our people might escape if we launch all emergency evacuation pods at once," he suggested grimly.

"Ninety seconds," Data said.

Picard shook his head. "Without warp capability, Traklamek would have days to pick them off one at a time."

Data looked up from his board. "Sir, I have just conducted an exhaustive analysis of all situations similar to this in the annals of Starfleet. It appears our only chance of survival, admittedly slim, is to throw ourselves on Traklamek's mercy."

"I know what Romulan mercy is like," Worf snarled. "Better to die a warrior's death in battle."

"Better not to die at all," Picard said, and he discounted his officers' suggestions and methodically continued to arrive at one of his own.

He told himself he was the captain of the *Enterprise*. Even now, with only seconds left in which to make his decision, he thought of the other vessels who had carried her name—all on the sculpted mural in his ready room. He thought of the company he kept: April, Pike, Kirk, Harriman, Garrett. They had never abandoned their ship or their crews. Picard would not either. There *had* to be some way out he hadn't considered. Some . . .

. . . Something deep within him spoke to him . . . an echo of Sarek's mind . . . an echo of another mind Sarek had touched . . . he couldn't be sure. But he was reminded at once that there had been other *Enterprise*s even before the ones that plied the stars. Other captains. Other . . .

Picard could almost feel the wind against his face, hear the flap of the sails, smell the smoke from the cannons as the seas raged all around him.

Something in him told him to change the rules of the encounter —not to concentrate on the *Enterprise*'s limitations, but on Traklamek's.

He *saw* the way.

Data gave the countdown. "Thirty seconds."

"Distance to Traklamek's Warbird," Picard said.

"Two kilometers," Data answered.

Picard stood behind Data, put his hand on the back of the android's chair. "Residual cloaking bleed, Mr. Data—how long does it last?"

Data angled his head questioningly. "A few tenths of a second, sir."

Picard nodded. "Then ten kilometers per second should do it. Mr. Data, transfer all power to the structural integrity field."

Data carried out the command instantly, but Riker moved to Picard's side to swiftly question him. *"All* power to the SIF? We're not in atmosphere, and without warp speed, the *Enterprise* doesn't even *need* the SIF."

"Where we're going," Picard said, "we don't need warp speed." He looked behind him to tactical. "Mr. Worf, target the dorsal bridge spine of Traklamek's ship. Then feed those coordinates to the helm. Now."

Worf immediately acted as directed, without questioning his captain's order. But Riker looked at Picard with wide eyes, at last understanding. "Captain, you can't be serious," he said.

"Five seconds to detection," Data announced.

"Number One," Picard said, "I have never been more serious in my life. Ensign McKnight—on my mark."

Then as he pointed his finger at the screen, he gave an order that had not been heard aboard an *Enterprise* for centuries—

"Ramming speed!"

Instantly the *Enterprise* sprang forward, her inertial dampers protecting all aboard from the monstrous force of the 10^3-gravity acceleration her impulse engines could achieve.

Traklamek's Warbird didn't have a chance.

Its defensive shields were tuned to the frequencies required to protect it from Federation phasers and photon-torpedo radiation. At relative rest under battle conditions, its navigational shields were configured to deflect dust and debris, and to leave energy available for weapons. They would only draw more power when the ship began to move again, or when sensors picked up incoming objects.

Undoubtedly, in the ship's last microseconds of existence, its sensors did pick up one incoming object—the 3.71-million-tonne mass of the *U.S.S. Enterprise.* But the residual cloaking bleed from Tarl's cloaking field distorted the *Enterprise*'s sensor image and Traklamek's computers automatically requested verification before altering the allocation of power to the shields under battle conditions. Romulan programmers had foreseen that danger might arise if shield frequencies were permitted to change in response to spurious sensor ghosts.

But even running at one billion operations per second, there was no time for confirmation of any sensor readings.

The *Enterprise* passed through the Warbird's navigational deflectors as if they did not exist.

The defensive shields set for radiation did not even register the *Enterprise*'s presence.

And on the Warbird's bridge, destruction was so swift that there was not even time for realization of their fate to form in the minds of the crew.

The leading edge of the *Enterprise*'s saucer section hit the dorsal bridge spine of Traklamek's ship at 36 thousand kilometers per hour. The Galaxy-class starship's internal forcefield system was designed to augment her structural integrity under the strains of warp acceleration. The system was tuned to the highest setting it would require to withstand velocities in excess of 1.78 *trillion* kilometers per hour—giving her a rigidity that rivaled that of degenerate matter at the heart of neutron stars.

Contact lasted less than one-hundredth of a second. If the *Enterprise*'s warp core had been active, the shock-wave feedback through the ship's structural integrity field would have triggered an instant antimatter compression wave, destroying the ship at once. But the warp core was off-line, and the *Enterprise* sliced the Warbird's head from its body and flew on intact.

In the Warbird's main hulls, the shock of the *Enterprise*'s passage crystallized duranium. The mechanisms of that ship's artificial singularity reactor shattered so suddenly that all gravitational containment fields failed at once in a massive implosion.

In the Warbird's bridge, all power conduits were severed at once. Immediately, its own inertial dampers and artificial gravity systems shut down. The force with which the accelerating bulkheads then hit the suddenly motionless crew members reduced them to superheated pulp in less than a thousandth of a second. Mere thousandths of a second after that, that pulp was consumed by the energy release of the singularity implosion erupting from the ship's other half.

In less than a second, there was nothing physical left of Traklamek's ship larger than an isolinear chip.

Resolute, the *Enterprise* flew on.

On the bridge, every alarm built into every console and piece of equipment sounded at once. Picard heard obscure warning chimes he had heard before only in simulations. All lights flickered, display screens rolled. The bridge speakers squealed as they were momentarily overloaded by the messages inundating them. The straining inertial dampers sent fluttering shivers through the ship as they tried repeatedly to reset themselves, making the superstructure creak and groan.

Picard blinked. It had taken no longer than that for the *Enterprise* to have obliterated her enemy. Then he moistened his suddenly dry lips. He glanced over at Ensign McKnight. Her face was drained of any color. Strands of blond hair hung in sweat-soaked tangles on her forehead.

Riker stared at Picard with an expression the captain could not read. "When Starfleet hears about this, I don't know if they're going to give you a medal or a court-martial."

"I'll settle for a refit," Picard said. He turned to tactical. Worf was also staring at him with a strange expression.

"Yes, Mr. Worf?" Picard asked.

Worf grinned, baring his teeth as only a Klingon could. His dark eyes sparkled beneath his heavy brow. "It is an honor to serve with you, Captain Picard. Songs will be sung about what you did here today." Then he went on speaking in *Hol,* so rapidly that Picard couldn't pick up any of it.

"Mr. Worf? Mr. *Worf!*" Picard said to interrupt what he took to be his tactical officer's praise. "Damage report, please."

Worf nodded and looked down at his board as he sighed. "It is difficult to know where to begin," he said.

In the end, it would have been briefer to list those ship's systems which had *not* sustained some type of damage in the collision. When Lieutenant La Forge was informed what had caused the severe shock to the ship, after a pause his response had been, "No, seriously, what just happened?"

But for all the overloaded circuits, the assaulted nerves, the delicate scientific instruments thrown out of alignment by the sudden surge in the SIF strength, the damage to the *Enterprise* was not major, just extensive.

Twenty minutes after the event, by which time the ship's damage-control routines were in full operation and power to the bridge had returned almost to normal except for the food replicator and the science stations, Data mildly observed that what Picard had had the *Enterprise* do did not even appear as a footnote in the ship's operational manuals. Starships had collided in the past, but never before with such bold purpose.

"Because I sincerely doubt that precise combination of conditions has ever occurred before," Picard said. *"If* Traklamek's ship had not been at relative rest; *if* his shields had not been set for battle conditions; *if* our warp core had not been shut down; *if* the *Enterprise* had not been cloaked; and *if* we had not been so close to him, the maneuver would certainly not have succeeded."

Data studied the captain carefully. "I am curious, sir: If those conditions had not all been present, what would you have done?"

"I have no idea," Picard answered truthfully. "We couldn't fight, we couldn't run, and a Romulan would never have accepted our surrender after we had already fired upon him." He glanced over at Riker. "Number One, make a note to refine this scenario for a training simulation."

Riker nodded. "It should give the *Kobayashi Maru* some stiff competition." Under his breath, he added, "Ramming speed," and shook his head.

Thirty minutes after the collision, the *Enterprise*'s redundant systems had almost completely restored the ship to normal operation. Sensor grids remained severely limited in capability until full realignment could be carried out, and the warp core remained to be reactivated. But in every other regard, Picard's *Enterprise* was whole.

She was also alone.

No trace of Commander Tarl's Warbird could be found. Only the widely dispersed ionized gas cloud that remained of Traklamek's ship, and the scattered debris from DaiMon Pol's *62nd Rule.* And without full sensor capability, the *Enterprise* was unable to detect either a warp trace or impulse exhaust trail to indicate where Tarl's ship might have gone.

Two hours after the collision, at the standard senior officers' debriefing in the observation lounge, Data offered a suggestion: "Commander Tarl's Warbird might still be nearby, provided it is cloaked at a distance beyond Counselor Troi's ability to sense its crew."

But Picard discounted that possibility. "It would make no sense

271

for her to stay near a site where two other Warbirds have been destroyed. Perhaps Commander Tarl really was serious about returning to the Empire to atone for her actions, or else she has gone off on her own. It could be that the idea of becoming a farmer or miner did not appeal to her."

"I think what we should focus our attention on," Riker said, "is that we now have both the Borg artifact and the Preserver object on board."

"Let's just hope it *is* a Borg artifact," La Forge said. "Especially after the lives it cost."

Everyone at the table turned to the engineer.

"Do you have some reason to doubt its authenticity?" Picard asked.

"I'm not sure, Captain." La Forge looked up at the ceiling as if searching for the best way to let Picard's hopes down gently. "The Borg ship we encountered in System J-25 was a hodgepodge collection of bits and pieces from other vessels, other machinery, all sorts of things jumbled together."

"Isn't that what the artifact in the shuttlebay is?" Riker asked.

"Well, yes it is, sir. But remember what Data said about the age of it."

"Approximately four centuries," Picard said.

"Exactly. The *entire* artifact. Every conduit. Every piece of mesh, wire, light guide, and photonic circuitry in it is the same age, *except* for the Preserver object."

"What's your point, Geordi?" Riker asked.

"Well, if all those parts had been assimilated from other vessels, they should show some variation in their age. I mean, as we've been taking it apart, it's clear we're dealing with material that's come from a lot of different cultures and levels of technical sophistication. But it's all the same age."

Data regarded the engineer without expression. "Geordi, are you suggesting that the artifact might have been deliberately aged? Perhaps by exposure to intense, non-ionizing radiation, in order to simulate the condition of having been in space for an extended period of time?"

La Forge made a half smile. "Something like that, Data."

Dr. Crusher looked perplexed. "Why would the Borg want to make their ships seem older than they really are?"

"Not the Borg," Troi said. "The Romulans."

Dr. Crusher wrinkled her brow as if the distinction made no difference. "Either one. What's the point?"

Picard looked at his engineer. "Any theories, Mr. La Forge?"

"Not really, Captain. If the artifact *is* a fake, it's a damned good one. It matches what we know about Borg construction exactly. Offhand, I'd say that the only way anyone could have faked it so perfectly would have been to take apart a real Borg artifact, replicate the pieces, then reassemble them."

"Which would account for the artificial aging it might have been subjected to after assembly," Data said. "Molecular-level replication would not accurately reproduce the age traces of the original components and it would be apparent we were observing a recently made duplicate."

"What about the Preserver object?" Picard asked. "Could that also be a duplicate?"

La Forge shook his head. "Oh, I doubt that, Captain. First of all, I can't identify the material it's made from. And most of it is opaque to every kind of sensor I can turn on it, *including* a neutrino stream which could penetrate a light-year's worth of lead. So it is definitely the product of a technology that we can't duplicate."

"How extraordinary," Picard said. "There is another so-called Preserver object, an obelisk that houses a graviton-beam generator. It also is opaque to neutrinos."

"That's good to know," La Forge replied. "The library computers are still down and I haven't been able to pull up any archaeological files to match against the object's configuration."

Picard straightened up with interest. "Would you like me to take another look at it?" Archaeology was more than a hobby for the captain.

"Give me an hour to cut it out of the artifact and you're on," La Forge responded immediately. Then he added more seriously, "Captain."

"So, I stand corrected," Riker said as he leaned back in his chair. "What we need to focus on is that we have a mystery on our hands."

"But what kind of mystery?" Troi asked. "Borg, Romulan, or Preserver?"

Picard looked out the observation room windows to see the stars, silent and impassive. Given those three choices, he couldn't shake the feeling that the real answer to the mystery would be something they hadn't yet considered. Or, perhaps, something that they all were unable to consider.

The unexpected had a way of continuing to turn up on this voyage. He decided he wouldn't be surprised if it did so again.

FOUR

U.S.S. ENTERPRISE NCC-1701
ENGAGED WITH THE ENEMY
Stardate 3855
Earth Standard: ≈ November 2267

Cochrane pushed himself up from the corridor floor, disoriented by the shifting angle of the walls, the screams of the sirens, the flashing red lights. He felt the officer named Kyle grab his arm and pull him forward. Captain Kirk's voice echoed from the corridor speakers.

"This is the captain. We are under attack. All hands battle stations. This is *not* a drill."

"Who's attacking us?" Cochrane asked as loudly as he could to be heard over the cacophony as he jogged beside Kyle. They passed a corridor intersection. Cochrane looked down it. It seemed to go on forever. No ship could be that large. "And where are we?" he added.

"You're on the *Enterprise,*" Kyle shouted back, not breaking stride. "And I have no idea who's bloody firing at us."

The floor suddenly shifted again, but the movement was weaker this time. As he and Kyle made their way along the corridor, Cochrane heard strange mechanical sounds reverberate through the walls. He even heard a rhythm that reminded him of the matter-antimatter generators he had used to power his superimpellors.

275

Kyle stopped when they came to a ladder on the wall. It extended up through the ceiling. Other men and women in uniforms like Kyle's raced through the corridor. Surely, too many for any one ship, Cochrane decided.

"C'mon," Kyle said, waving at the ladder. "This is faster."

Cochrane had no idea what the ladder was faster than. He began to climb.

"Two decks up!" Kyle called up from below him.

Cochrane smelled smoke as he passed the next deck. The floors lurched and he grabbed onto the ladder. "What was that room I was in?"

"Climb!" Kyle urged as the shaking ceased.

Cochrane's entire body ached but he forced one hand over the other, one foot above the next. He came to the second deck and stumbled off the ladder. This corridor was almost deserted. Kyle leapt out behind him. "This way!" He tugged Cochrane on again, double-time.

"Just tell me—how did I *get* here?" Cochrane gasped. One moment he had been locked in a stateroom on the liner, then something cold had passed through him, and he was suddenly standing on a glowing circular plate surrounded by the other prisoners he had seen when he had been captured. He was certain he hadn't been drugged, but he had no other explanation for how he had been moved from one ship to the *Enterprise,* whatever it was.

"You were transported," Kyle said unhelpfully as they rounded a corner. At the end of the new corridor, Cochrane could see a group of people, mostly in blue uniform shirts, gathered around other people on stretchers, arranged against the wall. He guessed this was sickbay.

"I *know* I was transported," Cochrane said with mounting exasperation. "But by what?"

"By *transporter,* what else?" Kyle answered. He sounded equally irritated and out of breath.

Cochrane gave up. Perhaps Kyle was under orders not to disclose military secrets. What other explanation could there be for such deliberately circuitous logic? They stopped again, near the people on stretchers. Kyle pointed through an open set of

276

doors. "You're to report in there," Kyle said. "I have to get to my station." Then he was gone, not wasting an instant.

Cochrane stepped out of the way as two blue-shirted crew members rushed in carrying an unconscious red-shirted woman between them. He followed them into the room. Finally, he saw a familiar face.

"Dr. McCoy!"

The doctor looked up from a patient stretched out on a bed. The patient's gold shirt was ripped open, smeared with dark red blood. Cochrane could see more blood pulsing weakly out through a charred, ragged gash on the man's chest. "What are *you* doing here?" McCoy said abruptly.

Cochrane felt even more confused. "I . . . I was brought here. Captain Kirk said the Companion would—"

McCoy didn't let him finish. "We're under attack. The captain's on the bridge and that's where you should be." He turned back to his patient, waving a glittering device over the bloodied chest as if he were some kind of witch doctor, never once touching the torn flesh.

"But *who's* attacking us?" Cochrane asked plaintively. He stared in puzzled fascination as the patient's bleeding seemed to slow, then stop, all without the doctor appearing to do anything but gesture at the wound.

"Damned Klingons!" McCoy muttered. He looked to the blond woman at his side. "Close this one up." He looked out over the room. "Where's the compound fracture?" A blue shirt waved the doctor over to another ravaged body on another bed. Some sort of medical display flashed and blinked above the second victim. Cochrane wondered how anyone could function in the room's chaos, yet somehow the doctor seemed to be in control of everything at once without effort.

He followed McCoy to his next patient. The doctor still wasn't touching flesh or bone as he treated the man with the broken leg. "Dr. McCoy, please—how do I get to the bridge?"

McCoy looked around angrily. Cochrane couldn't tell if it was real anger, or just the result of interrupted concentration. The doctor jabbed a finger in the direction of a young woman with her arm in a sling and a red uniform that consisted only of a shockingly brief dress. Cochrane wondered if she had been changing when she had been injured and hadn't had time to finish dressing. By the early-twenty-second-century standards of Centauri B II, the woman might as well have been naked. "Ensign!" McCoy barked. "This man's to report to the captain. Take him to the bridge."

The ensign was clearly in pain, but she instantly sprang to her feet and nodded at Cochrane. "This way, sir," she said, and led him rapidly past the crowd outside, then around another corner.

"What are Klingons?" Cochrane asked as he tried again to catch his breath.

The ensign glanced at him sharply. "Where're *you* from?" she asked.

Cochrane understood her reaction. Apparently, *everyone* knew what Klingons were. Except people from the twenty-second century.

"Never mind," Cochrane said. This wasn't the time for a history lesson. But maybe he had been wrong about Kyle's apparent reticence to discuss how he had come here. "Ensign, can you at least tell me what a transporter is?"

The ensign stopped in front of a set of flush-mounted doors. They sprang apart to reveal a tiny room no larger than a closet. After a moment, Cochrane realized it was an elevator, and felt foolish. He had been expecting more twenty-third-century wizardry.

"You been frozen or something?" the ensign asked curiously as she stepped inside.

"How'd you guess?" Cochrane said, grasping her question and seeing in it a chance to escape further suspicion. The technical manuals Kirk had left behind had contained only vague allusions to the politics of the day, and there had been so much to do in order to prepare to support himself and the Companion that Cochrane had never gotten around to reading the history updates. He hadn't been all that interested, either. "I'm from 2117. I don't know a thing past that."

The ensign whistled. "Twenty-one seventeen? That's a long time." She grabbed a downward-projecting handle and said, "Bridge."

The elevator doors closed and Cochrane felt the car move *sideways*. "What is this?" he gasped as he grabbed for another handle.

"Turbolift," the ensign said. "Like a . . . an elevationer, I think they were called back in your day."

"Elevator," Cochrane corrected. The car stopped moving sideways and began moving up. He watched the lights flashing by the frosted window, wondering if each flash could represent a deck. If so, the ship was monstrous. "So, what's a transporter?" Cochrane asked, no longer caring how out of touch he seemed. Information was information, and he'd always been a quick study.

"Matter-energy conversion," the ensign answered. She shifted her arm, apparently trying to find a more comfortable position than the sling would allow. "Converts you to energy, beams you to a new location, reconverts, and there you are."

Cochrane felt his stomach drop out of him, and it wasn't the turbolift. He stared at his hand. It *looked* like the same one he'd been born with.

"Are you all right, sir?"

"That's terrible."

"What?"

Cochrane was appalled. Had human life become so cheap? So meaningless? "Each time you're converted to energy, you're killed," Cochrane said. "What comes out the other end is just a duplicate that thinks it's the original."

The ensign gave him a wide-eyed look that she might have reserved for a child. "You're thinking about old-fashioned matter replication, sir. In replication, the original is destroyed so that duplicates can be reconstructed at any time. But the transporter process operates on a quantum level. You're not destroyed and re-created; your actual, original molecules are tunneled to a new location. You're still you, sir. Believe me. We do things differently these days."

Cochrane could believe it. He felt marginally better. The lift doors opened.

"Bridge, sir. This is where the doctor said you were to report."

Something flew at Cochrane. He whirled in time to see—

"Zefram!"

279

—the Companion.

All thought left Cochrane as he embraced her. The attack at home, the interrogation, the imprisonment, conversion to energy —all of it left him as if the universe itself no longer mattered. He held the Companion in his arms. He had been afraid to even think of what had happened to her, had not dared to hope of being reunited, until Kirk had said she would be here.

"Oh, Zefram, we were so frightened," she whispered into his chest.

"Shh," he comforted her. He placed his hand to her head, wincing as he felt the bandage there. "What's happened to you? How long have you been away from our home?"

She gazed up at him with one luminous eye, the other hidden beneath the sparkling fabric that wrapped her head. "Nothing's wrong, Zefram," she said. "And we have not been gone long. Dr. McCoy said we're strong, getting better. And we are, now that you're with us."

Then Cochrane was aware of someone standing outside the turbolift—the Vulcan who had accompanied Kirk.

"Mr. Spock," Cochrane said. "Is the captain here?"

"This way, please," Spock said. The ensign remained in the turbolift, most likely to return to sickbay.

Cochrane stepped forward, his arm securely around the Companion's frail shoulder, and his mouth opened in shock.

The bridge of Kirk's ship was larger than the total living area had been on the *Bonaventure*. He gazed at it with delight. Beside him, above a dedication plaque, there was a schematic of a vessel. He recognized the twin nacelles as a classic continuum-distortion configuration, but the rest of the clean design was a revelation. So many problems of distortion-field stability were solved just by comparing the proportions of the lead saucer to the secondary hull from which the superimpellor nacelles sprang. He wanted to reach out and touch the image. Could it really be he was aboard *this* vessel?

"Mr. Cochrane, if you please," the Vulcan insisted.

Cochrane moved forward, his fingers just brushing the image of the ship. Then the stairs took him by surprise. He nearly lost his footing when he reached them, so intent was his gaze at the viewscreen before him. There was some kind of wreckage displayed on it, rotating in microgravity—what had been another spaceship, he decided. Beyond the wreckage, three other ships hung poised in space, a different design from any other he had seen so far. But if the level of continuum-distortion propulsion today had been properly represented by the schematic back by the elevator, then the only reason the three ships on the screen looked the way they did—stretched out in two dimensions with a precariously long forward section—was that they were warships. That inefficient design could only be acceptable in order to provide a smaller target silhouette in head-on attacks. Cochrane had no idea about the politics of this era, but physics were physics.

With the Companion still nestled close at his side, Cochrane saw Kirk in the center chair. He realized he would have expected to see him nowhere else.

"Captain Kirk?" he said.

Kirk glanced at him, then moved his eyes back to the screen. "Glad to have you aboard, Mr. Cochrane. My apologies for the rough ride." He leaned forward. "Mr. Sulu, status on the shields on the number-three ship?"

An Asian human at the center console replied, "Eighty-seven percent, Captain. We won't be able to touch them if they try it again."

Kirk bit his lip, deep in thought. But for all the confusion Cochrane had seen so far, the captain was an oasis of calm and the bridge and its crew were a natural extension of him.

"Are those . . . Klingons?" Cochrane asked.

"They're Klingon ships," Kirk answered. "But since they don't appear interested in communicating with us, I can't tell you who's on board."

"What are they after?"

Kirk looked at Cochrane again. "They're after you."

Cochrane swayed, but the Companion steadied him. He closed his eyes. He had wanted this all behind him.

When Monica had died, he, too, had wanted to die, rather than continue the fight. It had cost him too much already. But then, when the Companion had found him, rescued him, he had allowed himself to believe that the battle that had consumed his life might, in fact, be over. The time spent with the Companion, even in the strangely appealing energy pattern in which she had originally appeared to him, had been like a second life, a dream filled with a contentment and satisfaction he had never thought possible; a sharing of thoughts and ideas and emotions so healing, he had been freed from his past, missing only, ironically, the rituals of conversation and social interaction that he had always avoided before.

Thus, when she had brought Kirk and the others to him, and the Companion had miraculously become flesh and blood in the form of Commissioner Nancy Hedford, Cochrane had felt his life move toward true completeness.

Finally holding the Companion in his arms, knowing that the pure mind that had captivated and delighted him was encased in a physical body that entranced him . . . he was overcome.

There was nothing more that he had wanted, nothing more that he—the scientist who had never felt there would be time enough to do and learn all that he might—felt compelled to do. Whatever name the poets wished to give the feeling that had come upon him then, it was to him one thing and one thing only—

Zefram Cochrane was at peace.

Once, as a child, he had dreamed of a bubble twisting within a bubble so that both twisted up together somewhere else. From that dream he had given humanity the stars.

But there had been another dream in Cochrane, a dream encoded in his cells, perhaps in the very structure of the universe that had caused him to come into being.

In the Companion he had found that dream made real.

But now his past was reaching out once more to steal that dream from him, as it had stolen the lives of his wife and his friends a century and a half before.

"They're not Klingons," Cochrane said with inexpressible sadness.

"Indeed," Spock said beside him.

Cochrane opened his eyes. An old woman stepped up to him.

She was dressed in a gold-shirted uniform like Kirk's, but the decorations on her sleeves were different, and the emblem on her chest was a rainbow-hued starburst, not the asymmetric field-distortion symbol Kirk and his crew wore.

"Am I to take it you know who's after you, Mr. Cochrane?" the old woman asked imperiously, as if she were used to being answered.

Cochrane looked at Kirk, seeking direction.

"This is Fleet Admiral Quarlo Kabreigny," Kirk said. Cochrane supposed he should be surprised, but the surprises of the twenty-third century were beginning to wear him down. He knew that in the late twentieth and early twenty-first centuries, women had literally fought to be in the military. But after the nightmare of World War III, with the preservation of the species at the forefront of everyone's minds, the conservative influence of the colony worlds had placed females back in a protected category. At the time, Cochrane had read that it was all part of some grand sociological cycle in gender roles, and he wondered now if the abbreviated uniform he had seen on the ensign was an indication of another move toward greater independence for women in this era. Still, for someone of his time period, he found it difficult to truly accept that this older woman was in a position to give orders to Kirk.

"The admiral has taken quite an interest in your career, *after* your disappearance," Kirk continued. "If you can clear up any of her questions, it will probably help all of us."

"Should I repeat the question?" the admiral said pointedly. Now Cochrane definitely had the feeling that the old woman was not used to having to repeat herself.

"That's not necessary," Cochrane said. "I had hoped that the Optimum Movement would have died out by now. That we would have grown smarter, stronger than that."

"The Optimum Movement?" Kirk said.

Spock placed his hands behind his back and began to recite historical facts. "The name given to a collection of loosely affiliated fascist political organizations that sprang up on Earth in the early to mid-twenty-first century," Spock said. "Among its adherents were the infamous Colonel Green—"

283

But Kirk stopped him. "I *know* what the Optimum Movement is, Spock."

Cochrane was puzzled that an alien would know so much about Earth history. Kirk had an equally puzzled expression. "Mr. Cochrane, the Optimum Movement's takeover of certain countries is widely considered to be a contributing cause of World War III. At the beginning of the reconstruction, the movement was thoroughly discredited. Its leaders captured and tried. It's dead and gone."

"It was still alive in 2117, Captain. They killed my wife and students on Centauri B II. I was supposed to be next."

"That's why you disappeared? To die in space?"

Cochrane felt his body tremble as the old sense of futility hit him again. He felt the Companion draw closer to him, wanting to protect him from all that was bad in this universe, in whatever time. It was unbearable to him that she, in turn, should be placed at risk, because of him.

"Keptin." A young Russian officer at the center console spoke up. "The enemy wessels are changing formation."

As Kirk glanced at the screen, Cochrane saw two of the three battleships change position. In the same instant, he suddenly realized that the wreckage on the screen was what was left of the spaceship he had just been on.

"Keep watch on their weapons readiness," Kirk said calmly. "Uhura, keep trying with all hailing frequencies." He looked back to the Vulcan. "Spock? Did you know that? That the Optimum Movement survived into the early twenty-second century?"

Cochrane was impressed with Kirk's ability to keep track of so many situations at once, much as Dr. McCoy had managed in sickbay. He wondered if all people of this time were equally capable, or if by some coincidence two of the best had ended up on the same ship.

"Records show," Spock began, "that the original Optimum Movement was destroyed during the postatomic horror. However, it would not be impossible for splinter organizations to have sprung up, much as neo-Nazi groups continued to arise for more than six decades after Earth's second world war. That likelihood is increased if we accept that some Optimum leaders were able to escape to the colony worlds, as the popular entertainment of the time repeatedly proposed."

Kirk looked back at the screen, keeping track of the warships. "What about the chances of the Optimum Movement surviving till today?"

"I would suggest that was highly improbable, Captain. There is not a world in the Federation where such a political movement would be tolerated. The Klingons, for all their barbarity, would find the Optimum ideals abhorrent for their lack of honor. And the Romulans would never support any political organization that did not originate with them."

"Which leaves us with our opening question," Kirk said. "Who's in those ships?"

"Sir," the Asian officer said, "we're being scanned again."

"Shields to full power," Kirk ordered. "Give them some feedback to confuse their readings."

The admiral ignored Cochrane for a moment. "How long are we going to hang here doing nothing?" she asked Kirk irritably.

Kirk shifted in his chair, and Cochrane was surprised yet again at the familiarity with which the captain addressed his commanding officer. Whatever organization ran this ship, it was unlike any military group he had ever encountered back in his time.

"Admiral, we've got a cracked dilithium crystal, damage to the port nacelle strut, thirty crew injured, and weapons capability less than sixty percent. Ten kilometers out there are three top-of-the-line D7 battle cruisers. Two are untouched, the other has shields at eighty-seven percent, and they're jamming every subspace frequency in the spectrum so we can't call for help. The only reason we're not in pieces like that spaceliner is that we backed away from the wreckage so they could scan it. My guess is that the only reason they didn't press the attack is that they don't know if we have Cochrane on board or not. Right now, I'm betting they're asking for additional orders from wherever their command center is. And each minute they wait before they come at us is another minute my engineer has to try and get us back into fighting condition."

Kirk turned back to Cochrane, apparently not concerned that if he had spoken to a commanding officer that way in Cochrane's time he would have been court-martialed. If anything, Cochrane thought, the ship ran along the same lines he had run his research facility on Centauri B II: he had been in charge, but everyone was free to question him, provided the work proceeded responsibly and on schedule.

"Now, Mr. Cochrane," Kirk said, "forget everything we've just told you about how history deals with the Optimum Movement. Who kidnapped you from the Companion's planetoid? What did they do to you on board the *Planitia?* And who the hell do you think is commanding those cruisers?"

Cochrane sighed. He directed the Companion to a seat on the upper level behind Kirk. He was grateful that she was content to remain a silent comfort to him as he struggled to interact with others of his kind in this new time. He knew, however, that she would be at his side the moment he faltered. As Cochrane turned to face Kirk, he felt more tired than he ever had when his body had been eighty-seven. "On the planetoid where you found me, I was attacked by humanoids with green skin. I had run up to their ship. It was small, like your shuttlecraft. I thought it might be you again. One of them had some kind of rifle. That's the last I remember of that night."

"Those men were Orion pirates," Kirk told him. The captain kept his eyes riveted on the screen. "The rifle was either a phaser or disruptor. Either way, it would shock your nervous system, knock you out. What happened next?"

"I woke up, sore, sick, on a large spaceship." Remembering what had happened was almost as unpleasant as what he had actually experienced. "I could hear people shouting, crying. The humanoids with green skins told me the others were hostages. To make sure nothing happened until . . . until some kind of trade was arranged."

"Who told you about a trade?" Kirk asked.

"A different type of humanoid. Definitely alien. Oily skin, black beard and mustache."

"That was a Klingon," Spock said.

"They're the enemy?" Cochrane asked. He could believe it. The alien had been objectionable from the moment he had stormed into Cochrane's stateroom and offered him a plate of still-wriggling worms. When Cochrane had refused, the alien had acted outraged, as if eating live worms was a great honor where he came from.

But the admiral apparently didn't agree with Cochrane's assessment. She interjected swiftly, "Let's just say that, so far, the Federation and the Klingon Empire have yet to discover common ground. At the moment, we're finishing negotiations—among the Klingon and Romulan Empires, and the Federation—to establish a joint colony on Nimbus III. It will become the Planet of Galactic Peace—a crowning achievement for interplanetary diplomacy at the highest level."

Kirk rolled his eyes at that; then he asked Cochrane to continue. "What else did the Klingon tell you? What kind of trade was he expecting?"

Cochrane shrugged. "At the time, he didn't say. I thought it was some kind of hostage situation, a mass kidnapping."

"Did they ever ask you your name?" Spock asked.

Cochrane shook his head. "No. That's why I thought I was just a random victim. Until Captain Kirk said those ships were after me."

Spock looked at Kirk. "Captain, we have yet to hear an explicit mention of Cochrane, or a specific demand for him. There *is* a slight chance this could all be a coincidence."

Kirk laughed. "Don't let McCoy hear you say that." He took on a thoughtful expression. "Mr. Cochrane, why was the Optimum Movement so eager to hunt you down in your own time? And how could that same reason possibly be valid today, one hundred and fifty years later?"

Cochrane hesitated, trying to think of the simplest way to tell Kirk what people had once thought the continuum-distortion field capable of. But before he could answer, the admiral stepped in front of him.

"Mr. Cochrane, the answer to that question is classified, and I insist you do not answer it."

Cochrane and Kirk both objected at the same time. Spock raised an eyebrow.

"Nothing is classified after a century and a half," Kirk said testily. He looked angry, and unlike the doctor's earlier mood, Cochrane could see that this anger was real.

"I am not a part of whatever organization you represent," Cochrane told the admiral. He could feel himself grow upset as well. "I can say whatever I want about my work." The military had not been able to restrain him back in his own time, and he was not about to allow them to begin now.

But the admiral was unlike any older woman from Cochrane's day. She stepped closer to him. She was a foot and a half shorter than he, but still she tried to stare him down. "The 'organization' I represent is called Starfleet, *Mr.* Cochrane, and this is a Starfleet vessel. By being present on it, sir, you are *compelled* to obey my orders. You will *not* answer Captain Kirk's question."

Cochrane glared down at the woman, forgetting her age. Arrogance, it seemed, had not gone out of fashion.

Kirk tried to reason with her. "What work could Cochrane possibly have done so long ago that it's still classified today?"

The admiral turned her fury on Kirk. "I've had enough of your interference, Captain. You will *not*—"

Cochrane had had enough. "The warp bomb," he said, and before anyone else could react, the admiral slapped him.

The Companion gasped and with surprising swiftness moved to Cochrane's side, pulled him back, inserting herself as a shield before him. She was half-crouched, hands out as if ready to physically attack the admiral. Kirk jumped out of his chair in the same instant. The entire bridge crew turned to see what had happened. Spock stepped to the admiral's side, ready to intervene from that position. The admiral herself stood with her hand still upraised, quivering with fury.

"I said *no,"* she shouted, voice quaking.

"Admiral," Kirk said quickly, trying to mollify her, "the warp bomb is an illusion. An engineering impossibility."

The admiral snapped her head around to confront Kirk. And in that moment, seeing the look that passed from her to the captain, Cochrane had the horrible realization that both he and the captain had been wrong—the warp bomb was *not* an impossibility.

Somehow, in this future time, it had become real.

And it was still a secret.

Kirk looked over at the Vulcan. "Spock, it *is* an impossibility, isn't it?"

Spock studied the admiral with interest. Cochrane guessed he had interpreted the look that the admiral had given the captain in the same way he had. "To the best of my knowledge," Spock said, "it is."

"Admiral Kabreigny," Kirk said quietly, "it is apparent that you are under a great deal of strain. With respect, I must insist that you explain yourself, or leave my bridge."

The admiral closed her hand into a fist. "Starfleet is all that stands between the United Federation of Planets and . . . anarchy, Captain. I am a Fleet admiral. I will not explain myself to you."

Kirk shook his head, as if trying to find something to say and not succeeding. "I'm sorry, Admiral. I really am." He touched the arm of his chair. "Dr. McCoy to the bridge. Medical emergency."

"You traitor," the admiral said to Kirk. Cochrane had the feeling he had stepped into the middle of a conflict that had been going on for years. If not between the admiral and Kirk, then between the two factions they represented. "You're part of it, aren't you? That's why those ships haven't attacked. Because they know you're going to turn him over!"

The admiral made a move as if to strike Kirk. Kirk grabbed her wrists, awkwardly holding her back. "Admiral, please," he begged her. "I'm not part of anything. I assure you I will not turn Mr. Cochrane over to—"

"Liar!" the admiral said. She struggled in Kirk's grasp, her situation all the more maddening to her because it was so evident that she did not have the strength to free herself.

Mr. Spock moved behind the admiral and put his hand on her shoulder as if about to give her an encouraging pat. But suddenly, the admiral groaned, arched back, then fell limp into Spock's arms.

Cochrane was appalled. The admiral had worked herself into a heart attack. Once again, his life's work had disturbed the balance.

JUDITH AND GARFIELD REEVES-STEVENS

Spock lifted the admiral into his arms as if she were a doll.

"Shouldn't you start CPR?" Cochrane asked. Surely that wasn't a lost art.

Kirk put his hand on Cochrane's shoulder. "It's not a heart attack. A Vulcan nerve pinch. The admiral's health is not . . . robust."

Cochrane twisted his head to see Kirk's hand on his shoulder. He had heard that Vulcans had strange mental powers. He wondered if they could be taught to humans.

Kirk saw what Cochrane was looking at. He removed his hand. "Relax. I can't do it. And despite what the admiral said, I'm not your enemy."

McCoy rushed out of the turbolift, followed by what Cochrane took to be two other medical workers in blue shirts. In moments the doctor was gesturing over the admiral's unconscious form with his glittering instruments while his assistants carefully took the admiral from Mr. Spock and laid her gently on the deck.

Spock told McCoy about the nerve pinch; McCoy agreed it had been a good decision, something about the admiral's heart; then he touched a standard spray hypo against her arm. Cochrane was surprised to see such an antique device in the doctor's arsenal. It looked barely different from the spray hypos he remembered as a child, though he assumed it had to be far more sophisticated on the inside.

"Could anyone tell me what all that was about?" Cochrane asked. He was beginning to think all he was good for any more was asking questions. But old habits died hard. Perhaps something he might learn would give him a clue to his role in this new age.

"Secrecy has taken its toll," Spock answered, after Kirk nodded at him to do so. "There is apparently some conspiracy afoot which involves both you and a purported warp bomb. The senior officers of this ship were concerned that the admiral was part of that conspiracy. On the other hand, it appears that she was equally worried that *we* were in fact the conspirators."

"So who *are* the conspirators?" Cochrane asked.

"Presumably, whoever is on those ships," Spock said.

290

Cochrane studied the viewscreen image of the three battle cruisers, as Kirk had called them. "And they won't talk to you?"

"Not so far," Kirk said.

"Because they can't be sure if I'm on board?"

"There has to be some reason why they didn't continue their attack," Kirk said. "If you go by the numbers, in our present condition we're no match for them."

Cochrane liked the qualification in Kirk's assessment, as if Kirk still believed he and his ship *were* a match for whatever they faced. "You don't strike me as someone who goes by the numbers very often, Captain Kirk."

Kirk grinned at him, and in that moment Cochrane felt again that they could be friends. They seemed alike in many ways, their different paths the result of their different times. Cochrane had had no rules to play by, everything about interplanetary exploration had been new. But Kirk also seemed to him to be the same unrestrained, questing spirit he himself had once been, though Kirk was obviously forced to work within a bureaucracy of exploration. Cochrane was bemused by the concept— interplanetary exploration becoming so commonplace that it was run by the twenty-third-century equivalent of civil servants.

"Do I detect a suggestion, Mr. Cochrane?"

Cochrane smiled back at the captain. His gradually returning calm was having an effect on the Companion, still vigilant at his side. She no longer looked as if she were ready to kill the admiral. "Let them know I'm here," he said. "Then they won't attack."

Kirk nodded thoughtfully. "I've considered that. The drawback is: What if they *want* to kill you?"

"Wouldn't they have done that on the other spaceship?"

"Not necessarily," Spock said. "At that time, you were in their control. If you had secrets, they could be extracted from you. However, now you are in our control. Depending on how valuable —or how dangerous—our opponents consider you, they might conclude it is better to kill you than allow you to remain in our hands."

Kirk gave Cochrane a commiserating look, as if those had been his thoughts exactly. "Do you have any such secrets, Mr.

Cochrane?" He nodded at the admiral's still form. "Admiral Kabreigny obviously thought you did."

But Cochrane shook his head. "None that I know of. Judging from those technical manuals you left me, my knowledge of what you call warp propulsion is at the same level as what a schoolchild probably starts with these days."

"So you never worked on a warp bomb?"

"I think those rumors go back to an accident at Kashishowa Station, back in the fifties. The *twenty*-fifties."

Kirk looked at Spock. Spock looked at Cochrane.

"What accident would that be, Mr. Cochrane?"

Without knowing why, Cochrane was troubled by the question. "It was a test facility on the moon's surface. About one hundred kilometers outside Kashishowa, but that was our base. Anyway, the lithium converter failed. We had a runaway continuum distortion too close to the sun's gravity well and everything in the field got pulled into what I think was a wormhole." He didn't understand Spock's look of concentration. "There must be records. That's when we moved all our research to an old ice freighter so we could work out past Neptune."

Kirk had the same expression of concentration, as if he were trying to recall hearing anything about the incident. "Check it out, Spock."

The Vulcan went back to the bridge's upper level to access what Cochrane assumed was some sort of computer. McCoy and his medical assistants carried Admiral Kabreigny to the turbolift. The rest of the bridge crew worked on with remarkable concentration as if there had been no change in their operating conditions.

"Did I miss something?" Cochrane asked.

"Probably not," Kirk said as he settled back into his chair. "But anything that might tell us what our friends out there are thinking could help us."

Cochrane again studied the battle cruisers on the screen. Combat, it seemed, had not changed much in the future, either. Long periods of waiting broken only by short bursts of violence. "Captain?" he asked. "What are the primary weapons of the day?"

"For this ship, phasers," Kirk answered, eyes also on the screen. "Um, phased energy rectification. Basically, a concentrated nadion beam that interrupts the nuclear binding forces, strong and weak. At low power, it can disrupt cellular processes to stun or kill. At high power, it can cause the constituent components of matter to disassociate without a resulting release of energy."

Cochrane had never heard of nadions, but he understood the implications of what Kirk described. If the Optimum had had a weapon like that . . .

"In addition to phasers, photon torpedoes. Essentially a matter-antimatter bomb, but with a warp-capable casing."

Cochrane understood the implications of that, too. "So you fight battles at warp speeds?"

Kirk understood the meaning behind Cochrane's question. "Technology is neutral, Mr. Cochrane. It's what we choose to do with it that gives it a military application or not."

"I've heard the argument," Cochrane said. He decided Micah Brack would have liked Kirk, too.

Then Spock looked up from the computer station he had used. "Captain, there is no record of a catastrophic warp research failure at Kashishowa Station in the 2050s, or at any time."

"But that's not possible," Cochrane protested. "I was there, two kilometers from the test dome, when it . . . it disappeared."

Kirk tried to explain. "Many records were lost in the Third World War, Mr. Cochrane."

"On the *moon?*" Cochrane asked. "On *Centauri B II?*"

"What about it, Spock?"

Spock looked thoughtful for a moment, then touched a control at the computer station. "Spock to Engineering. Mr. Scott, do you have a moment?"

A Scotsman answered. Cochrane found the distinctive accent and attitude reassuring. Like the spray hypo, engineers at least hadn't changed at all in this future time.

"Not bloody likely, Mr. Spock. Not if you expect me t' get this—"

"A moment only, Mr. Scott," Spock said, unperturbed. "In your studies of the history of warp propulsion, do you have any

recollection of an early setback, in the 2050s, involving the
inadvertent creation of what might have been an unstable static
warp field on the Earth's moon?"

"Aye," the Scotsman replied hesitantly. "As I recall, it was what
led Zefram Cochrane's team t' conduct further experiments out
of the sun's gravity well. Can I ask ye what this has t' do with
anything?"

Spock looked impressed, in a quiet, Vulcan manner. "Do you
happen to know when and how you first heard of the incident?"
he asked.

The unseen Scotsman sighed. "I canna tell ye, Mr. Spock. At
the Academy, perhaps, one of the first-year courses. Look, I've got
a lot of work t' do down here, and—"

"Very good, Mr. Scott," Spock said. "Please carry on." He took
his finger off the control and the engineer's voice cut out.

Kirk looked at Cochrane. "Curiouser and curiouser. It used to
be known to Starfleet, but now it's no longer in the computer. A
worm program, Mr. Spock?"

"Perhaps, Captain."

Cochrane was lost. Kirk saw the incomprehension on his face.
"In the past few days, we've discovered that Starfleet's main
computer system may have been infected with programs designed
to locate references to you," he explained. "And, perhaps, to
selectively erase elements of your work."

"What about printed records?" Cochrane said. "Or computers
not connected to yours?"

"Printed records would be unaffected," Spock said. "As for
other computers, it would depend on the nature of the worm
program itself, and whether or not it had the capability to move
between different systems and remain effective."

"But why?" Cochrane said. It made no sense to him. Both he
and Micah Brack had seen to it that the records of continuum-
distortion propulsion development were disseminated throughout the known worlds without restriction. How could anyone
hope to contain that information? Why would anyone want to?

"Theories, Spock?" the captain said.

"In the past, there have been many instances where a scientific discovery has been overlooked at the time data were accumulated, only to come to light when the data were reexamined. Lasers, so-called black holes, many astronomical sightings, naturally occurring transtator phenomena, all were found to be supported by experimental data obtained well before their 'official' discovery."

Cochrane didn't like the sound of that at all. "You're saying that a warp bomb *is* possible? That whatever happened at Kashishowa Station wasn't what I thought it was?"

"I merely suggest that other parties might believe that in your findings of the time, there might be data which would reveal a different explanation of the event if they were examined today."

Kirk seemed to be no more convinced than Cochrane felt. "After one hundred and fifty *years,* Spock?"

"Science is a gradual process, Captain."

Kirk shook his head dismissively. "Going back all that time doesn't sound like science. It sounds like obsession."

Cochrane didn't know what to believe. He squeezed the Companion's hand in his. "The Optimum Movement excelled at obsession, Captain."

But Kirk was not convinced. "Flawed organizations like that tend to reinvent themselves over time, Mr. Cochrane. There's no clear-cut set of ideals to be handed down from one generation to the next. Goals change, especially if they're based on political expediency. Even if the Optimum Movement did still exist today, it would be in name only. Colonel Green and his kind are long dead."

Cochrane pointed out the one key flaw in Kirk's argument. "I'm still here."

Kirk looked at him with a crooked smile, as if acknowledging the point Cochrane had made.

Then the Russian called out—"Keptin! Wessel approaching at high warp speed. Configuration matches the ship we destroyed earlier . . . *and* the ship that followed us to Babel, sir."

To Cochrane, it felt as if the bridge had been electrified, but Kirk betrayed no sense of urgency. "Ready on shields, Chekov. Let's not use full power until we have to."

"There, Keptin!" Chekov said as a twinkling orange dot of light flew across the screen and vanished behind the center battle cruiser. "Docking in progress."

Kirk spoke over his shoulder. "What do you say, Mr. Spock? Their commander has arrived to take care of things personally?"

"That would be a logical development, Captain." Spock sat down at the computer station. Cochrane saw him stare into the small viewer of what seemed to be a holographic display. He knew vulcans had developed an elaborate system of processing three-dimensional data. Cochrane remembered trying one of their viewers once, and only getting a headache. "There is increased intraship communication," Spock reported. "Hard to make out with all the jamming."

"Enemy wessels changing formation again, Keptin."

The Asian navigator added, "Weapons systems powering up."

"Keep what's left of the *Planitia* between us, Mr. Sulu," Kirk said. He touched a control on the arm of his chair. "Mr. Scott, we're just about out of time. What's the best speed you can give us?"

The Scotsman answered. "I can give ye warp factor seven, but only for a few hours, sir. Anything faster and the port strut will fracture; anything longer, and we'll lose our dilithium."

"Understood," Kirk said. He glanced at Cochrane.

"Warp seven," Cochrane said. "Is that a time-warp multiplier factor?"

Kirk nodded. "We called them time-warp factors in my cadet days. Now just warp factors."

"That's still pretty fast," Cochrane said.

"Those ships are faster," Kirk answered. "It won't pay to run."

"Even with a head start?"

"It would have to be a big one," Kirk said. "And even then it's only delaying the inevitable. Help's too far away."

Then the black woman seated at the station behind Kirk spoke. "Captain, they are finally responding to our hails. Requesting visual communication."

Cochrane sensed a quick feeling of relief from the captain. "Show us their visual, Lieutenant, but only send audio." He looked at Cochrane and held his finger to his lips. "Let's not give

FEDERATION

them any information we don't have to." Then he looked toward the screen.

"This is Captain James T. Kirk of the *Starship Enterprise* to unidentified Klingon cruisers."

Cochrane liked the sound of "starship." It had an almost magical connotation. He wondered if the people of this day thought the same, or if they had become jaded by the wonders of their age.

The captain continued. "You are in Federation space without authorization. You must identify yourselves."

Then the image on the screen changed, no longer showing the three battle cruisers, and Cochrane felt as he had when he learned he had been converted to energy and re-formed—completely disoriented, without any sense of order or control.

The face on the screen was as far out of time as Cochrane himself.

The commander of the alien force was Adrik Thorsen.

There was no escape from the Optimum.

297

FIVE

U.S.S. ENTERPRISE NCC-1701
ENGAGED WITH THE ENEMY
Stardate 3855
Earth Standard: ≈ November 2267

Kirk heard Cochrane's intake of breath and instantly knew that
the scientist recognized the commander of the Klingon ships. But
he had no idea how that was possible. And there was no time to
ask him, either.

"Give me Cochrane and I will spare your ship," the figure said
roughly, but with slow precision. He was humanoid, possibly
human, though because the screen showed him only from the
shoulders up, it was difficult to judge what form his body took.
His leathery skin was deeply lined, reminding Kirk of asteroid
miners he had met whose helmet visors hadn't afforded enough
protection from a star's ultraviolet radiation. His hair was lucid
white, cut almost to bristle length, and covered only half his scalp
as if part had been burned away, exposing old scars, almost
regular, as if they were a surgeon's work and not the result of
accidental damage.

But Kirk decided they were battle scars. The commander had
an unmistakable military bearing. He doubted any other human
could occupy the command chair of a Klingon vessel. If it truly
was a Klingon vessel.

"I repeat," Kirk said, "identify yourself."

The commander's face changed into what at first looked like a grimace of pain. But Kirk finally recognized the expression to be a smile, or at least an attempt at one. Only half the face moved, as if the rest had suffered irreparable nerve damage.

"Ask Cochrane who I am." He spoke the scientist's name as if it were the invocation of a demon.

"Who is Cochrane?" Kirk asked. If bluffing was good enough for Spock's father . . .

But the commander looked at something off the screen and snarled, *"pu'DaH! ghuH baH!"*

"Disruptors powering up," Sulu reported. "Leftmost ship. Shall I increase power to shields, Captain?"

Kirk shut off his audio transmission. "Negative," he said. "We don't want them to know we don't have one hundred percent." He switched the audio back on. "Klingon vessel: Take your weapons off standby and identify yourself or you will suffer the consequences. You will not be warned again." He switched off again, turned to Cochrane. "You recognize him, don't you?"

Cochrane nodded. The Companion looked up at him with attentive concern, clearly sensing more emotional turmoil than showed on the scientist's face.

But before Cochrane could say anything, the commander's harsh voice exploded from the speakers. "You have five seconds, *Enterprise. Vagh . . . loS . . . wej . . ."*

Cochrane hit the audio switch at Kirk's side and spoke before Kirk could stop him. "Shut it down, Thorsen. I'm here."

On the screen, the commander opened his mouth with a sound that was somewhere between a hiss and an exhalation of surprise. To Kirk, despite the commander's appearance, it didn't sound human.

"Go to visual, Uhura," Kirk said. If this was the way Cochrane dealt the hand, then Kirk would play along. Nothing could be gained by trying to hide Cochrane's presence any longer. "Who is this Thorsen?" he asked the scientist.

Onscreen, half of Thorsen's face reacted with dismay at what he saw as his own viewer came on.

"Adrik Thorsen," Cochrane said with revulsion.

The name was vaguely familiar to Kirk. Something historical.

"*The* Adrik Thorsen?" Spock asked. "Of Colonel Green's cadre?"

"That is not *Cochrane,*" Thorsen hissed.

Cochrane stepped in front of the Companion as if protecting her the way she had earlier protected him. "Look at me, Thorsen. You know who I am. The way I used to be. Think back to Titan. The first time I escaped you."

Whatever Cochrane had done to Thorsen on Titan, Kirk could see that the reference had the desired effect. Thorsen's face revealed recognition and hatred.

"But you're *young!* How is that possible?" he said. "After all these years?"

Cochrane apparently had no intention of feeding Thorsen's twisted interest in him. "How are *you* possible?"

Kirk heard Spock approach from behind. He spoke in a low tone. "Captain, computer records show that Colonel Adrik Thorsen died in a resistance attack in London, just prior to the onset of World War Three."

On the screen, Thorsen emitted a hollow drawn-out laugh. He held up a fist. Or what Kirk thought had once been a fist.

It was mechanical, three-fingered, the color of burnished duranium.

"Only *part* of Adrik Thorsen died at Battersea Stadium, oh six, two one, two oh seven eight," Thorsen said.

The mechanical fingers opened and flexed as the equivalent of a wrist socket rotated fully. At the same time, the image on the viewscreen changed its angle of coverage, so more of Thorsen was revealed.

"Fascinating," Spock said, as the full, horrifying extent of Thorsen's cybernetic transformation could be seen.

What flesh remained to him was supported upon and within a flattened exoskeleton, which ended at his shoulders. Both arms were mechanical, each with two elbow joints. Woven through the intricacies of the open chest, Kirk could see hanging pockets of skin connected by glistening, pulsating cords, as if human organs still remained, removed from no-longer-necessary muscle and bone. All that was flesh was encircled by tendril-like power

300

conduits and gleaming wire. And where metal made contact with flesh, the living parts were swollen, inflamed, encrusted with dried fluids.

What Cochrane had addressed as Adrik Thorsen now stood up from the modified command chair on three duranium legs. Behind the obscene apparition, Kirk saw two members of a Klingon crew, and an Orion. All were in civilian clothes; none of them wore uniforms.

"Colonel Thorsen appears to have made use of Grigari technology," Spock commented.

Kirk corrected him. "Outlawed Grigari technology."

"What have you become?" Cochrane said in disgust.

"What you have made me," Thorsen answered. His arms moved like the questing feelers of some enormous insect, twisting up to hold two clenched fists by his still human face as if to display them for their owner's admiration. "I have become *optimal.*"

Thorsen probed at his face with the mechanical pincers of his duranium hands. Kirk recognized their distinctive design just as Spock had. Each metal pincer ended with three smaller grippers inset at the tip, and each of those in three smaller ones, and so on, into the nanometer realm, giving each hand the capability to take apart living tissue on a cell-by-cell level.

Nanotechnology was the secret of the success of Grigari medical technology. Their molecular assembly devices could expertly weave together flesh and steel, uniting living nervous systems directly with computer-control circuits. But it was not a static situation.

The flesh of most life-forms would eventually reject the filaments of connection the Grigari devices wove. So the devices were programmed not to stop, in order to continually maintain the connection. Thus, as each layer of living cells became damaged, they were stripped away and replaced by more filaments of circuitry and steel. Eventually, the living body of a Grigari amalgam was completely discarded, replaced with an inexact, mechanical substitute.

The Grigari had proclaimed themselves as traders come to offer eternal life to the worlds of the Federation. But when their treatments had been investigated and found hideously flawed, the

Grigari ships had left as one, moving on to other, uncharted sectors, leaving behind only gruesome tales of the horrors their painful technology had wrought.

But for some people, Kirk knew, death was an even worse horror, and despite all that was known about what must inevitably happen when living matter and Grigari technology merged, there were still some worlds beyond the Federation's boundaries where the forbidden operations were available. For a price.

Adrik Thorsen, it appeared, had paid that price years ago, and what was left of him was paying it still.

"I don't care *what* you think you are!" Cochrane called out. His hand cut through the air in a forceful gesture, as if to ward off Thorsen and what he represented. "The Optimum Movement is *over,* Thorsen! You *lost!"*

Thorsen's pincers worried at the flesh of his face, distorting the expression of his frozen side. Kirk frowned at the sight. He doubted there was much of the original Thorsen underneath.

"I lost but a battle," the amalgam said. "The war continues."

Having observed the nature of his adversary, Kirk had already begun formulating his strategy, and now he began implementing it. "The Federation is at peace, Colonel Thorsen. The war you remember is long gone."

The pincers came away from Thorsen's face. The skin of his cheek was broken now, like the cracked bed of a dried river. But there was no blood. Only dark shadows, cutting deep, deeper. "There will always be a war, *Enterprise.* It is the nature of the beast. And only Cochrane can stop it."

"How?" Kirk asked. He quickly shut off his transmission and told Spock to confirm which of the three battle cruisers Thorsen's signal was coming from.

"He knows the secret of the ultimate deterrent," Thorsen said. His pincers fastened on his immobile eyebrows. The eyelids beneath the activity didn't blink. "He is the reason why the war was fought. Why Earth was devastated by the weak, who were cowards, incomplete, less than optimal. If he had listened to me on oh six, two one, two oh seven eight, Earth would be a paradise. None would have been able to oppose me."

"There is no ultimate deterrent," Kirk said, trying to keep this

302

deconstructing madman engaged in debate as long as necessary. Spock stepped in front of him, hands behind his back, gesturing to indicate that Thorsen's signal was coming from the leftmost ship, as Kirk had already assumed.

"Starfleet knows," Thorsen said as he placed the tip of another pincer against his unmoving eye. "I looked into their computers. Sent little strands of myself into their circuits." He treated them to his eerie half-smile, half-grimace again. "I can do that now, you know, Mr. Cochrane. Unlike you, I am much more than the sum of my parts."

Spock glanced at the captain. "I believe he is implying that he used Grigari nanocomponents to infiltrate Starfleet's main computer system. If so, by actually reconstructing themselves into duotronic circuits, the nanocomponents could create worm programs with impunity, making it appear that the network had been compromised by insiders, when, in fact, it was the system itself that was in control."

Thorsen inhaled with an oddly fluttering breath. "I *am* the system, now. I was always meant to be the system. And every time I reached out into the system, Starfleet moved against me, to classify more and more that had to do with Kashishowa Station. Now, Mr. Cochrane, I ask you, why go to all that trouble to hide a secret, unless there is a secret there to hide?"

Cochrane and Kirk turned to each other at once.

"Is that what this is about?" Cochrane asked.

On the screen, Thorsen sighed as he plucked at his unmoving eyelid. "I see it all, now," he whispered madly.

"It would appear so," Kirk said, answering Cochrane. To Thorsen he said, "The battle's been fought for nothing."

Kirk could see exactly how the scenario played out, even to the point of Admiral Kabreigny believing the officers of the *Enterprise* were involved in a conspiracy against Starfleet.

Thorsen, with the abilities of a Grigari amalgam, had somehow come into contact with a Starfleet terminal and created worm programs to search out information about the Kashishowa Station incident, believing it would reveal the secrets of a Cochrane-devised warp bomb. Kabreigny, or her staff, perhaps always on the alert for unauthorized weapons research, discovered that someone was digging into old science connected to long-since disproven rumors of the warp bomb. Concerned that someone else might know more than the Federation, that there was a chance that a warp bomb might exist, she had used her position to classify the results of Cochrane's early research and deployed worm programs of her own to selectively erase that data from the Starfleet computer network. But her response only confirmed what Thorsen had believed, so he began to intensify his search, trying to find some trace of information she might have forgotten, widening his areas of inquiry until it became a general inquiry covering anything at all to do with Cochrane, even down to the reference "Gamma Canaris." And each escalation Thorsen undertook must have convinced Kabreigny that she should take further measures in response, intensifying a secret war where no one knew who the real opponent was, and all fought over an ancient experiment that meant nothing.

"But however illusory the reason for the war," Spock said, "the stakes are very real." He glanced at the screen. So did Kirk.

Kirk felt nauseated. Thorsen had peeled away the skin around his eye to reveal more duranium.

"Look at him," Cochrane said. "He's insane."

"At his stage of transformation," Spock suggested, "it would be more proper to say he is malfunctioning."

"Give me Cochrane," Thorsen rasped. "I want him to appreciate what he has done." First one pincer, then another plunged deep within Thorsen's eye socket, but there was no sign of organic damage. To his sickened onlookers, if there was anything left of Thorsen that was human, it was no more than a vestige.

"Very well," Kirk said, forcing his eyes to remain on the screen. "But I want your word as an officer that you will then allow me to withdraw with the other rescued passengers from the *Utopia Planitia*. I have many injured who require immediate medical attention."

"No!" the Companion abruptly cried out as she realized what Kirk was doing. "We will not allow you to endanger the man!" She moved toward Kirk. Spock intercepted her, pulled her firmly away.

"Stand by for transport," Kirk said, his focus unshaken. "This might take a moment. *Enterprise* out." He killed the transmission, audio and visual, just as Thorsen's pincers began to withdraw from deep within his eye socket. Kirk felt better not knowing what they might have emerged with.

He stepped out of his chair. "Spock, it's all right. Companion: I will not harm the man."

"Thank you," Cochrane said. He went to the Companion as Spock released her. "But what *will* you do?"

"We have an edge, Mr. Cochrane," Kirk said, adrenaline flowing as once again he saw the way out. "The armaments and response time of those ships are handicapped by their commander. You saw the bridge personnel behind Thorsen. No uniforms. It's a smuggler's crew. Maybe he stole those ships, maybe the Empire's in such bad shape that they're starting to sell their battle cruisers, but we're not facing top Klingon warriors. That's a big advantage to start with."

Kirk went to the command console and reached down between Chekov and Sulu to check sensor readings. "Mr. Spock, have a shuttlecraft prepared for maximum warp on automatic pilot. We'll need a decoy in a few minutes."

"What heading, Captain?"

For that, Kirk didn't have an answer. Yet. "Mr. Sulu, we've got warp seven capability for only a few hours. Find us somewhere to go where we can disappear. Back to the asteroid belt in Gamma Canaris. A nebula. Somewhere we can avoid their sensors." Kirk left the console. "Then chart a course for the shuttle directly opposite that heading."

"Aye-aye, Captain."

"I thought we couldn't outrun them," Cochrane said.

"Not for long," Kirk replied. "But they're not the enemy I thought they were." He took his seat again. "Mr. Chekov, when I give the order, I want what's left of the *Planitia* blasted to plasma to create a sensor screen. Immediately after, we will concentrate all phaser fire on the bridge of the leftmost battle cruiser, and target all photon torpedoes on its warp nacelles."

Chekov acknowledged his orders enthusiastically.

"Hit and run?" Cochrane asked in disbelief at the daring of it.

Kirk nodded, smiling. "With luck, they'll be leaderless. And we've already seen that the crews of those ships won't take action without Thorsen's presence."

"Captain," Uhura said. "We're being hailed by Colonel Thorsen."

"Keep him offscreen, Lieutenant. Don't transmit visuals."

Thorsen's transmission was a single word, long and slow. "Cochrane."

"He's not cooperating," Kirk answered curtly. "Security is chasing him. We'll have him in a few minutes."

"One minute."

"All three ships are powering up their phasers," Sulu announced.

Kirk ended his audio transmission. "Do you have a heading, Mr. Sulu?"

"Three possibilities, Captain." Sulu turned around in his chair. "The Gamma Canaris asteroid belt is at the edge of our range, but once we got there, it would be cat-and-mouse until reinforcements arrived. Nothing to really confuse their sensor scans."

"What else?" Kirk asked. According to the chronometer, they had forty-five seconds before Thorsen opened fire.

"Epsilon Canaris. G-type star. Several planets including a gas giant. If we make it to Epsilon Canaris III, they have planetary defenses that could help us."

Kirk discounted that possibility at once. That planet was still in a precarious state as Federation commissioners continued to broker a peace treaty. The sight of the *Enterprise* rushing in, pursued by Klingon cruisers, would definitely be destabilizing to the fragile peace process.

"Third choice," Kirk said. Thirty-five seconds remaining.

"Shuttle ready for launching," Spock announced.

"I want the shuttle out of here the instant the wreckage is hit," Kirk said. "Mr. Sulu?"

"It's a singularity. T'Lin's New Catalog number 65813. Six hours at warp seven."

"A naked singularity?" Kirk asked.

"According to the survey charts, it has an event horizon."

Hope built in Kirk. A black hole could be just what he needed now. "Size?"

"Diameter is eight hundred kilometers."

Kirk saw that this had possibilities. Twenty-five seconds remained. "Mass?"

"Two hundred solar masses."

Kirk turned to Spock. "Can we use it to slingshot, Mr. Spock?" The right approach at the right warp speed around a massive enough object could propel the *Enterprise* back in time. Starfleet prohibited the maneuver except under controlled circumstances approved by the full Admiralty. But Kirk was willing to face them after the fact, if it meant he could get Cochrane and the *Enterprise* to safety, several days in the past.

But Spock put an end to that possibility. "The ship's present condition precludes a slingshot trajectory, Captain. Neither the remaining dilithium crystals nor the damaged port nacelle strut could withstand the strain."

Fifteen seconds remained.

"Keptin," Chekov said, "their targeting sensors are locking on."

"Spock: Will there be sufficient relativistic distortions near the black hole's event horizon to disrupt sensors?" Kirk asked.

"Without question," Spock answered.

Kirk made his decision, committed his ship. "Sulu, set course to TNC 65813. Chekov, ready on phasers and photon torpedoes."

Both men acknowledged. Ten seconds remained.

"Open a channel to Thorsen, Lieutenant," Kirk said to Uhura. "Audio only. Let's keep them off balance. Ready to fire on my mark, Mr. Chekov."

"Channel open, sir."

"Colonel Thorsen, we have captured Cochrane and are taking him to the transporter room. Which ship would you like us to beam him to?"

Thorsen appeared on screen. Half the skin remaining on his face now hung in fluttering strips. Where his eye had been was only a dark socket. "Beam him to me," Thorsen cackled in triumph. "We have a great deal of time to make up for. We both have secrets to share in the Pursuit of Perfection."

"Standing by in the transporter room," Kirk said. "We will beam him to you as soon as you lower your shields." He ended transmission.

Chekov next words were full of wonder. "Keptin, he is dropping his shields."

"Definitely not a Klingon," Kirk said. "Mr. Chekov, Mr. Spock, proceed with firing sequence and shuttle launch."

Instantly the deep hum of the phasers echoed through the bridge as Thorsen's image winked off the viewscreen, to be replaced by a split-second image of the *Planitia*'s wreckage just before it turned into an expanding field of incandescent plasma. The bridge of the *Enterprise* shook as the photon torpedoes launched, leaving glowing trails into the plasma cloud. Cochrane held tightly to the Companion, marveling at the audacity Kirk and his crew regularly displayed.

"Shuttle away," Spock confirmed. "Maximum warp."

"Phasers locked on Thorsen's ship," Chekov announced. The phasers sang again. "Registering hits but impossible to tell their shield status."

"Get us out of here, Mr. Sulu. Warp factor seven."

The bridge tilted as the *Enterprise* moved out of normal space and the plasma ball vanished from the viewscreen.

"No sign of pursuit, Keptin."

"That's it?" Cochrane asked. "We're at time-warp factor seven that quickly?"

Kirk smiled. His ship and crew had performed perfectly. "Warp readout, Mr. Sulu." The distant whine of the ship's engines increased.

"Factor five point five . . . point eight . . . six point two . . . point five . . . point nine . . . warp factor seven, sir."

Cochrane whistled. "In my day, it would take three hours just to get up to time-warp four."

"*These* are your days, Mr. Cochrane," Kirk said. "It's your engines driving this ship. You made all this possible."

"I also made Thorsen possible," Cochrane answered. "Like you said, Captain: Technology is neutral."

Chekov interrupted. "Keptin, I have clear sensor readings

around the *Planitia* wreckage. One cruiser crippled, sir. It has ejected its warp core."

"Good shooting, Mr. Chekov. What about the others?"

"One cruiser is in pursuit of our shuttlecraft decoy. Estimated time to intercept, fifteen minutes."

"If they don't think to scan it for life signs before that," Kirk said. "Last ship?"

"Staying within transporter range of the crippled wessel, sir. It appears they're beaming aboard the crew."

"Any sign of the Orion transport?"

"Negative, sir. It was docked with the damaged cruiser."

Kirk almost felt like relaxing. Each second the cruisers delayed chasing the *Enterprise* increased the odds of success. And they were finally out of Thorsen's jamming range. "Uhura, open a secure channel to Starfleet Command and request urgent assistance." Kirk thought about Admiral Kabreigny. She had been convinced that security at Starfleet had been compromised. But was it solely because of Thorsen, or did he have other accomplices? "Identify our attackers as Orion smugglers operating D7 battle cruisers. Make no mention of Colonel Thorsen for now."

Uhura acknowledged, and now that the immediate danger had passed, Kirk could see Cochrane looking around the bridge, eyes wide.

"All that about the condition of those ships behind us," Cochrane said, "you were able to detect it with . . . subspace sensors?"

Kirk nodded. "Would you like a tour?"

Cochrane stared at him in amazement. "Aren't we running for our lives?"

"Keptin, cruiser two is now in pursuit of the *Enterprise.*"

"Time to intercept?" Kirk asked.

"Five hours, ten minutes."

"Time to the singularity?"

"At present velocity, five hours fifty-five minutes."

The *Enterprise* would come under attack forty-five minutes before she reached safety. Cochrane was right. They were running for their lives. And the urge to relax left Kirk as quickly as it had come upon him.

SIX

☆

U.S.S. ENTERPRISE NCC-1701-D
EN ROUTE TO STARBASE 324
Stardate 43922.1
Earth Standard: ≈ May 2366

An hour after the senior officers' debriefing, three hours after the collision with Traklamek's Warbird, the *Enterprise*'s warp core was back on-line and Picard's mighty ship made way for Starbase 324, the heart of Starfleet Tactical's effort to develop a defense against the Borg. With his ship at peace once again, Picard arrived in the main shuttlebay as Geordi La Forge had requested, eager to examine the unexpected treasure that had been found.

By now, La Forge had completely removed the Preserver object from what might or might not have been a Borg artifact. The artifact itself was spread out over a section of the shuttlebay deck marked with a detailed grid. The grid's purpose was to aid in the analysis and reconstruction of damaged or destroyed vehicles and equipment. Optical sensors recorded the original position of each item on the grid from several different angles so the computer could create three-dimensional models to be studied in greater detail and under various simulated conditions. Portions of the Borg artifact were precisely laid out on that grid, and Picard knew that even now a compressed data stream containing everything La Forge and Data had managed to learn about it was being sent via subspace to Admiral Hanson at Starbase 324.

Picard only hoped that the information was not part of a Romulan effort to mislead the Federation about the Borg's true nature.

The Preserver object, however, was not on the reconstruction grid. La Forge had mounted it on several equipment cradles normally used to support shuttlecraft undergoing maintenance or repair. Though it was a purely subjective, emotional conclusion, the instant Jean-Luc Picard saw the object unobscured by the jumble of the Borg artifact, he felt certain that the object was authentic, and made by the same hand as the Preserver obelisk. It was, to Picard, a thing of beauty.

"Quite a sight, isn't it?" La Forge asked as he approached the captain, wiping his hands with a cleaning cloth.

"Oh, it is, Mr. La Forge, it is," the captain said.

Perfectly displayed against the stars that streaked to a vanishing point past the open shuttlebay doors, sealed only by an atmospheric forcefield, the object seemed to glow with a polished silver sheen beneath the bright shuttlebay lights. Its proportions, far more subtle than just the first reported gross measurements of two meters by three meters by five meters, included graceful indentations and curves that made it resemble a shaft of liquid cut from a magnificent wave of molten metal and frozen in a sparkling instant of time. Picard gazed at it and saw visions of oceans. The reservoirs of life. From what seas had the makers of this object emerged? How distant in time and space?

"You can almost hear the ocean roar, can't you?" La Forge said quietly.

"It's . . . magnificent," Picard replied, knowing the word did no justice to the depth of his feeling. "I cannot believe that this was constructed by the Romulans."

"And that's not all of it," La Forge continued. "Check out the other side."

They walked together, and on the far side of the object, where Data and Wesley Crusher worked with elaborate molecular probes held against the object's surface, Picard saw what he could only consider as an ugly scar that marred the object's beauty. It was a dark and ragged scrape a meter square which appeared to

311

have broken off a corner of the object, just where the eye—and the heart—demanded its curves should continue to a graceful conclusion.

"It's some kind of stress fracture or abrasion," La Forge said as they stopped beside the wound. "The outside skin is so tough I can't think of anything that could have done this short of a supernova, but sometime in the past three and half billion years, this thing suffered quite a shock."

Picard held his fingers above the abrupt demarcation line between the smooth outer surface and the dark indentation. "May I?" he asked.

La Forge nodded. "There's no danger. I can't tell yet if the dark material is what happens to the silver covering when it's subjected to intense heat and deformed, or if it's the normal appearance of whatever's inside. Data thinks we're actually looking at a tightly packed, molecular quantum computer of some kind, so complexly interconnected that it appears to be a solid. If that's true, this object could contain more computing power than . . . all the computers in the Federation combined." La Forge pointed to a textured section of the scar. "Now, over here, you can't see it, but with my VISOR I can detect a pattern of microscopic holes, almost like wiring conduits. This is the interface area where the Borg artifact had tapped into the object to draw power."

"It's still generating power?" Picard asked.

"Somewhere. Somehow," La Forge sighed. "Wesley's suggested that when we get to the starbase, we might see about creating a specialized type of nanite to crawl inside and look around."

"A splendid idea. Just so long as Mr. Crusher doesn't create the nanites onboard the *Enterprise* this time," Picard said. He remembered all too well what had happened with the acting ensign's last experiment in nanotechnology.

"I'll make sure of that," La Forge agreed. "Anyway, Data and Wesley are going over the undamaged surface to see if there are any interface areas that are intact."

Picard was intrigued. "Do you think this object was made for the purpose of interfacing?" The Preserver obelisk, which had been studied so intensely, and so ineffectively, seemed to be designed specifically to *not* give up its secrets. The idea that this

Preserver object was purposely constructed to communicate was tantalizing, to say the least.

"That's what Data thinks." La Forge pointed to the front of the object. "Come take another look at the inscriptions."

The object was now oriented so that Picard could identify the markings on its forward face without turning his head. He had no idea what the inscriptions meant, of course, but he did recognize them.

La Forge pointed to one of the geometric drawings that appeared among the Preserver cuneiform markings: the first drawing when the sequence was read top to bottom. "Does this look familiar?" he asked.

Picard was startled by the question. "Should it?"

"It did to me, as soon as Data pointed it out. It's surprising how obvious it is."

Picard studied the drawing, all the more baffling now that he knew it should have some obvious meaning. He traced the open border around it, ran his fingers over its sequence of vertical lines . . .

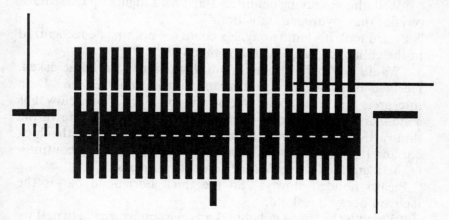

. . . but its pattern meant nothing to him.

"Are you suggesting this is similar to the old space-probe data records?" Picard asked. At the dawn of space exploration, humans had affixed various data-storage media to its space probes in the unlikely event they were ever recovered by aliens: first, analog audio and visual recording disks, then diffraction bars, and finally molecular bristle tubes. But no matter the technology of the recording, each data record had been sent out into space with an "instruction" plate. The plate was engraved with what behaviorists at the time had hoped would be universal symbols, each derived from basic physical constants that could be interpreted by any spacefaring culture. The purpose was to show the recordings' place and time of origin, and to indicate how the data should be interpreted to produce sound and pictures. Earth's historical societies were still asking alien cultures to try decoding replicas of those variously packaged space messages. To date, none had succeeded. Though the Vulcans had come close.

"Data thinks it's a possibility," La Forge confirmed, "though it's intended for a more sophisticated level of interpretation."

"I can see that," Picard said. "As I recall, the engraved plates our ancestors sent out began with the depiction of simple hydrogen transition states, to establish basic increments of time and distance, based on the law of mediocrity, the assumption that even alien systems would be based on similar laws of nature."

"Well, this engraving definitely starts a bit higher up the scale of physics than hydrogen transitions."

Picard took his hand away. He could see nothing he recognized in the collection of lines. "How much higher?"

"Would you believe continuum distortion?" La Forge asked. He held his finger to the diagram, starting on the left. "Data interprets this inverted T marking and the four dashes below it as a standard tachyon decay event." He drew his finger down the thin vertical line. "Here's the tachyon." He jumped over the thick bar and tapped the dashes. "And after the tunneling discontinuity, here are the tachyon's four constituent quarks."

Picard nodded slowly. "So the thick horizontal bar is the tachyon decay threshold."

"Which is the speed of light," La Forge confirmed. "Then, if we consider these two short, thick lines on either side of the vertical line pattern to represent the speed of light . . ."

Picard saw it instantly. It was in two dimensions, without a logarithmic or any other kind of curve, but the ratios looked right. He touched the thin, clear vertical line that cut through the horizontal bars above the speed-of-light markings. "Then this represents a state of infinite energy," he said.

"You've got it," La Forge agreed.

Picard dropped his finger to the set of horizontal dots that extended below the speed of light. "And this is the energy required for movement into warp space, which is less than infinite."

"And," La Forge continued, indicating the three clear vertical bars on the diagram's right, "once you're in warp space, here's your offset of the theoretical peak power consumption at one hundred percent efficiency."

"Do the ratios work out?" Picard asked.

"Data measured the width of each line and the spaces between them to within an angstrom. This diagram was engraved with precision particle etching that gives the numerical relationships of all warp ratio values to five decimal places. Captain, the diagram on this object is just a bare-bones version of this." La Forge tapped his chest beside his communicator pin, which was fashioned in the shape of Starfleet's familiar delta design. "It's the basis of warp physics established by Zefram Cochrane—a diagram of the asymmetrical distortion field function, missing one of its axes."

Picard was impressed. "If this is true, then whoever built this was indeed counting on a considerable level of achievement from those who found it."

"I'll say. Especially considering this is just the first diagram of twenty-four."

Picard rubbed at his chin. The power-consumption relationship depicted by the diagram was as obvious to him now as it was in the Starfleet insignia he wore, just as La Forge had said. But there were still parts of the diagram that didn't fit. "If the vertical line on the left is a tachyon decay, what about this vertical line on the right?" he asked.

La Forge shrugged. He pointed to the right-hand line and the vertical bar at the center bottom. "Data's best theory is that these lines have something to do with zero-point energy extraction." He indicated the horizontal line cutting across the six upper bars on the right. "And these lines might have something to do with transwarp propulsion in other dimensions."

"My word," Picard said. "Getting energy from a vacuum has eluded our scientists for generations. And Starfleet abandoned the whole idea of transwarp propulsion as impractical decades ago."

La Forge touched his finger thoughtfully to the diagram. "You know, Captain, if Data's right about this, if it *is* some sort of message that's set up for extremely technologically advanced cultures to interpret . . . it sort of makes me wonder if we were supposed to find it yet."

Picard had also been thinking exactly that. "You mean, somehow the object was damaged, perhaps, as you suggested, by a supernova. The Borg then incorporated it into their vessel without recognizing it for what it was, and the Romulans acquired it by accident, by destroying the Borg vessel."

"If the Romulans did acquire it from a Borg vessel. I'm still not convinced of that."

Data and Acting Ensign Wesley Crusher came around the corner of the object, molecular probes switched off.

"Hi, Captain Picard," Wesley said. He grinned at the object, eyes full of wonder. "Isn't this incredible?"

Uncomfortable as he was with children, even those as old as Wesley, Picard appreciated the acting ensign's youthful enthusiasm for an archaeological find of the first order. It indicated that the youth showed promise, which Picard had always suspected. "That and much more, Mr. Crusher," Picard said. He looked at Data. "Were you able to find an intact interface area?"

"No," Data said, "but that does not mean that one does not exist. Regrettably, I suspect it is simply beyond the means of our technology to identify."

"Do you agree with Mr. La Forge, then?" Picard asked. "That we have come upon this object before we are technologically able to understand it?"

"That is a distinct possibility," Data agreed. "I have used my subroutines to analyze the diagrams as Wesley and I have been working. It is the equivalent of the way in which humans consciously put aside problems so their subconscious can work on solving them without conscious effort." Data paused and looked

FEDERATION

to the side. "Though in my case, since I remain conscious of everything, the analogy does not hold."

"Data," La Forge said gently, "let's not keep the captain waiting."

"My apologies, Captain," Data said. "In any event, this first diagram is understandable."

"We've been over that diagram, Data," La Forge said.

Data looked at the object, indicating the path of the inscriptions and the diagrams along its front panel. "The diagrams that follow this first one clearly increase in complexity. I believe the next in the sequence relates in more detail to zero-point energy extraction, though to our knowledge of physics, it appears to be a mathematical description of a perpetual-motion machine."

"If we ever create the technology for extracting zero-point energy," Picard said, "we *will* have perpetual-motion machines."

"In a manner of speaking," Data allowed. "The third diagram bears some connection to the second, but I cannot comprehend its meaning at all. The fourth diagram appears to relate back to the first, referring again, I believe, to other spatial continuums beyond the one in which warp drive operates. I then do not have the slightest conception as to what nineteen of the remaining twenty diagrams mean, though judging from the preponderance of prime numbers in the ratio of line thicknesses to length, I presume they elaborate profound relationships of nature. Relationships which, as of now, are beyond our present level of science."

Picard nodded thoughtfully. Then he realized what Data had said. "Nineteen of the remaining twenty? Then you *do* understand another of the diagrams?"

"That is problematic," the android replied. He crouched down on his knees to point to a diagram at the bottom of the first row of inscriptions. Its position marred the otherwise symmetrical arrangement of the double columns.

"Quite clearly," Data said, "it is related to the first diagram in the series, though according to the established pattern, it should be much more complex, and thus indecipherable."

317

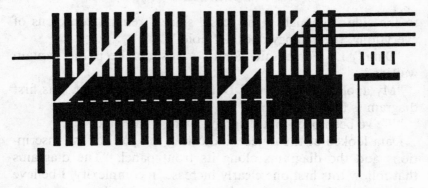

Picard knelt down beside Data to examine the engraved lines. "But you feel you understand what this one means?"

"Taken in context, I believe the clear diagonal lines relate to the infinite power release once thought to accompany unstable warp fields."

Picard tried to place that within his knowledge of the development of warp propulsion. It had been a long time since he had taken that class at the Academy.

But Wesley spoke up impulsively. "You mean, what they called the 'warp bomb'?"

"Precisely," Data agreed. "It was Zefram Cochrane, the human father of warp propulsion, who early on in his research faced the possibility that a warp field might be used to create a near-infinite energy release in a confined area."

"I'm pretty sure the captain is familiar with Cochrane's work," La Forge said.

Picard got to his feet again. "I am, but please continue with any insights you might have."

"As an interesting historical corollary, when human researchers developing the first explosive atomic-fission device originally performed their calculations of the chain reaction they sought to create, they determined that there was a chance the chain reaction might extend from the enriched uranium in the device into the Earth's atmosphere, igniting the atmosphere and consequently ending all life on the planet."

Picard could see La Forge's impatience building but was eager to know what else Data had concluded about the Preserver ob-

318

ject. "And how does that relate to the object at hand?" Picard asked.

"Before detonating the first fission explosive, the researchers had managed to detect the flaw in their theory and were fairly confident that the Earth's atmosphere would not ignite."

"Fairly certain?" Picard repeated.

"Scientific rigor was not the same in the nineteen hundreds, sir. In any event, it was quickly seen that there was no possibility of an atomic chain reaction extending to the atmosphere. In the same way, Zefram Cochrane and his team were eventually able to definitively prove that even the most unstable warp field could never generate a destructive force greater than could be achieved by an ordinary matter-antimatter reaction. Yet," Data concluded, "according to this diagram, such a reaction *is* possible."

Picard re-created the steps of Data's argument. He didn't see what the problem was. "However, you think the earlier diagrams show that zero-point energy extraction and transwarp propulsion are possible, if technologically beyond us for the moment. So why is it a warp bomb does not fall under the same category?"

"Because," Data said, with no hint of exasperation, "zero-point energy extraction has been known to be theoretically possible since the first mathematical descriptions of inertial damping in the early nineteen-nineties. Similarly, when Starfleet abandoned its transwarp propulsion studies, it was for reasons of practicality, reliability, and efficiency. If in the future the unlimited resources of zero-point energy ever become available, transwarp propulsion indeed might be feasible. But the warp bomb is as much a scientific impossibility as igniting Earth's atmosphere with an atomic bomb."

"Which raises the question," Picard concluded, "of why this particular diagram is included on the object."

"Since the warp-bomb diagram differs from the others and seems out of place in the sequence, it is possible that it was added much later, by someone other than the original manufacturers of the object."

"To what end?" Picard asked, frowning.

"Though I feel I have some expertise in the analysis of technical information, when it comes to understanding the motivation of

319

JUDITH AND GARFIELD REEVES-STEVENS

sentient beings, I must defer to those who have had firsthand experience." Data looked at La Forge.

"Mr. La Forge?" Picard said encouragingly.

La Forge in turn looked at Wesley Crusher. "Well, actually, Captain, Wesley is the one who came up with the idea."

Picard tugged on his tunic. "Very well. Mr. Crusher?"

Wesley looked uncomfortable in a gawky, adolescent way. "Well, sir, I've been spending a lot of time getting ready for the Academy, and . . . I think it might be a test."

"The object?" Picard said. "A test?" He stared at the object, trying to see it in this new light.

"Some of the entrance exams I've had to take were completely visual," Wesley explained in a hurry. "You know, pattern matching, spatial orientation, identifying mathematical functions . . . Maybe that's what this is. Sort of."

"And the purpose of it would be . . . ?" Picard prompted.

Wesley looked embarrassed, shrugged, and said nothing more.

"Wesley thinks that like the old Earth space-probe instruction plates," La Forge said quickly, covering for the young man, "these diagrams might be the instructions for how the object operates. And if we can figure out how it works, then maybe we could use it to communicate with whoever built it."

Picard eyed Wesley dubiously. "So you think this might be some sort of subspace . . . or shall we say, *trans*-space radio?"

Crusher's cheeks burned bright red and Picard was genuinely sorry that he affected the youth that way. "More likely a computer of some sort, sir," Wesley mumbled as he glanced down at the shuttlebay deck. "At least, according to what Data said about it appearing to have molecular quantum circuitry."

Picard looked at Wesley until the acting ensign glanced up and caught his eyes. "Mr. Crusher, I consider your idea a valid theory. To be part of the Starfleet team, you should never hesitate to contribute or to speak your mind. Good work."

Wesley abruptly beamed, though he still looked slightly disconcerted.

"But, unfortunately," Picard went on, "if this *is* a test, it seems unlikely we are in any position to pass it." The captain rested his hand on the object. For a moment, he suddenly recalled Wesley

320

when the young man had been unsuccessful in his first attempt at the Academy entrance exams two years earlier. But Beverly Crusher's son hadn't abandoned his goals then. He had simply applied himself to study harder for the next opportunity to retake the exams.

"The next opportunity . . ." Picard said to himself.

"I beg your pardon, Captain?" La Forge asked.

Picard smiled. "The Romulans failed the test," he said.

Data, La Forge, and Wesley just looked at him uncomprehendingly.

"Don't you see," the captain said, "this has nothing at all to do with the Borg. I think Geordi was right." Picard missed La Forge's reaction to his sudden use of the engineer's first name, a sign of the captain's enthusiasm. "That Borg artifact over there probably is just a replicated duplicate, built solely for us, so we would believe that we stumbled upon this Preserver object on our own."

"But why not just give us the Preserver object?" La Forge said. "Why go to all the trouble of wrapping it up in part of a Borg ship?"

Picard smiled as the logic of it became clear. "Because the Romulans correctly assessed our weakness—our *need* for new knowledge. Imagine if they had tried to give us the object alone. We would have been suspicious, mistrustful. We probably wouldn't have allowed it on the *Enterprise,* fearing some trick." The captain patted the object now. "But a piece of *Borg* technology would receive a different reception. Starfleet wants something like that so badly that we were bound to be less critical when it was offered.

"And the whole scenario of coming to *us* directly—not leaving it in a space lane where someone else might have come across it—but bringing it directly to the attention of the *Enterprise,* the first ship to have engaged the Borg, how could we resist? And approaching us through the Ferengi—pure genius. We were so busy trying to avoid being cheated by DaiMon Pol that we didn't bother to examine what he was saying very carefully."

"But, Captain," La Forge pointed out. "All those Ferengi . . . they were killed, sir."

Picard frowned. He was aware of the specter of death surrounding this object. "Dead men tell no tales, Mr. La Forge. Whoever was behind this plan wanted no witnesses."

"And what about Traklamek?" La Forge continued. "I can understand the Romulans deciding to sacrifice Ferengi, but not their own people."

Picard nodded in agreement. "Traklamek's fate might very well have been a miscalculation on the Romulans' part. In hindsight, Commander Tarl did seem too eager to return home to the Empire. It's possible that it was intended from the beginning that she would be 'recaptured' by Traklamek, leaving us with the Borg artifact and feeling fortunate that we had escaped with it. Remember, Traklamek made no mention of the artifact, nor did he attempt to destroy our shuttlecraft when we were bringing it aboard. However, he was not prepared for our commitment to helping Tarl escape to a new life."

"Which would mean Tarl is probably halfway home by now," La Forge said, "thinking we've fallen for her story hook, line, and sinker." At that remark, Data looked at La Forge as if the android were about to ask a question, but La Forge held up his hand and said, "I'll explain later, Data." The engineer addressed Picard again. "*I'll* admit it makes sense, but you've got to admit it's an incredibly complex plan."

Picard agreed with La Forge's sentiment, but he said, "Think of the incredibly high stakes, Mr. La Forge. This object could open a window onto technology centuries, if not millennia, in advance of our own."

"That's another problem," La Forge said. "If it's so valuable, why give it to us?"

"So we can do what the Romulans could not," Picard answered. "Unlock its secrets."

Data rejoined the discussion. "If that is true, Captain Picard, then the Romulans must have devised a second part to their plan, to allow them to reclaim this object once we have determined its function, if we are able."

Picard had already considered that. "A very good point, Mr. Data. Would your investigation of this object have uncovered any Romulan listening devices?"

"Without question," Data said. Then he looked over at the reconstruction grid on the shuttlebay deck. "However, there is no telling what may be hidden in the complexities of the apparent Borg assembly. I will require some time to scan that assembly detail."

"In the meantime," Picard said as he studied the mound of parts already removed from the Borg-like material, "perhaps it would be wise to surround the entire artifact with a security field, in order to disable any hidden sensing devices."

"I'll get on it right away, Captain," La Forge acknowledged. "But what should we do about this?" He indicated the object.

Picard studied the inscriptions carefully. If he were to follow the rules apparently inscribed on it, he would turn the object over to Starfleet, where a science team would begin analysis and trial and error. It could be decades before any results might be forthcoming, if at all. But as his attack on Traklamek had shown, sometimes the rules could be changed.

"Is it possible," Picard asked, "that the conduits used by the Borg to tap the object's power might also be used to link it with a computer?"

La Forge nodded. "That's why we were scanning for an interface area on the surface."

"Why not try to access the object from the exposed interface area?"

Wesley was the one who answered. "Wouldn't that be like . . . cheating, sir?"

Picard shook his head. "In this case, we're making up the rules as we go along, Mr. Crusher. I see nothing wrong in exploiting every opportunity which presents itself."

La Forge looked thoughtful. "I could hook up a type-three interface connection between the ship's computer and the object in just a few minutes, sir. It won't tell us anything immediately, but at least we could start probing the object's circuit structure."

Picard nodded. "Make it so."

A half hour later, the Borg-like artifact was encased in a sparkling forcefield that would prevent any type of monitor from recording the events on the shuttlebay deck and transmitting them to any potential Romulan spy.

At the same time, beside the Preserver object, La Forge, Wesley, and Data had set up a portable engineering computer-console. A thick bundle of monofilament induction leads ran from the console to a universal connector that was attached to the interface area on the object's scarred section. Picard had watched his crew set up the equipment with interest.

Finally, La Forge looked up from his tricorder and flipped the tiny device shut. "We're getting positive signal strength from all microscopic conduits, sir."

Data spoke from his position at the console's controls. "I have established a program which will allow our equipment to probe each conduit in terms of signal strength and its interrelationship with other conduits. It will be a trial-and-error method at first, but in time we should gain a basic understanding of the circuit logic used within the device, which might lead to our being able to communicate with it."

"Splendid," Picard said to his team. "Any idea how long it might take?"

"On the order of hours to days, sir. Assuming that we are correct in identifying the object as containing computational ability."

Picard had been hoping for faster results, but it would take the *Enterprise* more than two weeks to reach Starbase 324, so at least there was a chance of achieving some breakthrough before then. "Please proceed, Mr. Data."

Data ran his fingers over the console's control panel. "I am now completing the connection."

Status lights flickered over the console's displays and on the universal connector.

"Intriguing," Data said as he studied the readouts.

Picard stepped closer to look over the android's shoulder. He could see that patterns were already beginning to emerge.

"Look at that," Wesley said, standing on Data's other side. "The object is probing our equipment the way we were trying to probe it."

"Is that right, Mr. Data?" Picard asked.

"It is, sir. It appears the object is considerably more sophisticated than I anticipated." He pointed to the largest display screen on the console, where geometric shapes created by multicolored lines swirled like mixing water currents. "The data-relay pattern that is developing is similar to that which was created by Dr. Ira Graves when he downloaded his intellect into the ship's computer."

Picard reacted with alarm. "Is the object attempting to *download* information?"

Data angled his head, eyes fixed on the displays. "It is unlikely that—"

Riker's voice came from Picard's communicator. "Bridge to Picard." He sounded troubled.

Picard tapped the Starfleet delta on his chest. "Go ahead, Number One."

"Sir, the *Enterprise* has just changed course."

"Under whose authority?" Picard asked.

"That's just it, sir. No orders have been received or given. We simply . . . changed course and the helm no longer responds."

Picard looked at the universal connector attached to the Preserver object. He had been in space long enough to guess what had just happened. "Disconnect the interface at once," Picard ordered. Perhaps the object wasn't to blame, but the interface could always be reestablished later.

Data quickly entered commands on the control surfaces. Picard heard the *Enterprise*'s engines begin to whine.

"Sir," Data said, "the interface no longer appears to recognize our abort commands."

"Captain Picard," Riker announced. "We're at warp eight and continuing to accelerate."

"Mr. La Forge!" Picard called out as he pointed at the universal connector.

But Wesley was closer and immediately saw what the captain meant. He grabbed the monofilament fibers attached to the connector.

"Wesley, no!" La Forge warned.

Too late. The instant Wesley yanked on the fibers, sparks erupted from the connector, traveling along the fibers to flare around the youth's hands. He cried out as he was flung back to land heavily on the deck. The connector, now free, clattered on the deckplates.

La Forge and Data rushed to Wesley's unconscious form. Picard hit his communicator. "Number One—what's our status?"

Sparks continued to flutter over the surface of the connector, along the monofilaments, and onto the console itself. None of the controls could be touched now. The engines continued to increase their pitch.

"We've just hit warp nine!" Riker answered tensely. "All bridge controls are locked."

Picard glared at the Preserver object. "Will—listen carefully. Our computer has been invaded by an override program. You must shut down *all* computer functions. We will have to reset the—"

Picard's communicator squealed. He tapped it again. "Picard to bridge?" But the connection had been severed. It made perfect sense. All communications on the ship were controlled by the computer.

A few meters distant, Wesley moaned as La Forge and Data succeeded in helping him to his feet. Picard moved swiftly to an equipment locker and pulled out a phaser. As he jogged back to the console, he set the weapon to level nine to vaporize the interface console and keyed in his security override command to permit that level of power discharge on board. But as he raised the phaser to take aim, all lights in the shuttlebay went out at once.

Picard held his finger over the phaser trigger button, loath to fire when he could not see Data, La Forge, and Wesley. It took a moment for his vision to adjust to the emergency storage lights that came on-line. They were independent of the computer system, but would only provide a few hours of low-level illumination.

"Stand back!" Picard warned his crew. Then he fired at the portable computer console. It took only a few seconds for the console to dissolve beneath the phaser's fury.

But the scream of the *Enterprise*'s engines still rose.

La Forge ran to the captain's side, shouting to be heard above the din. "Sir, if something has taken over the computers and can control all the ship's systems, we have to get out of the shuttlebay *now!*"

Picard was about to ask his chief engineer why. But then he became aware of the characteristic sputter of a forcefield being shut off and he looked in horror at the hangar-bay opening. For an instant, time stopped for Picard as he realized what had happened.

The atmospheric containment field had been shut down.

The wind began to howl as the bay began to explosively decompress.

Picard felt himself yanked forward, feet sliding across the deck, as the wind propelled him inexorably to the vacuum of space.

And oblivion.

SEVEN

U.S.S. ENTERPRISE NCC-1701
APPROACHING TNC 65813
Stardate 3855.5
Earth Standard: ≈ November 2267

The first phaser volley struck Kirk's *Enterprise* ten minutes before she had reached her destination. Mr. Scott had managed to coax a few extra decimal places of warp propulsion out of the engines, but it was not quite enough to avoid interception. Still, Cochrane saw that Kirk was pleased that his ship would now only be vulnerable for ten minutes, and not forty-five. But as far as Cochrane could tell, a starship could be destroyed in seconds, so the difference between ten and forty-five minutes seemed inconsequential.

Cochrane and the Companion were back on the bridge when the attack began. Spock had prepared a station for them, two chairs close together by unused environmental controls. They had managed to clean up and eat in the interim. They had toured the *Enterprise*'s vast engine room. Some of the basic components Cochrane felt he could understand, but most had been a mystery to him. Mr. Scott had been quite kind in attempting to explain key systems, but Cochrane had realized the pressure the engineer had been under and had left as soon as possible.

He and the Companion had even found a few moments to themselves, and Cochrane had immediately apologized to her.

They were to have had years together, full of peace, uneventful, and yet, after only six months, this had happened.

But for the Companion, she regretted nothing. "When we became as we are," she had told him, "we knew each hour with you was numbered, each moment spent was a moment less in the time we would have. But we have had those six months, and we will have years more to come before we are no more."

Cochrane had held her then, admiring her strength. For one who had come so late to understanding humanity and the brevity of human lives, she had courage enough for them both.

But Cochrane had heard the hidden tension in Kirk's words these past five hours. He had seen the intent expressions on the faces of Kirk's crew. He had realized that it wasn't just Kirk and McCoy who were the best in their roles on board this ship—each member of the crew he observed excelled in the same way. Whether that meant Starfleet had discovered staffing methods unknown in Cochrane's time, or whether in the face of interplanetary exploration humans had actually begun to change in the past century and half, Cochrane couldn't be sure. But despite the talent on board the *Enterprise,* despite her near-miraculous technical capabilities, Cochrane knew that the captain felt their situation was precarious.

Yet if the Companion was not capable of detecting that tension in others, Cochrane did not feel it was his place to take her hope from her. Let her dream of a peaceful future with him. He owed her that much, not because of duty, but because of the love he felt for her.

Cochrane wanted to protect her as she had protected him. But as the bridge trembled beneath the pursuing cruiser's first phaser hit, all he could do was hold her hand. At least her smile told him it was enough. For now.

"Damage report," Kirk said. He sat in his chair as a king would occupy his throne. All power emanated from that one position.

"They're still too far away to inflict damage," the Russian, Mr. Chekov, reported. "No damage to ship or shields."

"Time to the black hole?" Kirk asked.

"Nine minutes," Mr. Sulu replied.

"Status of second cruiser?"

"Thirty minutes away."

The second cruiser had intercepted the decoy shuttle, destroyed it, then doubled back to join the pursuit of the *Enterprise*. Thus far, there was no way to know which of the two cruisers carried Thorsen, or even if Thorsen had survived the attack on the third.

The bridge shuddered again. "Minimal damage," Chekov reported without being asked. "Shields stabilizing."

"Transfer all power to aft shields," Kirk said. "Those hits are going to get worse."

"Photon torpedoes launched from pursuing wessels!"

"All hands stand braced for impact," Kirk broadcast throughout the ship. "Ready on phasers, Chekov."

But Chekov did nothing. He spoke with a question in his voice. "Torpedoes passing us, Keptin."

"Damn," Kirk said. "Full power forward shields!"

Instantly the viewscreen flared with orange energy as the *Enterprise* bucked. A moment later, sirens sounded as she shook again.

Chekov called out above the cacophony. "No damage from impact with photon torpedoes! But direct phaser hit on port nacelle and hangar-deck doors."

Spock also raised his voice to be heard through the inundation of noise. "Shields at sixty percent."

Cochrane realized what had happened. As soon as Kirk had reduced the strength of his forward shields, the pursuing cruiser had launched torpedoes on a trajectory that would carry them in front of the *Enterprise* to detonate where her shields were weakest. Then, when Kirk had recognized that strategy, when he had strengthened the forward shields, the cruiser had taken advantage of the starship's exposed aft by firing again.

As damage reports filtered in through the bridge speakers, Kirk said, "At least we know Thorsen isn't on that ship."

Cochrane agreed. The attack had been too well thought out. Whatever else Thorsen had become in the past century and a half, Cochrane doubted he was capable of that kind of sophisticated strategy.

"Arm photon torpedoes," Kirk ordered. "Let's be ready when they try that again."

"Cruiser has launched again," Chekov said.

"As soon as they pass us, drop from warp and launch our torpedoes at the aft of the cruiser," Kirk said.

"Torpedoes passing . . . *now!*" Chekov said.

The *Enterprise* shuddered as she dropped to sublight and the sounds of her torpedo launching tubes echoed. On the screen, Cochrane saw the pursuing cruiser pass in a blur, and even as he braced for impact, he tried to analyze the computer imaging that enabled him to see an object moving faster than light.

But no impact came. Instead, a double set of silent explosions pulsed from the screen.

Chekov raised his fist in victory. "Got them! Fore and aft, sir! They ran into their own torpedoes just as ours hit. Reading heavy damage."

Kirk remained calm. "Go to maximum warp, Mr. Sulu."

"Cruiser is coming about, sir."

"Maintain course. Chekov, ready on phasers."

Then impact finally came as the *Enterprise* swept past the damaged cruiser and both ships exchanged torrents of phaser fire. Cochrane saw an eruption of plasma on the cruiser's starboard flank, and then it was gone from the viewscreen.

Spock reported. "We took no significant damage from that barrage, but our shields are now at forty-three percent."

"Status of the damaged cruiser?" Kirk said.

"Still in pursuit," Sulu answered. "But only at warp five."

"Time to destination?"

"Seven minutes, fifteen seconds."

Cochrane watched as Kirk stretched, and was amazed at the captain's ability to remain so focused on the moment. Cochrane knew that with the differences in their speeds, the *Enterprise* would make it to the singularity before the cruiser could attack again. But even though that next attack was minutes away, Kirk behaved as if his work was finished. Cochrane decided that was the only way a starship captain could approach his work. If he really stopped to think about the power he controlled and the danger he faced on an ongoing basis, he'd be paralyzed.

Kirk slipped out of his chair and headed for Spock's science station. "Uhura, status on Starfleet's response?"

"The *Excalibur* and *Lexington* are en route, priority one. ETA: *Excalibur,* fourteen hours; *Lexington,* twenty-two hours."

"What do you think, Mr. Spock? Can we elude both of Thorsen's cruisers for fourteen hours?"

Spock remained seated at his station as the captain approached. "We need only elude them for thirteen hours, twenty-two minutes," he said.

Kirk smiled. "That makes me feel so much better." Then he became serious again. "What are our chances, really?"

Spock considered his answer for a few moments. "For the entire period, virtually nonexistent."

Kirk didn't seem fazed by his science officer's pronouncement, though, as if he had already come to the same conclusion. "How long can we last?"

"Two, perhaps three hours," Spock said. "If we manage to destroy or cripple one of the cruisers, we might be able to survive an additional four hours. However, sublight maneuvers close to the singularity's event horizon will exert a sizable strain on our structural integrity field. Even if we avoid additional weapons damage, we will be forced to leave the vicinity of the singularity at that time."

Kirk rubbed his eyes, the first indication Cochrane had seen of the exhaustion he must feel. He also rubbed at a spot on his back, wincing as he did so.

"I am open to suggestions, Mr. Spock."

But Cochrane spoke first. He needed to understand exactly what kind of danger he was exposing these people to. "What's a structural integrity field?" was his first question.

"An internal forcefield system that augments the mechanical strength of the *Enterprise*'s spaceframe," Spock answered. "The stresses involved in moving from sublight to warp velocities, in changing course at high-impulse speeds, typically are in excess of what the ship's physical components can withstand. While we are close to the singularity's event horizon, we will need considerable power from both our artificial gravity generators and the structural integrity field in order to overcome the intense, gravitational tidal forces we will experience."

"Is this giving you any ideas, Mr. Cochrane?" Kirk asked.

"Couldn't we last longer if we didn't move as close to the horizon? The gravitational stresses would be less."

"True," Spock said. "But as gravitational stresses decrease, so does the distortion effect on the cruisers' sensors."

Cochrane understood. "Like a submarine," he said. "The closer to the event horizon we are, the harder we are to detect, but the more pressure we're under."

"Very apt," Spock agreed.

"And if we hit bottom," Kirk said, "we get smeared across the event horizon of a black hole with two hundred times the mass of the sun collapsed into . . ." Kirk looked at Spock. "What's the estimated size of the singularity at the heart of TNC 65813?"

"No more than a meter," Spock said.

Cochrane shook his head. "In my time, we had no way of knowing what was inside a singularity. It was the point at which our understanding of physics completely broke down."

"In our time as well, Mr. Cochrane," Spock said. "There are many valid theories worked out in considerable detail, and we have discovered some technologies that allow singularities to be used and manipulated as power sources. But since there is no possible way to extract useful information from inside a singularity, no attempt to probe one, or to see inside one, has ever yielded results. Thus, no theory can be tested."

"Destination in four minutes," Sulu announced. "TNC 65813 onscreen."

Cochrane looked at the screen and saw a luminous whirlpool of glowing gases and dust slowly expanding as the *Enterprise* neared it. At almost ninety degrees to the spiral arms of the whirlpool, solid shafts of light shone top and bottom, slowly precessing like sweeping searchlights. And in the center of the whirlpool, right where the gas and dust reached maximum velocity in their long fall into the singularity hidden at the black hole's center, where their kinetic energy should make them glow the brightest, right at the edge of the event horizon, there was only a black disk.

"Incredible," Cochrane said, overcome by the sight.

The black disk marked the point at which the gravitational attraction of the singularity within accelerated everything to the speed of light—including light itself. No matter, no electromagnetic impulse, could ever have enough energy to emerge from that point. The black hole would inevitably swallow everything which came near, pulling it endlessly down to the inconceivably dense singularity at its heart.

"Have any ships ever been this close to this object?" Kirk asked.

"Automated probes only," Spock said.

"Then let's put all nonessential sensors on 'record,'" Kirk said. "We shouldn't waste the opportunity."

Once again, Cochrane was impressed. Only minutes from a life-and-death struggle, Kirk was concerned with science, with exploration.

"'O brave new world,'" Cochrane said, softly enough that only the Companion could hear him.

But Spock looked at him and nodded, as if acknowledging the sentiment, and Cochrane decided the shape of Vulcans' ears must be more than purely decorative.

Kirk kept his eyes on the screen, but Cochrane doubted he was taking in the beauty of the sight. "Mr. Spock, is there anything we can do to add to the sensor confusion we're trying to exploit? So we can stay farther above the point of no return as Mr. Cochrane suggested?"

"An interesting proposal," Spock said. He joined the captain in staring at the screen, and again Cochrane was certain that it was not to appreciate the power of nature.

"By setting photon torpedoes to explode just above the event horizon, it might be possible to cause it to oscillate, setting up gravitational disturbances. Using the transporter to deposit small amounts of antimatter within the gas and dust could also create gravitationally distorted sensor echoes indistinguishable from the Enterprise, which should serve as effective camouflage." Spock turned to his station. "I shall attempt to work out the details."

Kirk nodded at Cochrane. "Good work, Mr. Cochrane."

Cochrane appreciated the captain's sentiment. He was making the outmoded scientist feel like part of the crew, a talent Kirk used on all the people under his command. Cochrane knew he had only made a wild suggestion. It was Kirk and Spock who had applied the suggestion to the situation at hand and found something useful in it. Still, it encouraged him to try again. Who knew what other wonders of technology this age held?

"If you're trying to create a real disturbance," Cochrane said, "is there any way you can rig one of your torpedoes to detonate just *under* the event horizon?"

Kirk angled his head in forbearance. "The force of the explosion could never emerge on this side of the horizon," Kirk explained.

"I know," Cochrane said. He let go of the Companion's hand and went to Spock's science station. "But a matter-antimatter explosion a few meters underneath the horizon could make it ring like a bell, setting up gravity shock waves all around the black hole, like waves in a pond."

Kirk looked at Spock. His expression said he had no argument against the suggestion.

Spock raised an eyebrow, indicating significant surprise, Cochrane knew. He began to adjust controls on his computer interface. "That is an admirable tactic. But there would be relativistic time-dilation effects to take into account, and they would delay the appearance of oscillations on this side of the horizon."

"What about detonating the torpedo at warp velocity?" Cochrane said. "The continuum-distortion field eliminates time dilation."

"Unfortunately," Spock said, "the torpedo's warp drive would be destroyed at the instant of detonation, causing time dilation to return."

Cochrane frowned. Spock was right. But then Kirk raised a finger.

"Put the torpedo in something, Spock! A shuttlecraft!"

Spock raised both eyebrows. "Of course. If a shuttlecraft containing the torpedo pierced the event horizon, the torpedo could be detonated inside the shuttlecraft's warp field. The explosion would proceed in real time for the few nanoseconds before the shuttlecraft was destroyed."

"Provided the warp field is still within contact of the event horizon!" Cochrane added excitedly. Then his elation left him. "But how do you get something the size of a shuttlecraft through an event horizon?"

"Theoretically, that is not difficult," Spock said. "It has artificial gravity and inertial dampening systems in place, as well as a structural integrity field. Since it can withstand the stress of moving from sublight to warp speed, it can assuredly survive the transition through the event horizon. In terms of overall acceleration, this would be several orders of magnitude less stressful." Spock hesitated for a moment. "Once inside the event horizon, though, the shuttlecraft's power plant would only be able to power the necessary systems for an hour at most."

Kirk looked pleased. "But we'll only need a few seconds, Spock. Have the hangar-deck crew load photon torpedoes with timers onto the remaining shuttlecraft."

"Coming up on TNC 65813," Sulu said.

Onscreen, the black disk flared and sparked with flashes of energy as dust particles collided at relativistic speeds above it.

"Close orbit, Mr. Sulu. Five thousand kilometers to start."

"Dropping to impulse," Sulu said.

Cochrane could hear the ship's engines strain. He understood that without the *Enterprise*'s artificial gravity, inertial dampening systems, and structural integrity field, the ship would already be breaking up under the black hole's tidal forces the way the gravity of planets like Saturn created the dust and debris of its rings by breaking up larger bodies that passed within the Roche limit—the critical distance any object could remain without being torn apart.

Cochrane went back to the Companion. "Don't be frightened," he said.

"When we are with you, we fear nothing," she said.

"I wish the captain had someone like you to draw strength from," Cochrane said.

The Companion watched Kirk take his chair, saw the way his

hands found their way to the arm controls. "He does," she said. Cochrane wasn't sure he understood what she meant.

The screen was awash in streaks and flares of energy as the *Enterprise*'s navigational deflectors pushed the high-speed dust and debris orbiting the black disk out of the way.

"How much longer till those cruisers arrive?" Kirk asked.

"Cruiser one in six minutes. Cruiser two in twenty," Chekov answered.

"Does that give us enough time to test one of the torpedoes in a shuttlecraft?" Kirk asked Spock.

"I would recommend against it, Captain. If the technique works, we will need each of our remaining shuttlecraft to deliver torpedoes to the black hole. If it does not, testing will not matter."

"Very well. Have the hangar crew stand ready for launching shuttlecraft on automatic pilot. Mr. Sulu, change orbits as soon as we're out of line of sight of the cruisers, then scan for regions of high sensor distortion. We've got six minutes to find a hiding place."

The ship began to buck, just a gentle rhythm, but noticeable nonetheless. Cochrane looked at Spock.

"That is the expected operation of the inertial dampeners," Spock said in response to Cochrane's unasked question.

"What would happen if it wasn't the expected operation?" Cochrane asked.

"At this distance from the singularity," Spock replied calmly, "we would be little more than thin layers of organic paste, smeared on opposite sides of the *Enterprise*'s ruptured hulls."

"She's quite a ship, isn't she, Mr. Spock?"

"Indeed she is," Spock said; then he turned his attention back to his computer.

On the screen, Cochrane had difficulty orienting himself. There were only flashes against utter blackness, but no indication of the curve or size of the object they orbited.

"Out of line of sight," Sulu announced. "Changing orbital planes. Picking up sensor distortion nodes directly ahead."

"Very good, Mr. Sulu," Kirk said. "Let's try to sneak into one."

As Cochrane watched, the orientation of the screen image

changed so that he saw a large black ellipse at the bottom, against
glowing auroras of scintillating gas and dust. Directly ahead, a
twisting knot of glowing yellow light, dropping streamers of red,
slowly grew larger. Cochrane decided it was the sensor distortion
node, rendered into something the human eye could make sense
of by the *Enterprise*'s computers. He could believe a starship
could hide in one. Once again, Kirk had come up with a worthy
strategy.

But he wasn't the only one.

As the image grew larger on the screen, collision alarms
sounded and a dot of orange light flew out from the node.
Cochrane just had time to see the flash of blue phaser fire erupt
from the closing light, and then the universe exploded around
him.

EIGHT

☆

The instant the Orion ship hurtled out of the distortion node, Kirk realized his mistake.

Because there'd been no sign that the high-speed transport had been pursuing the *Enterprise,* Kirk had assumed he'd crippled it in his attack on the Klingon cruiser it had docked with. But obviously, Thorsen, or whoever was now commanding the attacking force, had anticipated the *Enterprise*'s destination and had sent the Orion ship on ahead in a circuitous route.

The strategy was obvious, but Kirk's recognition of it was too late.

The screen flared white as the collision alarms sounded and for a moment Kirk feared the *Enterprise* had been rammed. She could withstand considerable mechanical stress under normal operating conditions, but her structural integrity systems were already strained to the limit by being so close to the singularity.

But the *Enterprise* held. Kirk gripped the arms of his chair as the bridge twisted beneath him. He smelled smoke and fire and the chemical spray of the fire-suppressor systems. But the *Enterprise* held.

"Track it, Chekov!" he called out over the alarms.

339

"Coming back at us!"

"Photon torpedoes—two, four, six! Make him break off."

Kirk clenched his teeth as he waited. He heard only two torpedoes fire and knew there must be damage in fire control.

"Hit, sir!"

"Onscreen!"

The viewscreen jumped to a port-side angle. Kirk saw the Orion transport engulfed in a nimbus of glowing plasma, streaming off to the dark curve of the event horizon below.

"It's venting antimatter, Keptin. We must have hit its engineering section."

Kirk was surprised. Where were the transport's shields? Unless its configuration required too much energy to be transferred to its own structural integrity field . . .

"Power failing, Keptin. It's—"

Chekov stopped as the orange glow of the Orion ship winked out, leaving only the angular silhouette of its hull. An instant later, that silhouette stretched out like taffy, one point shooting downward toward the event horizon, the other arcing away until the strand of distant metal broke apart into glittering fragments, all at different trajectories, but all falling.

Kirk took a deep breath. What happened to the transport was exactly what would happen to the *Enterprise* if her power failed. He wondered if Thorsen had been on board.

Kirk called for a damage report. At the same time he heard Spock call for a medical team to the bridge. As the damage reports came in, Kirk turned to see Cochrane cradled in the Companion's arms. The sleeve of his technician's jumpsuit was charred. Transtator current feedback from the environmental controls, Kirk guessed. But Cochrane was obviously alert. His hand could be healed.

Whether the *Enterprise* could be was a different matter.

Only two photon-torpedo launch tubes remained functional, and the forward phaser banks had been completely shut down. The Orion transport had aimed its weapons well, and left the *Enterprise* almost defenseless.

But at least Kirk knew the distortion nodes did manage to fool sensors. They still had a chance.

Then Scott called the bridge.

"Captain—we've lost another crystal, sir. We canna keep up with the power demands for more than another hour."

That wasn't what Kirk wanted to hear. "Scotty, we have to hold out for *thirteen* hours."

"Captain, when the last crystals go, our matter-antimatter reactor shuts down and there's nothing t' be done about it. We'll be on batteries only, and under these conditions, they'll only hold us together for a few minutes at best, without the chance to go to warp."

"Any good news, Scotty?"

"Aye. When the structural integrity fails, we'll be flattened so fast we won't even know it."

"Do what you can." Kirk went to break the connection, but Scott kept talking.

"Just so ye know, Captain. I'm fresh out of miracles down here. The *Enterprise* is a fine ship but she was never meant for this kind of strain. If ye want her t' hold together for another thirteen hours, then you'll have t' get her well past that bloody singularity's Roche limit. And if we stick to impulse—which I recommend— that means we'll have to break orbit a good thirty minutes before the last crystals fail to be sure we have enough power to get there. You understand what I'm saying, Captain?"

"The *Enterprise* leaves orbit in the next thirty minutes, or she doesn't leave at all."

"Just so ye know, Captain. I'm sorry."

"So am I, Scotty. Do what you can. I'll get right back to you." And then there was nothing more to say.

"Entering the distortion node," Sulu said.

"Hold her steady," Kirk ordered. He went to Spock. "You heard Mr. Scott?"

"Yes," Spock said. "His report adjusts the odds of our survival. Dramatically. Downward."

"Why don't you carry more dilithium?" The question came from Cochrane. He was back in his chair at the environmental station, looking dazed. The Companion had dressed his hand with a first-aid kit.

Kirk shrugged. "I ask that question myself, Mr. Cochrane. And

341

JUDITH AND GARFIELD REEVES-STEVENS

Starfleet tells me the operational life of a set of starship-grade dilithium crystals is twenty years and that I should take better care of them because there's not enough to go around."

"Any way to go back to an ordinary *lithium* converter, the way it used to be in my day?"

Spock shook his head. "Ordinary lithium crystals cannot operate at the efficiencies required for modern starship operation."

"So," Kirk said, facing what he thought he would never have to face—the inevitable. "We have thirty minutes to come up with a way to get past Thorsen's cruisers. Other than relying on a lucky shot."

"There is no way," Spock said. "We do not have the weaponry available to fight. We do not have the warp capability to flee. We do not have the energy capacity to remain hidden. Therefore, we have only one option."

Kirk knew what that option was, but he rejected it. "The *Enterprise* will not surrender."

"She doesn't have to," Cochrane said. He stood up, still groggy, steadied by the Companion at his side. "If he wasn't in that ship that was destroyed, Thorsen wants me. So turn me over. I volunteer."

The Companion spoke for them all. "No. You cannot."

"It's the only way," Cochrane said. "The only reason Thorsen even came after the *Enterprise* is because I'm on her. I . . ." Cochrane stopped as he saw Kirk and Spock look at each other. "What is it?"

"Can he leave the ship?" Kirk asked. "In a shuttlecraft with a torpedo aboard?"

"A suicide mission?" Cochrane asked. Was this finally how he would end?

But Kirk said, "No. When you're close enough to Thorsen's ship, we'd beam you back, then detonate the torpedo."

"Even if a single torpedo detonation were enough to overload the structural integrity field of Thorsen's ship, that would still leave the second cruiser," Spock said.

"It would double our chances," Kirk said.

"Twice zero is still zero," Spock replied.

FEDERATION

"Captain," the Companion suddenly said. "If the man were not here, would you be safe?"

Kirk looked at the Companion intently. She had said so little since he had rescued her from her planetoid that he had begun to think of her only as a silent extension to Cochrane. But he reminded himself that within her, no matter what the origin of her alien half, there were still the mind and skills and talents of a Federation commissioner. "There *is* a chance that Thorsen or his followers would leave us alone. Slim to none, but still a chance. Why?"

"Then let us hide, away from you, as we hid with the man so long ago."

Kirk didn't understand. He looked at Cochrane for enlightenment, but he seemed no more certain than Kirk.

An intercom hail sounded and McCoy's voice asked, "What's the situation on the bridge? You still need medical up there?"

Cochrane held up his bandaged hand. The glittering fabric was stained with blood.

"Affirmative," Spock said.

"Emergency?"

"No."

"All right. I'm finishing up in phaser fire control. Tell the captain, no fatal casualties. I'll be up soon. McCoy out."

Cochrane used his good hand to hold one of the Companion's. "There is no place where the captain can take us to hide," he said quietly to her.

The Companion looked troubled. Her brow creased in concentration. "Part of us understands. But part of us . . . remembers what it was like to fly among the stars."

Spock leaned forward. "Companion, when you were in your energy state, before you merged with Commissioner Hedford, you were able to move at warp velocity. Can you do so now?"

But the Companion shook her head with a gentle smile. "No. We have become human. We no longer fly among the stars, but we know love. It is a fair bargain."

"What are you trying to tell us?" Cochrane asked her. "Do you know of a place to hide?"

343

The Companion pointed with her free hand. All eyes followed in the direction she indicated. The viewscreen. The dark ellipse.

"There," she said. "Where light stops."

"If you go there," Kirk explained, "you can never come out. That doesn't make it a good place to hide."

"But we can come out," the Companion insisted. "Part of us knows that place. Part of us understands what you said to the man about fields and torpedoes and shuttlecraft. Between our two halves, we know it can be done." She pulled herself close to Cochrane. "Zefram, please, in a shuttlecraft, we can go in to the place where light stops, and we *can* come out again. We know this to be true." Her face twisted, as if in pain, as if struggling with some inner fight. "Zefram, *I* know this to be true."

Cochrane looked surprised. He turned to Kirk. "She hasn't said 'I' for months, Captain."

Kirk had neither Spock's logic nor McCoy's passion to guide him now. His ship was in danger. Only minutes remained before Thorsen's cruisers would arrive and the *Enterprise* would have to leave the protection of the distortion node, putting herself at their mercy. If ever there was a time to change the rules, this was it.

Kirk looked at Cochrane. Somehow, he felt he saw himself, in a different era perhaps, fewer rules, fewer choices, but a kindred spirit just the same. "Do *you* trust her, Mr. Cochrane? With your life?"

Cochrane didn't hesitate. "With all my heart, Captain Kirk."

Kirk made his decision. He did the unthinkable.

He put the fate of the *Enterprise* in the hands of the Companion.

NINE

U.S.S. ENTERPRISE NCC-1701-D
DEEP SPACE
Stardate 43922.1
Earth Standard: ≈ May 2366

Even as the stars called out for him, Picard felt a hand with the strength of molybdenum-cobalt alloy close on the back of his collar, restraining him against the gale that rushed from the shuttlebay to empty space. Debris blew all around him—cleaning cloths, tricorders, the smaller wire and mesh segments of the Borg-like artifact no longer contained by their security field. But Picard was held in place and he knew why.

Data.

Picard twisted to see the android behind him, unaffected by brief exposures to vacuum, standing immovably on the deck. Data's other hand held Wesley Crusher firmly by the collar, the youth's face wide-eyed with fear but impressively without panic. La Forge had wrapped his own arms around one of Data's to grimly hold himself in place.

The wind vanished, the air completely gone, and though artificial gravity still held them to the deck, only seconds remained to Picard, La Forge, and Wesley before lack of oxygen claimed them all.

Already Picard felt his lungs demanding that he breathe. Wesley's mouth gaped open, trailing tendrils of sublimated vapor.

345

Picard could see him beginning to struggle like a drowning swimmer. Starfleet trained its members to remain conscious for a minimum of ninety seconds after explosive decompression events, but Wesley hadn't had that training yet. Picard realized with chagrin that for himself, it had been too long since his last refresher course.

In the eerie total silence of the vacuum, Data started forward, pulling his captain forward across the deck. The android still kept hold of Wesley under one arm, legs dragging. La Forge stumbled alongside him, still clutching Data's arm. Picard could not hear the *Enterprise*'s engines or the clatter of their boots, but he felt the vibrations of his ship through the deck and they seemed to match the flickering of the black dots at the side of his vision.

Data stopped and Picard was dimly aware that they stood before a door—exactly where, he couldn't tell in the dull illumination of the emergency lighting. La Forge dropped to his knees, hands at his throat. Picard felt cold, a cooling prickling sensation over all his skin. His eardrums ached with the pressure within them. He tried to blink to relieve the pressure building in his eyes, but his lids were stuck as if frozen open.

Data's hand moved to a door panel control. Picard tried to warn him not to open it—that he would only decompress the rest of the corridor beyond. But no words came out. As some part of him, the composed and thoughtful part he had shared with Sarek, fought to deal with the knowledge that he was suffocating and had only seconds of consciousness remaining, Picard finally came to the realization it didn't matter what Data did. Every door on the ship was under computer control. Whatever had taken over the *Enterprise* would never allow them to be opened. They were trapped on the shuttlebay. Picard would never draw breath again, and as he faced his death in those final moments, his one overwhelming regret was that he would never know the truth about the Preserver artifact.

His legs gave way as his vision shrank through a well of darkness. He felt as if gravity had been switched off and that he was tumbling down without end. Then a bright light gathered him up in a blinding luminescence. He felt surprise. Could the stories of the moment of death be true?

He felt himself thrust upward into the light. He welcomed it. The adventure *would* continue after all.

His body spasmed. Safety carpet bristled into the side of his face. He inhaled with one last shudder. Safety carpet?

He tasted air.

Picard's vision was blurred, his eyes were still stuck open, but as what they gazed upon became evident, he saw enough to understand just where he was, where Data had brought him.

Inside a shuttlecraft.

The light had been the craft's interior being revealed as its door had opened wide. That same door was now shut tight.

Picard's lungs heaved as he gasped hungrily for more air and he heard the sounds of life again as the craft was repressurized: La Forge and Wesley breathing deeply, Data's footsteps on the shuttlecraft deck.

"Please do not be alarmed," Data's calm voice announced. "We are on board the *Gould* and I have disabled all communication with the *Enterprise*'s computers. We are quite safe. I will now pass out decompression treatment kits. Please use them as you have been instructed."

Picard resisted the incredible impulse to laugh. Data sounded like a flight steward on the Earth-moon shuttle. La Forge did laugh, though, presumably for the same reason. Wesley still wheezed deeply, hoarsely.

Picard took the small first-aid kit Data handed him, opened it, and instinctively reached for the parabolic cups that would treat the surface of his eyes, damaged by the sudden sublimation of their moisture. That part of his basic Starfleet training he did remember, and within a minute he could see clearly again and was sitting in the pilot's chair of the shuttle.

Data was beside him. La Forge sat behind them with Wesley. The acting ensign's throat had been damaged by his understandable attempt to hold his breath in the vacuum. The resulting explosion of air from his lungs would remind him what to do in the next incident of explosive decompression better than any Academy training program.

"Are you able to pick up anything from the *Enterprise?*" Picard asked as Data scanned the sensor readouts. "Any signs that the rest of the ship has been depressurized?"

"Shuttlebays two and three are also exposed to vacuum," Data said. "But the rest of the ship appears to be intact. Since life-sign sensors indicate many unconscious bodies in the immediately adjacent pressurized areas, it would appear that whatever is controlling the *Enterprise*'s computers has flooded the ship with anesthezine gas."

Picard felt relief at that. He had feared that the entire crew had been exposed to vacuum. But the only harm that had been done was that they would awaken with splitting headaches.

"Are we able to communicate with the bridge?"

Data adjusted some controls without effect. "That does not appear to be possible. All computer-mediated communication capabilities are off-line."

"Can you tell where we are heading?"

"The shuttlecraft controls display our course, but without contact with the *Enterprise*'s main navigational library, I do not know what our likely destination might be." Data glanced at his captain. "However, to anticipate your next question: We are not traveling toward the Romulan Empire."

"That *was* my next question," Picard said. He took a deep breath. His lungs still ached from exposure to vacuum. "Well, there should be environmental suits in the storage lockers on the shuttle, so perhaps we can move along the outside of the hull to a manual airlock and gain entrance to the bridge that way."

"Would it not be better to transport to the bridge from the shuttlecraft?" Data suggested. "As we are traveling inside the same warp field, we would not experience any spatial disorientation."

Picard had thought of that possibility, but had ruled it out. "Check the corridors for security forcefields. With anesthezine released, I think you'll find all are in active mode."

Data did so. "You are correct, Captain. It would be impossible to beam directly to the bridge through the forcefields now in place in the decks above us." Then Data paused. "However, since the security forcefields in question are limited to protecting specific doors and corridor pathways, it should be possible for me to maneuver this shuttlecraft to a position beside the bridge, so that we may beam directly through the hull."

La Forge leaned forward. "Data, are you sure you can keep the shuttlecraft close enough to the *Enterprise* to remain in her warp field?" he asked. "If we get too far away and slip out of it, the downwarping stress will tear this thing apart."

"I have already calculated the necessary safety margin, Geordi. We shall be safe within the *Enterprise*'s warp field. At the same time, we will also be within her navigational and defense shields, so there will be no impediment to the transporter." Data looked at Picard. "Do you wish me to proceed with the appropriate flight path, Captain?"

"At once," the captain said.

With a barely detectable thud, the *Gould* made hard contact with the *Enterprise*'s hull directly behind the observation lounge. Picard looked out the shuttlecraft's forward canopy and saw through the observation windows that emergency lights were operating in the lounge. But the doors were closed, so it was impossible to see what condition his bridge was in.

"Deploying magnetic grapple," Data warned, and two louder thuds echoed in the shuttlecraft. "Switching off interior gravity." At once the shuttlecraft seemed to move to a gentle slant, matching the angle of the saucer hull she had landed on. "I believe we are now firmly anchored, sir."

Picard adjusted the life-sign sensors to scan the bridge only meters away on the other side of the lounge. Six unconscious bodies were present. The apparently abnormal readings from one of them indicated the body in question was Worf.

Picard stood up, leaning against the seatback to keep his balance on the angled deck. "Gentlemen, this shuttlecraft will not be safe if whatever's in control of the *Enterprise* decides to shake it off, either through violent maneuvers or with a tractor beam. Therefore, we will all beam over to the bridge, taking with us the shuttlecraft's emergency supplies and setting the transporter here for automatic return, just in case. Any questions?"

"What about the anesthezine gas?" Wesley asked, then coughed.

Picard had already checked the shuttlecraft's medical locker. Among the hypospray ampules included in it was an anesthezine antagonist. The three of them would be safe from the gas's effects, and the unconscious crew members could be roused.

Two minutes later, hyposprays in hand, Picard and Data materialized on the bridge. In addition to Worf, the other crew trapped on the bridge when the ship had been taken over were Riker, Dr. Crusher, Ensign McKnight, Counselor Troi, and Miles O'Brien, who was slumped over at the ops station.

Thick white anesthezine mist still floated low to the deck, but other than that, the bridge looked relatively normal. Emergency lighting here maintained normal illumination levels, and all screens and displays showed standard function. At once Picard and Data began using their hyposprays on the unconscious bridge crew. Wesley and the emergency supplies beamed in a few moments later, followed after another short delay by La Forge.

Only after insuring that all life-support functions continued to operate throughout the Enterprise, and confirming that none of the ship's controls would respond to their input, Data and La Forge began the tedious process of disconnecting nonessential bridge systems from the ship's computer by physically pulling out isolinear chips from control consoles. By the time bridge environmental systems were under manual control and the anesthezine gas had been vented, Picard had briefed his bridge crew on what he believed had happened—the suspected Preserver object had somehow downloaded an override program into the Enterprise's computers.

"What would be the purpose of such a program?" Worf growled. He was barely containing his angry frustration at the fact that none of his tactical or security controls were operational.

"Ensign McKnight," Picard said, "can you identify any likely destinations for us on this heading?"

The young ensign was back at the conn beside Mr. O'Brien. She called up a navigational display. Because the request did not interfere with the Enterprise's operation, it was not affected by the override program. McKnight put a computer graphic of their destination on the main screen.

"Our present heading will take us directly to this, Captain," the ensign explained.

On the screen, Picard recognized the classic glowing gas disk and twin ionized polar jets of a singularity.

"It's listed as the Kabreigny Object," McKnight continued. "Also on the charts as T'Lin's New Catalog number 65813. I, uh, can't pull up anything on it from the library computer, but if this black hole's got a name as well as a number, it's been studied."

"What is our estimated time of arrival?"

McKnight checked her board. "We're doing warp nine point six, sir. That'll put us there in just under six hours."

Riker approached the screen, holding the side of his head. "Why would a three-and-a-half-billion-year-old Preserver device want to take us to a black hole?"

Data, on the upper level of the bridge with Worf, said, "Perhaps we should ask it, sir," Data said.

Riker looked at him, bewildered, one eye fluttering with the pain of what Picard recognized as an anesthezine hangover. "I beg your pardon?" Riker said.

"As I noted in the shuttlebay, the Preserver object appears to have downloaded not just a program, but a personality matrix. Since the *Enterprise* has been taken over in a precise and logical manner, without pushing her systems beyond their limits, I believe it is likely that the personality matrix will share enough common thought patterns that we might be able to converse with it in a meaningful way."

Dr. Crusher sat on the bench beside Counselor Troi to the captain's left. "You mean, you could just talk to it as if it were the ship's computer?" she asked.

"It is a possibility," Data said noncommittally.

Picard glanced up from his position in the center chair. "Computer: What is our heading?"

In its familiar feminine voice, the computer answered, "Food replication services are temporarily suspended. Please rekey selection."

From his position in the center of the bridge, Riker spoke. "Computer: Identify command override authorization preventing bridge crew from controlling the *Enterprise.*"

"Rook to king's level four," the computer replied. "Touchdown."

Without a hint of embarrassment, Data commented, "It would appear the computer's verbal interface functions have not yet been fully integrated by the personality matrix."

Riker smiled ruefully. "Any other suggestions?"

"It might be possible for me to interface directly with the computer, processor to processor," Data said.

"No way," La Forge protested. He was on his back, head jammed into a service opening beneath the first science station. Wesley worked with him, keying in commands on the input panel. But La Forge sat up as he continued his objection to Data's plan. "If the personality matrix or override program or whatever it is could take over the ship's computer, it could easily do the same to you, Data."

"It is possible to make the connection one-way, Geordi. In effect, write-protecting my memory so that no new program can be input."

Picard didn't like the idea of risking Data's life, or his operational status, but neither was he prepared to sit back while his ship operated under something else's control. "What would you hope to accomplish from a one-way connection?" he asked the android.

"At the very least," Data replied, "I might be able to identify the source of the personality matrix. Romulan programming techniques are quite recognizable."

Troi looked surprised. "Data, do you still think this all could be part of some Romulan deception?"

"That does not seem unlikely, Counselor. A three-and-a-half-billion-year-old Preserver object would have few motives for taking over a starship," Data replied.

"But what motive would the Romulans have?" Dr. Crusher asked.

"That is what I would hope to find out," Data answered.

"Likely it is connected to the singularity we are approaching. But how, I do not know."

Picard gave permission for Data to attempt the linkup with whatever controlled the ship's computer, provided the android could convince La Forge that the interface would indeed be one-way. Life-sign indicators continued to show that the rest of the crew was incapacitated throughout the ship, and that all doors were locked and security forcefields in operation. However, the *Enterprise* maintained her speed at warp nine point six, a strain, but within her operational limits, at least for the length of time it would take to arrive at the black hole. For the moment, it was only frustration that drove Picard, not danger. But all that might change soon.

Eventually, La Forge was convinced that Data had taken sufficient safeguards to protect his own memory pathways. The android sat at a science station on the upper level, ringed by La Forge, Picard, and Riker. Troi, Worf, Dr. Crusher, and her son remained off to the side. McKnight and O'Brien held their stations at their command consoles, in case control of the ship should return unexpectedly.

Outwardly, there was no change in Data. During normal operations, he had the capability to communicate directly with the ship's computer through short-range radio. He would do so now, though the communications loop would consist of Data's transmitting to the computer by internal radio, then watching for any response through visual images displayed on the main science-station screen. With no physical or radio connection between them, the risk of Data's being exposed to the personality matrix was zero.

La Forge adjusted the science-station display to show a visual representation of a specific area of memory within one of the *Enterprise*'s three main computer cores. For now, the image was a rapidly shifting random flurry of light and dark pixels, each corresponding to a specific memory location in a communications processing node. Data would transmit to that section and see what response, if any, was forthcoming. If there was no response, he was prepared to isolate warp-drive operations from the rest of the computer, then transmit a shutdown code to the entire system, effectively erasing the personality matrix.

"I will begin now," Data announced. He cocked his head and his eyes seemed to focus on something past the display screen.

The screen immediately flashed to nonrandom patterns. Picard saw dark diagonal bars roll down through alternating squares of light and dark. Clearly a directed signal was being received by the computer—Data's transmission.

"Curious," Data said. "The patterns being displayed are simply my signal. There is no response from the computer, as if the personality matrix is no longer present."

"Ensign McKnight," Picard called out. "Drop to sublight."

The sound of the engines didn't change.

"The helm will not respond," McKnight said.

"It was worth a try," Troi told the captain.

"I will attempt to make contact again," Data said.

An intricate pattern of curved lines flashed over the screen, creating a strobelike image of white circles flashing in a spiraling curve.

"That is interesting," Data said as he gazed at the screen. "Something is generating a recursive feedback loop."

La Forge looked at Data with alarm, but Picard did not know why. "Data, slow down your visual-recognition subroutines. Don't let that feedback . . . Data?"

Data was frozen in position, staring at the screen, the light from its rapid flickerings painting his yellow skin.

"No!" La Forge shouted as he placed both hands over the display, blocking the pattern. "Pull him away!"

Riker slapped both hands on Data's shoulders to haul him back from the screen. Picard moved in to help. But Data's right arm came back like lightning, his elbow driving into Riker's leg. Picard heard a wet crunch and Riker cried out in sudden pain, falling back into Worf. At the same time, Data's left hand grabbed both of La Forge's, crushed them together, then twisted so that the engineer was thrown to the side.

The remaining crew members could only watch as the science-station display screen went dark and Data turned away and slowly got to his feet.

Methodically he scanned the surrounding area, fixing his gaze on each crew member in turn. Then he looked down at his own hands, turning them over, flexing them, as if he had never seen them before.

Even before Data spoke, Picard knew what had happened. Somehow the personality matrix in the computer had generated a visual signal which had compelled Data to adjust his settings and allow two-way communication, permitting the matrix to download itself into the android's positronic neural pathways. Data was now under the same control as was the *Enterprise*. But by what kind of matrix? And for what purpose?

"Better," Data said, and there was a different quality to his voice, deeper, slower. "Much better to have a body again. Especially one without flesh."

Picard stepped forward, putting himself between Data and the rest of his crew. "Identify yourself," he demanded.

Data, or the thing that had been Data, stared at Picard, then smiled as if somehow amused.

"I do not take orders from you, Captain Picard." His hand shot out, grabbed the captain by the collar of his tunic, then twisted so hard that Picard couldn't breathe. "You will take orders from me."

Picard wrapped both hands around Data's hand but couldn't budge it. Worf leapt onto Data, but the android's free hand shot out and with an open-palmed shove forced the Klingon back to flip over his tactical station.

"If anyone else tries to interfere," the Data-thing stated, "the captain will die."

Those crew members still on their feet stepped back, showing they would do nothing to endanger their captain.

"A wise decision," the Data-thing said. "Most optimal."

He let go of Picard and the captain staggered back, gasping for breath as he clutched at his throat. But he glared at the Data-thing in controlled outrage. "Whoever you are, return Lieutenant Data to me at once!"

The Data-thing gave Picard a thin smile. "Lieutenant Data isn't here, Captain Picard. I am. You may call me . . . . Thorsen."

TEN

U.S.S. ENTERPRISE NCC–1701
CLOSE ORBIT TNC 65813
Stardate 3856
Earth Standard: ≈ November 2267

"I will not let you go alone," the Companion said.

Cochrane stood by the doorway of the shuttlecraft *Ian Shelton*. "If you're sure this plan will work," Cochrane told her, "there's no need for you to come. The captain can take you back to your planetoid. You'll be safe until I return. A few days and we'll be together again."

But the Companion would not release his hand. "Our lives are entwined, Zefram Cochrane. I can no more leave you than I can be what I was."

Spock stepped forward. "We are ten minutes from our point of no return," he said. "You must leave now if the plan is to have any chance of success."

Cochrane understood the Vulcan's understated urgency. It had all gone perfectly up to now. The *Enterprise* had contacted Thorsen when his cruiser had arrived in orbit of TNC 65813. Thorsen had eagerly agreed to the exchange Kirk had offered, backed up by visual images of Cochrane bound and gagged in the custody of security. Kirk had convinced Thorsen he didn't know what had happened to cause the explosion of the wreckage of the *Planitia*. Perhaps the warp core had finally lost its shielding. But

356

when the explosion had occurred, what else could Kirk do but fire his torpedoes and run for safety? Surely, Thorsen could understand.

Kirk had told Cochrane that it was a story that would never have played out with a Klingon. But Thorsen had accepted it, blinded by his desire to obtain what he had searched for through the years, what he had cheated death to obtain. How could he *not* believe when what he desired was so close at hand?

"What chance?" McCoy grumbled. He had been late getting to the bridge and had come to treat Cochrane's burned hand on the hangar deck.

Cochrane looked at him with an unworried smile. "Doctor, if the Companion says it will work, then I believe her."

"Black holes and the laws of physics are one thing," McCoy replied. "But that madman Thorsen is another. How do we know he won't blast you out of creation the instant you're outside the *Enterprise*'s shields?"

"Because he's obsessed, Dr. McCoy. He has always wanted to see me die with his own eyes. Or whatever he's been using to see these days. To pay me back for what he thinks I did to him almost two hundred years ago. Adrik Thorsen *wants* me aboard his ship."

Kirk's voice came over the hangar-deck speakers. "How are we doing there, Mr. Spock?"

Spock gestured to the door. "They are just boarding now, Captain."

Cochrane realized he couldn't argue with the Companion without continuing to endanger the *Enterprise*. He looked at Spock. "When the *Excalibur* recovers us, we'll have to get back home in two days," he said. The Companion could remain apart from her planetoid no longer than that and still live.

"It shall be done," Spock promised. "Admiral Kabreigny has said she will make it her personal responsibility."

"Will she be well enough to do that?" Cochrane asked.

"The admiral is still not convinced that our conclusions concerning Thorsen's responsibility for compromising Starfleet's computers are correct, but her health is good. Now, please, sir."

Cochrane stepped onto the shuttlecraft. The Companion followed. He turned to see Spock raise his hand and hold it palm out, fingers split in the center. Cochrane guessed it was a twenty-third-century wave and waved back. Then he and the Companion went forward to the pilot and copilot seats.

"I remember this," the Companion said after a moment as she looked around.

Cochrane smiled at her as they took their seats. He still wasn't used to hearing her say "I" so often. But he understood what her increased use of the singular personal pronoun meant. Somehow, all these months after the energy being had merged with Nancy Hedford, the two disparate parts of her had finally reached a total consolidation. Her voice still had its unusual harmonic, as if two voices spoke at once. But she was clearly an individual now, part alien, part Nancy Hedford. In a way, he supposed, what had happened to them in the past few days had caused her to grow. To grow up, even.

He shook his head. He didn't know how it was possible, but just thinking about her made her even more a part of him and his continued existence.

A voice came from the shuttlecraft's control console. "Mr. Cochrane, this is Sulu. Are you ready for launch?"

"Yes, sir," Cochrane answered.

"Very good. We're opening the hangar doors now. I'm going to fly you out on remote control and toward Thorsen's ship."

Cochrane felt the shuttlecraft shift below him. He looked out the front viewport and saw they were moving closer to the immense hangar doors. The doors were parting and he wondered how the machinery of the *Enterprise* managed to depressurize the deck so quickly. He hoped he'd be back to find out.

Sulu kept talking. "I'm going to keep control until we're sure that Thorsen has scanned you and confirmed that you're on board. Then I'll initiate the autopilot as we've programmed it. The ride will feel turbulent. Internal gravity will be a bit higher than normal to help hold you together. Mr. Spock tells me that passage through the event horizon will be like breaking the sound barrier. The flight should smooth out considerably past that point."

The hangar doors disappeared to either side as the shuttlecraft slipped between them.

"Shuttle away," Sulu said.

The small forward windows didn't give Cochrane much of a view. He could see part of a glowing, gaseous arm, then the huge cylinder of the *Enterprise*'s starboard nacelle as the shuttlecraft eased past it.

"Thorsen's ship should now be dead ahead," Sulu said.

And it was. About a kilometer distant, framed by a distant, rippling aurora of glowing gas, the ominous silhouette of the Klingon battle cruiser hung before him, growing larger with each moment.

"You're being scanned," Sulu told Cochrane. "And Thorsen is hailing you. I'm switching you to an audio and visual signal directly to his ship. I'll stay off the circuit until it's time to make our move."

Cochrane glanced at the Companion. She reached her hand across the aisle between them and took his.

"This will work, Zefram. Have no doubt, no fear."

"Never," Cochrane said. He was surprised to discover he meant it.

Then, what had been Adrik Thorsen appeared on the viewscreen on the shuttlecraft's control console.

"I've thought of you each night since Battersea," Thorsen said, his voice a terrible low whisper, as if the power of speech was eroding as quickly as the last traces of his human origins. The skin Cochrane had last seen hanging in ragged strips from Thorsen's face was now back in position, tiny silver scars marking where it had split and where the Grigari nanocomponents had repaired it. But the eye that had disappeared was now a glowing emerald orb, completely inhuman. "We have so much to talk about. Old times. Optimum times I still see the laser you shone at me."

"We have nothing to say to each other, Thorsen. Starfleet has confirmed that there is *nothing* to the warp bomb. You're insane if you think—"

"Silence! There is still time to remake the worlds. Old dreams need not die. Order. Salvation. Red banners wave and black eagles fly. There can still be a bright future for humanity."

Thorsen's breathing was disturbing. It hissed and bubbled, hinting of further internal changes.

"You missed your chance, Thorsen. You're like I am—a dinosaur. We shouldn't be in this age."

"This age shall be remade in my image," Thorsen said. "And my first—"

The audio and visual feed ended. Sulu's voice returned on the secure and scrambled channel. "Here you go," the navigator said. "Make it look good and we'll see you in twenty hours—or thirty minutes from your point of view. Smooth sailing, sir."

The shuttlecraft rocked. The forward boom of the Klingon cruiser swung by the viewports as the *Ian Shelton*'s orientation suddenly veered away. Cochrane held the Companion's hand tightly in his. He cleared his throat. Then he activated the communications link. And just as Spock had coached him, he screamed out in panic.

"Enterprise! Enterprise! This is Cochrane! Thrusters have malfunctioned! We're headed for the horizon! I can't control it!" Seeing the flashes just above the ominous darkness of the event horizon inspired Cochrane to make his cries sound real.

Sulu's voice returned to the console speakers, transmitted so that Thorsen could hear him as well. "Shuttlecraft: This is *Enterprise*. Stand by for tractor beam."

Just as Kirk had surmised, the next voice was Thorsen's. "Stand back, *Enterprise!* Zefram Cochrane is mine!"

A blue glow came through the viewport. Cochrane had been told to expect it. It was the radiation signature of a focused linear graviton beam. The Klingon cruiser was using it to attempt to drag the *Ian Shelton* back on course. But just as Spock had calculated, it was almost impossible for gravitons to remain focused this close to the event horizon. The sharply climbing gravity gradient smeared the beam, dropping its effectiveness.

"Warning," the onboard computer announced. "Approaching event horizon. Impact in twenty seconds."

But Cochrane saw that the blue glow of Thorsen's tractor beam did not diminish. Instead, it intensified.

"Course altered," the computer said. "Impact in fifty seconds."

The Companion said, "Zefram, that is wrong."

Cochrane knew it.

The blue glow grew even brighter. Spock had said that Thorsen's tractor beam would fail.

"Course altered. Impact in three minutes."

They were being pulled away from the event horizon. Cochrane swung the spherical tactical viewer from the side bulkhead and peered into it. A portion of the display screen showed an aft view. Thorsen's ship was closing on them. Spock had said the Klingon vessel couldn't operate this close to the event horizon. That Thorsen wouldn't risk coming after the shuttlecraft. But there he was, close enough that his tractor beam was working.

"What can we do?" the Companion asked.

Cochrane felt the onboard gravity increase. According to the autopilot, they should be just seconds from entering the event horizon. But they were minutes away because of Thorsen's interference.

Cochrane reached out his hand to the controls. He had to tell the *Enterprise* what was happening. They had to change the program, recalculate the trajectory inside the event horizon. Everything depended on the shuttlecraft describing a perfect parabolic arc around the heart of the black hole and then coming back to within a few meters of the event horizon in twenty-two hours. For Cochrane and the Companion, because of relativistic time dilation, the total flight would be no more than thirty subjective minutes. But the trajectory had to be exactly as Spock had calculated it, and now, because of Thorsen's interference, there was no chance it would even be close.

A ready light glowed on the control console even as Cochrane's hand shook against the increased gravity, trying to switch on the communications circuit. The light showed that the shuttlecraft's warp engines were powering up.

"No," Cochrane gasped. "The trajectory is wrong." In the tactical viewer, the Klingon battle cruiser filled the screen.

"No!"

The ready light stopped flashing. Cochrane heard the whine of the *Ian Shelton*'s warp engines begin. He looked straight ahead through the viewport. The blue glow of Thorsen's tractor beam vanished. Darkness rushed at him, enormous, unstoppable, swallowing everything.

"Impact," the computer said.

Zefram Cochrane and the Companion passed through to the place where light stops.

ELEVEN

U.S.S. *ENTERPRISE* NCC-1701
CLOSE ORBIT TNC 65813
Stardate 3856
Earth Standard: ≈ November 2267

One instant, the *Ian Shelton* was on the main screen, a glowing spot of blue light barely ahead of the Klingon ship. The next instant, it was gone.

"I could not override," Spock said.

"Where is he?" Kirk demanded.

Spock had set the shuttlecraft's trajectory personally. It was supposed to pass through the event horizon on a parabolic curve that would bring it around the singularity and return it to just beneath the horizon in time to rendezvous with the *Excalibur*. At that time, if the *Ian Shelton* were limited in its movements to only normal space-time and electromagnetic phenomena, it would never be able to return to the other side. But the small craft carrying Cochrane and the Companion had warp capability and could easily move past any barrier that light could not escape.

But Thorsen's obsession had gone beyond the limits of even what Kirk had counted on. When it had become apparent that the *Enterprise*'s shuttlecraft was beyond rescue as Spock had planned, Thorsen had followed it toward the event horizon.

At first, Spock had not been concerned by Thorsen's cruiser's change of course. He said that the structure of the Klingon ship was designed for combat, and did not have the integrity of the *Enterprise*.

But Thorsen's ship had held together. His tractor beam had deflected the *Ian Shelton* to a new trajectory.

For all Kirk knew, Cochrane could be on a direct descent into the singularity itself—the point of absolute mass and pressure where physics broke down and from which not even the technology of the twenty-third century could rescue him.

"Spock," Kirk repeated, *"where* is he?"

"Sensors indicate the shuttlecraft has entered the event horizon, Captain. I am detecting no increased level of Hawking radiation from the boundary layer; therefore, we may assume the *Shelton* has survived the passage intact."

Kirk couldn't remain seated. "I *know* it survived, Spock. The *whole* plan was based on the fact that it *would* survive. But what's its trajectory?"

Spock finally looked up from his station. His expression was pained, and not just in a subtle Vulcan way. "At the angle it entered, it will spiral into the singularity within ten of our subjective hours."

Ten hours. The *Excalibur* wouldn't even have arrived by then.

"How long will it seem to Cochrane and the Companion?"

"As they approach the singularity, their relativistic velocity will approach the speed of light, and the corresponding time dilation will, from the perspective of the outside universe, stretch out their final seconds to infinite length."

Kirk felt as if he'd been kicked. Stars would form and die. Whole cultures evolve and become extinct, and Cochrane and the Companion would still be falling to their deaths. There was nothing they could do. Nothing Kirk could do.

He refused to accept it.

Spock suddenly pointed at the viewscreen. "Captain, Thorsen is attempting to follow the shuttlecraft."

Kirk wheeled in time to see the Klingon battle cruiser flash into the absolute darkness of the event horizon. "That's suicide. Isn't it?" he turned to Spock. "Did he make it?"

"Scanning for Hawking radiation . . . scanning . . ." Spock

looked up, making no attempt to hide his surprise. The tension of the moment was bringing out his human half. "No radiation."

"He made it," Kirk said. The concept was sickening. The pursued and pursuer trapped in an endless, infinite fall. But if the Klingon ship could do it . . .

"Spock! You said the D7s weren't built for the stress the *Enterprise* can take." Kirk pounded his fist on the railing separating the upper level of the bridge from its center. "If Thorsen can do it, we can!"

Spock's expression of Vulcan calm returned to him. "Captain, I understand your desire to save Mr. Cochrane and the Companion. But they are but two individuals, and the *Enterprise* has a crew of—"

"Don't tell me about my crew!" Kirk shouted. "If Thorsen can go in there, then he can come out with Cochrane! And what happens if the warp bomb is possible? Are you willing to risk it being put into that madman's hands? Can the Federation risk that?"

Kirk's heart was pounding. He *knew* he was right. "Calculate an angle of entry, Spock. Now!"

The intercom whistled. "Engineering to the bridge," Mr. Scott said. "Captain, if we don't start out within the next two minutes, we won't have the power t' be out of range when we lose the crystals."

"We're not leaving, Scotty."

"Captain? We've only got another thirty minutes in our crystals. Less than a second if we try to go to warp."

"That's all right, Scotty. We'll be here when the *Excalibur* and *Lexington* arrive." Kirk went to the rail by Spock's station. "Won't we, Mr. Spock?"

"Captain Kirk," Scott protested, "those ships are hours away. We'll never last that long out here."

"Understood, Mr. Scott. That's why we're going into the event horizon."

Scott said nothing.

Kirk continued. "With time dilation, we can spend a day down there and have only thirty subjective minutes pass."

"Aye," Scott said, sounding definitely unconvinced. "She'll hold together on the way in, but to come out again, she'll need to go to warp, and the crystals will never take the strain."

"Will they give us a second of warp, Scotty?"

"After thirty minutes on the other side of the event horizon, we'll be lucky to get a tenth of a second."

Kirk looked to Spock. He knew a tenth of a second would be close, but he couldn't be sure. Spock exhaled, as if making a decision. Kirk waited to hear if the next words to come from his science officer's mouth were to relieve him of command.

"Spock here, Mr. Scott. We will only need to move faster than light for a distance equal to five times the ship's length, once we return to the event horizon. Can you guarantee us warp propulsion for even one one-hundredth of a second?"

Scott replied as if a phaser had hit him. "Guarantee?! Mr. Spock, no ship has ever gone through an event horizon before and come out to tell the tale! Can you guarantee a ship this size can even make it through?"

"We have just witnessed a D7 Klingon battle cruiser do exactly that, Mr. Scott."

"What?!" Scott squealed. "You're saying a tin can piece o' junk D7 can make it?"

Kirk grinned. "One hundredth of a second, Scotty. Just a small miracle."

"Aye," Scott sighed. "And if I don't come through, we'll never know it."

"Is that a guarantee, Scotty?" Kirk knew what he wanted to do. He knew what he thought his ship and crew were capable of. But if his chief engineer couldn't be convinced, Mr. Spock was right—he couldn't throw away the lives of 430 crew members and the rescued passengers from the *Planitia,* even for the sake of the Federation, without a guarantee.

"It's as close to one as you'll get from me," Scott finally said. "Keep a clear channel open so I can hear what foolishness you'll be dreaming up next."

Kirk gave Spock a questioning look. "Is that good enough for you, Mr. Spock?"

A corner of Spock's mouth actually twitched up in a partial, unpracticed smile.

"It would not be good enough for my father," Spock said, "because there is little logic in the decision. But it *is* the right thing to do." Spock looked past his captain. "Mr. Sulu, I am transferring trajectory coordinates to your navigation system. Please follow them exactly."

At the command console, Kirk saw Sulu and Chekov exchange a glance of surprise, perhaps even of excitement. "Aye-*aye,* Mr. Spock," Sulu acknowledged. "Trajectory plotted."

"Are you ready, Mr. Scott?"

"As I'll ever be," the engineer replied.

Kirk returned to his chair. His course was set. "Uhura, launch a flight recorder with a transcript of everything we've just said here, along with complete sensor records of the flight paths of Thorsen's D7 and the *Ian Shelton.* I want the recorder sent on an intercept course to the *Excalibur* so they'll know what to be looking for when they get here." He settled into position. "Mr. Chekov, what is the position of the second Klingon cruiser?"

"It has withdrawn to a higher orbit, sir."

"Perhaps waiting to see if the other cruiser emerges," Spock suggested.

"Flight recorder away," Uhura announced.

"Any sign that the second cruiser spotted it?"

"No, sir," Uhura answered. "There's so much interference, I doubt anything that small could be scanned."

Kirk glanced back at Spock. Spock nodded. It was enough.

"Mr. Sulu, take us in."

Sulu's hands hovered over his controls. "Coming up on trajectory entry in eighteen seconds."

Except for the sounds of the ship herself, the bridge was silent. No one spoke, because there was nothing more to say.

At five seconds, Sulu began a countdown.

Kirk tightened his grip on the arms of his chair. He had changed the rules once again, and now it was time to see if the universe was playing the same game as James T. Kirk.

"Two," Sulu said. "One . . ."

Impact.

TWELVE

U.S.S. ENTERPRISE NCC-1701-D
APPROACHING TNC 65813
Stardate 43922.2
Earth Standard: ≈ May 2366

"Who the hell is Thorsen?" Riker asked.

The first officer was on the floor, leaning back against Worf's inoperative tactical console, as Dr. Crusher applied a nerve masker to his broken leg.

"You will lose your ignorance soon enough," the Data-thing said. "Ensign McKnight: Course and speed! Report at once!"

But McKnight said nothing. Picard could see the young woman's back stiffen in determination as she kept her eyes fixed on her board.

The Data-thing grimaced. "Captain Picard, while part of me retains professional admiration for the command structure your crew follows, the rest of me will tear Ensign McKnight's head from her body if she, or any one else on this bridge, does not follow my orders as they would your own." Slowly, chillingly, he made a fist. "You know this body has the capability to do that."

"Ensign McKnight," Picard said. "Tell Mr. Thorsen our course and speed."

The Data-thing glowered directly at Picard, who found it unnerving to see such emotion play over Data's usually placid features. The Thorsen personality matrix was even more turbulent than Data's brother, Lore.

"And it isn't *Mister* Thorsen. It's *Colonel* Adrik Thorsen." A sudden smile brightened the android's face as he glanced about the bridge. The sudden changes were unsettling. "The next one to forget that will die."

"Ensign McKnight," Picard said, not looking away from Data's yellow eyes, "report to Colonel Thorsen."

"On course for TNC 65813," the ensign said. "Velocity at warp factor nine."

The Data-thing looked suspicious. "This ship is capable of greater speed."

"Not without an engineering crew," La Forge said. He still nursed his hands against his chest. Picard could see that the engineer's fingers could move, though with obvious pain. He could also see anger beginning to build once again in the android's face.

"You did have us traveling at the ship's top speed," Picard said quickly, trying to defuse the situation. "But that requires constant adjustment of the warp core, which we are unable to carry out without a full complement of crew members in engineering."

The Data-thing hesitated, then pushed past Picard to the propulsion system station. Rapidly, his fingers moved over the flashing control surfaces. Then he turned to La Forge. "I have vented the anesthezine from engineering and opened a communications channel to that section. Your crew will be awake in a few more minutes. You will then supervise them to have this vessel operate at its maximum speed for the remainder of its journey."

La Forge looked at Picard.

"Don't look at *him!*" the Data-thing ordered. *"I* am your commander now!"

Picard could see that La Forge couldn't help the sneer that briefly touched his lips. But the engineer said, "Yes, *sir,"* and sat down at the station.

The Data-thing looked pleased with himself. Then, without warning, he reached out and grabbed Counselor Troi by her thick hair, twisting her around until he held her tightly against him, back to front, with one hand crushing her neck. "I shall keep this half-breed alive for three minutes. At the end of that time, I expect to see every phaser on this bridge stacked up on that chair." He grinned as he tightened his grip on Troi. "Two minutes fifty-nine seconds, fifty-eight seconds . . ."

With Wesley's assistance and before the time limit was up, all phasers from the bridge storage lockers were on the chair. The Data-thing discarded Troi by dropping her to the deck, then methodically picked up the phasers and crushed them, one by one. His concentration on the task allowed Picard to analyze their position. He surprised himself by thinking things didn't seem as grim as he had feared they'd be.

In terms of crew, O'Brien and McKnight were unharmed and at their stations. Worf was on his feet again, with a minor concussion Dr. Crusher wanted to treat in sickbay. Riker was pain-free, though it would be at least a day before the first officer's broken leg was healed, and he would not be capable of much walking for at least the next twelve hours.

Except for a raspy throat, Wesley had recovered from the explosive decompression in the shuttlebay, and remained close to his mother, helping her with her medical duties. La Forge was reduced to activating controls with only two fingers, but could still function adequately. And the counselor, though her neck was bruised and she appeared shaken, was otherwise unharmed.

Most important, however, was the status of the unusual personality matrix that had taken over Data the way it had taken over the *Enterprise*. Picard was sure he had heard the name of Colonel Adrik Thorsen before. He had some recollection of the man as an underling in Colonel Green's cadre in the period of upheaval directly preceding Earth's third world war. How or why a machine intelligence would take on that persona, Picard had no idea. But where there was reason for hope was that Thorsen now had to *ask* for information about the *Enterprise*'s status. Whatever kind of phenomenon Picard was facing here, the personality matrix that had taken over the ship was no longer operating in the ship's computer system. If Data could be overcome, then there was a chance the Thorsen personality could be defeated.

The only difficulty would be in physically overcoming the most powerful member of Picard's crew without causing any permanent damage that could compromise the safety of the real Data. Picard hoped that personality was still somewhere in the android's body and could, at some time, be restored.

The last crushed phaser clattered to the deck, scattering pieces of its casing, as the Data-thing turned to face Picard. "I'm fully aware of the strengths and weaknesses of this body, Captain Picard. I have access to the full range of what you call Data's memory. If any of you attempt any action—absolutely anything —that is intended to harm me, I know I can remain operational long enough to kill several of you and seriously damage your ship."

Picard studied the Data-thing for a moment, then deliberately adopted a belligerent tone. It was worth taking a chance if he could provoke the Thorsen personality into another round of erratic emotional responses—anything to keep him off balance. "First of all, *Colonel* Thorsen, I know you will not cause any damage to the *Enterprise* because you need her to get to the black hole. And second, you won't kill anyone because you need us to operate her."

The Data-thing cupped his chin in a thoughtful pose, then chuckled. "Jean-Luc, just as a friendly reminder: I don't need the Wesley child to run the ship; this body I wear doesn't need the doctor; and I certainly don't need the empath. So if I do need to make an example of anyone, they'll be the first to die. Are there any other threats you'd care to make?"

"Why are you doing this?" Riker asked from his position on the floor.

"Don't question your orders," the Data-thing warned.

"You're not my commanding officer," Riker said.

The Data-thing looked at Riker in confusion. "What kind of army is this? Do you *all* question your superiors?"

"This is not an 'army,'" Picard said forcefully. He was beginning to wonder if it *was* somehow possible that the personality of a twenty-first-century military madman had survived to the present. If so, it might give him a clue as to how to reason with Thorsen. "We're explorers, not soldiers."

"You mean you're weak," the Data-thing said contemptuously. "You'll never be optimal."

371

"Optimal? Do you honestly expect us to believe that you're *the* Adrik Thorsen from the Third World War?" Riker asked in disbelief. Picard was pleased that his first officer had made the same connection to Thorsen's name as he had. Perhaps Riker also realized that there was a chance to regain control of the ship if anyone could get close enough to Data.

"I am *more* than Adrik Thorsen ever was," the Data-thing said. "I contain the core of him, the best of him, spread out to realms undreamed of in his day. I have transcended the Thorsen flesh and become the one true Optimal."

"What's so optimal about having to threaten to kill people to get them to do what you want?" Wesley asked, making no attempt to hide his angry frustration, though it was still tempered by fear.

"I forgive you your doubts because you are not yet formed," the android replied. "If you survive to serve me, you will learn."

"Serve you in what way?" Picard asked.

"You shall be the soldiers in my army in the war to come," the Data-thing said emphatically, swept up in the grandeur of whatever perverted vision he held. "Old dreams need not die. Red banners wave and black eagles fly. I shall remake this age in my image. A new order among the worlds. Peace in my time. Salvation from chaos."

"You're too late," Riker said dismissively. "The worlds of the Federation *are* at peace. There is no chaos in our affairs."

"Commander Riker, you forget, I have all the knowledge of your Data. I know the true condition of the Federation. Treaty disputes, planets on the brink of war, inefficient resource allocation—you're just a duplicate of Earth and her colonies before the atomic cleansing. Your Federation is crying out for order. Nothing has changed except the size of the battlefield."

Picard stepped closer to the android. "Colonel Thorsen, no planet in the Federation has been on the brink of war for decades. You're thinking of the nonaligned worlds. As for treaty disputes, they are a given in any collection of thriving civilizations. The wants and needs of cultures change from generation to generation. The Federation exists to accommodate those changes in the most peaceful and equitable manner, and we do. And however inefficient our allocation of resources is, we do a better job of it today than we did ten years ago, and we will be doing a better job again ten years hence." Picard could not help himself. He felt his voice become more powerful, as if he were speaking to an audience far greater than just Thorsen. "The Federation is not static, which is what gives us our strength. The Optimum Movement's backward, inhumane dreams of a society made perfect because every regimented member looks alike, behaves alike, and believes alike was recognized for the hateful abomination it was centuries ago and rightfully abandoned.

"I don't know what you really are or how you came to be in this time, but no matter how you threaten us, we have outgrown you and you no longer have a place among us."

The Data-thing looked around at Picard's crew in sarcastic amazement as they regarded their captain with pride. "A philosophical debate about humanity's *maturity?* On a starship with weapons enough to destroy *entire* planets?" The android turned back to Picard. "Captain, this is an argument I am destined to win for one very simple, very self-evident reason."

"Which is?" Picard demanded, taking another step closer, preparing to make the one move he hoped the Data-thing would not anticipate.

"This," the Data-thing said. And then his fist moved up so quickly that Picard never saw it coming.

"How are you feeling?" Beverly Crusher asked.

Picard blinked up at her. The lower half of his face felt numb. He touched his chin.

"Careful," the doctor said. "You've got two broken teeth so I had to switch off a few of the nerves."

Picard realized he was flat on his back, though he could hear the steady sounds of the bridge and knew where he was. He started to sit up and Dr. Crusher helped him. On the main screen, he saw the glowing gas spiral of TNC 65813, but it was no longer a computer graphic—it was a real-time sensor image.

"Beverly, how long—"

"Almost six hours," Crusher said. "He didn't hit you that hard, but he decided you would not be 'conducive to the smooth running of the mission' so he had me use a neural blocker on you." Crusher frowned, apologetic. "I'm sorry, Jean-Luc, but if I hadn't, he would have medicated you himself."

"You did the right thing," Picard assured her as he got to his feet. "But why am I being allowed to awaken now?"

"We've arrived at the black hole," the doctor said softly, "and there's another ship here."

Picard saw the Data-thing sitting in his command chair, legs crossed, hands cupped around one knee. The other seats in the command area were empty. Except for McKnight and O'Brien, the remaining crew were on the upper level, looking grim, ready to fight.

"So good of you to join us," the Data-thing said to Picard. He indicated the seat beside him. "Join me."

"Are we about to rendezvous with your partners?" Picard asked as he walked slowly toward the android, carefully rubbing his jaw.

"And who would those partners be?" the Data-thing asked.

"The Romulans, of course."

The Data-thing laughed scornfully. "Captain, the Romulans are just pawns. Commander Traklamek was even easier than you to convince that he had found an authentic Preserver device."

"So the object in the shuttlebay *isn't* what it appears to be?"

The Data-thing shrugged. "Maybe it is, maybe it isn't. The point is, it's so old and so badly damaged that it's completely inoperative. I've been searching space for a long time, Captain, and it's surprising the things that can be found in it. That object, half-destroyed as it is, is just one of many unusual items I've salvaged. Originally, I had planned to use it as a test. I added a diagram of my own to its inscriptions, to see if anyone could build the warp bomb for me. But once I had contacted the Romulans, and learned that they had their own reasons for seeking a Galaxy-class ship, I had only to add a power source and some . . . 'appropriate circuitry' to the object to get me passage on your ship."

"What was Traklamek expecting out of all this?"

"What else?" the Data-thing replied. "Your ship. Traklamek thought he was dealing with a machine intelligence eager to be transported to the vessel from which it had been separated. So we worked out an 'arrangement.' If Traklamek could get me aboard the *Enterprise,* then I would seize control of it, send it into the Neutral Zone to initiate certain aggressive acts, and then make certain that he could capture it relatively intact."

"And in return?"

"I told Traklamek that I knew where the rest of 'me' was, and if he would take me there, I could reunite with my own ship and be free to go home." The Data-thing grinned nastily. "Romulans have such childlike devotion to their home that Traklamek believed me without question. Such a gullible people."

"So you coming aboard the *Enterprise* was his idea," Picard asked. He still wasn't any closer to understanding what the Thorsen personality was after.

"Of course not," the android replied in irritation. "Being here, now, was *my* goal from the beginning. I just had to do it in a way that would guarantee you would connect me with your computers. And if you had just 'happened' to find me floating by in space, you would have been far too cautious to ever allow that.

"No, the Romulans were very clever to use the Borg artifact as a Trojan horse. And to bring in the Ferengi to add further layers of deception designed to lull you into acceptance. But it is *my* goal which has been achieved."

"What about Commander Tarl?"

"She was Traklamek's wife. Those fools had visions of becoming proconsuls or some such together. I really couldn't spare much attention for their backward culture."

For a moment, Picard didn't know what to say. If Tarl and Traklamek had been mates, then Picard was surprised that the instant the *Enterprise* had destroyed Traklamek's Warbird that Tarl hadn't attacked in revenge. He wondered if the Thorsen entity was actually speaking the truth. Picard was certain no Romulan mate could leave such an outrage unavenged.

"So who *is* meeting us around the black hole?" Picard asked, hoping that Data's possessor would continue to shed light on his actions and thus help Picard and his crew to outmaneuver him somehow.

"That's why I called you back from the void, Captain. *I'm* not expecting to find anyone around the black hole. I believe the ship that is there is one of yours. And I want you to deal with it."

"In what way?"

The Data-thing's eyes glittered. "It seems to be a Federation vessel. Feel free to order it to withdraw. And if it doesn't, destroy it."

Picard stood in front of the android. "If you want me to do anything, get out of my chair. Anyone who sees a lieutenant commander sitting there with the captain beside him is going to know something's wrong."

The Data-thing shrugged and moved over to sit in Counselor Troi's position. Picard watched the move with increased interest. The Thorsen personality hadn't moved to the first-officer position. If he had access to all of Data's memories, he should have known that that was where he belonged as operations manager in the first officer's absence. Perhaps the slipup meant that while he had *access* to Data's memories, he wasn't in the habit of looking up every detail in them. That might be another advantage to be exploited.

Picard made himself comfortable. Just by being in this seat, he felt the situation was halfway back to being salvageable. "Mr. O'Brien, status update, please."

From his position at the ops board, O'Brien replied, "We're operating on ninety-percent automatic controls, sir. Engineering is under direct control of the engineering crew. The majority of the crew remains unconscious after exposure to anesthezine. The ship remains closed off by locked doors, security fields, and inoperative communications."

"None of that is your concern," the Data-thing warned. "I want that Federation vessel gone."

Picard tried to ignore the android beside him. "Do we have identification of the vessel in question?"

"None, sir," O'Brien answered. "It appears to be an Oberth-class starship, now orbiting one thousand kilometers above the singularity's electromagnetic event horizon. Without access to the computer, I can't call up any Fleet records so I have no way of knowing which ship she is or what she's doing there."

"Where are *we,* exactly?" Picard asked.

"Three million kilometers away and closing on impulse."

"Mr. Worf," Picard said. "Open a hailing frequency."

The Klingon's response was terse. "Communications remain inoperative, sir. Colonel Thorsen has placed lockout codes on all key functions."

Picard looked at the Data-thing with a shrug. The Data-thing shrugged theatrically in return, swung around a command console, and entered a series of commands.

"Subspace communications back on-line," Worf said. "Hailing the unidentified vessel."

The main viewscreen image of the plasma jets and gas disk was suddenly replaced by a transmission from a Starfleet vessel. A young human captain sat in her command chair, brushing crisp brown hair from her forehead. "Hello, *Enterprise* and Captain Picard," she said cheerfully. "Captain Bondar, *U.S.S. Garneau.* I knew this recovery operation was big, but I didn't know it was *this* big. Glad to have you along."

Picard didn't recognize the woman, though she obviously knew of him. "Greetings, Captain Bondar," he began. "What recovery operation do you mean?"

The Data-thing spoke in a menacing whisper. "Tell her to leave or you will destroy her."

Captain Bondar shifted position in her chair, suddenly taking on a more formal demeanor. "Excuse me, Captain Picard, but you *are* here as part of the recovery mission, aren't you?"

Picard could see that the Data-thing was about to speak again, so he replied quickly, before he could be stopped. "We have no knowledge of any recovery mission."

"Last chance," the Data-thing said.

"We are, however, on a classified mission," Picard continued. "And we require you to leave your position at once."

Bondar looked stern. All sense of friendly welcome was gone. "Under whose authorization?"

"Admiral Hanson," Picard said, grabbing the first name to come to mind. "Starbase 324."

Bondar reacted with dismay. "Oh, damn, it's something to do with the Borg, isn't it?" She motioned to someone out of the viewer's range to come closer. "Captain, you're presenting me with a real conflict. We've been on station here as a priority-one science mission for the past three months, and we're coming up to a critical time in the mission profile." A Bolian commander stepped up beside Bondar, giving her a padd as she continued speaking. "Our command authorization is such that I am going to have to request verification of your orders from Starfleet Command. I hope you—"

"Viewscreen off," the Data-thing said. He tapped more commands into his console. "Phaser banks on-line. Tactical officer will now target the *Garneau*."

"Captain Picard," Worf said in consternation. "I cannot fire on a Federation vessel."

Picard turned to the Data-thing. "Why is it so important for us to be here and that ship not to be?"

"The *Enterprise* will be going into hiding soon, and the fewer who know her last location, the better." The Data-thing looked up over his shoulder. "Now, Klingon, destroy that ship or I will do it myself and kill one of you as an example."

Picard clenched his fists. "Mr. Worf, fire a warning shot across the *Garneau*'s bow."

"Locking phasers," Worf replied.

"What pathetic weaklings this species has become without leadership," said the Data-thing, shaking its head in disgust.

The phasers hummed.

"Low-level burst detonating one kilometer in front of the *Garneau*," Worf reported. "Captain, we are receiving an urgent hail."

Picard stared defiantly at the Data-thing. "Onscreen," he said.

"What the *hell* do you think you're doing, Picard?!" Bondar was on her feet, shouting into the viewer. "You are interfering in a classified Code One Alpha Zero rescue operation! Back off now or we will return fire!"

Picard didn't understand Captain Bondar's use of the code. One Alpha Zero meant a spaceship was in distress. But there were no other ships in the area. What did she mean?

The Data-thing's voice rose sharply. "Go to battle stations at once. That puny vessel is no match for this ship."

"This ship has no crew," Picard snapped. "If we go into battle relying on automatic controls only, that puny vessel could blow us out of space."

The *Garneau*'s captain stared out from the viewscreen in confusion. "Picard? What was that about having no crew? Are you in some kind of operational difficulty?"

Picard started to answer but the Data-thing stood up in front of him.

"There is no difficulty," the android said. "Worf! Fire!"

Picard saw his chance. He reached out for the android's back and—

The Data-thing's hand moved in a blur and closed around Picard's right wrist. With a burning twist, Picard felt bones crack and he cried out in shock.

"Fire!" the android shouted.

"All hands battle stations!" Bondar ordered on the viewscreen. Then she added quickly, "Listen *Enterprise,* whoever's in charge, just remember the gravitational environment you're in. No ship can survive being crippled this close to the event horizon. One shield fluctuation and the tidal forces will stretch you to taffy. This is your last chance. You must withdraw!"

"Fiiire!" the Data-thing screamed, and he wrenched Picard forward to throw him on the deck of the bridge at the same time.

Picard hit and rolled with a gasp of pain. His right hand hung useless. He saw the Data-thing spin to face Worf, but Worf took his hands from the tactical controls. He refused to fire.

Incoherent with rage, the Data-thing rushed to the side of the bridge rail, leapt over it, and threw himself at Worf. The Klingon bravely stood his ground, got in one powerful though ineffectual blow to the android's head, and then was smashed sideways into a control console, which exploded in the impact. Worf slumped senseless to the deck as Troi, Wesley, and Dr. Crusher ran to his aid. Riker, clutching his leg on the floor, could only watch in helpless frustration.

The Data-thing took over Worf's console, and the *Enterprise*'s phasers fired. Picard pushed himself up to look at the screen.

The bridge of the *Garneau* rocked with the hit it took. Picard heard warning sirens sound on the science vessel. "Captain

Bondar!" he called out. "The *Enterprise* has been hijacked! It is no longer under Starfleet control! Withdraw at once!"

The *Enterprise* lurched as three photon torpedoes from the *Garneau* burst across her primary hull shields. Damage warnings sounded on his own bridge.

"This is a rescue operation, Picard! We cannot withdraw," Bondar shouted.

"Where is the other ship you're to rescue?!" Picard demanded as he heard the Data-thing fire phasers again.

"Beyond the event horizon!" Bondar answered. She held on tightly as her command chair shuddered. Picard saw sparks erupt from a console behind her. "It's a science package Starfleet launched ninety-nine years ago. We've got to—" The transmission washed out in a wave of static, then came back half-strength. "Damn you, Picard! Can't you take responsibility for your own ship?!"

Picard groaned in pain and frustration. Why wouldn't this captain realize the danger she was in? He heard the twang of photon torpedoes launching even as the *Enterprise* trembled beneath the *Garneau*'s phaser blasts. "Get out of there, Bondar! Starfleet can always launch another science package!"

"You don't understand!" the captain said. "There is a passenger on board it! He is crucial to the security of the Federation! He is—"

The transmission ended without static, signifying a complete shutdown of the *Garneau*'s communication system. But from the view of the gas disk that returned to the main screen, Picard could see no indication of the science vessel's fate.

But he knew the real mission of the Thorsen personality.

Picard confronted the Data-thing. "You want that passenger, don't you? Whoever he is, he's from a century ago; you're from almost three centuries in the past . . . you're still fighting some war that ended generations ago."

The Data-thing contemplated Picard. Its rage was no longer evident. "Very impressive, Captain, except that the war continues. And I will triumph."

"How?" Picard asked. "By leaving the passenger inside the event horizon? Trapped forever?"

But the Data-thing slowly shook his head. "Oh, no, Picard, I came to 'rescue' the passenger myself. I saw him go in there, and I intend to bring him out. Personally."

"Why? Who is it?"

"He is a man who dared claim that I exist because of him. So I want him to see what he has made of my existence, before I destroy his."

"You're mad," Picard said. It was the only explanation.

"The entire universe is mad, Captain Picard. That's why it needs me to lead it. I'm going to protect the rest of you from yourselves." The Data-thing looked past Picard. "Mr. O'Brien— status of the *Garneau*."

"No readings," O'Brien reported sullenly.

"Destroyed?" Picard asked.

"This close to the event horizon, sir, I can't be sure. Half of our sensors are still off-line."

The Data-thing walked purposefully down the ramp to the command area again. "That's all right," he said. "I understand the environment beyond an electromagnetic event horizon is quite simple. Sensors will not be taxed."

With those words, for the very first time, Picard also understood why the Thorsen personality had come for the *Enterprise*.

"No," Picard said. "You cannot do this."

"Correct," the Data-thing agreed as he walked past Picard and casually reached out to snag McKnight's uniform and toss her from her station. "I cannot. But the *Enterprise* can."

Picard stood helplessly by the android as he watched the new heading entered into the navigation controls. "The *Enterprise* has just experienced a collision," he said. "Her crew is incapacitated. Her structural integrity field has been overloaded."

The Data-thing glanced up at Picard with contempt. "I have had subroutines monitoring Starfleet computers for decades, Picard. I know this ship was designed to withstand warp tunneling through electromagnetic event horizons."

"Theoretically!" Picard insisted. "Event horizon missions have only been carried out by remote probes—never by crewed vehicles." He looked up at the main screen. The giant, dark ellipse of the event horizon curved across the bottom of the image, lit by blinding flashes wherever gas and dust and debris fell in, accelerated to light-speed by the monstrous gravitational pull of the singularity deep within it.

"Then it appears I know something you don't," the Data-thing gloated. "Where we are going, we will not be the first."

Collision alert sirens sounded.

"But we will be the last."

Absolute darkness filled the viewscreen.

Impact.

Part Three

☆

WHERE NO ONE HAS GONE BEFORE

THORSEN

Adrik Thorsen's dream had consumed him until only that dream remained.

What once had been human had died on Earth, centuries before, as humanity had stood on a threshold and rejected him and his kind, moving forward.

What once had been human, restored, augmented, and enhanced by the products of human technology, had brooded and plotted alone in space, until the Grigari had offered their bargain, the age-old trap—life eternal in exchange for all that made life worthwhile.

What once had been a Grigari amalgam, the last vestiges of flesh augmented by blindly programmed, self-organizing machines, had hunted for revenge. Only to find itself a silent witness to the events of TNC 65813, stardate 3856, orbiting in the second Klingon cruiser, watching all that played out below him.

Cochrane had escaped that day. Revenge was denied. Incomplete. Non-optimal.

But knowledge burned deeply within what remained of Thorsen, as painful as the laser burst forever etched within his optic nerve—the knowledge that though Cochrane had escaped, Cochrane, in time, would return.

Thorsen vowed to be there when he did.

And then the Grigari bargain claimed its final payment and all that was left of the original Thorsen died.

But the evil that had spawned him lived on. Hatred, intolerance, unrestrained greed, all those qualities which had once defined humanity so well, proved fertile still, even in this day when they had been vanquished in so many others.

Blindly, the Grigari machines continued their work, replacing the necrotized flesh in its entirety, maintaining the form and the function, following the most basic program that had fueled Thorsen in his life. The desire to destroy Cochrane and all those like him whose very humanity now mocked the travesty that pursued them.

To fulfill Thorsen's purpose, the Grigari machines spread out, an invisible, mechanical plague, infecting computers and starships, scanning for any clue or event linked to Zefram Cochrane and the time of his return.

Eventually, the time of the fabled scientist's return was calculated by Starfleet, and the Grigari machines knew. They brought their information back to the construct that they served, the construct that existed now with only one program, an echo from a distant past, a version of a personality driven by desires no longer based in living thought or tissue.

A mathematical duplicate of Thorsen's intellect devised the plan. A Galaxy-class starship must be found to survive the mission to recover Cochrane, to save him, and then destroy him. A long-lost alien object would be the bait for the trap. The Romulans, caught up by hatreds of their own, proved willing accomplices. Thorsen's personality matrix would continue, jumping from one storage device to another, as blind in its desires as were the unknowing machines that had formed it.

As of stardate 43922.2, there was no conscious thought behind this goal of hateful destruction, and no humanity.

But then, in truth, there never had been.

ONE

☆

TNC 65813
$t = \infty$

The turbulence ended.

Zefram Cochrane was aware only of the low whisper of the shuttlecraft's air circulators, the soft hum of her engines, the warmth of the Companion's hand in his.

He looked out through the forward windows and saw darkness, limitless, featureless, broken only by a faint blue glow to port.

"We survived?" the Companion asked.

Cochrane smiled. "Did you doubt we would?"

She returned his smile and Cochrane felt the peace of this journey fill his heart because the Companion was with him.

"I only knew I had to be with you," she said, "whatever happened."

Cochrane felt relief that for the first time since they had been reunited, the Companion seemed to have finally relaxed. The bandage over her eye, the condition of her hair, all might be part of some avant-garde fashion on a world he had never visited. He marveled at Kirk and Spock and McCoy for devising this plan, for making it possible. The human race had changed so much in his extended lifetime, become so strong. He could hear Micah Brack telling him he should take credit for at least part of what had

387

happened to humanity and those who joined them in their future, for giving them the stars. For in reaching out to explore the heavens, all had found themselves, as if the stars were where they were always meant to be.

Cochrane himself would never forget taking off his mask on the plains of Centauri B II, drawing that first breath of alien air.

Unencumbered.

For the first time, Cochrane could see that Micah Brack had been right but not in the way he had expected. All else in human history had followed from that moment, and Cochrane could finally admit that he *had* done something extraordinary—that he had given Earth's peoples a way to achieve what they had always searched for—freedom, growth, the unending adventure of living. Yet all that mattered to him now was that in exchange for his gift to humanity, the events of his existence had brought him the gift *he* had searched for: the Companion, who gave to him all that made the adventure of life worth living. Love.

For a moment, Cochrane was overcome by the path he had taken to reach that final understanding of his life's journey, that acceptance—from a child's dream beneath a tree on Earth to the uncharted and complex dimension that lay within a black hole in space, all so he could arrive at such a simple destination, such a simple understanding.

"I love you," he said to the Companion.

Her smile was answer enough. Journey's end.

She glanced through the forward windows. He saw her eyes as she gazed off to port.

"What causes that glow?" she asked.

"Photons above us," Cochrane said, admiring the line of her precious face, so softly lit by the glow from the shuttlecraft's instruments. "The ones falling toward the singularity that we'll swing around. We see nothing ahead of us because no light can escape the singularity from that direction. But we *can* see the blue-shifted light beginning its fall."

"But not all the light is blue, Zefram."

From his position, Cochrane could not see as far to port as the Companion could. He swung the spherical tactical monitor out from the bulkhead and checked the aft view.

He gasped.

Directly astern, flaring from within a rainbow-streaked halo of gravity-smeared light, a Klingon battle cruiser raced straight for him.

Even here, even now, there was no escape from the Optimum.

The turbulence ended.

Kirk eased his grip on the arms of his chair, a parting caress. The *Enterprise* might just as well have been flying at half-impulse through normal space.

"We have tunneled through the event horizon," Spock announced.

"Scotty," Kirk asked, "how's she doing?"

"Captain Kirk," a Scottish lilt answered back, "considering we're in a region o' space where nothin' bigger than a molecule should be able to exist, th' fact that we can have this conversation at all should be answer enough for ye."

It was. The *Enterprise* had done it again. Her crew had done it again.

Kirk had done it again.

"Mr. Chekov, any sign of the shuttlecraft and the Klingon cruiser?" he asked. The main screen was black and Kirk could see Chekov working frantically on his sensor controls, trying to establish an image.

"There is no forward optical information available to us in this environment," Spock said. "I am switching all sensors to subspace ranging-echo only."

Instantly, the main viewscreen came to life with a collection of indistinct green splotches—an irregularly shaped blob to the lower right, and two much smaller dots to the upper left.

"Analysis, Spock?"

"In the upper left of the screen, I believe we are seeing sensor returns indicating that both the shuttlecraft and the Klingon vessel survived the event horizon. However, I am also recording extreme quantum compression waves that correspond to no known theory of gravitational singularities. Those waves are preventing me from obtaining finer display resolution."

"Range to Klingon vessel?" Kirk asked. He sat forward in his chair. At least he could see that the small dots were expanding. The *Enterprise* was gaining.

"Keptin," Chekov said plaintively. "Sensors indicate the Klingon vessel is more than *one million* kilometers away."

"Impossible. The diameter of this event horizon is only eight hundred kilometers."

"The quantum compression waves are to blame," Spock explained. "They are distorting spatial dimensions, though not as theory predicts."

"Then how can we set a course in here?" Kirk asked. "How can we target that Klingon ship and save Cochrane?"

"I am attempting to create a conversion program for our navigational routines. However, the compression waves are erratic. It appears our presence here is disruptive and the computer cannot cope with the changing spatial conditions."

Kirk hadn't come all this way to be stopped by a computer shortcoming. "Dammit, Spock—what's the source of those waves?"

Spock adjusted controls at his science station, and the image on the main screen expanded to show the irregularly shaped blotch from the lower right corner. As the green shape filled the screen, it became better defined, until Kirk could see that part of its distortion came from movement—it appeared to be pulsating with three expanding and contracting lobes.

"That is the source," the science officer answered. "It is the *subspace* event horizon. The boundary from which not even warp engines could return us to normal space-time."

"But why isn't it a sphere, like the electromagnetic event horizon we passed through above?"

"Unknown, Captain. Our sensors cannot obtain any information from beyond that boundary. However, judging from the pulsations, I suspect that instead of one singularity being at the heart of this black hole, there are in fact three. They appear to be linked into tight orbits of each other, at what would, from necessity, be faster-than-light speeds."

Kirk turned to look at his science officer to be sure he had heard correctly. *"Three* singularities? Orbiting faster than light?"

Spock made a dismissive expression. "I do not pretend to understand how such a thing could exist at all."

"All right. It's there. How can we deal with it to stop the Klingon ship?"

"I would suggest launching a photon torpedo. Its onboard guidance system can perform necessary course corrections in flight."

Kirk turned back to the screen. "Put the cruiser and the shuttlecraft on the screen, Mr. Chekov."

The pulsating tri-lobed shape disappeared, replaced by two green, rough-edged silhouettes. One was little more than a few pixels across, showing no detail, but the other image was identifiable as a D7 battle cruiser.

"Lieutenant Uhura," Kirk said, "can we use subspace radio in here?"

Uhura frowned as she listened carefully to her earpiece. Her expert fingers moved swiftly over her controls. "Barely, sir. There is considerable interference."

"Try to hail the cruiser. We'll give it one warning at least."

"The ship is not responding, sir."

Kirk turned to Spock again. "Any way to know how shock waves will travel through this region? If we do destroy the cruiser, what might that do to our shuttlecraft?"

"Shock waves will not propagate here faster than the relative velocity of the shuttlecraft. It will not be harmed."

Kirk took no pleasure in what he knew he must do next. It might be better if the Klingon ship had tried to fight back. "Does the cruiser even know we're here?" he asked.

"Each ship in this region experiences time at a different rate. It could be that their sensors cannot even perceive us," Spock said. "The compression waves we've disturbed are creating pockets of temporal distortion as well as spatial ones."

Shooting at a blind enemy didn't make it any easier for Kirk, but he knew he could delay no longer. "Mr. Chekov, target the Klingon cruiser."

"Cruiser targeted, sir."

"Fire photon torpedo, self-guided mode."

The sound of the torpedo launcher hummed through the bridge. Kirk watched as a tiny point of green appeared on the screen, then seemed to spiral in the general direction of the cruiser, making constant course corrections.

"As I suspected," Spock said, "as the torpedo passes through different compression nodes, its sensors are perceiving the Klingon ship in different locations at different times. This is a most fluid environment. Quite fascinating."

The tiny green dot moved past the Klingon ship. Kirk tensed, worried the torpedo would lock on to *Ian Shelton*. But the dot doubled back, merged with the cruiser's silhouette, and then both were gone.

"That's it?" Kirk asked.

"As soon as the torpedo disrupted the cruiser's structural integrity field," Spock said, "tidal forces would have reduced the ship to little more than a molecular mist."

"Then Cochrane and the Companion are safe?"

"Only if we can adjust their trajectory, and ours. For the moment, both our vessels are being drawn down toward the linked singularities and the second horizon."

Kirk was too fueled by adrenaline to remain seated. He paced the area behind Chekov and Sulu. "Mr. Sulu, match trajectory with the shuttlecraft." He glanced back at Spock. "At least we'll be able to beam them back aboard."

But Spock shook his head. "There are too many temporal distortions present, and we are creating even more as the compression waves bounce off our shields. Our transporters would never be able to hold a coherent signal, even at close range."

"Then we'll use tractor beams," Kirk said.

"If we are able to generate sufficient power."

Kirk heard the unspoken message in Spock's tone. "*Are* we going to be able to correct our trajectories, Spock?"

"I do not believe we have that capability, Captain. We are too deep within the gravity well."

Kirk stopped pacing. "Even if we go to warp?"

"The condition of our dilithium crystals is such that we cannot remain in warp long enough from this position to reach the event horizon. If we even make the attempt, our crystals will burn out within a second, our structural integrity field will collapse, and—"

Kirk finished it: "—we'll be reduced to a molecular mist, like the ship we just destroyed." He tapped his fist against his open palm, brain afire with possibilities. "Can we adjust our trajectory enough to slingshot us *past* the linked singularities and use the velocity we'd gain to carry us upward to the first event horizon?"

"I am endeavoring to calculate that course," Spock said. "But the compression waves are reducing the amount of space we have in which to maneuver. The closer we approach the singularities, the more problematic course corrections become."

Kirk could see he shouldn't interrupt Spock again. If there was a course correction they could make, Spock would find it. But only if he had time.

Kirk sat back down, forcing himself to remain calm. "Uhura, try to raise the shuttlecraft so we can at least let Mr. Cochrane and the Companion know what's going on."

He tapped his fingers against the arm of his chair. There had been a way into this black hole, there would be a way out. All he had to do was find it.

"No response from the shuttlecraft," Uhura said. "Too much interference."

"Keep trying," Kirk said. He watched the tiny dot on the screen slowly expanding as the *Enterprise* drew near. At least wherever they were bound, they would all get there together.

Uhura suddenly murmured with surprise and Kirk turned to see her pull out her earpiece.

"Sorry, sir. I just got a flood of interference."

"Keptin," Chekov called out. "Sensors are picking up the presence of *another* wessel! It has just passed through the event horizon above us."

Kirk's jaw tightened. "Ready photon torpedoes," he ordered. He had been half expecting this. The second Klingon cruiser had finally arrived. And by being in the higher orbit, it had the upper hand. "Onscreen," he said.

The screen flickered as an aft view was displayed. Instead of a black background, the screen was alive with flashes of color and light, the result of the infall of photons and subspace signals from above. In the middle of the visual confusion was the smeared, irregular silhouette of the third vessel.

It looked wrong.

"Can you make that any clearer?" Kirk asked.

"Trying, sir," Chekov said, but no matter what adjustments he made, the level of interference remained the same.

The third ship was gaining, its silhouette growing larger. "That's not a Klingon cruiser," Kirk said. The silhouette showed a distinct saucer section and twin nacelles. "Spock, have we been down here long enough for that to be the *Excalibur*?"

"It is possible," Spock said. "The temporal-distortion nodes are interfering with normal time-dilation effects. I will attempt to trace the vessel's trajectory to calculate its time of entry."

"Keptin, the wessel is making course corrections, matching our trajectory."

"Uhura," Kirk said, "open hailing frequencies to that vessel. Warn them away from our trajectory."

"Too late, Keptin. They've matched it precisely."

Uhura went to work on her board. Kirk was too impatient to wait for Spock. "Come on, Mr. Spock—is that the *Excalibur* or the *Lexington*?"

Spock looked up from his science viewer with an expression of un-Vulcan-like bemusement. "Captain, it is neither. According to my calculations, that ship is from the future."

Kirk's eyes widened. "How far in the future?"

"A century at least," Spock said. "And it is trapped in the same fatal trajectory we are."

The turbulence ended.

For Picard, it was as if the *Enterprise* had moved into the eye of some galactic hurricane. All he was aware of was the gentle background symphony of normal bridge functions. And his throbbing, broken wrist.

The main screen flashed with static as the sensors reset themselves. When the image cleared, Picard could see that most of it was computer-enhanced, as if very little of what the sensor grid was able to perceive would make sense to human eyes. Picard guessed that, for the most part, he was looking at subspace sensor returns. But of what?

The Data-thing shouted commands to O'Brien at Ops, telling him how to adjust sensor readings to improve the screen image. Unfortunately, the sensor grid had not been reset since the Romulan collision and O'Brien was unable to comply with the settings he was ordered to make.

Finally, though, the blurred images coalesced on the screen. In the lower right was a bizarre, three-lobed object which appeared to pulsate. Picard guessed it was the subspace event horizon, though could not explain the shape and movement unless the second, lower horizon hid three singularities linked in close orbit—which would require velocities in excess of the speed of light. Picard remembered reading abstracts about multi-singularities as an exotic new form of gravitationally collapsed object, but whatever phenomenon the *Enterprise* was now facing, this was no ordinary black hole.

To the upper left of the screen were two much smaller objects. One was only a dot of light, presumably the science package the *Garneau* had been on station to recover. But the second object was clearly a starship—and the *Garneau*'s captain had not mentioned that. In addition, it was clear that both objects were spiraling down toward the subspace event horizon, and not away from it. Picard didn't know how the *Garneau* had been expected to recover either.

"I compliment you on your ship," the Data-thing said. "It is hours away from failure."

The main screen images changed their position as the *Enterprise* changed course.

"Captain Picard . . ."

Picard turned at the sound of Worf's voice, weak and shaky. He had a bad cut across his warrior's brow, being treated by Dr. Crusher even as he leaned over his tactical board. "The course we are on . . . we are heading for the singularity . . ."

"Just for the time being," the Data-thing said. "First there is a shuttlecraft we must rendezvous with. And then your mighty ship will take us back."

"We'll never make it," La Forge said urgently. He was still at his engineering station but Picard could see science displays on his screens. "Captain, the Kabreigny Object is a *multi*singularity. The closer we get to the subspace event horizon, the more the quantum metric of space will be compressed around us. It won't matter how much power we have for our engines—we just won't have enough space left to maneuver in!"

The Data-thing looked over his shoulder, about to speak. But he didn't. Picard could guess what had happened. The Thorsen personality had accessed Data's onboard data banks and discovered that La Forge was right.

"Take us back now," Picard said. "You know we can't make it back if you take us further in."

The Data-thing remained silent, looking as Data often had, eyes to the side, as if engaged in some internal conversation. "I will never surrender," the android said at last. He looked at Picard. "I must destroy him, no matter what the cost." He turned back to his board, rapidly entering more commands. Picard heard the *Enterprise*'s impulse engines increase their output.

"What are you doing?!" La Forge cried. "Captain! He's drawing power from the SIF to give us greater speed."

For the first time since passing through the event horizon, the great ship shuddered. Picard heard creaking from the superstructure around the bridge. The images of the two objects on the screen were becoming larger as the *Enterprise* gained on them. She shuddered again.

"I can't override him, Captain!"

"You'll destroy the ship!" Picard shouted at the Data-thing. "What can be worth that?"

"To prove I am right," the Data-thing said.

An ominous vibration started as the engines began to whine. Picard felt the full weight of command descend upon him. More than a thousand crew members depended on him to get them back to safety. But there was nothing he could do. The Thorsen machine could not be reasoned with. It could not be swayed. It could not be stopped.

In frustration, Picard swung his left fist against the Data-thing's head. *"Give me back my ship!"*

Slowly, the Data-thing rose from his position. Picard did not back away. He would not face death cowering. This monster from the past would have no power over him.

"I will kill you now," the Data-thing said.

"At least I'll die knowing that you've been stopped," Picard shot back. "Swallowed forever by this black hole. Exactly where you belong."

The *Enterprise* shuddered again as the Data-thing raised his fist.

"Stop!" Beverly Crusher stepped in front of Picard, medical tricorder in hand. Her son was beside her, carrying a first-aid kit. "Can't you see the captain is delirious?" the doctor said to the Data-thing.

The Data-thing paused, distracted by the interruption. "All the more reason for him to die. He is nonoptimal."

"But you'll need him when we get out," Dr. Crusher insisted. She responded to the android's expression of confusion. "I heard Worf and La Forge talking. The ship has enough power to get out of here. They were just trying to scare you."

The Data-thing's eyes flashed dangerously. He glared at La Forge and Worf on the upper level. "Is that so?"

The *Enterprise* lurched. Wesley almost lost his grip on the medical kit.

"Yes," Crusher said. She aimed the medical tricorder at Picard. "I mean look at this. His brain functions are all scrambled by pain. He's not responsible for—" She stopped suddenly, then turned the tricorder on the Data-thing. "Oh, my," she said. "Do you feel all right?"

The Data-thing drew back from her in disdain. "I am not organic."

"Some of you is," Dr. Crusher said, adjusting the tricorder controls. "Check your design specifications. You've got several biological components and I'm picking up a disturbing break-down in functions."

The Data-thing slid his eyes to the side again.

"Here, look at this," Dr. Crusher said. "Goodness, you're facing a major system shutdown."

The Data-thing seemed to struggle to bring his eyes to bear on

397

the tricorder. "No! I am optimal! I am beyond the flesh!" He snatched the instrument from Dr. Crusher's hand, twisted it around, rightside up, and—

—crashed to the deck, immobile.

Wesley Crusher stood behind the space the Data-thing had just occupied, a single finger extended. Where it had activated Data's Off switch.

The *Enterprise* lurched heavily, throwing those standing to the side.

Picard lost his breath with the sharp stab of pain from his wrist. Recovering with difficulty, he ordered McKnight back to the conn. "Status report!" he called out over the whine of the engines and the creaking of the deck.

"SIF at seventy percent!" La Forge answered. "Switching power back from impulse engines."

"Sir!" Worf added, "we are still in a direct trajectory toward the singularity."

Crusher slapped a hypospray to Picard's wrist, startling him. But moments after it hissed, he felt blessed relief, though his hand hung limp and useless.

"Can you identify those vessels?" Picard asked as he moved back to his command chair. Troi was helping Riker down the ramp to join the captain. Wesley dragged Data's inert form to the side of the bridge. Worf remained leaning against his tactical console, La Forge near him at engineering.

The *Enterprise* bucked as if she had hit something solid. Collision alert alarms sounded.

"SIF feedback!" La Forge shouted as the *Enterprise* seemed to careen into a spiral, vibrating coarsely.

"We passed through some sort of molecular dust cloud," O'Brien yelled out. "Reads like vessel debris."

"Another vessel?" Picard exclaimed. "Why all this interest in *this* black hole?"

Then Riker was beside him, broken leg held tight in a splint, and Troi sat to the captain's left. Picard's bridge was fully staffed. With engineering, this crew was the *Enterprise*'s last hope.

"Routing power," La Forge called out as the *Enterprise* continued to angle, inertial dampers straining to hold the interior together, hull metal screaming all around them as the structural integrity field fought the staggering tidal forces straining to tear the ship apart.

"Sir," Worf boomed, "sensors have identified the larger ship below us. It is a Constitution-class vessel!"

"Constitution-class?" Picard repeated. "They've been out of service for at least fifty years."

"Captain Bondar said the scientific package was launched a century ago," Riker said. "Maybe the starship's part of an earlier recovery attempt."

"Is it possible we're being exposed to temporal distortions as well as spatial ones?" Picard asked. He raised his voice. "Worf, plot a four-dimensional point-of-origin solution to the starship's entry point."

Computer graphics flickered over the viewscreen. Then the line tracing back from the Constitution-class vessel began to flash.

"Sir," Worf replied in loud and obvious consternation. "Trajectory calculations indicate the vessel penetrated the upper event horizon from a point approximately eighty to one hundred years in the past."

"Mr. Worf," Picard said, as the shaking of the ship seemed to quiet. "Can you identify that vessel?"

"Scanning for identification codes . . ." the Klingon said. "Scanning . . ." Then it seemed as if the universe itself became still as Worf spoke again, his voice filled with disbelief and awe. "Captain Picard, the other ship is the *Enterprise* 1701. And sir . . . her captain, James T. Kirk, is hailing us. . . ."

TWO

TNC 65813
$t = \infty$

At the precise instant that he felt sure all was lost, Zefram Cochrane saw the Klingon battle cruiser ripple in a flash of golden light, then dissolve into a sparkling band of luminescence. As quickly as the threat had come, it had vanished. For a moment, the shimmering remains of the cruiser reminded Cochrane of the stars he had watched from beneath the dome at Christopher's Landing, as if they were the common thread woven through his life.

"Zefram, what happened?" the Companion asked.

"James T. Kirk," Cochrane said, not even considering any other possibility.

There were giants in these days.

He felt fortunate to have lived to have seen them.

Uhura's clear voice rang out over the confusion of the bridge. "Sir, I am picking up a Starfleet standard identification code from the vessel."

Kirk and Spock locked eyes. A Starfleet vessel. From the future. There was only one thing they could do.

"Uhura, cut communications!" Kirk ordered.

At the same time, Spock downgraded the resolution of the main screen. Where the image of a familiar, saucer-and-twin-nacelle–style starship had been taking shape in greater detail the closer it approached, only a handful of blocky pixels remained to indicate the future ship's position.

Reluctantly, Uhura shut down the automatic hailing sequence. She turned to the captain. "But what if they're our only way home?" she asked.

Kirk held up his hand to tell Uhura he would answer her in a moment. "Spock, how much longer to impact with the subspace event horizon?" he asked.

"In subjective time, perhaps an hour. However, we will only be able to maintain our structural field integrity for another twenty-six minutes."

The turbolift doors opened and McCoy came onto the bridge.

"Then we still have a few minutes to decide what to do," Kirk said to Uhura. "But if that ship *is* our only way home, it will be to our home in the next century."

"The next century?" McCoy said. He looked at the screen. "Damn. We're past the event horizon, too, aren't we?"

"And we've just made contact with a Starfleet vessel from at least a century into the future."

McCoy raised an eyebrow. "Really? Did you communicate with it?"

Kirk shook his head. He knew Starfleet's standing orders. Time travel to the past was possible. The *Enterprise* had done it herself. Now all Starfleet vessels had been given procedures to follow in the event they encountered a ship from the future and those procedures forbade communication. The reason was that the Prime Directive worked both ways. Just as Starfleet did not want to interfere in the normal development of other cultures, neither did it want anyone else to interfere in the normal development of the Federation. If information from the future were to be inadvertently transmitted to the past, new timelines might develop, ones that diverged from the Federation's natural evolution. Even a detailed sensor image of a ship from the future might transfer advanced design knowledge to the past, so Starfleet had decreed that all viewscreens must be set to low-resolution modes in the event of visual contact.

JUDITH AND GARFIELD REEVES-STEVENS

But there was one exception to the no-contact rule: If a present-day vessel faced certain destruction, contact was permissible provided the present-day crew abandoned their own era and went forward through time with their rescuers. Only in this way could all knowledge of the future be kept from those still in the past.

Kirk knew that the logic of the situation meant that it was the ship from the future which must make first contact. The future-day crew were assumed to be in a position to know the historical circumstances they were involved with. If their history showed that a ship had been lost in the past, then the ship from the future was authorized to make a rescue attempt.

Kirk also knew that whatever was going to happen to his ship in the next twenty-six minutes was already ancient history to the vessel above him. According to regulations, he had to trust to them to act accordingly. And he would.

For a few more minutes at least.

But then, regulations be damned.

"Captain," Worf said, "the 'Enterprise' has stopped hailing us."

"Was it a live hail, or a recording?" Picard asked. He clung to his chair as his Enterprise continued to shake all around him. But the movements were becoming less severe.

After a moment's delay to compare the sound signatures, Worf reported that they had received an automatic recording.

"Respond anyway, Mr. Worf."

"Our send capabilities are locked out, sir. Colonel Thorsen only keyed open our channel to the Garneau."

"Damn," Picard said. "Can our sensors show if there is any crew on board?" Picard asked.

"There is too much interference at this distance to be sure, sir."

Troi asked, "What makes you think there wouldn't be a crew?"

Picard sighed. "This trajectory is carrying that Enterprise to certain destruction," he explained. "And history shows that that ship was destroyed under Captain Kirk's command. But for the life of me, I can't remember when. Do you, Number One?"

Riker shook his head. "It's been a long time since I read Admiral Chekov's books," he said.

402

La Forge announced that the SIF had been restored to full power. The whine of the ship's impulse engines dropped back to a steady thrum and Picard's *Enterprise* regained her stability.

Picard leaned forward. "Wesley, have *you* read the accounts of Kirk's missions?"

"Yes, sir," the young man replied promptly. "I know that the original *Enterprise* was destroyed by Captain Kirk himself, in . . . twenty-two . . . eighty-five. I think. But it was on a classified mission so I don't know where it happened."

"Seventy-nine, eighty years ago," Picard said, growing more annoyed with himself. "Just within the margin of error Worf calculated." He tapped his temple. "This is maddening. Have we come to depend on the computer and Mr. Data for all our historical needs?"

Troi looked even more perplexed. "I don't understand your problem, Captain."

Picard pointed at the screen with his uninjured hand. "That is James T. Kirk's *Enterprise* and it will be destroyed within minutes. It may be within our capability to save it. Yet, we might be observing it in the mission in which it *was* destroyed, so if we *do* change its fate, then we are changing our past." Picard shifted in his seat again. "Mr. La Forge, ask your engineering crew if any of them recall the exact circumstances surrounding the destruction of Kirk's *Enterprise*. And see if there is any way to get even some of the ship's library computers on-line."

La Forge began polling the crew members in engineering, still locked behind the isolation doors that were immovable without the lockout codes devised by the personality that had taken over Data.

Picard instructed Ensign McKnight to bring their *Enterprise* closer to Kirk's, to see if their sensors could pick up *any* sign of life on board.

"Why are life signs so important?" Troi asked.

"Because there was no loss of life when Kirk's *Enterprise* was destroyed. If we find there *are* crew members on board, then the ship is not meant to be destroyed here, and we are free to attempt to rescue it."

"Captain Picard," O'Brien said, "the faster we go along this course, the more difficult it will be to return. The quantum compression waves are beginning to pile up like waves breaking against a shore. And they're starting to limit the amount of space we have to maneuver in."

"What is our point of no return?" Picard asked.

"We'll hit it in twenty minutes, sir."

"Can't we go faster?"

"Not if we want to match trajectories. If we gain too much velocity compared to the other *Enterprise,* we'll slip out of their relativistic time frame and never get near them."

La Forge reported that no one in engineering had any information to share, beyond confirming Wesley's recollection of the year of the original *Enterprise*'s destruction on a classified mission.

"I can sense nothing in these distorted conditions, but perhaps they'll hail us," Troi suggested.

"Not if they're following Starfleet standing orders," Picard said. "Regulations are quite clear that in these situations involving Starfleet vessels, it is the ship from the future which must make the first contact, in accordance with recorded history. And here we are, without any access to recorded history." He tugged at his tunic, grimacing as he inadvertently moved his broken wrist.

"There's always another possibility," Riker suggested.

Picard looked at him expectantly.

"We all know what regulations say. But if I remember my history correctly, Captain Kirk wasn't all that much for regulations. If he's on that ship, and he knows we're here, he'll contact us. All we have to do is wait. Regulations be damned."

THREE

TNC 65813
$$t = \infty$$

"Computer," Cochrane asked. "How long until we make contact with the singularity?"

"Unable to calculate," the computer replied.

"Why?" Cochrane asked.

"Standard navigational functions do not permit the use of infinite values in calculating estimated times of arrival."

The Companion looked at Cochrane with concern. "What does it mean by 'infinite values'?"

Cochrane knew. Time would become so relativistically dilated for them that the moment of impact with the heart of the black hole would stretch out to infinity. The rate of the passage of time would come to equal zero.

"It means we'll be together forever," he told her.

"Do you promise me that?" she asked.

"With all my heart."

"I don't understand it, Keptin. The other vessel is accelerating along our course. If they're coming from the future, I would think they'd know as much about conditions down here as we do."

Kirk looked at Spock. "Could it be damaged? A runaway? Do you think there's anyone aboard her?"

405

"Under present conditions, our sensors are not up to the task."

Kirk looked at Uhura. "Anything?"

Uhura sighed. "Captain, they could be hailing us on all frequencies right now and I wouldn't hear it through the interference."

McCoy stepped in front of Kirk. "Contact *them,* Jim. At least you'll know you tried."

Kirk nodded. He had waited long enough. "Open hailing frequencies, Uhura."

The communications officer shook her head. "I doubt they're going to have much better luck hearing us." But she tried.

"Fascinating," Spock said, apparently in response to nothing.

Kirk and McCoy stared at him intently.

"What's so fascinating?" McCoy asked peevishly. "The fact that in twenty minutes we're going to be relativistic dust?"

Spock ignored the doctor and spoke to Kirk. "I have detected a pattern to the compression waves rebounding between us and the linked singularities."

"It took you long enough," McCoy said.

Spock gave him a withering glance. "Doctor, the pattern was not established until the other vessel matched our course. Under the circumstances, I believe I have—"

"Spock, the pattern?" Kirk said to get his science officer back on the subject. "What's the significance?"

Spock shrugged as if he were discussing the color of the bridge carpet. "It should be possible to time a maneuver such that we would cause our leading compression wave to combine with the compression wave of the vessel from the future, in effect stealing spatial distortion from it the way we would steal kinetic energy if we attempted the maneuver in normal space-time."

McCoy looked pained. "What the *hell* does that mean, Spock?"

"He means slingshot around it, Bones," Kirk said.

"Essentially, though in higher dimensions. A better metaphor for Dr. McCoy, perhaps, would be surfing. Allowing the compression wave to do the work of moving us."

"Whatever, does it mean we could get out of here?" McCoy asked.

"It does, and within the limits of our power consumption," Spock answered.

McCoy was smiling but Kirk had one more concern. "What about Cochrane and the Companion?"

"If we time the maneuver correctly, we should pass by them closely enough to be able to snare their shuttlecraft with our tractor beam, then hold them within our deflector shields, taking them with us."

Kirk was pleased. It almost seemed simple. Like the best of ideas. "Let's do it. Feed the coordinates to Sulu."

"However, there is one other factor we must consider," Spock added.

"Why did I know he was going to say that," McCoy moaned.

"In stealing spatial distortion from the other vessel, we will be accelerating them downward into the subspace event horizon beyond the ability of any technology to save them."

"So it's them or us," Kirk said. "And they already know the way this turns out."

"If there *is* anyone aboard her."

Kirk rubbed at his back. The knife wound throbbed, making it difficult to concentrate on the problem facing him. If he did destroy a ship from the Federation's future, at the very least he would not be changing his own timeline. But what about the future's timeline? How many people might be on a ship that size? There were too many variables to handle at once. Even for him.

"When can we make the maneuver?" he asked.

"Anytime. And the sooner we perform it, the greater our margin of safety."

Kirk looked at the screen, and the block of pixels that represented his only hope of survival. "Is there no other way, Spock? Anything at all?"

"If we were able to communicate with the other vessel," Spock allowed, "there would be another option."

"And . . . ?" McCoy urged with exasperation.

"In seven minutes we will be coming up to a triple-compression-wave overlap pattern. If both ships were to maneuver together, precisely at the moment the triple wave is exactly between us, we could both slingshot around each other. The result would be that both ships would steal spatial distortion from the linked singularities, enabling us to exit upward through the electromagnetic event horizon together."

"If we could communicate," Kirk said. "Which we can't."

"What happens if the joint maneuver isn't done precisely?" McCoy asked.

"The slightest miscalculation on the part of either ship," Spock said, "will accelerate both our descents with no hope of escape."

"The Prisoners' Dilemma," Kirk said.

"Precisely," Spock agreed.

Kirk saw McCoy's look of incomprehension. "It's an old problem in strategy, Bones. In this case, the first prisoner to act selfishly goes free while the other remains in prison. But if we both cooperate, we both go free. The trick is, we can't communicate with each other. So neither prisoner knows what the other is thinking."

McCoy held out his hands to Spock. "This is no time for story problems. What does your damned logic say to do?"

"In the Prisoners' Dilemma, the solution is quite clear," Spock said matter-of-factly. "Logic dictates that the first player to act selfishly will always fare better."

"I've always hated your logic," McCoy said. "Now I know why." He looked at the captain. "Jim, if you do act first, you could be condemning a ship full of our descendants to an infinite death."

"I know that, Bones. I also know that if it turns out there *is* no one aboard that ship and I wait, then I'm condemning my ship and all of us to the same fate."

McCoy displayed all the agitation that Kirk felt. "Is there no way to find out if there's someone on that blasted ship?"

"No, Doctor," Spock said with finality. "We have all the facts we shall ever have. All that remains is for the captain to make his decision."

Kirk looked away from the eyes of his crew to stare at the screen. The lives of everyone aboard the *Enterprise* rested in his hands, balanced against the lives of people he might never know, never see, but also, who might not exist at all.

The guarantee of survival at the cost of strangers' deaths?

Or the chance of cooperation, which might lead to joint survival or meaningless death for all?

It was the ultimate command decision.

The one he had been born to make.

And in that moment before he gave his order, he felt free.

"The Prisoners' Dilemma," Picard said as he studied the three trajectories Ensign McKnight had brought up on the main screen. "The first one to act gets away at the cost of the other's freedom. If they cooperate, they both escape."

"But there's no way to know if there's anyone on that ship to cooperate with," Riker said.

"And even if we did know if there were someone on board," Troi added, "we wouldn't be able to communicate with them to plan the maneuver."

"That wouldn't be necessary," La Forge said. "The physics of the maneuver remain the same from any viewpoint. If anyone on the other *Enterprise* sees the opportunity and does the calculation, that is."

Picard stared at the screen. They had drawn close enough that even with the intense interference brought on by spatial compression, the sensor return image had more detail. There was an old-style shuttlecraft leading the original *Enterprise* toward the heart of the black hole. Picard had already concluded that the shuttlecraft was the scientific package the *Garneau* had expected to recover. Someone was on it. Someone vital to the security of the Federation. Was that why Kirk's *Enterprise* was chasing it? But then, what had happened eighty to a hundred years ago? Obviously Kirk's *Enterprise* hadn't succeeded in saving the shuttlecraft, otherwise the *Garneau* wouldn't have been dispatched in Picard's time. But then, what had happened to Kirk's *Enterprise*? Was this how Kirk had destroyed it on its final mission? What would happen if Picard interfered in the outcome? There were too many variables. Even for him.

"Captain Picard," Worf said suddenly.

Picard turned to face the Klingon.

"The original *Enterprise* exploded, sir."

Everyone was looking at Worf now. "Are you certain?"

"Yes sir. I just remembered. Something my father taught me. In Admiral Chekov's book, in the other histories of Kirk, everyone makes the point that Captain Kirk destroyed the *Enterprise* without causing any loss of life."

"That's what I remember," Picard said impatiently, wondering what point his officer was trying to make.

"But that was not true," Worf continued. "What the books meant was that none of Kirk's crew died. But there was loss of life. A Klingon boarding party."

Picard understood. "At the time the incident took place, at the time those books were written, the Federation and the Klingon Empire were deadly enemies."

"I know, sir. That's what my father taught me. That once we were such great enemies that the Federation did not consider the deaths of Klingons to be the same as the deaths of humans."

"We have changed a great deal since then, Worf."

Worf nodded carefully, trying not to dislodge the healing emitters Dr. Crusher had attached to his head wound. "I know, but I remember more about the story, from the Klingon side. The Klingon boarding party died in an explosion. Therefore, because that *Enterprise* we see on the screen is still intact, it is *not* on its final mission."

Picard eagerly seized on the scrap of information. "Splendid, Worf. That's it!" He turned back to the screen. "Captain Kirk is on that ship! He must be saved. He obviously *was* saved for us to have read about his latter exploits."

"But are we the ones to save him?" Riker asked from his chair.

"If not us, then who?" Picard asked.

"The only way *we* know how to save him is to perform a risky joint maneuver that must be executed with precise timing. How do we know Kirk even knows about that maneuver?"

Wesley turned with an excited smile. "Sir, if Captain Kirk is on that *Enterprise,* then Commander Spock is with him. He'll have figured out the maneuver. He was incredible."

"Even given that," Riker said skeptically. "How can we be sure

Kirk will elect to perform the joint maneuver? Maybe he's going to choose the selfish maneuver any second, as soon as Spock works out the math. Maybe Kirk survived in the past because he consigned us to the linked singularities."

"As Mr. La Forge has said, Number One, the physics are the same. The law of mediocrity still holds. Kirk will understand what must be done for us both to escape."

"As I remember history, Kirk was not noted for being a team player, sir."

Picard paused in thought. Riker was correct. Kirk was entirely capable of doing the unexpected to survive, no matter what the cost.

"Captain," Ensign McKnight said, "we're coming up on our point of no return. Either we break away within the next minute, or we will have to wait for the triple compression wave. And that joint maneuver will be our last and only chance to escape."

"Understood, Ensign," Picard said.

Picard looked away from the eyes of his crew to stare at the screen. The lives of everyone aboard the *Enterprise* rested in his hands, balanced against predicting the decision of a man who had been revered for his unpredictability, who had been perfectly capable of consigning a ship from the future to an endless fall in order to see his *Enterprise* survive.

Picard's options were clear. The guarantee of survival at the cost of consigning a hero to death, before that hero could do the same to him. Or waiting for the chance of cooperation, which might lead to joint success or, if Kirk acted first, to senseless defeat.

It was the ultimate command decision.

The one he had been trained to make.

And in that moment before he gave his order, he knew what duty compelled him to do.

FOUR

TNC 65813
$t = \infty$

"Zefram," the Companion said, "sing to me. As you did when we lay beneath the stars. Sing to me, so I will remember you forever."

Darkness loomed before the shuttlecraft once again and Cochrane knew it was the singularity that would claim them in an endless fall. Even the Companion knew that.

But their hands were entwined and would remain so for as long as stars still shone.

"Sing to me, Zefram."

He did.

> *"Amazing Grace, how sweet the sound*
> *That saved a wretch like me*
> *I once was lost, but now I'm found*
> *Was blind, yet now I see. . . ."*

She joined him and their voices rose together in the tiny bubble of light and warmth, poised on the brink of oblivion.

And together, there was nothing that they feared.

"Mr. Sulu, prepare to initiate the triple-wave maneuver on Mr. Spock's mark. Mr. Chekov, stand ready on those tractor

412

beams to bring Cochrane's shuttlecraft into our shields as we pass."

McCoy took Kirk's arm. "Are you sure, Jim? That's a big risk to take, counting on someone who probably hasn't been born yet."

Kirk had no doubt. "That's a Starfleet vessel out there, Bones. That means a hundred years from now, the Federation is still there, too." Kirk took his chair. He felt nothing but confidence. "That's what I'm counting on. Not a person. But tradition. An ideal."

Kirk settled back, decision made, course set, with no possibility of failure.

"Your reasoning is most illogical," Spock said.

"In this case, my reasoning doesn't have to be logical," Kirk said lightly. "It just has to be right." He looked behind him at his science officer and friend. "Your father might not agree with that, but I'll bet you could persuade him."

Spock inclined his head as he thought for a moment. "It would require a bluff," he said.

"Ensign McKnight, prepare to initiate the triple-wave maneuver on Mr. Worf's mark. Mr. O'Brien, stand ready with tractor beams to catch the shuttlecraft as we pass."

"Are you certain, Jean-Luc?" Riker asked. "You're taking a big risk gambling on someone with Kirk's reputation."

Picard had little doubt. "Whatever his reputation, Number One, James T. Kirk remained a part of Starfleet for almost fifty years. He wasn't the kind of man to make that kind of commitment without feeling something for the institutions he was sworn to defend." Picard took his chair. He was fairly certain he had made the right choice. "That's what I've based my decision on. Not the person. But tradition, and the ideals he served."

Picard settled back, decision made, course set, with little possibility of failure. "I believe it is a logical course of action," he said.

Riker looked at him closely. "Another echo from Ambassador Sarek?"

Picard was startled by the sudden feeling that Riker was

somehow correct. He had a flash of another bridge surrounding him—smaller, cruder.

"Will, I think you're right," Picard said. "I think that sometime in the past, Ambassador Sarek did touch the mind of Kirk."

"Any memory of how this turned out?" Riker asked.

Picard concentrated but found only fleeting impressions. "No," he said at last. "We're going to have to discover that for ourselves."

FIVE

☆

TNC 65813
$t = \infty$

The triple compression wave moved through the *Ian Shelton* first, unfelt and unnoticed by Cochrane and the Companion. Their shuttlecraft was too small, their absorption in each other too strong for anything in this universe to disturb them.

Their course was set. They flew on.

The triple compression wave moved through Kirk's *Enterprise* next, following close behind the shuttlecraft, though the nature of space in this environment defied ordinary units of distance and time. Spock measured the wave as it pulsed through his instruments, and he started the countdown.

On Picard's *Enterprise,* Worf undertook the same countdown, his forward tactical sensors pushed to their utmost limits to obtain even the weakest reading of the wave's progression.

When the wave reached the exact halfway point between the two ships, Worf and Spock both gave their signals at the same instant. On those signals, Sulu fired his impulse engines in full reverse, slowing Kirk's *Enterprise* just as McKnight fired her impulse engines for more forward velocity.

Picard's *Enterprise* crested the triple compression wave and rushed forward, balancing the countercompression caused by Kirk's *Enterprise.* Thus the triple wave rolled on between the two starships, restored, unchanged, and for all values of velocity and compression to remain equal in that environment, energy was stolen from the linked singularities. Just as Spock and La Forge had predicted.

Both ships used that energy to alter their courses in the tightly compressed space, to swing past the black hole's pulsing, triple-lobed subspace horizon and loop around it, accelerating up toward freedom and the electromagnetic horizon separating them from their destinations.

Kirk's *Enterprise* and Picard's *Enterprise*—they flew together, side by side, the *Ian Shelton* nestled between them, securely cradled by the tractor beams of both ships.

Space flowed around the two starships as they moved together, coming so close that their shields merged in a sparkling of shared energy on a common course.

Protected together, protecting each other, the *Enterprise*s escaped their fate, linked not by the captains who commanded them, but by the ideals that were common to both.

The event horizon loomed above them, and on Kirk's *Enterprise*, Spock determined that they were being drawn along the wrong worldline, to a time that was not their own. On Picard's *Enterprise*, La Forge calculated the same.

It was suddenly imperative that momentum be exchanged between the ships and the means to do it was obvious to both.

Communicating, indirectly, by common knowledge of the unchanging laws of physics, the universal law of mediocrity, Kirk's *Enterprise* gently released her hold on the *Ian Shelton*. Just as gently, Picard's *Enterprise* took up the task.

Minutes from the event horizon, the shuttlecraft and its momentum safely exchanged, the ships parted, Kirk to his time, Picard to his own. But just before their handshake across time was broken, before their relativistic frames of reference grew too separated in the mesh of temporal distortions, someone on the bridge of Picard's ship, someone whose straitlaced aura of correctness concealed just a touch of Kirk's rebellion, that someone happened to touch a control that sent out an automatic hail, in complete and utter defiance of Starfleet's strict standing orders governing the transmission of information from the future to the past.

On the bridge of Kirk's *Enterprise,* Uhura caught the hail, faint, almost nonexistent as the separation in time grew larger.

But she did hear enough of it.

She took her earpiece out. Wide-eyed, she turned to her captain. She told him what she had heard.

"Captain Kirk," she said. "They sent a hail." She smiled in awe. "The other ship . . . it was the *Enterprise,* sir."

Kirk nodded. And silently sent his thanks out through time itself to the someone who had broken regulations to send that small acknowledgment, that tiny confirmation that the future was secure.

And on Picard's *Enterprise,* Picard himself nonchalantly moved away from a communications control panel where he had just happened to find himself with his uninjured hand resting by the automatic hailing frequencies controls, unaffected by the coded lockouts. He returned to his chair. Troi smiled at him. She knew. She understood.

The years once again grew between Kirk and Picard but in the grand scale of things, there was little that separated them.

Each to their own time, both servants of the Federation, they reached the upper event horizon, and together yet apart they made their way back to their separate times and the destiny they served . . .

. . . the United Federation of Planets.

The stars burst like fireworks before Cochrane's eyes and he blinked in surprise and excitement.

"We're free!" the Companion exclaimed. "Oh, Zefram, we can go home!"

Cochrane could still not believe what had happened. He had seen two starships, the *Enterprise* and one twice its size, fly in formation to either side of the shuttlecraft. He had seen the *Enterprise* veer off and disappear in the murk of the environment beyond the event horizon. He guessed that some rescue had been organized. Perhaps the larger ship that kept the shuttlecraft safe was the *Excalibur* or the *Lexington,* both of which Kirk had said were on their way to help.

There was no sense of movement as the gas disk of the black hole fell away from beneath them. They were in warp space, heading away from the tidal forces of the singularity. It had all worked out.

Then, in the moment of his rejoicing, Cochrane saw a shimmering of green light through the forward windows, and as he watched in utter astonishment, a green starship materialized out of the vacuum, and flew at him, weapons firing.

The stars burst like fireworks before Kirk's eyes and he knew they were free from the event horizon.

An instant later, the bridge lights dimmed and damage alarms sounded.

"Och," Scotty said from engineering, "there go the crystals. And after what we've been through, we've only got a minute of power left."

"Shut down every system!" Kirk commanded. "Communications, environmental, everything! Put it all into propulsion, Mr. Sulu." Kirk knew they had to get as far away from the region of the black hole's crushing tidal forces as they could, before his ship's structural integrity field failed and the *Enterprise* was torn apart.

Spock was to Kirk's right. "I regret to point out that we do not have sufficient reserves to escape the Roche limit," he said flatly. "These efforts are useless."

McCoy was on Kirk's left. *"You* regret it?"

"Scotty will get us out of here," Kirk said. Scotty always did.

But Scotty said, "Not this time, Captain. With no matter-antimatter reactor, I've got nothing more t' draw from. I'm sorry, sir."

Kirk straightened in his chair. There were no more options. No more rules to change. The odds could only be beaten so many times before the law of averages made itself known. The journey was over. As simple as that.

"You warned me, Scotty," Kirk said, uncharacteristically

quiet, the fire gone from him in this moment, accepting that even he had limits. "We took this ship into a black hole and we brought her out again. Maybe this is the way we're supposed to go out."

"Being the first," Spock said.

"And the best," McCoy said.

Scott started the countdown from engineering. "Thirty seconds, Captain."

"I'm proud of you, Scotty. You kept her going when no one else could."

"Glad to have been aboard, sir," the chief engineer replied softly. "Twenty-five seconds. The lights will go first. The SIF will fail a moment later. Just so ye know."

Kirk touched the intercom control on the arm of his chair. He spoke to his crew, to his ship, telling them of his pride in all of them. He spoke to the passengers he had rescued from the *Planitia,* telling them of his sorrow. He ended the broadcast and in the privacy of the bridge said his farewells to Uhura, to Chekov, to Sulu.

He was surprised that in the end there were no real regrets.

"Ten seconds," Scott said.

"I never thought it would end this way," McCoy said.

Kirk forced a smile as he stared at the screen, wondering what he might see the instant before it happened, and the instant after. "I never thought it would end, period," he said.

"Five seconds," Scott announced. "I'll see you in Valhalla, gentlemen."

Beside him, Kirk heard Spock sigh. "At least it can be said that it was f—"

A blinding blue flash flared from the viewscreen. A second flash followed, and with that all systems failed—the lights, the displays, the engine roar. Only battery lights remained, offering dim illumination for the final second.

Which became the final two seconds.

The final five seconds.

"Why are we still here?" McCoy asked.

"She didn't go!" Chekov exclaimed.

JUDITH AND GARFIELD REEVES-STEVENS

"Obviously," Spock commented.

And instantly Kirk realized what had happened. The flight recorder he had launched! The twin flashes of blue light!

He turned in his chair. "Uhura! Full battery power to communications! And get that screen going!"

A moment later, Captain Harris of the *U.S.S. Excalibur* was grinning from that screen. "Welcome back, *Enterprise.*"

Kirk felt like laughing, felt like crying, both together. "Tom. Hello. Glad you could make it."

"I'll bet you are," Harris laughed.

Another voice came over the speakers. "Jim, you old spacedog. Am I reading my sensors right? You've got no power, no crystals, no nothing?"

The screen image changed. Commodore Robert Wesley appeared, front and center on the bridge of the *Lexington.*

"Hello, Bob," Kirk said to his old friend. "Thanks for the lift, and the tractor beams, and the shields."

Wesley shook his head in admiration. "Hold on tight, Jim. We'll be taking you to warp as soon as we calibrate with the *Excalibur.*" Wesley looked off to the side, grinned back at Kirk. "I tell you, Jim, from the damage statistics we're getting from your ship, you'd better hope Starfleet doesn't decide to deduct the damages from your salary. You could be flying these things for the next thousand years."

Kirk leaned back in his chair. "I'd settle for a hundred," he said. "That would be just about right."

Then, like a wounded warrior carried victoriously from the field, the *Enterprise* rested in the shields of her companions. Flanking her, supporting her, but adjusting their beams so she had the honor of leading the way, the *Excalibur* and the *Lexington* delivered the *Enterprise* from the gravity of TNC 65813, and returned her to the stars where she belonged.

The stars burst like fireworks before Picard's eyes.

They had succeeded.

"Congratulations," Riker said to Picard.

"To us all, Number One." Picard turned to his engineer. "Mr.

420

La Forge, can we handle warp speed long enough to get us away from here?"

"We should be able to manage a few light-hours, Captain."

"Mr. O'Brien," Picard continued. "What is the status of the shuttlecraft?"

"Two strong life signs," O'Brien answered. "One human, one . . ." He shrugged. "Not human, I guess."

"Two? The captain of the *Garneau* was aware of only one passenger," Picard said. "Will the tractor beam hold them till we get away from here?"

"Yes, sir. For an hour or so at least."

"Very good," Picard said. Already the next course of events was becoming clear to him. A brief warp flight to empty space. Then, a complete shutdown of the *Enterprise*'s computer system so they could bring it back on-line without the lockout codes the Thorsen personality had somehow programmed into it. To begin, work crews could get around the sealed doors and security screens by using the personnel transporters in the several shuttlecraft the ship carried. Those transporters could also be used to bring aboard their mysterious passengers from the past. "A day or two and we should be able to get underway for Betazed," Picard said. There was no sense in delivering a counterfeit Borg artifact to Admiral Hanson. "In time for the trade conference. And then we can see what we can do about restoring Mr. Data."

Riker carefully touched the splint on his leg. "And the rest of us," he said.

"Ensign McKnight, plot a general heading toward Betazed, warp factor three."

"Course plotted, sir."

"Engage."

With only a slight hesitation, the *Enterprise* came to life around them. The gas disk of the Kabreigny Object began to shrink in the viewscreen.

"I wonder if that black hole was named after Admiral Quarlo Kabreigny?" Picard asked. "I have always found her essays about the dual nature of Starfleet most compelling."

"We'll know as soon as we get our computer back," Riker said.

A collision alarm sounded.

"Warbird decloaking!" Worf called out.

There could be only one explanation. "Tarl!" Riker said.

The viewscreen flickered as a phaser burst hit the ship.

"Shields at forty percent!" Worf announced.

"Captain," La Forge said, "without a crew, we're not going to be able to maintain even that strength for long."

"Maybe we should have brought Kirk into our time," Picard said. "Mr. Worf, ready on phasers! Ready on photon torpedoes!"

"The Warbird is coming around," Worf said. "Our phasers are at fifty percent."

"Prepare for evasive maneuvers," Picard warned his crew.

The Romulan Warbird filled the screen. The *Enterprise* shook from the fury of its attack.

"I'm all out of tricks," Picard said. "The only thing we can do is—"

The Warbird's port side flared with a phaser hit. The ship twisted with the sudden vaporization of its hull plates. Two streaks that could only be photon torpedoes swept in through the shield opening and slipped between the double hulls. Then golden light flared within those hulls and the Warbird split in half, top and bottom, with her bridge tumbling forward until it, too, disintegrated in a fireball.

"Good shooting, Mr. Worf," the captain said, impressed.

"I did not fire," Worf answered, perplexed.

Picard and Riker looked at each other with startled glances, a single name on their lips. *Had* he come back with them? Could it be—

"Sir, we are being hailed by Captain Bondar of the *Garneau*," Worf announced.

Picard sighed. It had been too much to hope for that he would ever have a chance to meet Kirk in the flesh. "Onscreen, Mr. Worf."

The captain of the *Garneau* was far different from her first appearance on the screen. She was forbidding, implacable. "Who's in charge of your vessel now?" she said bluntly.

"Jean-Luc Picard," the captain answered. "We have regained control."

"Good," Bondar said. "Otherwise, after what you did to my ship, you would have been next. Any idea what that Romulan wanted?"

"It's a long story," Picard replied.

"What about that shuttlecraft you're carrying in your tractor beam?" she asked. "Did you bring that out from the event horizon?"

"Yes, we did," Picard confirmed. "I believe it is the science package you were supposed to retrieve."

Bondar frowned. "I hope not. It looks like the Romulan shot it up pretty bad."

The next few minutes were confusion compounded by frustration. With the entire *Enterprise* at his disposal, Picard was unable to have the ship do anything.

The *Garneau* beamed aboard the two passengers from the damaged shuttlecraft. The *Garneau* beamed Dr. Crusher to its own sickbay to examine the passengers. The *Garneau* then beamed La Forge to the *Enterprise*'s engineering section and a team of computer technicians from the areas in which they were trapped to the *Enterprise*'s computer cores.

Dr. Crusher reported back to Picard twenty minutes after boarding the *Garneau*. Both passengers were seriously injured.

"Severe radiation burns," Dr. Crusher said from the main viewscreen. "The male will require major organ replacement. And the female, well, she seems human but I'm getting strange double readings. To the naked eye, she's in just as bad shape as the male, but on my tricorder, she doesn't seem as badly off for some reason."

"Will they survive until we can take them to a starbase?" Picard asked.

"That's just it, Jean-Luc. The female says they can't go to a starbase. She has to go home, or she'll die. She says home is where Captain Kirk was taking them."

"Where is her home?"

"A planetoid in the Gamma Canaris region. Designation five two seven."

Picard nodded. "We're very near. Will there be medical treatment available for her there?"

"That's the impression I get," Dr. Crusher said. "I've got her sedated. She was quite upset when she was beamed aboard."

"Do you know who she is?" Picard asked.

"She gave the name Nancy Hedford. The computer over here lists a few humans with that name from her time period and we're running a picture match. But Jean-Luc, I don't think she's the passenger Starfleet was so concerned about."

Picard was intrigued. "Do you know who the male is?" he asked.

Dr. Crusher looked out from the screen as if apologizing in advance for what she had to say next. "She says the man's name is Zefram Cochrane."

Picard felt a chill lift the fine hairs on his neck. *The* Zefram Cochrane?"

"His features are very close to the portrait in one of the engine manuals they have over here. Much younger, but he would have been well over two hundred years old in Kirk's time period, so there might be something at work here we don't know about."

"That, Dr. Crusher, is an understatement if I have ever heard one." Picard shifted in his chair. His broken wrist was beginning to regain feeling. But there would be time enough to deal with that later.

"Ensign McKnight," Picard said, "lay in a course for the Gamma Canaris region, planetoid designation five two seven. Mr. Worf, get me Captain Bondar."

"We're not taking them to a starbase for medical treatment?" Riker asked.

Picard shook his head. "Captain Kirk was taking them home, Number One. After what he did for us, the least we can do is complete his mission."

SIX

U.S.S. ENTERPRISE NCC-1701-D
APPROACHING THE GAMMA CANARIS REGION
Stardate 43923.8
Earth Standard: ≈ May 2366

Cochrane remembered the light and the pain of the Romulan's attack and he thought he was on the *Bonaventure II* again, life ebbing, the light enveloping him, bringing him peace, bringing him—

He awoke.

On the *Enterprise* again.

But not the *Enterprise*.

Kirk's ship he had felt he could *almost* understand. He had glanced at some of the technical manuals Kirk had left with him on the Companion's planetoid. He had seen the ship's design on the plaque, seen it in space from the shuttlecraft. The lines made sense. There was a logic to its construction that clearly derived from his work.

But this *Enterprise* . . . it made him think of Clarke's law, that any sufficiently advanced technology is indistinguishable from magic.

That's what this *Enterprise* was.

Magic, pure and simple.

The first night, he had sat up late in his bed in sickbay, scanning the manuals La Forge had flagged for him. More than a thousand

425

crew. Matter replicators. A top speed beyond what his most optimistic projections had ever predicted would ever be possible.

And there was still no end in sight.

The first night on this ship, this miracle, he had held on to the Companion's hand as she sat beside him by his bed. He had drifted in and out of sleep, in and out of fragments of his life. He was increasingly sure that there was a path there, one he could see, and the feeling only added to a sense of completeness he felt building within him. But he knew now the path itself had begun before he had been born and he could see it would continue after his death. His own life had only intersected for a moment with that larger path, already filled with so many others' journeys.

Three hundred and thirty-six years he had seen. Three hundred and thirty-six! He wondered what his friend Micah Brack would have said to that. If he would have been jealous.

What wonders he had seen. What wonders he knew were still ahead.

The second morning he awoke smiling, thinking of those wonders, cradling the Companion in his arms.

She had slipped into her coma shortly after. The ship's doctor had been concerned, but Cochrane had convinced her not to worry. When they returned to the planetoid, all would be well. The Companion drew her life from that place. She would do so again.

Picard came for him that morning as the Companion slept in Cochrane's arms.

They had been moved from sickbay and given an ordinary stateroom. One of unthinkable luxury to someone used to the twenty-first century.

To Cochrane, Picard seemed a serious man. Almost too controlled, as if he had a touch of Vulcan blood inside him.

"We have arrived," the captain said.

Cochrane nodded his thanks. It was difficult to talk. The doctor said that he had been badly irradiated. That he would need drastic medical treatment. But Cochrane had not been worried. Once the Companion was well, there would be time enough for him.

"And I have some rather bad news," the captain continued.

Cochrane tightened his embrace of the Companion. She didn't stir, though he could hear her, feel her breathe.

"The planetoid is no longer there," the captain said. "Instead, at its coordinates, we're reading rubble, almost a century old. With a high degree of some unusual energy matrix our scientists have been unable to identify."

Something in Cochrane slowed and was still. Three hundred and thirty-six years. He was not surprised it was coming to an end.

"From what you have told us about the Companion, in her first form, we're wondering if it is possible she had some symbiotic relationship with her home. You said she could maintain the temperature, and air, and gravity as long as she was there, but when the Orion pirates injured her, her control failed. That could be a sign that she was bound to that place and that place was bound to her."

Cochrane nodded. Life and habitat were always intertwined. Anything was possible. His existence was proof of that.

"We can take you to a starbase where there are medical facilities more advanced than what we can offer."

Cochrane smiled sadly. He had seen this ship's sickbay. Medical facilities more advanced than these belonged only to the gods.

Perhaps that was where the larger path led. Eventually.

Cochrane swallowed, preparing his throat for the effort of speaking. Picard waited attentively, respectfully. In his mind's eye, Cochrane saw Kirk stand beside him. That man would have been raging, consumed with frustration at not being able to save his passengers. He wondered at the difference between them. Two so unlike, yet so much the same. One so full of timeless youth and confidence, forever searching, full of passion. One so seasoned by his years and measured doubt, forever considering, full of timeless wisdom.

Youth and maturity. Not just the men but the culture they inhabited. A common culture. The Federation. But at different stages. Following its own larger path.

And it was time for Cochrane's interception of that path to end. He knew that now.

"Could you move the ship?" he asked in a whisper. "So we can see the stars as we would see them from the planetoid."

No rage. No bluster. Acceptance. "Of course," Picard said gently. "I will make it so."

Cochrane thanked him silently. He was weary. The Companion lay warm and at peace in his arms. But just once more, he wanted to see the stars.

Who knew? Perhaps they would sing to him one final time.

SEVEN

In the conference room, at the end of two hours, Admiral Kabreigny offered Kirk a cup of coffee. Kirk took it as a good sign. Maybe some progress had been made during this meeting after all. The nerve pinch had not been mentioned at all.

Spock declined her offer. McCoy accepted, but he looked as if he'd rather be having a mint julep.

"And so," Kabreigny said, staring intently at Kirk, "I will be able to report unequivocally to Starfleet that no information about the future was transferred to our present?"

"None," Kirk said firmly. His bridge crew had been sworn to secrecy. The name of the ship that they had encountered in the black hole would never be revealed. In that way, Kirk could be truthful in saying no information had been passed from one age to another. After all, he would never lie to Command.

Kabreigny appeared to accept his assurance and sipped her coffee.

"I am curious, Admiral," Mr. Spock said. "What *will* you report?"

Kabreigny shrugged. "I will have to seek out advice on that matter. Obviously, since a ship from the future penetrated the

429

event horizon in a trajectory that brought it to you and the shuttlecraft, someone in that time knew that the shuttlecraft would be there. I don't want it publicly known that Zefram Cochrane is on board, so we'll keep your secret of your meeting with him as you originally intended. The last thing we'd need is for one of Thorsen's collaborators to drop a few antimatter bombs through the event horizon to try and destroy him. Before he gets rescued the way you observed he already has been rescued—*will* be rescued.

"Perhaps we could say that Starfleet dropped a science package into the event horizon," she continued. "We could then ask that it be recovered on whatever date the shuttlecraft's original trajectory would have brought it closest to the event horizon."

Spock looked skeptical. "You are treading close to a causal loop, Admiral."

Kabreigny actually smiled at Spock. Kirk thought it was the first time he had seen a real smile on her face. "Which is why I will seek out advice, Mr. Spock. Starfleet is very cautious when it comes to time travel. And this is a good example why."

Kirk saw his opening and decided to take it while the mood was auspicious. "How does Starfleet feel about conspiracies?" he asked.

The smile left the admiral's face. "It would appear that I need to seek out some advice about that as well."

"At least there *was* a conspiracy," McCoy said, trying to be helpful. "It wasn't just some paranoid delusion." His smile faded, too, as he realized no one was sharing it with him.

"The conspiracy didn't originate *within* Starfleet, Doctor. For which we can all be grateful. But Colonel Thorsen was able to exploit an unsuspected weakness in our security and it could take years to build in the proper safeguards."

"In the meantime," Spock said, "Adrik Thorsen might still be at large."

That possibility did bother Kirk. When the *Lexington* and *Excalibur* had escorted the *Enterprise* from TNC 65813, there had been no sign of the second Klingon battle cruiser, and no way to know which of the two cruisers Thorsen had been on. He might have died in the cruiser the *Enterprise* had destroyed in the black hole. Or he might still be free. Free to pursue Zefram Cochrane.

"I don't think we'll have Thorsen to worry about much longer," Kabreigny said. "The Grigari nanomachines will take care of him, cell by cell."

"Still," Kirk said, " 'the evil that men do . . .' "

Kabreigny shook her head. "There's no room for evil in the galaxy anymore, Captain."

"Science isn't enough to guarantee that," Kirk said.

Kabreigny put down her cup. "Captain Kirk, after all we've been through, is it going to end like this? With us still on opposite sides of the old debate?"

"It doesn't have to," Kirk said. "If your secret committee had shared with the rest of Command your concerns about a possible military plot in Starfleet, revolving around Cochrane and the Klingons and a warp bomb, we might have been able to stop this before it escalated as far as it did."

"Knowing what we knew at the time, how could Starfleet's science divisions trust the military branch?" Kabreigny asked.

Kirk folded his hands on the conference table. "Knowing what you know now, about how that lack of communication led to such a profound division between us, how can you not trust them?" Across the table, Kirk and Kabreigny faced one another. Neither ready to give way.

"You must not remain on opposite sides of the debate," Spock said to the two of them.

"You can't afford to," McCoy added, damned if he was going to allow Spock to be the peacemaker.

"Admiral, we're both part of Starfleet," Kirk began after a long moment. "Perhaps the question is not whether or not we have to label ourselves as a military organization or a science organization. Perhaps we should just say we're Starfleet and leave it at that. Something new. A label all its own. Let the conflict go. With Thorsen and the Optimum. Where it belongs. In the past."

Kabreigny stood. Regal. "Somehow, I don't think we're going to solve this problem today, but, Jim, my thanks for trying." She paused, then held out her hand dramatically. Kirk stood to shake it with equal flourish.

"I wonder what kind of galaxy Zefram Cochrane's going to find a century from now?" Kabreigny asked.

"A better one," Kirk said. "I guarantee it."

Kabreigny looked at him as if she were going to ask another question, perhaps to check again that no information had come back from the future. But she seemed to think better of it.

"Your guarantee," she said. "That's good to know."

She gathered her data wafers together and slipped them into her attaché case. "The *Lexington* is going to take me back to TNC 65813 before you get to Neural III," the admiral said. "I have a feeling I'm going to be studying that particular black hole very carefully in the next while, trying to figure out where—and when—Cochrane's going to come back."

McCoy grinned. "Well, who knows? Maybe they'll name the black hole after you, Admiral."

Kabreigny simply stared at the doctor, then said good-bye to Kirk and Spock, and left.

As soon as the doors had slipped closed behind her, Kirk turned to McCoy. "Naming a *black hole* after an *admiral?* What were you thinking of?"

McCoy looked hurt. "That's not any black hole. We're in it. And Cochrane is in it. And that other *Enterprise* is in it. Right now. And for the next century." McCoy's smile returned. "Sort of makes you think, doesn't it?"

But the concept stopped Kirk cold. He put a hand to his temple. "Gentlemen, I hate time travel."

"It is not logical to have an emotional reaction to what is a natural outgrowth of the laws of physics."

Kirk started for the door. "Mr. Spock, I think it's time you took a long, relaxing leave. We'll send you back home to visit your parents."

As the doors swept open before them, Spock fell into step to one side of the captain, McCoy to the other.

"Good idea, Jim," McCoy agreed. "Spock and Sarek can discuss logic all day, and play poker all night."

"Doctor, I do not understand why you continually—"

But Spock stopped talking as Kirk suddenly laughed, for no other reason than that he was alive, and on his way to the bridge of his ship.

There was still so much more to be done.

And he intended to do it all.

EIGHT

U.S.S. ENTERPRISE NCC-1701-D
THE GAMMA CANARIS REGION
Stardate 43924.1
Earth Standard: ≈ May 2366

"How are you feeling?" Picard asked.

"That is not an appropriate question," Data replied, "considering that I have no feelings to begin with."

Picard smiled. La Forge looked up from his tricorder. "That's Data, all right. No sign of the Thorsen personality at all."

Data looked around the shuttlebay. The Preserver object was where Picard had last seen it, on the equipment cradles, near what was left of the counterfeit Borg artifact.

"Where is the Thorsen matrix?" Data asked.

"Back in the Preserver object," La Forge answered.

"I can detect no programming residue from the Thorsen matrix in me," Data said. "Is the ship's computer system similarly free of residual effects?"

La Forge closed his tricorder. "Completely. A personality matrix isn't like a program. It's like human brain waves—analog, not digital—so it can't be duplicated the same way. Only transferred. Like you and Lore."

La Forge disconnected the positronic leads from Data's open scalp and closed the access port there, carefully positioning Data's hair back into place. "Of course, when the Thorsen matrix

434

downloaded itself from the computer into you, it left programming codes behind, blocking access to certain ship functions, but that was all. And those codes were erased when we did a full restart of the system."

Data got up from the workbench he had been lying on and checked his hands and arms, assessing his condition.

"The last thing I remember, I was sitting at the science station, trying to communicate with the matrix."

"And as soon as it realized that you were a better host than the ship's computer, it downloaded itself into you."

Data moved his head back and forth in a series of short, jerky movements. "Geordi, have I been struck recently?" he asked.

La Forge looked away. "Uh, Worf tried to push you away from the controls."

"I hope I did not do anything inappropriate while I was not myself," Data said.

"You bear no responsibility for what happened," Picard replied.

Data gave him a curious look, concentrating on the splint on Picard's hand and wrist. "Geordi, how did you induce the matrix to leave my system and return to the Preserver object?"

La Forge finished stowing away the delicate tools he had used on Data. "You were switched off, Data. When I made the connection back to the object, the matrix was drawn to the system where it could function. I didn't switch you back on until all connections were broken. Your backup subroutines restored your own matrix, and Colonel Thorsen, or what used to be Thorsen, is now trapped."

"What will you do with the object now?"

La Forge looked at Picard.

"One of the hardest things I will ever do," Picard answered.

He walked over to the wondrous silver object and for the final time put his hand on it, wondering what other hands had touched it when it first had been forged. There was still not enough evidence to tell if it was a true product of the Preserver culture or not. Picard tried to tell himself that that should make what he had to do easier. But it didn't. The only positive side to acquisition of the object was that he had had full sensor recordings made of its inscriptions, and of its provocative diagrams of science as yet unimagined. The real archaeologists would appreciate those. Though how they'd react to the news of what an amateur had done to the object was something Picard would rather not deal with at the next conference he attended.

He slipped off his communicator pin and placed it on the object. Two versions of the same warp function now adorned it—the Cochrane delta of his pin, and the alien version inscribed in its surface.

He stepped away.

Data was beside him. "Is it necessary to destroy it, Captain?"

"It nearly destroyed this ship, Mr. Data. And the creature inside it nearly destroyed humanity three centuries ago when it had its chance to control the world." He looked at the android, knowing how human in fact Data was because of the compulsion Picard now felt to explain himself. " 'The evil that men do lives after them,' " he quoted. "Thorsen died centuries ago; now it's time for his evil to die as well." He spoke to the air. "Picard to Transporter Room Four."

"O'Brien here," the transporter chief answered.

"Lock on to my communicator, Mr. O'Brien. One object. Unknown composition. Set for wide-beam dispersal. Maximum range."

"Transporter locked," O'Brien acknowledged.

Picard took a last look at the object, so hauntingly beautiful, so full of mystery, of promise. "Watch carefully, Mr. Data," Picard said, overcome with deep melancholy. "This is a lesson in life. Checks and balances."

"Good and evil," Data said. "I understand the equation, even if I do not feel the deeper meaning behind it."

Picard nodded. Three and half billion years of history about to vanish. When would this chance ever come again? He looked at Data. "Then . . . could you . . . Mr. Data?"

"I understand, sir." The android looked at the object. "Mr. O'Brien: Energize, please."

The transporter harmonic filled the shuttlebay. The silver

object dissolved into mist, into time, taking with it the past and the future.

Picard sighed and turned away from the empty equipment cradles. The galaxy was safer now that it had been a moment ago, but that didn't help make him feel any better.

He left the shuttlebay, thinking that some days he didn't like his job at all.

Beverly Crusher called him hours later, during the middle of ship's night. She told him it was urgent. He came at once to Cochrane's stateroom.

Dr. Crusher was there, in her blue medical coat. A medical kit lay on a table nearby. And in the bed, Zefram Cochrane, a giant of his time, now out of time, his eyes turned to stare without seeing to the stars beyond the viewports, just as they would have appeared to someone on the surface of planetoid 527, one hundred years ago. The Companion lay beside him, her hand in his, eyes closed, barely breathing.

"They're going quickly," the doctor whispered.

"Is there nothing you can do?" Picard asked. There had been too much death this voyage. Any death was too much.

Crusher shook her head. "I told him earlier that we could try putting them both into transporter stasis and get them to a starbase to try some experimental treatments, but he said no. And I have to respect that."

"He's come so far," Picard said. "Done so much."

"No one ever does it all," Crusher said softly, to comfort him.

"No," Picard agreed. "I suppose not."

He sat with the doctor then, at her side, in the darkened room, keeping watch on the passengers from another age.

Sometime in the hours that followed, beneath the starlight, the doctor took the captain's hand. It felt right. To reaffirm life so close to death.

Sometime in the hours that followed, Jean-Luc Picard stared out at the stars, trying to remember the first moment he had noticed them. As a child, he supposed, in the fields near his home. Walking out with his parents. He would always remember his

parents. One generation to the next. But now even more generations whispered within him, the final echoes of Sarek and the
minds the legendary Vulcan had touched in his long life. Picard
reflected upon that expanse of time, and wondered what his own
legacy would be. How it could possibly measure up to all that had
gone before.

Sometime in the hours that followed, Beverly Crusher squeezed
his hand. "Jean-Luc," she whispered. "Look."

Picard turned his eyes from the stars and looked across the
stateroom where Cochrane and the Companion lay.

But there was something different. Something about the
lighting . . .

The bed was glowing. Their forms were glowing.

Picard stared in amazement. A glowing halo of some dazzling
golden energy was rising from the Companion's frail body. It
danced in delicate rhythms, casting flickering fairy light on all
that was in the stateroom.

Cochrane slowly turned his head to the light. Picard could see
the strain on the man's face as he looked up into that energy.
Cochrane let the Companion's fingers slip from his grasp and
raised his hand instead to touch the cloud.

The cloud coiled around him, ephemeral, translucent, heart-
breakingly alive with color.

Cochrane turned his head back to the windows, to look out to
the stars, a smile of wonder growing on his face as all sign of
struggle left him.

The cloud slipped down the length of his arm, merging with
him just as it had separated from the Companion. His entire body
shone with a steady inner light.

"Can you hear them?" he whispered in a voice full of love.

And to Picard's amazement a voice that was more than a voice
answered back with equal love, *I do.*

Cochrane lowered his arm. Slowly the glow faded from his
body. Slowly Picard realized that Zefram Cochrane's journey had
at last come to an end.

Picard sat there a long time in the ship's night, with Beverly
Crusher beside him. Both touched by the incredible sense of

peace and completeness in what they had witnessed. He put his arm around her. She rested her head on his shoulder.

There was still so much more to be done.

But just for now, just for this stolen moment, they could rest.

The Federation would endure.

Part Four

REQUIEM

ONE

☆

CHRISTOPHER'S LANDING, TITAN
Earth Standard: March 19, 2061

As the guests gathered around the musicians on their dais in the assembly hall, Zefram Cochrane stepped outside the governor's home and into the comparatively vast space of the dome built beside it.

He could smell rich soil, reminiscent of Earth but with a faint after-scent of something different, something alien. In time, he knew, the area beneath this dome was intended to be a park.

Cochrane stepped off the patio and onto that alien soil. It felt loose and crumbly beneath his boots, but in the light gravity of Titan, he did not sink into it as much as he had expected.

As he walked across the thus-far barren soil, he thought of the gravity of Titan, of Mars, of the moon, and of Centauri B II. He had walked on all of them, felt the pull of four different worlds. How many more would he feel in his lifetime?

He stopped beneath the center of the dome. At the age of thirty-one, he had accomplished a feat of which humans of centuries past could not conceive, and which humans of centuries to come could never repeat.

He should be content with that, he knew.

But he wasn't. Not yet.

As the music started up in the governor's home, Cochrane looked up through the slabs of transparent aluminum, to where the floodlights outside the dome lit the thick, churning clouds of Titan.

Most of the time, this moon's atmosphere was completely opaque, but with night coming on, Cochrane had heard that there was a narrow window in which a high-pressure ridge moved with the terminator, clearing the sky for only a few minutes, sometimes creating a brief opening through which to see the stars.

That's what Cochrane wanted to do right now, to be away from the meaningless noise and confusion of the party held to honor him.

He longed to see the stars again, only hours after he had seen them last.

It was a foolish desire on his part, he suspected. But who could explain the needs of the human heart?

He waited expectantly beneath the dome, eyes fixed on the heavens, so far unseen.

In time, he knew, he'd have to go back to the party. He had to talk to Micah Brack. He should catch up with events on Earth over the year he'd been gone. But that was all in the future.

For now he would see the stars. It was as simple as that.

Long minutes passed as he gazed up at the twisting of the atmosphere, watching the spikes of illumination from the floodlights disappear into dark shadows as the gaps between the blowing cloud banks grew larger.

He thought of all that countless humans had accomplished to make it possible for him to be standing here this evening. He thought of all that would happen in the future because of what he had done.

He wondered how many others might stand here after he was gone, just as he did now, looking up, seeking the stars.

The distant roar of the wind diminished.

Between the day and the night, the clouds lessened.

The sky above turned dark.

FEDERATION

High above Zefram Cochrane, the stars began to appear, and for just one moment, a fleeting instant of the time his life would span, Zefram Cochrane was certain he heard those stars sing.

He wondered if anyone else could hear them.

Someday, he decided.

But for now, it mattered only that they sang for him.

TWO

CHRISTOPHER'S LANDING, TITAN
Earth Standard: ≈ March 19, 2270

Admiral Kirk stopped just inside the dome of Founder's Park and took a deep breath. He was surprised by how much like Earth the air smelled. But Christopher's Landing was an old colony, and its tailored ecosystem had had time to become as complex as the one it had sprung from, more than a century ago.

Birds of Titan sang as he resumed his way along the worn stones of the path through the grass. He could hear the laughter of children on their swings, the splashing of a fountain, the rustle of the fan-driven wind through the . . . Kirk squinted at the grove of tropical trees at the edge of the dome.

Fig trees, old and robust, with their own bank of dedicated ultraviolet lights above them.

He wondered who had brought them here. One of the first colonists, he decided. Trying to make an inhospitable world more like home.

Kirk adjusted the slim package under his arm and walked along the path to the monument standing beneath the dome's exact center. McCoy was already waiting for him there, looking outlandish in his civvies and a patchy beard. Kirk tried to suppress a smile as he shook hands with the doctor. He saw

McCoy suppress the same smile at seeing Kirk in his admiral's uniform.

"I never thought you'd stay an admiral for so long," McCoy said.

"I never thought you'd stay retired for so long," Kirk answered.

McCoy gave a short mirthless laugh. "There's about as much chance of my coming back to Starfleet as there is for Spock."

"Have you heard from him?"

"Why would I? Probably taken some damned Vulcan vow of silence for his pursuit of *kohlin*-whatever."

Kirk smiled with understanding. "I know, Bones. I miss him, too."

McCoy looked alarmed. "Now look here, I—"

But Kirk shook his head and pointed at the monument so that McCoy had no choice but to stop talking and look at it as well.

"What do you think?" Kirk asked.

A twice-life-size bronze statue of Zefram Cochrane stood on a base of granite brought from Earth. The scientist was looking up, eyes fixed forever on the heavens. In one hand he carried a laurel branch, curved to suggest it was one half of the frame of the Great Seal of the Federation. With the other hand, he gestured, as if inviting the viewer to follow him.

"The cheekbones aren't right," McCoy complained.

"I don't think that was the point," Kirk said.

On the granite base, a simple plaque had been inset:

ZEFRAM COCHRANE
Human scientist, inventor of the warp drive
B. 2030 A.C.E.—D. ?
Erected by the Christopher's Landing Historical Board
to commemorate the 100th anniversary of the founding of the
UNITED FEDERATION OF PLANETS
and the 200th Anniversary of
Zefram Cochrane's triumphant return to his home system
following humanity's first faster-than-light voyage to another world.
March 19, 2261

Kirk liked it. There were similar statues on more worlds than he could remember, but this one had special meaning because this marked where Cochrane himself had returned.

"He might have stood right where we're standing now," Kirk said.

"Was this dome even built back then?" McCoy grumbled.

Kirk didn't know. It didn't matter.

McCoy scratched at his beard. "You ever regret going by the book on that one, Jim? I mean, not trying to communicate with them earlier. Before the interference got in the way?"

Kirk smiled. "I can communicate with them," he said.

McCoy looked perplexed.

Kirk held up his package, started to open it.

McCoy felt the stationery sheets that Kirk withdrew. "Is that real paper?"

"Hand-made," Kirk answered. "A little shop in San Francisco still makes it. They supply the Vulcan Embassy."

McCoy raised an eyebrow. Kirk didn't dare mention where the doctor had undoubtedly acquired that expression. "You're going to write a *letter* to the captain of the other ship?"

"That's right. I've put it off too long. He deserves to know the whole story behind his mission."

"Jim, he probably hasn't been born yet. If you set down what happened—what *will* happen—and he reads it . . . you're telling him his future. He might not do exactly what he did before—will do—good Lord, no wonder Starfleet doesn't like time travel."

Kirk laughed. "That captain won't get it until well after the date Spock calculated his ship came from. I'm including a few years' margin of error, just in case."

"Starfleet Archives, I suppose?" McCoy asked.

"Their security has been much improved. I've taken a personal interest in it."

McCoy stared back up at the statue of Cochrane. "And then what?" he asked. "After the letter? What are you going to do?"

Kirk shrugged. "Get back to work. The refit is progressing nicely but Mr. Scott still needs some strings pulled from time to time. And I have to begin reviewing candidates for . . . her new captain."

McCoy stared at Kirk. "I don't believe you."

Kirk didn't know how to respond. "About what?"

"You're going to take her out again. And you know it."

"Bones, they don't give starships to admirals."

"That's right. And the *Kobayashi Maru* is a no-win scenario."

Kirk sighed. He held up his stationery. "Care to make any other predictions for future generations to judge? I could add them as a footnote."

McCoy put his hand on Kirk's shoulder. "Just don't think that when you're writing that letter to the future, that you're somehow writing your epitaph. I don't approve of this . . . this mood of summation you're moving into. As if you're about to give up or something. You're thirty-six. Almost thirty-seven. Too young to be an admiral, too young to be behind a desk. You belong where that letter's going." He looked up at the dome where Zefram Cochrane's eyes were forever aimed. "Up there, out there, anywhere but here."

Kirk looked up, too. The engineering of Titan's atmosphere was proceeding on schedule and the thin clouds just after sunset let the stars shine down in almost all their glory. He wondered if the dome *had* been here when Cochrane had arrived. He wondered if Cochrane might have had even a glimpse of the stars from the surface of Titan. Probably not, he decided. But the same stars had shone down on them just the same, and they always would.

"Want to get some dinner?" McCoy asked. "I know this little place over by the shuttlebays."

"Later," Kirk said. He held up the package of stationery and glanced over to the side of the dome. "Right now, I'm going to go sit under those trees and write my letter."

"Just don't fool yourself that you're writing your memoirs, Jim. There's still a lot of life left in you. Even if you are an admiral."

Kirk said his good-bye to his friend and made his way to the grove of fig trees. There was a bench there and he arranged himself on it, the package balanced on his knee as a writing surface.

He wrote the date on the first page, then stopped to think how to proceed. McCoy was probably right. The captain of the other ship was most likely not yet born, wouldn't be for decades. And yet his actions—or her actions—or its actions—had made it possible for Kirk to escape the event horizon of a black hole and be here. He found it troubling to think how actions in the future could ripple through time to have an effect in the past. But given all he had seen in his career, he supposed that quirk of the universe made as much sense as anything else.

So how then to reply to the captain of the other ship? What message should he set down on these pages, what wisdom from the past, what revelation of hopes and fears deserved to be preserved and passed into the future, to thank someone who did not yet exist, for actions not yet taken?

Kirk sat for a long time on the bench beneath the trees. He heard again the noisy laughter of children playing, saw lovers strolling alone in their intimacy, watched old couples sitting comfortably on other benches by the splashing fountain as they, too, savored the signs of life in all its stages that flowed around them. And invariably, everyone Kirk saw, at some point or another, looked up past the dome, in the direction Cochrane had shown them, and he knew for a certainty that countless others just like them looked back from different distant worlds.

Kirk stared at Cochrane's statue. Someday that question mark about his death would be filled in, all truths would be known. But until that day . . . he followed the scientist's gaze upward.

He looked at the stars.

And soon he knew exactly what to say.

Alone on his bench, under some long-ago colonist's trees, Kirk began to write. It was many hours before he looked up again. And when he was finished, the letter complete, he knew McCoy had been right.

One way or another, when her refit was completed, he was going to take the *Enterprise* out again.

The stars demanded it of him.

He could almost hear them calling.

THREE

☆

CHRISTOPHER'S LANDING, TITAN
Stardate 48988.2
Earth Standard: ≈ May 28, 2371

Picard closed his eyes for a moment as he stood in the center of the Founders' Park dome. The rich scent of Titan's air, the rustle of the leaves, the songs of the birds—all reminded him of what had happened on Veridian III, of all he had lost there. And of the millions of lives that had been gained in return.

But he was here now. For whatever reason, fate and the universe had conspired to keep him moving forward, to bring him to this moment while others were left behind. His whole life could be viewed that way, he knew. For whatever reason, he had had experiences and adventures of which humans of centuries past could not conceive, and which humans of centuries to come could never repeat. If he considered the progress of his life that way, he was content.

Picard opened his eyes and gazed upon the unchanging face of Zefram Cochrane. He found it comforting.

Five years had passed since the scientist had come aboard the *Enterprise* for his final voyage among the stars. His body had been returned here since, and lay buried deep within the soil of Titan, with the granite of Earth his marker, this bronze statue his monument.

451

Picard read the plaque inset in the stone. The numerals giving his date of death were brighter than the other letters in the metal, attesting to how recent their addition had been.

Picard heard familiar footsteps approaching, so easily recognized after eight years.

"Hello, Will," he said a moment before Riker spoke.

He could hear the smile in Riker's voice as he replied. "Captain."

They stood together, gazing up through the dome, seeing what Cochrane would see forever—the stars, brightly flickering through Titan's cleansed atmosphere, a jeweled band around Saturn's majesty. This moon of Saturn was still far too cold for anyone to venture out without an environment suit, but the citizens of Titan had begun a geothermal venting project, and in a few more centuries, who knew? This whole park might be open to the night sky. Picard wondered what Cochrane would have thought of that.

"A most remarkable man," Riker said.

"A most remarkable life," Picard agreed.

They remained together in silence, contemplating the monument and what it represented. For all that they had been captain and first officer for eight years, for all that they did not know what the future would hold for them now, they were friends, and the silence between them was as meaningful as any conversation.

In time, another set of footsteps approached, ones that Picard did not recognize. He and Riker turned together.

The visitor was a Vulcan in a red Starfleet uniform and short-cropped hair. She was approaching middle age for her species, no more than one hundred Earth standard years. The attaché case she carried was embossed with the emblem of the Starfleet Archives.

"Captain Picard?" she asked.

"Yes?"

"Forgive me for intruding." She opened the case and removed a clear aluminum cylinder. Fixed inside there appeared to be an old-fashioned envelope. Made from real paper, it seemed.

Picard was immediately intrigued by the object, even more so when the Vulcan handed it to him. "This is for you, sir."

Picard held the cylinder in his hands, turning it to read the careful handwriting on the envelope inside. "What is it?"

"It is a personal communication, sir. A letter. Deposited in Starfleet Archives one hundred standard years ago."

"I don't understand," Picard said. "How could it be for me?" There was no name on the envelope, just a series of handwritten dates and coordinates.

"The letter is addressed to the commander of the Starfleet vessel who took part in a special recovery operation within the event horizon of TNC 65813, on or about stardate 43926."

Picard felt a sudden chill of recognition as he heard the Vulcan speak. Those words were exactly what was written on the outside of the envelope, and the time and place they referred to had never been far from his mind. Picard's eyes met those of the Vulcan. He dared not ask the question he knew he must. The potential answer was more than he should hope for.

"The letter was contained in a personal log vault, marked for release this year. The person who deposited it was apparently following Starfleet regulations regarding the temporal transmission of information in other than a causal manner."

"In other than a causal manner . . ." Picard repeated as he realized what he might be holding. "And the person who deposited this letter?"

The Vulcan nodded her head slightly, a subtle sign of respect for the name she spoke. "James Tiberius Kirk, sir. At the time it was written, Admiral, Starfleet Command."

Picard slowly drew in a breath of anticipation, surprise, wonder, he wasn't sure which. In the years since his ship and crew had recovered Cochrane, he had had the opportunity to discuss the incident within the event horizon with Ambassador Spock, and with Montgomery Scott when he had come aboard the *Enterprise*. But when Picard had spoken with Kirk on Veridian III, even at the time he had been overwhelmed by the feeling that there was so much more they should be saying to each other, so much more they had to share, even beyond the events of TNC 65813. But time had been too short, it was always too short. Like a law of nature.

The cylinder seemed to float in Picard's hand. The envelope within seemed to glow.

"I met him once, sir," the Vulcan said. "Admiral Kirk. Captain Kirk," she amended. "After he had retired. At the Ellison Research Outpost."

"Did you?" Riker replied, saving Picard the pain of describing the circumstances of his own meeting with Kirk on Veridian III.

"A most remarkable man," the Vulcan said.

"A most remarkable life," Riker agreed.

The Vulcan nodded, her silence acknowledging how little words could convey about some subjects. She closed her case. "The cylinder is filled with nitrogen," she explained. "It would be best if, after opening it, you used archival storage methods for the letter inside. I would be pleased to provide the latest guidelines at your convenience."

Picard thanked the Vulcan and she departed.

"Well? Aren't you going to open it?" Riker asked.

Picard ached to do exactly that. But he said, "Not here, Will. Up there. Where his words belong."

Riker smiled softly as he nodded. "I understand."

Picard held the cylinder as Cochrane held the laurel branch, as if it were the frame of something much bigger, unseen, still in the future. "The three ages of the Federation," he said softly. "Cochrane, Kirk, and us." The envelope was fat. The letter inside must be long, rich with detail, with . . . who knew what secrets there were to be shared only by those who commanded starships?

"I wonder what the next ages will bring?" Picard asked. "And to whom they'll bring it?"

For a moment, he could almost hear the stars answer him.

THE ARTIFACT
New Stardate γ 2143.21.3

The ship moves through domains of space unimagined by Cochrane, powered by engines incomprehensible to Scott or La Forge. But all three engineers would recognize its destination, deep within the voids between the galaxies.

The captain of the ship holds up her hand to the main bridge view wall and with her thumb blots out the Milky Way as it recedes from her, sidewarp factor 55.

"Beacon signal converging as predicted," her data officer announces. "Dropping to warp speed." The ship slows to a relative crawl as the main viewer switches to the forward scan. Against a sprinkling of distant galaxies, one blue beacon stands out as the ship closes. "Moving to sublight . . . and relative stop."

The ship hangs tens of millions of light-years from any star, from any matter larger than a grain of dust, except for the silver structure dead ahead, the structure whose presence was made known to them by sidespace radio after the final inauguration ceremony and all spacefaring cultures in the Milky Way had been joined in one grand Federation. That, so the current theory went, had been the trigger for the invitation.

The translator tanks identify markings on the side of the structure as consistent with similar markings recorded on so-called

455

Preserver artifacts. The Cochrane delta is there among them. Science tanks confirm that the radiation signature is consistent with postulated controlled-access corridors to multiple universes. The captain shakes her head in amazement. "Multiple universes," she says to her data officer, the words, the entire concept, still unreal to her. The data officer holds his hands ready over the control surfaces. "Do we accept the invitation, Captain?"

The captain stares into the beckoning doorway of the silver structure between the galaxies, contemplating an infinite ocean of time and space into which life could expand, its fate no longer tied to a single world, a single galaxy, or now, even a single universe.

"Helm, full ahead," she orders. "Let's see what's on the other side." Like another explorer centuries before her, who stood on the brink of an equal adventure, her eyes blur with tears even as she laughs, the reason for either response a mystery to her, rooted deep in that which makes her human.

In the language of the time, the ship is called Enterprise, *and she slides forward, accepting the invitation, once more going where none has gone before.*

For even here, even now, the adventure is still just beginning. . . .

EPILOGUE

ON THE EDGE
OF FOREVER

ELLISON RESEARCH OUTPOST
Stardate 9910.1
Earth Standard: ≈ Late September 2295

Kirk took his hand from the Guardian and for a moment felt as if he had forgotten how to breathe.

The Guardian seemed to spin around him. Vortices of stars. Images of gateways unimaginable. Paths and possibilities and *multiple* universes—

"Captain?"

He became aware of the Vulcan standing close to him. The impossibly young lieutenant commander with the tricorder slung against her hip. He had not heard her approach over the duraplast sheeting.

"Did you require something, sir?"

Kirk tried to answer but his throat was dry as dust, as if he hadn't spoken for days. It struck him that he had no idea how long he had been standing by the Guardian, listening to . . . to what?

"How—" He coughed to clear his throat and began again. "How long have I been here?" he asked. He glanced over his shoulder to see the Vulcan attempt to hide her concern.

"Beside the Guardian, sir?"

"Touching it," Kirk said.

The Vulcan's hand played over her tricorder. Kirk could see she was struggling with her desire to turn it on.

"Only a moment, sir," she said. "I thought you said something to me so I came back and . . ." She fixed him with an expression of curiosity that was more familiar to Kirk than she would ever know. "Sir, did . . . something happen?"

Kirk shook his head. He could say that he had asked a question and the Guardian had answered, but whatever had been related had apparently been only for him.

If it had happened at all.

Kirk closed his eyes again and the myriad images the Guardian had somehow shown him burst across his mind's eye as if a dam had burst.

. . . as if a dam had burst . . .

He heard the echo of Micah Brack saying those words to . . . to . . . Zefram Cochrane? Had it really been Cochrane he had seen, there on Titan? Was Brack really Flint, the immortal human Kirk had met so many years ago? Or had some trick of the Guardian, some alien static charge somehow flashed through him, weaving together his own disparate memories of forty-five years in Starfleet, creating an illusion, nothing more?

Kirk heard the Vulcan switch on her tricorder, heard it scanning, and made no move to stop her. He had no idea at all how much of what he had seen, experienced, imagined, been shown, was real. Perhaps the tricorder would have an answer.

"Is anything different?" Kirk asked.

"No, sir." Kirk's trained ear could hear her disappointment, though few others who were not from her world could have done the same.

Kirk held his hands together, squeezing his fingers. The hand that had touched the Guardian felt stiff, as if he had held a position too long, for centuries.

Then he realized he had felt this way before.

Ten years ago, in San Francisco, when Sarek had come to his apartment seeking information about Spock, his son.

Kirk had undergone a mind-meld with the ambassador that night, and the aftereffects had been much the same as what he

460

felt now—memories not his own colliding with half-remembered dreams from all the other minds Sarek had touched in his life.

The other captain had felt the same way, Kirk suddenly remembered. The other captain in the other ship, the other *Enterprise.*

For an instant he had an impression of that other captain, standing by a monument of . . . of . . . it was gone as quickly as that.

Kirk rubbed his hands across his face, as if waking from a long sleep. The tricorder still trilled behind him but he suddenly felt certain that it would discover nothing.

Had he really seen a past he could never have known? Had he really seen a future that he would never be part of? A future now seventy years distant, a thousand years distant? Was there a difference in whatever time stretched on beyond his own years? Could he believe anything he had seen or was it all just an indulgent dream of self-justification?

Sarek would know, Kirk thought. He felt certain that the ambassador's thoughts were somehow woven through all of this, as if through the Guardian the normal limits of space and time and causality had been sundered and a mind-meld of a different order had occurred, between Kirk, between the other captain, between the Guardian itself, all minds linked by some agency unknown.

He tried to recapture the details, but they were lost in the tapestry the Guardian had woven for him, until he only saw the larger pattern, the grand design.

The need for life to continue.

The certainty that life would.

Above the gentle wind, the subtle silence of the ancient stones, Kirk heard faint, familiar music play.

He turned to see two shimmering pillars of light swirl into existence upon the dust of this world. And as the figures within took shape, became whole, through a trick of the transporter nimbus that surrounded them, he seemed to see them as they had been almost three decades ago.

Commander Spock. Dr. McCoy.

At the beginning of their adventure.

Then the transporter effect vanished and his friends as they were now came for him.

McCoy stood by his captain's side and stared at the Guardian. Spock nodded politely to the young lieutenant commander and then it was as if she did not exist.

"Captain Sulu sends his regards, Captain. The *Excelsior* is at your disposal."

Kirk took a last look at the Guardian.

"C'mon, Jim. It's time to go home." McCoy reached out to touch Kirk's shoulder.

"I know," Kirk said, "I know," and with his friends at his side, he walked to the edge of the sheeting, stepped again onto the soil of this world, and readied himself for what would happen next. Whatever it would be.

The story that the Guardian had shared still resonated within him, and even as the details fled, he was left with what he had always known—that his journey would be ending soon.

But he realized at last that one thing *had* changed—perhaps the Guardian's gift—the new recognition he had that though *his* journey would be ending soon, *the* journey itself would never end.

However small, that knowledge made a difference.

Kirk stood between his friends. Held the communicator. The last time for so many things.

But not for everything.

"Kirk to *Excelsior*," he said. "Three to beam up."

The gentle chime of the transporter claimed them then, Kirk, Spock, and McCoy, and together they dissolved into the quantum mist and were swallowed by the light.

The young Vulcan stared a moment into the space the three legends had occupied. Looked at their footprints in the ancient dust, then shook her head as if suddenly chiding herself that what she thought wasn't logical.

She turned her back on the Guardian and walked to the research huts.

Alone once more in its solitude, the Guardian watched her go, waiting patiently, silently, as it had for eons, until another would come who was worthy to ask it a question.

It would be a long wait, the Guardian knew. But eventually another would come.

There was so much of the story still to be told. And not even the Guardian knew how it would end.

ACKNOWLEDGMENTS

We first proposed *Federation* to our then editor, Dave Stern, in a letter dated May 18, 1987. At the time, with *The Next Generation* still in preproduction, the idea of involving Captain Kirk in events spanning hundreds of years of Federation history was considered to be a bit ambitious, and we went on to other proposals.

Over the years, *Federation* made its way to the publisher and to Paramount in several different revisions, in long outlines and short outlines, and was consistently turned back, not with the judgment "No way," but with the comment "Not yet."

Finally, in a refreshing turnabout, from the writer's point of view, five years after we had first suggested *Federation,* the publisher called *us* and asked if we would like to resubmit once more because the time was finally right.

Would Gene Roddenberry have approved of this mixture of his two creations, not only in this novel but in the *Next Generation* episodes "Unification, Parts I and II," "Relics," and the motion picture *Star Trek: Generations*?

We think so, and here's why.

Of all the many STAR TREK projects that might have been, truly one of the most unusual and intriguing would have been the "Star Trek Opera," conceived as an event to commemorate STAR TREK's twenty-fifth anniversary. In the opera's very preliminary stages, Gene Roddenberry reviewed our STAR TREK novel *Prime Directive,* and a *Next Generation* comic book story we had written, and approved us to write the opera's "book." As for the story the opera would tell, Gene Roddenberry had said in the summer of 1990 that it

ACKNOWLEDGMENTS

was time to bring the crews together, and the opera would be an opportunity to do so.

Though the opera never went forward, Roddenberry's wish for his crews to be brought together did come to pass in a variety of ways, and we're proud of his confidence in us, and happy to have had this chance to offer our own small extension of the worlds and characters he created.

As always, in writing this STAR TREK novel we have drawn on the work of many writers who have shaped and expanded Gene Roddenberry's STAR TREK. Chief among them are Gene L. Coon, who created the characters of Zefram Cochrane, the Companion, and Nancy Hedford in the Original Series episode "Metamorphosis"; Dorothy Fontana, who created the character of Sarek in the Original Series episode "Journey to Babel"; and Harlan Ellison, who created the Guardian of Forever in "The City on the Edge of Forever." Flint, who may or may not have been Cochrane's mysterious Micah Brack, was created by Jerome Bixby in "Requiem for Methuselah." Ambassador Sarek was first brought into the time of *The Next Generation* in "Sarek," written by Peter S. Beagle, from an unpublished story by Marc Cushman & Jake Jacobs.

In those episodes, Zefram Cochrane was portrayed by Glenn Corbett, Nancy Hedford by Elinor Donahue, Flint by James Daly, the voice of the Guardian by Bart LaRue, and Sarek, of course, by the incomparable Mark Lenard.

Moving from the written word to the visual symbol, the famous STAR TREK arrowhead symbol, first seen on the uniforms of the *Enterprise* crew, and later throughout Starfleet, was created by the Original Series' costume designer, William Ware Theiss.

Given the time span encompassed by this novel, it is clear to us that we could never have written it in its present form without the use of that magnificent triumvirate of STAR TREK reference works: *Star Trek: The Next Generation Technical Manual,* by Rick Sternbach and Michael Okuda; *Star Trek Chronology: The History of the Future,* by Michael

466

ACKNOWLEDGMENTS

Okuda and Denise Okuda; and the remarkable *Star Trek Encyclopedia: A Reference Guide to the Future,* by Michael Okuda, Denise Okuda, and Debbie Mirek. The thoroughness, good humor, and respect with which these works have been written have made them invaluable resources for STAR TREK writers everywhere, and we are indebted to their authors for their scholarship.

Though we have drawn on established STAR TREK lore for many of the events in this book, we must add that much of the early history of the Federation, and Cochrane's adventures prior to and after inventing the warp drive, are extrapolations solely of our own creation and thus could be superseded by official adventures in the years to come. Until then, we hope the audience will enjoy reading this one possible STAR TREK adventure as much as we enjoyed writing it.

On a personal note, we must again extend our thanks to Mike and Denise Okuda for their encouragement and unfailing efforts to suggest possible answers to questions not contained in their works.

We are also indebted to Paula Block of VIACOM Consumer Products, the licensing arm for Paramount Pictures, whose insightful comments on early versions of this story helped us remain true to the original intent of the romance of Cochrane and the Companion; and to John Ordover of Pocket Books for encouraging us not to forget important parts of our first proposals.

Finally, our sincere appreciation to Dave Stern, for his enthusiasm at the beginning, and Kevin Ryan for his own enthusiasm, help, encouragement, and never-flagging support in all the years since, for this book and many projects still to come. He's the number-one reason why we'll be back.

J&G